THE WIDOW MAKERS: STRIFE

DEDICATION

To my much loved son
Simon John Newby

THE WIDOW MAKERS: STRIFE

JEAN MEAD

bwthyn
GWASG Y BWTHYN

ISBN 978 1 907424 14 4

The publisher acknowledges the financial support
of the Welsh Books Council

Published and printed in Wales
by Gwasg y Bwthyn, Caernarfon

CONTENTS

1860–1874

CHAPTER ONE

A bitter March wind, blown from the Russian steppes, shrieked through the galleries of the immense Garddryn Quarry. There was enough ice in it to cut through flesh and chill the marrow of Joe Standish's bones, as he worked at the cliff-face, suspended on a rope reeking of resin. His craggy face set in a grimace, as the glacial draught crawled beneath his fustian coat and penetrated the three layers of flannel bound around his midriff.

The wind came in gusts, blowing with such force that the rope trembled, swinging around. Kicking viciously at the vertical rock face, Joe dug the toecaps of his boots into the formed rut to steady himself.

With a quick glance at the sky, he estimated he had a few minutes to finish drilling the bore hole before the next deluge began.

Digging his boots hard into the rock face, sending slivers of slate and mud cascading down, he worked fast to complete the hole.

The grey sky darkened to granite, although it was hardly mid-morning; the dim light of a winter evening closed upon the mountain. A fine mist soaking the slate to ink black.

Joe poked the sharp metal bore into the pocket of his coat.

Reaching into his other pocket, the movement tightening the rope entwined around his thigh, he fumbled with cold, numb fingers for the small pouch which held the explosive powder. Carefully he drew it out.

Another fierce gust caught him. Tucking his head further into his coat collar, he gave the sky a malicious glance.

With little feeling in his fingertips, he untied the drawstring awkwardly. Upending the pouch, he trickled a small amount of the grainy stuff into the small hole.

Fishing deeper into the pocket, he pulled out a Bickford fuse and pushed it into the powder, scagging his knuckles on the razor sharp slate. Cursing he sucked beads of blood off the open skin, tasting the acrid bitterness of the gunpowder. The vileness would remain on his tongue all day, ruining every morsel he ate.

The first spots of rain fell from a thousand feet and vanished into his coat. His long drawn out sigh was lost on a fierce blast of wind.

The warning siren wailed, alerting quarriers of an imminent blast. Glancing up to the topmost point of the workings, Joe saw the red flag flying, a bright blazon dancing against the wet slate.

Hurrying, he struck a Lucifer. Shielding the tiny flame with his cupped hand, he put it to the fuse.

Playing the hemp rope out, dropping to the gallery floor, he moved fast. His old boots tearing slivers of slate off the face, sending it rattling after him in a small grey avalanche. Reaching level ground he untwined the rope quickly and ran. The soles of his boots slipping and sliding on broken shale.

Setting explosives was no longer new to him but he still felt a tingle in his belly in the moments before the burning fuse hit the powder.

Stumbling, grazing the palms of his hands on stones, he lost a precious second. Rising clumsily he looked at the weathered door he was making for. It stood closed against the rain. In a flash of doubt he imagined it locked. Two fast strides and he grasped the brass knob. The door opened and he breathed a great sigh of relief, the air cold enough to rasp in his labouring lungs.

Safely in he banged the door shut. Putting his back up against it, he hunched over, waiting for his rapid heartbeat to steady. As the panic passed he smiled at the absurdity of it.

Tense, he waited for the eruption of the explosion. The only one scheduled for ten o'clock. But there was only a long-drawn-out infinite silence.

Although it went against his better judgment, he grabbed the doorknob and pulled the door open. Peering through the drizzling rain he looked towards where he'd set the fuse. A flash of flame, brighter than sunrays, boomed out of the rock.

'Bugger me,' he murmured, his eyes lighting with amusement.

With a noise like cannon fire, great boulders of slate plummeted to the gallery floor, an avalanche of stones and soil tumbling after it.

'Bugger me,' he said again. Praying no one had ignored the warning siren.

The all-clear sounded.

With a reproachful glance at the sky, he turned up his collar against the slanting rain, and stepped out from the shelter.

Shoulders hunched he started back down the slope.

Reaching the fairly even pathway, he took a breather and checked his pockets for the pouch of gunpowder. The stuff was safe. As was the Bickford's and Lucifers. Moving on, he made for the site of his explosion. In his rush to be away he'd dropped his tools and abandoned the canvas satchel that held his midday meal and bottle of cold tea. Finding his stash he collected it together and slung the damp bag over his shoulder.

The stones were wet and slippery; he took a few cautious steps to the edge of the cliff and looked down the ragged precipice. Fallen boulders blocked the gallery floor.

The size of the harvest surprised him. The men of his team were already clambering over it inspecting the quality, looking for that elusive perfectly grained slate. The hunt was noisy, jocular. The yield obviously good.

Joe called down, 'A bit more there than I bargained for.'

Tudor Williams, Joe's long time friend and workmate, laughed. 'Often is, Joe. It'd be a daft sod that didn't heed the siren when you're firing the rock.'

Joe grinned. 'You buggers can stand me a couple of ales in the Half-Way, later on.'

Tudor laughed. 'We'll be glad to, Joe. If this slate's as good as it looks, there'll be more than a couple in it for you.'

'I'll look forward to all of 'em.' Joe grinned.

Gathering his tools, hitching everything into the crook of his elbow, he walked towards a large boulder on the periphery of the rock face. Wrapping the hemp rope tied to the base of the rock around his thigh, he walked backwards, playing out the rope until he stood at the edge of the precipice. Stepping off, he shimmied down to the lower gallery.

Twenty years ago, on his arrival in the Garddryn, he'd begun work as a rubbler, a bad-rock man. Shifting tons of waste rock so the team he worked with could get at the good slate. As the years passed he'd crept up the workers hierarchy until he was competent enough to prepare and light the charges. It was a job he enjoyed. There was a grim satisfaction in tearing another great wound in the mountain that had claimed his youth, the lives of comrades, and his friends.

Working in the quarry hadn't been easy. There were times when he felt a complete outsider. An Englishman working in a Welsh industry. The task made harder by his son's success.

Tommy had been in charge of the quarry for the past two years. There wasn't a harder taskmaster or a bigger penny pincher to be found from Nantlle to Blaenau Festiniog. If he had a sixpence for every time he'd been shamed by his first-born, Joe reckoned he would be a rich man.

* * *

Tommy Standish, principal of the quarry, shook his wet hat before handing it to the nearest underling hovering in the office foyer. Oakley, the quarry manager, took Tommy's black outdoor coat from him and draped it on a peg on the wooden clothes stand.

Haughty, Tommy straightened his long-skirted jacket, pulling at the hem. Satisfied that the garment sat well, he proceeded to make his way to his comfortable office. The underling and the manager anxious to do his bidding, at his heels.

Servants, employees and quarryman were well used to bowing their heads to Tommy Standish. He demanded obedience without question.

As a boy he had fostered ambitions to be the owner of the Garddryn. Educated by Bertram Bellamy, the former quarry owner who had spotted his quick mind and great potential, Tommy had grasped the opportunity to spend time at Plas Mawr, the Bellamy mansion. Working hard, learning all he could to further his objective. Turning his back on his family and humble origins when they became an embarrassment to him.

Seducing Bertram Bellamy's innocent daughter, making her pregnant, was part of his plan which led to him mar-rying into the wealthy family. From the very beginning, before the boy was born, it was obvious to his in-laws that the union was not a safe match.

Disappointed in his protégé, Bertram Bellamy thwarted Tommy's aspirations and at the reading of his Last Will and Testament, the Garddryn, the quarry he desired above all other possessions, was snatched from him.

Upon this betrayal, for that was how Tommy saw

Bertram's decision to bequeath the fortune and the quarry to his baby grandson, Tommy Standish became embittered, resentful of his wife and the little boy.

The Will guaranteed Tommy the position of directing the quarry's fortunes until his son Edward reached his majority.

Twenty-four hours after the reading of the Will, Tommy reached a decision. As he had nineteen years to amass his own fortune stealthily from the Garddryn, albeit under the noses of the trustees and solicitors employed to examine the accounts in his son's interest, he would do so.

If by the end of that time he did not wish to relinquish the Garddryn to his son he would not part with it. Twice in the past he'd come close to losing the quarry. Millie Barker forfeited her life when she threatened his position. Bertram's only son, George, an inveterate gambler had come close to endangering the stability of the business and it had been necessary to remove the young man from the line of inheritance. George was now an incapable, dribbling imbecile living with his mother and his nurse in Chester. Far enough away from the Plas Mawr mansion not to be an embarrassment to Tommy.

These people were not in Tommy Standish's thoughts on this wet and bitingly cold March morning. But then they rarely were. He was pondering on the journey and which carriage he would use to get to a funeral in Bangor. From there he must travel to Penrhyn Castle.

Tonight, Edward Douglas-Pennant, owner of the castle and the great Penrhyn Quarry, was holding a dinner for several friends.

Tommy was looking forward to a lively and entertaining evening. Edward, a generous host, was also an intelligent raconteur.

In his mind Tommy pictured the plump and generous kitchen maid, Sadie, lying naked in his bed, her soft thighs circling his hips. He shivered with arousal.

Bringing his attention back to the moment, he lifted his

coat-tails and sat in the comfortable green leather chair, mindful of his expensive tailoring.

His eyes didn't meet Oakley's as he waited for the manager to place the mail in his outstretched hand. Hired help didn't warrant acknowledgement or civility.

He spoke brusquely, 'I will be leaving here at eleven.'

His glance turned to the unfortunate junior. 'I expect you to have everything ready for my departure. I will hold you personally responsible if arrangements do not run smoothly.'

Nervous, subservient, the junior clerk bent at the waist, his longish hair making a sweep of his thighs. 'Yes sir, Mr Standish.'

Tommy flicked his eyes away. If only everyone would be as submissive. There had been another embarrassing scene with Henrietta at breakfast and he had been forced to banish her from the table. It was fortunate that he wasn't returning to Plas Mawr tonight. He might be tempted to confiscate the laudanum and opium she was so fond of, if she continually harangued him about his visits to Penrhyn Castle.

Turning his attention to the manager, he spoke crisply, 'On my return I want a full report on the troublemakers spouting ideas of strike action at Bethesda chapel yesterday. Give me the names and I'll dismiss them myself.'

Oakley's stomach sank. His own son had been shouting his mouth off about deteriorating conditions at the quarry. As had Joe Standish. The fact that Joe was Tommy's father would not cut any ice with Tommy Standish. Joe would be out of the quarry without a brass farthing if anything he'd said came to the master's ears.

Oakley's heart began to pound in a worryingly familiar way. It would be his own neck on the block for keeping the senior Standish on after the last row. A great speechmaker bloody Joe Standish was becoming. Frank, his other son, was no better. A right pair of English rabble rousers. At

13

every opportunity they were shouting *Union* like it was a holy grail. Buggers!

The young clerk was backing towards the door, a bend in his back. If he didn't get to the privy soon he feared there'd be an embarrassing accident. A steely look from Mr Standish had the power to turn his bowels to water. After such a close encounter with the master he could look forward to rushing in and out of the privy for hours.

Whilst Tommy had his eye to the quarry correspondence, the clerk made a furtive escape, dashing towards the low building at the back of the office.

With the lad occupied it fell to Oakley to summon the steward, Rees Roberts, to the office. Leaving the building to search for the man, with no time to collect his coat, his best jacket became soaked as he made a dash across the yard, trying to avoid the puddles.

The rain was ceaseless, horizontal. Smoke lowering down from the chimney pots clung to the slate roof, tainting the wet air.

He was still cursing the apprentice for his absence, when he saw Rees Roberts rounding the corner of the storage sheds.

Beckoning, he called, 'Roberts, you're wanted in the main office.'

Without waiting for the steward's reply, Oakley went quickly back to the shelter of the office building.

Minutes later, Roberts left the office with a grin on his usually surly mouth. Striding across the yard, mindless of the inch deep lake collected in the depression where vehicles turned. He was a man with an objective and not an altogether disagreeable one. Oakley had handed him a list of the suspected dissenters. He'd scanned it in the manager's presence, aware that Oakley's son's name should be on it. Oakley had made a vague remark about it, then dismissed the matter with a pithy comment. Now he was expected to forget the young rascal's culpability. A smile crawled across his mouth as he thought of old Oakley, beholden. What favour might he extract in return for his silence?

It took him thirty minutes to reach the workings. Time enough to add a few names of his own to the list, men that had done him some disservice or not treated him with the respect his position of Letting Steward warranted.

Climbing over a pile of broken slate, he made his way to the crest of the top gallery. From here he'd have a good view, take stock, and discover which quarrymen were shirking. With luck, he'd have a dozen more culprits to hand over to Tommy Standish when he returned from Penrhyn Castle tomorrow.

As soon as Roberts left the building, Tommy called for his carriage.

Unprepared for the inclement weather, Tommy had arrived at the office from Plas Mawr in the half-hooded vehicle and was now forced through lack of time to travel in it to Bangor. Beneath the leather hood, he sat in brooding silence, listening to the beat of the mare's canter. Watching the rain disappear into the groom's coat and droop the cockade on his hat. He considered the wisdom of sending the steward, an untrustworthy man, to hunt down the dissenters hell-bent on forming a Union. It was a job he should have undertaken himself, interrogating the men he suspected and imposing the appropriate punishments. When he returned tomorrow, he would deal with the problem himself.

A small private smile came to his mouth. Before his return he would have shared a bed with Sadie, a sensual, passionate, submissive woman who enjoyed pleasuring him. Sadie was all Henrietta was not.

The half-smile was scrubbed from his face as he thought of his wife and the debacle in the breakfast room this morning.

If only he could transplant Sadie into her place. Then there'd be co-operation, sexual intercourse on demand, passive compliance. Sadie bent to his will. Henrietta was devious and suspicious regarding his fidelity. Nothing pleased her more than harping back to when her papa was alive and how wonderful her girlhood had been.

Only once, during an argument, had she made a disparaging remark regarding his humbler beginning. She wouldn't repeat it, not after the beating he'd given her. His heart rate increased and his face flushed remembering how on that occasion she had tried to flee him with a bird-like quickness and he had caught her by the arm and clouted the side of her face. Stupidly she had raised her eyes and he had seen the hatred and contempt in the grey pools and he had drawn back his arm and hit her for a second time. Moments later he had her straggled across the bed, her drawers torn, and as he thrust his naked hips forward her insolence had evaporated.

The recalled incident renewed his anger and it came welling up inside him like an unwelcome guest, a red rage, tightening his jaw and making fists of his hands.

His antagonism turned to Bertram Bellamy. The reading of his Will had been intolerably humiliating. Anger long suppressed threatened to burst from him, and lifting his hand to his brow he brought it down wet with perspiration.

In the time it took to travel the next two miles he recovered his equilibrium. Finding it beneficial to mentally assess the wealth he had accumulated upon his marriage. Somewhat calmer he began to chaff at the length and time it took to make the journey to Bangor. With his eye to the back of the groom's wet coat and dripping hat, he blamed the man for his incompetent tardiness that prolonged the agony of travel.

On reaching Caernarvon, away from the shadows of the mountains, the sky cleared and it ceased to rain and the ebony-black mare picked up her pace.

With the improvement his thoughts turned once more to Sadie Pearson and her lush thighs and he dwelt on fantasies until repetition began to irritate. Then he turned his thoughts to the sumptuous dinner and social introductions that the evening might bring at Penrhyn Castle.

He was still musing, mentally holding a conversation in the elaborate library, when the carriage reached the outskirts of Bangor and joined the other equipages on the reasonably straight track of road.

The brightening weather had brought out many of the city's pedestrians and wreathed in winter garments they dashed between the moving vehicles, stepping over the deep puddles formed in the ruts in the road.

The rain kept off for the burial. Within an hour of arriving at the church, Tommy made his way to the nearby hotel. Arrangements had been made for a light repast and a glass or two of best brandy.

In the mountains the rain persisted throughout the day, thick cloud swept in from the ocean and reaching the high peaks descended into the valleys as wet mist; visibility was virtually zero.

Before four-thirty, as the daylight diminished, work at the Garddryn came to a halt.

There wasn't a man that wasn't wet to the skin. Tempers were running high. The steward's manhunt had disrupted work and antagonised the men. Twelve workers had been sent home early with orders to report to Tommy Standish on the following day.

Rumour had it that Tommy Standish had gone to Penrhyn Castle. If this were true he wouldn't be seen back at the quarry for a day or two. It was common knowledge that he was philandering with a wench there. She had him by the balls by all accounts. The salacious gossip raised many a smile in the Half-Way, but not if Joe Standish were present. Joe had a fierce temper when it came to Tommy's shenanigans.

With work finished for the day, the early knocking-off cheering no one, a crowd of disgruntled men, shoulders hunched and necks sunk into wet coat-collars, strode along the track making their way out of the quarry. Conversation centred on the steward and his nefarious *list*. Someone brought up the name of his predecessor, who was killed when a lump of rock landed on his head. Speculation as to the chances of history repeating itself, brightening the homeward journey.

Tom Hughes, head down against the rain, listened but kept his own counsel, making no comment about the meeting scheduled for later. It didn't do to let all the men know *Union* business. Nosy buggers some of them, ready to run to management with a tale, guaranteeing an extra shilling in their pay come Saturday Reckoning.

Whilst Joe walked to the Half-Way, his wife Emily was preparing supper at the table in the kitchen-cum-parlour. Placing several pigs' trotters into an earthenware pot she covered them with onions and haricot beans and poured on a meat stock. The firelight cast a glow on the corner of the table where she stood; there was just enough light to see by.

Glancing through the small window, she looked out on the murky afternoon. With the light fading early there was a chance that Joe would be home soon, if he didn't pop into the Half-Way for an ale.

As she covered the pot with the lid, she saw that it had acquired yet another chip on the rim. The discovery brought Frank, her youngest son's face into her mind as the possible culprit.

As she opened the bread oven door, heat wafted out. Placing the pot in the centre, she pushed the door closed. Checking the time on the black mantel clock she added two hours to the present time. The pot roast would need that if the meat was to fall off the bone.

Supper would be at six o'clock, same as always. Joe would be back by then. He wasn't renowned for being late for his meal. She could not say the same for young Frank; he was courting a girl in the village and he was likely to get waylaid. When that happened she kept his plate over a pan of hot water until he appeared famished, grinning with embarrassment. The lad was so different from his brother. Tommy had done his courting in a furtive manner and married that way too.

Noticing a crease in the rag rug in front of the fire, she bent to straighten it. It was time she made another rug; the colours were fading in the old one and the strips of material had suffered at the corner where Joe took off his old boots every night.

Lighting the lamp, she put it in the centre of the table. Throwing the spent spill into the fire. As she pulled the curtains closed, the afternoon was too gloomy to look at, her eye caught a movement in the far hedge.

For a moment she watched the spot intently, she wasn't nervous for her personal safety, but there were foxes and tinkers about that would steal one of her hens in a flash. If a tinker was about he would try to steal the pig. Not that he was likely to get away with it. Old Jake would squeal for Wales if anyone got near. Darkness fell as she stood at the window; one moment there was a glimmer of light on the horizon far out to sea, then it was as dark as it would get.

Drawing the curtains together, she shut out the shadows.

Five minutes went by and she couldn't rest; whatever or whoever was under the hedge had probably crossed the field by now, got into the pen and let out the chickens. The idea set her to action.

Slipping her feet into her old boots, she fastened them so quickly she missed several of the black buttons. Pulling a shawl off the hook at the back of the door, she threw it over her shoulders, knotting it quickly.

She wondered if she should carry a lantern. Should she alert whoever was out there? Deciding that it would be better if the tinker made a run for it, she took the lantern from the mantel. Her fingers trembling slightly as she lit it.

Grabbing the poker off the hearth was an afterthought.

19

But it made sense. She'd need something to clout the trespasser with should they decide to stand their ground.

Prepared she went out of the door, before she had a change of heart and let the scoundrel make off with one her precious chickens. Outside was blacker than a coal shed. The lights in the windows of the other cottages were dim and far away.

Emily and Joe's home was the last cottage of the village. Built by Frank and Joe two years previously, it sat well back from the lane. Close by was Bryn Tirion; the cottage had once been their home, it was empty and almost derelict now.

The wind soughed through the trees, rattling the broken slates on the ruined roof of her old home, and drew icy fingers through her long loose hair.

The blackness was infinite, the sky an unimaginable expanse and the darkness of the lane endless, trees, hedges, road, ditch and the grass verge melded into a sloe-black darkness.

The gleam of the lantern hardly broke into the shadows. Beyond the fuzz of light, her eyes searched for a sight of Joe. The flickering flame cast a small yellow circle around her, bright enough for him to see her if he was close. As there was no friendly shout or hurried steps to herald his appearance, she started up the narrow lane. Imagining him sitting in the warmth of the inn, comfortable, laughing with his friends, supping a glass of ale. She cursed the vagaries of men that generally put them away from home when they were most needed.

Clutching the solid brass handle of the poker like a club, ready to clobber the vagrant she expected to find beneath the untidy hedge.

With her night vision ruined by the light of the lantern, she scanned the ditch and dark place where the grey trunks of the blackthorn buried its roots into the soil.

A sound quickened her heart and dried the spittle in her mouth. Holding her breath, she edged forward, raising the poker she swiped the blackthorn viciously breaking several winter brittle branches.

The crack was startling. Several birds leapt fluttering into the air, the beat of their wings matching the thumping of her heart. Terrified that an immense dark shadow would lunge from beneath the hedge, she grasped the poker tightly. There was nothing but silence and the air left her lungs in a long sigh of relief.

She felt foolish; there was nothing but fled birds and terrified rabbits watching from a safe distance.

From the corner of her eye she saw a small fluttering movement and more in surprise than fear she thrust the poker into the hedge. Hooking an old coat, she hauled it out. The dirty lining was a pale cloth. Caught up on a low branch it had flapped in the wind. So there was no chicken murdering vagabond ready to snaffle her prize layer. Screwing her nose in disgust, she dumped the coat in the ditch.

A moment later she was running towards home, the lantern swinging and rattling. If she could reach there before Joe, he might never learn of the escapade. She felt enough of a fool, without him telling her how big a one she was. She'd never hear the last of it if he discovered she'd risked life and limb and been ready to commit murder for an old hen; or as it turned out an old coat. She'd never live it down. Young Frank would be no better than his father. The lad would wear a silly grin for a fortnight of Sundays.

Undetected she made it to the front door and with a sigh of relief went into the cottage. Safe, feeling a little sheepish, she placed the poker in its usual place, propped on the old brass fender.

The lantern went back onto the mantel. Opening the tiny glass door she blew out the flame. Touching the still hot glass with the backs of her fingers, she prayed that it would cool quickly.

Flinging her shawl over the hook on the door, she crossed

the room, her boots noisy on the slate floor. Taking up the apron she'd discarded earlier, she slipped it around her waist and tied the cords.

Grinning she muttered, 'Just fancy me doing summat that daft, I'm still as silly as a young wench at times.'

Catching her image in the misty mirror above the mantel, she saw her hair was windswept and tangled; deliberately ignoring the silver threads now running through the long and once dark locks, she tied it back with a green ribbon.

Joe's footfalls on the path startled her. There wasn't time to change her boots and don the ancient clogs left warming at the fireside. Glancing around the room, she checked that she had left no evidence of her escapade.

As the front door opened, dark smoke wafted down the chimney.

Emily turned to see him enter. With a hint of guilt in her voice, she said 'Joe, you're back early. I thought you'd stay a bit longer in the Half-Way.'

Turning back to the fire she flapped the corner of her apron at the lingering smoke.

His eyes went to the chimney piece. 'Wind's turned to the east again.'

She grinned. 'Is that why you're back early?'

He wasn't in the mood for humour. 'Course not. The chaps were having a bit of a chinwag and as the conversation turned to our Tommy, I came away.'

Slipping out of his drenched coat, he draped it untidily over the fireguard.

Any mention of Tommy brought a slight nausea to Emily's stomach. She was almost afraid to ask as she said 'Why, what's he done?'

Joe's frown deepened. 'Nowt out of the ordinary for him, just more of the usual. He's locked men out of their place of work and victimised the weakest.'

A grunt escaped him as he slumped onto a wooden chair

by the fireside. Bending, he unlaced his sodden boots and pulled them off, leaning them against the fender to dry.

Looking up he saw her standing with her hands still clutching the skirt of her apron. The smile was gone from her face and he was sorry he'd come in like an old curmudgeon.

To put matters right he tried to sound more cheerful. 'It's only fair to let the poor sods talk in peace. And anyway, I wanted me supper. I'm famished.'

The truth was he was embarrassed when conversation turned to his elder son and he would walk out of the ale house at the first mention of his name. Although it was his choice to walk away, he always had a sense of being excluded, even mistrusted as he turned his back. He had never discussed this with Emily. She had her own demons where her son was concerned, without adding his to the pile.

Taking his coat off the fireguard, she gave it a shake over the hearth and then draped it so that it would dry more effectively. It steamed immediately.

Bending to the oven, she said 'It's a good job I put an extra trotter in the pot if you're half-starved.' Bringing out the earthenware dish she stood it near the hot hob.

Joe sniffed the meaty aroma. 'That smells good. I'll take me wet things off and change into summat dry.'

She gave him a half-smile. 'It's not quite ready, so you've time for a dip. The water's simmering.'

'I'll not bother. I'll only get in your way whilst you're cooking if I bring the old bath in.'

Taking a cloth, he lifted the lid off the pot. 'This smells bloody good, Emily, you've surpassed yourself, lass.'

'You'll not be in my way. Supper won't be for another half-hour.' She glanced at the clock. 'Did our Frank say what time he'd be in?'

Joe filched a bean out of the steaming gravy. Biting into it cautiously, he spoke as he tossed it around his tongue. 'Not till later. He's taking that girl of his to see her sister,' he said pinching another bean.

'Put that lid back on, our Joe. There'll be no beans left in the pot if you keep fishing them out.'

Sitting again, still chewing, he took his boots off the fender and slipped his cold feet into them. Without bothering to tie the laces, he made his way to the scullery door.

Outdoors the rain was sloughing from the sky in horizontal rods. Ducking his head against it, he covered the tiny yard in three fast strides. As he unhooked the bath off the privy wall icy water trickled beneath his shirt sleeves, the freezing runnels streaming to his elbows. Hastily, he manhandled the bath through the back door, bashing it against the doorpost as he came into the kitchen-cum-parlour. Tripping over his soaking laces, he practically dropped the tin bath onto the rug in front of the fire.

He was laughing. His wet hair plastered to his head and water dripping off the end of his nose.

'It's absolutely pouring down out there. I'll get wet through again when I go out to hang the darn thing back up.'

Five minutes later, Joe inched down into the hot water and gave a long satisfied sigh.

'Amos should call tonight,' Emily said. Laying knives and forks on the table.

Amos Ridley, a peddler of books, visited Garddryn village regularly and although nearly blind he still traipsed from village to village, considering himself a weary pilgrim to knowledge and erudition.

Joe had come to the pleasure of reading books late. When Tommy and Frank were youngsters there had been no pennies to spare for such extravagance. The mystery of the written word eluded Emily, but sometimes she would take Joe's discarded newspaper and struggle to fathom the gist of the local news.

The aroma drifting from the pot on the hob, was enough to shift Joe from the water.

Sufficiently thawed through, he stood, drying vigorously.

Looking towards Emily, he said 'Maybe the rain will keep poor old Amos at home tonight.'

Emily's brow furrowed. 'When did the weather ever stop Amos Ridley?'

'Aye, you're right there. He's a bugger for punishment, always has been.'

Joe dropped the damp towel on the rag-rug, then stepped onto it. The heat of the fire was on him as he dressed in the clean clothes left warming on the fireguard. It was a great pity, he thought as he pulled up his combinations, that he had to go back out in the rain. But the bath had to be emptied.

Emily was prodding boiling potatoes with a fork, when she heard footsteps on the path. 'That sounds like Frank.'

As Frank opened the door the wind blew into the room, sweeping the Chronicle newspaper off the corner of the table. A pall of grey smoke came down the chimney bringing the smell of damp soot into the room. The flame in the oil lamp gutted then settled.

'There's a real gale blowing up,' Frank said, unbuttoning his coat.

'Aye, we felt it, Frank,' Joe said tersely, buttoning his trousers.

'Sorry about that, Da.' Picking up the separated pages of the Chronicle, Frank put it back in order and then slapped it down on the table.

Emily picked a wet leaf off the floor and flung it into the fire. 'Don't take your coat off, our Frank. You can help your father take the bath out.'

Between them they carried the old tub outdoors. As they tipped the contents into the fast flowing stream, a spray of water flew back, soaking Frank.

Emily heard their snorts of laughter and the clang of the bath as it was hooked onto the wall.

They came in fast, still grinning.

Emily looked up from cutting a loaf. 'Get by the fire, our Joe. You'll catch your death going out so soon after a bath.'

Frank shrugged out of his wet coat and draped it next to his father's on the fireguard. 'What's for supper, Mam?'

'Pigs trotters and beans.'

Frank grinned. 'Pettitoes! We haven't had those for ages.'

With a cloth around the hot handle, Emily carried the steaming pot to the table.

Pulling out a chair, Joe sat. His taste buds working overtime as Emily ladled the rich lava of gravy, meat marbled with fat, and haricot beans onto a plate.

Frank pulled the corner off a slice of bread and held it poised ready to dip into the gravy. 'I'm starving, Mam.'

Handing him a plate, she smiled. 'So what's new?'

For several moments no one spoke. Emily broke the silence. 'Amos will be here soon.'

Frank swallowed, wiping gravy off his lips with the back of his hand. 'I'll miss his visit. I promised the minister I'd go to fiddle practice at Bethesda chapel.'

Emily scooped beans onto her fork. 'I haven't seen the old minister for an age. How is he keeping?'

Frank grinned. 'Same as he always is, all except for his hair.'

'What's up with that?' Joe dunked bread into the gravy on his plate.

'It's gone dark brown.'

'Well I never,' Emily said surprised.

Joe grinned. 'When did that happen?'

Frank spoke with his mouth full. 'About the time he started walking out with Nelly Bainbridge.'

Joe and Emily's eyes met over the table. Emily giggled and Joe grinned.

'Nelly Bainbridge has changed a bit too,' Frank said seriously.

'How's that then?' Joe was close to laughing.

'She's started wearing bright colours and her hair's different.'

Joe grinned. 'Not darker?'

'No curlier.'

Frank changed the subject. 'We haven't had cowheel for a long time, Mam.'

Emily dabbed her mouth with the corner of her apron. 'Why is it you men are always thinking of the next meal before we've finished the one we're eating?'

'He's right though, Emily. We haven't. I like a bit of cowheel for me supper,' Joe said, scooping beans onto his fork.

'It's best when it's cooked really slowly with barley and carrots,' Frank said, looking to his father for support.

'Give over, you soppy lad.' Emily stirred what was left in the pot. 'Do you want the last of the gravy, Frank?'

'Let Da have it. He's worked harder than me all day.'

'We can share it between us, lad.'

'No, you finish it. I want to leave room for me pudding.'

With supper finished, Frank, his ancient fiddle wrapped in an old coat to shield it from the rain, left for Bethesda chapel.

Emily busied herself in the scullery, soaking dried lentils for tomorrow's soup, and inspecting a jar of gooseberries she'd bottled last autumn.

Joe settled in the chair beside the fire with his pipe and the Chronicle, his ear cocked for Amos Ridley's footsteps on the path.

Joe was an enthusiastic reader, particularly of fiction, enjoying the escapism, the pearl of a good story, or so Amos Ridley was fond of saying.

Hearing footsteps, Joe folded the newspaper, and rose.

Sheltered by the small overhang of the porch, shoulders

hunched against the miserable night, Amos Ridley lifted the wooden knocker and clouted the door.

Opening it almost at once, Joe put his head out. 'Evening, Amos.' He glanced at the sky. 'Still raining?'

'Aye, it is that.' Snorting with disgust, Amos removed his ancient stovepipe hat and shook drops of water off the near-threadbare fabric.

Wiping his boots thoroughly, he stepped indoors. 'A dreadful day, will winter never end? March and still the wind has us in his grip.'

Joe took the heavy bag from him. Wondering not for the first time, how the elderly chap, nearer blind than sighted, managed to trek about the countryside with such a cumbersome load and in all weathers.

'Hand me your coat and sit yourself down, Amos. Thaw through. It's not fit for a dog out there.'

Fingers swollen with rheumatism, Amos fumbled with the bone buttons. Shucking off the old fashioned caped coat, he handed it over.

Shaking drops of rain from it, Joe draped it over the fireguard.

With near unseeing eyes, Amos watched the blurred image of Joe as he tended the garment. The coat would be near enough dry by the time he came to wear it again. He and Joe were likely to chat for a couple of hours.

Sighing contentedly, Amos eased his old bones into the more comfortable chair. It didn't escape him that Joe had offered his own favoured seat. But that was the way of Joe Standish, a generous and honourable man, scholarly, although self-educated.

Pulling another chair near the blaze, Joe saw that Amos's ancient boots and the bottom of his trousers were sodden.

Hot tea spiked with something stronger was called for; it would thaw him through quicker than anything. Joe's eyes went to the scullery door. Emily was still shifting pots about.

He was about to call her, and then thinking better of it, he put the kettle to the hob.

'You'd like a brew, Amos, wi' summat added?'

The old man's eyes lit. 'Aye, it'd be most welcome.'

Rising, Joe went to the dresser and opening the door of the cupboard, he brought out a bottle of whisky.

Amos bent to his bag. 'I've brought something that might interest you.' Rooting for a moment, his eyes narrowed to slits, he found what he was looking for. 'I knew that I could not have forgotten to bring it.' Straightening, he offered the magazine.

Joe scanned the cover. 'Punch?'

Amos tapped the periodical with his forefinger. 'It's what's inside that will interest you.

Opening it, Joe flicked the pages.

Amos eyes were on him. 'There's an excellent article detailing the incidents and calamities of the American war. I haven't read a better description of the goings on there or the impact of the blockade. With shipments stopped and the cotton industry here grinding to a halt, thousands will starve in Lancashire.'

In his mind, Joe saw the faces of people he had known in the slum streets. In twenty years most of those folk would have moved on one way or another, but their bairns would still be there. Those and thousands like them would have sought employment in the cotton mills that had sprung up like weeds. The overcrowding would be more unbearable than it had been in his time. He thought back to the unemployment when the infamous Galloway, death trap mine, had closed. Then people had gone hungry, begging on the streets for a bit of bread and more often than not going without. What would it be like now?

Amos went on passionately, 'It was always a mistake for the cotton industry to be so concentrated in one county, Lancashire. All that investment should have been channelled into something besides.'

29

Joe's eyebrows lifted. 'There's still coal there.'

'Aye, there might be. But the mines don't take women and children any longer and they need employment just as much as men do. Thousands will starve. It's in England's heartlands that America's battles will be felt hardest.'

'I fear you're right, Amos. But we have to take into consideration the plight of the slaves ...'

'Aren't we slaves?'

'Aye, but here we are free to come and go. We're not shackled to the job.'

Amos smiled. 'Joe Standish, I thought you were a union man. Isn't working in the Garddryn near enough to slavery?'

Joe's eyes twinkled. 'You have me there, Amos. I think I can recall saying summat like that not so long ago.'

'Change the subject, shall we?' Amos chuckled.

The kettle came to the boil, splattering drops of water onto the flames.

Whilst Joe made the brew, Amos dipped into his bag and pulled out a pamphlet. The black edged paper was a tribute to the Prince Consort, dead for over a year.

'These are still cropping up,' he said grimacing.

Joe's thoughts had been with the squalor and hunger of Manchester, his birthplace. The costly pamphlet contrasted greatly with the predicament of the people living there and for a moment his strong royalist beliefs faltered.

More out of habit than sympathy, he said 'I wonder how the Queen manages? They reckon she'll not come out of deep mourning.'

Amos sniffed scornfully. 'It's something other women could learn from her. Merry widows, most of 'em. No sooner have they buried their old man and they're cavorting with the next. That vixen, Mildred Fr...'

Coming into the room, Emily caught the end of Amos's words. 'Evening, Amos. Who's cavorting?'

Caught gossiping, Amos looked up sharply. 'Nobody as I

know of. Your good husband and I were just discussing the Queen.'

Crossing to the fire, Emily warmed her cold hands. 'Oh, I thought I heard you mention the poor widow, Mildred Francis. It's nearly six months since she lost her husband. Doesn't time fly by?'

Emily had heard that Mrs Francis had *entertained* a gentleman recently. The spinsters and matrons of the village were suitably scandalised. Emily hadn't repeated the gossip to Joe. She was giving the woman the benefit of the doubt.

Smoothing down her apron, she spoke sympathetically, 'Talking of the Queen, it's said that she's not recovering from Albert's death, she's taken it very hard.'

She sighed. 'I don't expect there's much cavorting going on for poor Victoria. I wonder if she's up in Scotland? '

A republican to the core, Amos didn't comment.

Joe poured tea into three mugs.

Amos was looking forward to a shot of whisky and wondered if it would be forthcoming now that Emily was in the room.

Joe must have read his mind. Picking up the bottle he poured large measures into two mugs.

Nodding his thanks, Amos opened his bag; fumbling through several books, he pulled one out. 'Mill on the Floss,' he said turning the book over to read the reviews.

'I read something about it. Is it good?' Joe said taking it from Amos.

'Champion, especially if you enjoy reading about rural matters.'

Emily hoped Joe would buy the book. It was a while since he'd read to her. The long dark nights when it was impossible to work outdoors were monotonous. A good tale could make the hours between supper and bedtime fly by.

Noticing the pamphlet lying on the floor beside Amos's bag, she picked it up and studied the picture of Albert, circled in black. The artist had been kind. The Prince looked handsome, better than on other pictures. Quite splendid in his uniform. She sighed, sorry for the Queen who was without her husband.

The mantel clock ticked off another hour before Amos felt ready to leave.

Joe stood on the doorstep, watching the old man trudge down the lane, until he was lost to the darkness.

When Joe came back into the living room, Emily was tidying up.

Banking the fire, he put a pan of oats and cold water on a trivet, ready for tomorrow's early breakfast.

He made a trip to the privy, a small shed built over the fast flowing stream. Inside there was a polished plank of wood with a round hole cut into it. It was always freezing inside at this time of year, a breeze blowing over and under the door.

It was much too cold to linger; he was back indoors in moment.

Emily popped out but came flying back in, her cheeks flushed with cold.

Joe was warming his back at the fire. A steaming mug of tea in his hand. 'Your tea's on the table, Emily,' he said giving her a smile.

She glanced at the clock on the mantelshelf. 'Frank should be in at any moment.' Her thoughts went to her elder son, Tommy. She wondered what he was doing at that moment.

CHAPTER TWO

The carriage carrying Tommy Standish approached Penrhyn Castle in the early evening. The first shades of dusk were fading from the landscape and he was sorry to miss the astounding view of Snowdonia. A great portion of the rugged mountain range was Penrhyn land. The panorama gave an idea of the immensity of the domain belonging to the Pennants and the great wealth they possessed.

The last of the light was on the ocean and he glimpsed the treacherous, fiercely tidal water of the Menai Strait that raced between the mainland and the isle of Anglesey, with Puffin, magical small isle at the maw. In the far distance lay the Great and the Little Orme with the isthmus of Llandudno between.

Although he had missed the best of the view, there was still the show of great wealth to be appreciated on the mile long avenue and the park beyond, planted with hundreds of exotic species of flora from around the world.

At the end of the avenue, on the incline, the equipage slowed before sweeping around to the gate-house. At the change of direction he looked out; the indigo shadows of twilight darkened the castle walls. The utter stature and immensity of the edifice took his breath away.

Moments later, reaching the carriage forecourt the vehicle slowed. In the new darkness, Tommy fumbled for his primrose gloves, hat and cane. Collecting them together he held them in his hand preparing to alight.

The great oak door of the entrance gallery opened and

light spilled out. A liveried footman, his neck sunk into his coat collar against the chill air, trotted towards the carriage holding a lamp aloft.

Releasing the door latch, Tommy stepped down to the gravel. The journey had taken longer than he had anticipated and he was glad to stretch his stiff legs. Perhaps he should have heeded the advice of the coachman and used the copper foot warmer that Henrietta swore by on her journeys.

The coachman climbed down and retrieving Tommy's leather bag handed it to the second footman. Bidding his master goodnight, he took his seat again.

Tommy glanced at his servant as the man lifted the reins. 'Goodnight, Robinson.'

The equipage turned, the wheels raking up the stones as the driver headed it towards the stables.

The liveried footman held the lamp high. Walking in the small circle of light, Tommy made for the open door. The breeze sweeping off the mountains was brisk enough to lift his short brown hair and ruffle his grey silk necktie.

Crossing the gravel, Tommy reached the sanctuary of the entrance gallery. The large room was lit with candelabrum, the flickering flames creating long shadows on the dressed stone walls.

Tommy slipped the fashionable calf-skin gloves inside his tall hat and passed it to a waiting servant, along with his silver topped cane.

The first footman helped him out of his heavy coat. He missed the warmth of it immediately; the temperature was little different from the outdoor air.

The gallery had been designed to replicate a Norman cloister and therefore had little comfort. Some time ago, the Colonel had explained that the simplicity was meant to accentuate the impact of the grand hall. The doorway from the gallery had been deliberately offset to hide the impressive view. Tommy had gone back to see for himself and made a mental note to do the same if he should ever build a grand mansion.

The footman was beside him and Tommy detected the scent of oranges on his breath as the man said, 'The Master is waiting in the library, sir.'

Familiar with the layout of the castle, Tommy turned in that direction. As he did so his eye caught a watching servant and from the man's offensive expression guessed that he had connections with a Garddryn worker or a deposed dissenter.

Dismissing it as unimportant, Tommy followed the footman, his shoes clattering on the stone floor, whereas the soft, rabbit skin shoes of the servant, made no whisper.

Colonel Edward Douglas-Pennant, Member of Parliament for Caernarvonshire, had arrived in the library only moments before, the unusual tardiness due to mislaying an important letter, later found in the pocket of the frockcoat he was wearing.

In the rush, his valet had tied his green silk necktie quickly; it was less than perfect. Looking into an ornate mirror, Edward was putting this to rights as Tommy was shown into the library.

Turning around, he smiled. 'Tommy, it's nice to see you again, come and warm by the fireside. How was your journey?'

'It was bloody cold, bumpy and took too long.'

Edward laughed. 'I hope dinner makes up for the discomfort.'

Phillips the butler, recently transferred from the Pennants' London residence to the castle, hovered in the shadows. A lift of Edward's eyes brought him forward.

'Phillips, bring a couple of large malts, if you would.'

With a slight bow the man retreated silently.

Edward gestured towards a chair near the chimneypiece. 'Let's make ourselves comfortable, Tommy.'

Careful of his expensive tailoring, Tommy settled, crossing his legs at the knees.

Edward took the huge burgomaster chair opposite, a favourite of his when in the library. Leaning forward, Edward explained, 'The other guests have congregated in the drawing room. I thought that we could have a drink here before joining them.'

Lowering his voice conspiratorially, Edward glanced to the further recesses of the room to check that no guest had strayed in. 'It allows us to talk quarry business before the ladies take command of the conversation and turn it into a discussion on the merits of furbelows and bonnets.'

Tommy gave a short laugh.

More seriously, Edward asked 'How are things at the Garddryn? Have you made a decision about connecting to the tramway? It would be the thing to ...'

Interrupted by the return of the butler, the men fell silent, as he set glasses on small tables at their elbows.

When they were alone again, Tommy detailed the suggestion made by the Caernarvonshire Tramway Company and the cost it would incur.

Edward was enthusiastic about new innovations. Penrhyn Quarry set the lead when it came to getting the slate off the mountains and down to the shore.

'Although initially it'd be expensive, Tommy, better transport will improve Garddryn production in the long run. The industry is flourishing and it'll get better. We must move with the times; abandon the practise of hauling the slate down as it has been done for generations. Fast reliable transport is needed to get the product to the marketplace in Britain and foreign ports.'

The conversation turned to the existing track the wagons ran on at the Garddryn.

Tommy didn't mention that two men had been killed, crushed by a runaway wagon a few days before. Edward was aware of the accident and the dissent it had caused at the quarry.

Tommy's father, Joe Standish, was up in arms about the incident. Edward had learned of the row from his own quarry manager. The senior Standish blamed Tommy for the accident, saying that he was working the men for too many hours, in bad conditions. For sometime now there had been bad blood between father and son. Joe Standish was a radical, fighting for a union. Tommy was a profiteer. What chance had they of uniting?

Rising from the chair, Edward glanced at the elaborate clock above the fireplace. 'I think it's time to join the company.'

Tommy downed the remainder of his drink. Putting the glass aside, he rose. 'Do I know your guests?'

'You may be familiar with two or three of the men. Griffith the surgeon ...' As he explained who was present, Edward laid his hand on Tommy's shoulder steering him towards the door.

Although Tommy had visited the castle often this was the first time he had entered the drawing room, a room generally reserved for the ladies. Crossing the threshold he was struck by the predominately crimson furnishing. Candlelit, the room had an ambience of warmth and comfort.

Edward presented him to the four gentlemen who had congregated near the window to enjoy a pre-dinner drink. Tommy was acquainted with the two solicitors present. He'd had dealings with them in the past.

The elderly surgeon from Penygroes, standing in the centre of the group relaying a witticism Palmerston had made in Parliament, was no stranger to Tommy. Politely he stopped mid-flow in his story and extended his hand to Tommy, but the humour that had been in his eyes only moments before, had fled.

'Good evening, Mr Standish,' he said, dipping his entirely bald head.

Their eyes met and held for a long second, both men recalling their meeting of the previous day, when they had discussed the death certificates for the two recent deaths in the quarry.

'Surgeon Griffith,' Tommy said civilly, but he had already started to turn to the man standing beside the surgeon, a quarry owner from the neighbouring county.

With Tommy's arrival there was a slight shift in the convivial mood of the masculine group. Tommy had a powerful charisma, a force of energy that wasn't completely benign and it made the men prick with unease. His rise to their ranks had been meteoric. Bertram Bellamy, dazzled by the young man, had placed him in a position of power and had awarded him the greatest prize of all, his only daughter. Everyone expected that Tommy Standish would be the old man's heir, but Bellamy had left his vast estate to his baby grandson. Not that this had made any outward difference to Standish. He had carried on as before, running the quarry and fielding the financial colossus that Bellamy had left behind him.

Breaking away from the men, Edward and Tommy crossed to the four ladies seated on a matching pair of sofas. The women's eyes were on the handsome young man as the two men approached.

One woman stood out, a butterfly amongst moths. She had passed her youth but *joie de vivre* shone in her sparkling eyes. Expensively gowned in kingfisher-blue silk, the close fitting bodice heavily beaded with iridescent seed pearls, she looked exquisite.

From the moment Tommy had entered, her eyes were on him. He was the most attractive man she had seen for some time. He carried himself with confidence, the type of man other men would stand aside for. She felt a frisson of excitement at the thought that her husband was safely packed off to Italy, leaving her free for a short dalliance.

Taking her hand, Edward gave a little bow. His voice rich as he made the introduction.

Tommy gave an elegant bow of his own, his eyes hardly away from Lady Isabelle's for a second. It would have been very pleasant to remain beside her, but he was aware of the other woman awaiting an introduction and dutifully he turned to her.

She was older than Lady Isabelle by some years. The dark green gown she wore didn't compare in style or status to the costly garment of Lady Isabelle, but it fitted her well, showing what remained of her charms to the best advantage. His eyes were drawn to the tendrils of frizzy ginger hair haloing her plump face.

Seated on the sofa, she grinned up at him. 'And I'm Josephine. Plain old Josie. No posh title, Mr Standish.'

There was something about her that was appealing and after being introduced to the two other women, Tommy came back to her and they chatted until dinner was announced.

Lady Isabelle rose at precisely the same moment as Tommy. Placing her elegant hand upon his coat sleeve, she contrived that he would lead her to the dinner table. A footman was ready to pull out her chair, but it was Tommy that she inveigled to assist with arranging her voluminous skirt around it. It was natural that he should take the seat beside her. Mentally congratulating the Lady for her stage-management, Tommy left the opening of the conversation to her.

Lady Isabelle didn't disappoint, launching into a sparkling account of London entertainment, she had recently attended the Theatre Royal to see a John Buckstone production. 'Mr Standish,' she said animatedly, eyes glistening 'have you seen the play Our American Cousins? A wonderful comedy.' Repeating a line spoken by the actor, Edward Southern, she bent towards Tommy. Her rounded and pale as ivory breasts, tantalisingly close to his hand.

Listening with half-an-ear, the feminine display was too arousing to concentrate on her witty account. His thoughts were of her naked body splayed across his bed sheets. The erotic fantasy was disturbed by two footmen as they entered the room to serve the entrée.

The delicious aroma of the quail terrine reminded Tommy that he was hungry. His attention moved from Lady Isabelle to the Minton china plates being put before the guests.

Lady Isabelle was somewhat disappointed that his attention should be diverted so easily. She had thought he was as interested in her, as she was in him. Picking up a silver knife and fork, she picked at the food on the plate.

Discreetly and silently, the liveried servants poured wine.

It was maddening being ignored, and Lady Isabelle tried to focus on the dull comments of the dreary solicitor seated opposite. Throughout the tedious ordeal, she was constantly aware how close Tommy's thigh was to hers.

It amused Tommy, alert to her fidgeting and poorly disguised tiny sighs of boredom, to pay no attention to Lady Isabelle. The woman to his left, although she did not compare in beauty to Isabelle, was passably attractive. He was quite enjoying her intelligent and animated account of the Queen's visit to Penrhyn Castle. Fortunately she was in a position to give interesting little nuggets of information of the likes and dislikes of Victoria, which he listened to without interruption.

Silently, on soft soled slippers, the footmen cleared the Minton.

Looking around his table, Edward was pleased with the selection of guests and the choice of food and wine. It had been sometime since he had entertained at Penrhyn. Dinner engagements held recently had been at his London residence.

Sitting beside him, the Penygroes surgeon made a comment. Edward laughed, his eyes bright with amusement.

The door opened, and the servants brought in the next entrée.

The level of conversation around the table dropped, whilst the sea bream was served.

It gave Tommy a grand sense of wellbeing to belong to such high society and to be a favoured guest at the magnificent castle. His thoughts went to his parents' cottage. What would that lowly branch of the Standish family be supping on tonight in their pitiful abode? It was probably one of his mother's interminable stews, or a pathetic plate of salt herrings. Whilst he dined on sumptuous fare fit for a king, they made do with food only fit for pigswill. How he abhorred poverty and the shameful lack of expectations it bred.

Lady Isabelle seized the first opportunity to bring an end to the conversation with the solicitor. Turning towards Tommy, she touched his sleeve lightly. 'You look very deep in thought, Mr Standish.'

Pitching his voice low, so as not to be overheard, Tommy lied flawlessly, 'Lady Isabelle, my thoughts were with a new friend and how best I might persuade her to spend a little precious time with me.'

A slight flush travelled across Lady Isabelle's breasts. 'I'm sure your new friend would be delighted to spend a few hours with a man of your presence and charm.'

Tommy gave an almost imperceptible nod of his head, before turning back to Josephine.

Lady Isabelle was left wondering if he meant to come to her room later.

Sadie, Tommy's lover, a servant at the castle, entered the

room carrying a tureen. Tommy's presence was a complete surprise to her; cautiously she tried to catch his eye.

A silver serving dish was carried in by the first footman. As he placed it on the sideboard, Sadie went back to the kitchen.

During the carving of the rib of beef, whilst waiting for the plates to be filled, the discussion around the table turned to the merits of beef. Scottish as against beasts reared on Welsh grass. Opinions differed, but all agreed that more animals of high standard should be bred in Wales.

During the meal, Josephine, a clever raconteur and an amusing dinner partner, if a little daring, kept the guests amused with a selection of the titillating stories of foreign meals and foreigners abroad.

It was during the climax of one such story that Sadie returned to the dining room on the pretext of checking that the plates could be cleared.

At that moment, Lady Isabelle leaned close to Tommy. Her eyes blatantly sexual she caught and held his gaze. Tommy touched the delicate flesh of her upper arm with the back of his fingers.

Sadie, who only a moment before had been ecstatically happy, looking forward to a rapturous night with the man she loved, froze. Unable to look away, she glared at him in fury.

Infuriated that a lowly servant should look at him in that way, Tommy's expression was venomous.

Turning quickly, Sadie hurried from the room.

Lady Isabelle didn't miss the glance that passed between the maid and Tommy. The malevolence in his eyes increasing her excitement.

Tommy's eyes raked the other guests, checking to see if anyone had witnessed the embarrassing moment, but conversations were still in full flow. No head was raised questioningly. His greatest fear was that Edward, at the head of the table, should have noticed, but he was chuckling at something his neighbour said and had missed the scene.

Furious that Sadie had risked putting him in an embarrassing position with his peers, Tommy was pleased that she was distressed. She deserved it. The stupid wench had got above herself. Who did she think she was, flinging filthy looks his way? Nobody showed him disrespect and went unscathed.

Interested in what had taken place, Lady Isabelle watched his face and saw the malevolence still in his eyes.

The dining room door opened and three male servants entered carrying trays.

Tommy was disappointed that Sadie was not amongst them; he wanted to see her distress.

A moment later, she appeared, red-eyed from crying. She couldn't resist glancing his way.

Smiling, Tommy took Lady Isabelle's hand off the tablecloth, and kissed the tips of her fingers.

Sadie fled the room.

Edward, turning his head towards the closing door, whispered to the footman, 'Is something amiss?'

Speaking as close to his master's ear as his lowly station would allow, the servant said, 'The girl has something in her eye, sir. Cook did try to remove it but was unable to do so.'

Rising, Edward pushed back his chair. 'I'll go and see what I can do.'

The footman urged, 'Please do not disturb your guests, sir. I will deal with the matter myself.'

Sitting again, Edward said, 'Thank you, Ransom.'

Furious at Sadie's tearful return to the kitchen, Cook began a tirade. 'I spent hours preparing a dinner fit for the Colonel's guests, only to have my creations ruined by an upstart of a girl making a show on herself. Explain yourself, you little minx.'

Sadie hardly heard Cook's words, her sobs were bordering on hysterical.

The housekeeper gave Sadie a brisk clout across the ear.

Shrieking, Sadie covered the burning sting with her hand.

The housekeeper ran a tight ship. She was proud of her reputation as a Tartar.

An expert at bullying without raising her voice, she set about Sadie with outraged superiority. 'You'll be quiet at once, or I'll give you something to cry about. One more sound out of you and you'll be packing your bag and removing your sniffling face from my presence. Do you understand?'

Sadie sniffed loudly, choking back sobs.

Mrs Turnbull's hand rose, ready to strike again. 'I'll land you another one, if you don't shut up.'

Picking up the hem of her apron, Sadie wailed into the starched linen.

Mrs Turnbull turned to the cook. 'If the stupid girl carries on another minute, so help me God, I shan't be responsible for my actions.'

Cook sighed. 'Sadie, you had better stop this minute. It can only be man trouble that's upset you so.'

She glanced at Sadie's midriff. 'I hope you're not in the family way.'

The mere mention of such a calamity occurring in Penrhyn Castle flustered Mrs Turnbull. 'She'll be out on her ear, if she is. Neither the Colonel nor I will stand for that sort of nonsense. It's an outrage. Girls today, they're as bad as one another. Not like it in my day. Girls knew how to behave then.'

'I'm not in the family way,' Sadie sniffed.

Folding her thick arms, Mrs Turnbull harrumphed. 'That's good for you then. I'll not tolerate immoral goings on in my domain. Do you understand?'

'Yes, Mrs Turnbull.' Sadie sniffed back tears. Her head was throbbing. All she wanted was to curl up on her bed, cover her head and weep.

It was late. Sadie had been into the dining room several times and on each occasion she had successfully kept her eyes off Tommy's face. No one was more thankful than Sadie when the company rose from the table. The ladies moved to the drawing room, where small dishes of ices were brought to them. The gentlemen retired to the library to smoke cigars and drink brandy.

Before retiring for the night, the housekeeper hauled Sadie before her. 'As punishment for your dismal behaviour,' she said harshly, 'you will remain on duty until all the guests have gone to their chambers.'

Tired and unhappy, Sadie nodded bleakly.

The kitchen servants including Cook, filed out of the kitchen. The maids went to their quarters. As they walked down the narrow corridor, speculation as to Sadie's unhappiness was rife. Baffled by the show she had made of herself, they gathered at the end of the corridor to discuss the possibility of Sadie's imminent dismissal.

Cook went to her private sitting room. Pouring a large sherry, she sat before a blazing fire. Removing her soft shoes, she put her swollen feet upon a gout stool. Turning her face to the glow of the fire, she sipped the sherry. Content that the Colonel had enjoyed his dinner, she sat remembering past dinner parties.

Leaving Sadie in the kitchen, looking forlornly at the floor, Mrs Turnbull went to her own sitting room. Sitting beside the fire, kept blazing by the effort of a downstairs maid throughout the long evening, the housekeeper mulled over the problem of Sadie Pearson. For the life of her she couldn't get to grips with what had upset the girl so.

A plate of dainty cakes had been placed on a small table; reaching for it, Mrs Turnbull began to eat.

Sadie sat miserably in a wooden chair beside the big range. Near tears, she was thinking of Tommy in the library with the Colonel and his guests. At least Lady Isabelle isn't with him, she thought, sniffing back fresh tears. But to make matters worse, if that was possible, Mrs Turnbull had ordered her to wait upon Lady Isabelle when she retired.

Lady Isabelle had arrived without a maid. There was no one available in the castle to wait upon her ladyship. Three of the Penrhyn upstairs maids were at Mortimer House in Belgravia. The other two were ill and had been ordered to bed to stop the spread of infection.

Mrs Turnbull had been half-way through the door, on her way to her private quarters, when she had stopped and given fresh orders to Sadie. Being particularly harsh, she had shouted, 'Lady Isabelle's gown is exceedingly costly and I expect you to take special care. Also groom the Lady's hair, if she should so wish.'

Exhausting her catalogue of orders, Mrs Turnbull had slipped through the door. Leaving Sadie with the last of the dishes to wash.

Still sitting, her eyes on the red ember beneath the range, her troubles and the reasons for them tumbled like wild horses in Sadie's mind.

Eventually she came to the conclusion that the best thing to do was to ignore what she had seen and ask Tommy to forgive her childishness. Getting Tommy back on any terms was better than not having him in her life.

Now that she had calmed down, she saw that the woman had been leading him on. It wasn't his fault. What man wouldn't be flattered by the attention of an attractive woman, although she was twenty years his senior? This thought brought her upright in the chair. Why would Tommy want a woman so much older than himself? The episode in the dining room had been a figment of her imagination. Restless, she got out of the chair and began to pace.

The scene she had witnessed, Tommy taking Lady Isabelle's hand and planting a kiss on the tips of her fingers, was just a gentlemanly thing. It might be a new fashion. Trust the gentry to start a new mode.

Ignoring the little worm of doubt, her mind raced forward. Tommy might do it all the time. She didn't know how he was expected to behave. They didn't mix in the same social circles. She almost laughed out loud. Their time together was spent in bed. Apart from the wonderful episode when they had enjoyed several days together in Chester. Remembering that idyllic time, her eyes lit and she hugged herself, smiling happily. Tommy loved her, he wouldn't purposely hurt her. Tommy was incapable of harming a fly. All she had to do, when he climbed into his bed, was be there for him.

Looking forward now to the night ahead, she hummed as she crossed the kitchen and put the kettle to the hob. Whilst she waited for it to boil, she washed her face in cold water in the sink. Feeling much better, she went to the marble slab to get milk.

She had almost finished her tea, when she heard the company moving, saying their goodnights. Hurrying, she put her cup with the unwashed dishes on the draining board; she'd rise really early and do the lot tomorrow, before Mrs T. came down. Crossing the room, she doused the lamp on the table. There was another burning near the door; picking this up, she made for the back-stairs leading to the maids' quarters. Lifting the hem of her skirt, she went quickly up the staircase. The lamplight drew grotesque moving shadows on the stairway walls. Imagining that her progress was watched by long dead eyes, she trod lightly to lessen the sound of her footfall.

As quickly as she could, she went down the long narrow corridor. Reaching the bedroom she shared with the other girls, she listened at the door for the soft murmur of sleep coming from within.

Lowering the lamp to the floor, she opened the door slowly, cautious of the squeaky hinge.

The room was as familiar as the room she shared with two sisters at home, Beatrice and Maud. With the door ajar, there was a small amount of light, enough to see that two of the black iron beds were occupied, course linen sheets and grey blankets humped over the occupants. Her bed was against the wall, neatly made up, a wooden trunk her father had made wedged under it. Each bed had a wooden locker beside it, and a chamber pot beneath.

A simple washstand stood under the window, with a green jug and a white basin. An untidy assortment of hair clips lay strewn on the painted wood. In the centre of the room stood a table, the boards scratched and scarred. A solitary candlestick with a doused half-burned candle stuck in the melted wax stood on the unpolished wood.

The floor was bare-board, apart from the small rag-rugs placed at the side of the beds. The window was tight shut. The room was stuffy, although a cold draught blew in from the bleak corridor.

With her eye on Matilda, always a restless sleeper, Sadie untied the cords on her apron. Crossing to her own bed she draped it over the iron bedstead. Careful not to make a sound, she opened her locker and took out a comb. Without benefit of a looking glass, she ran it through her hair.

A few minutes later, carrying the glowing lamp, she made her way from the housemaids' tower towards Lady Isabelle's room. In her mind was the thought that Lady Isabelle would not be pleased to have been kept waiting and might see fit to punish her in some way. The lack of apron and cap might displease her. But looking nice for Tommy was too important to worry about what might be said.

The long corridors and stone stairways were gloomily silent. The footmen and other staff had retired long ago. The butler, she supposed, was in his comfortable quarters, probably enjoying what had remained in a wine bottle off the dinner table. Cook and Mrs Turnbull would both be asleep in their beds.

Just about everybody was off duty; it was unfair that she had been told to wait on Lady Isabelle, it wasn't her job to do so. She might at this moment be in Tommy's arms had

Mrs Turnbull not decided to punish her with this errand. It was a mystery why the housekeeper had ordered her to assist at dinner. It was most unusual for a maid to be seen in the dining room. With luck, come tomorrow, Mrs Turnbull would be questioned by the Colonel as to how it had come about.

On the last flight of stairs, she slowed to get her breath. Looking down into the well of the staircase it was possible to make out the fantastic carving in the stonework, eerie and horrible in the dim flickering light of the single lamp.

Coming to the immense door of the state bedroom, she knocked gently. She was terrified of disturbing Lady Isabelle if she had already climbed into bed. She waited until the lamp grew heavy in her hand, then plucking up courage she opened the door a little and looked in.

The heavy curtains at the window were open. The moon high in the ink black sky drenched the bed with wet light. Clothes lay in a tangle on the floor. A lady's elegant shoe kicked off had landed near the chimneypiece. Tommy's waistcoat lay draped across the arm of a chair, the bright silk drained by the light of the white moon.

A sob rose in her throat and her heart contracted in her chest.

From the elaborate carved bed came a sigh of passion and an answering light chuckle.

Fleeing the awful scene, Sadie ran along the corridors and passages that had taken on a nightmare quality, the walls and floor distorted by her tears. How could she have been such a fool? She had given him the benefit of the doubt, dreamed up excuses and absolved him from all blame. Fool! Fool! Fool!

The opulence of hallways and staircases ended. Pushing open the heavy oak door to the servants' quarters she dashed through, her footfall heavy on the bare boards.

Her first thought was to escape to the sanctuary of her bed. Now in the dark passage she saw how impossible it would be to have privacy, with the other two girls in the room.

Frantic, she stopped, looking back the way she had come, to the oak door; if she went through it, where would she go? Out into the grounds? Impossible! To the kitchen? What comfort would she find there?

An image of the room she had just left came to her, and a pain gripped her heart till she could hardly catch her breath. There was no way but forward, and forcing her weak legs to move, she went to her bed.

Undressing mechanically, she flung her clothes on the floor and saw *his* clothes tangled with *hers* on the moonlit carpet. In contrast to the exquisite silks, hers lay in a crumpled heap, the smells of the kitchen on them. She wept silently.

CHAPTER THREE

Astride his mount, a black glossy mare, Tommy sat solitary on a hilltop looking into the far distance to the dark-blue silhouette of the Snowdonia Mountains against the sky. Between lay a wilderness of plain, thousand upon thousands of acres of boulder strewn non-arable land, a lake of rock buried beneath. Turning in the saddle, the warm leather creaking, his eyes roamed the misty green vales and soft hills.

The late morning was perfect, the air still, scented with gorse and broom growing like yellow fires in the reedy grass. The sky was cloudless, the early May sun warm on his face.

It was good to be alone, away from Henrietta who had been senseless on opium before breakfast. Infuriated by her stupidity, he had come away from the house and ridden frantically for a while, before calming down and ambling to this place.

It was not a familiar spot, a good way out of his usual domain, but it was interesting. The terrain spoke volumes of the rocky structure beneath. A seed of an idea took shape and shifting in the saddle he looked to the middle-distance to where an outcrop rose out of the moorland.

Grinning widely, he shouted 'By jove! It could just be ...'

Steering carefully, mindful of the boulders and stones lying hidden in the grass, he walked the animal towards the projection. Dismounting, holding the reins loosely in his hand, he looked over the stony ground until he found what he was looking for, slate.

Grinning, he clasped the grey shard tightly and began a

wider search. A pace behind him, the horse snatched at the tips of the less than tender grass.

Within minutes he struck treasure. Almost buried, with only the tip visible, was a chunk of the highly prized red slate. Using a sharp stone he scraped around it until he had enough leverage to tug the wedge free. Abandoning his fastidious nature he brushed away the damp soil, home to several thread-thin worms, to examine the find. It was an age since he'd seen anything like it, rare even in the largest quarries. The Garddryn had never birthed such a specimen.

His pulse tripping, he drew a handkerchief out of his pocket and wiped the remaining dirt off the piece. Truly revealed it was incredible, the red-gold particles in the sheered edges glistening in the sunlight. It looked perfect, the grain lying just as it should.

Pocketing it, he scanned the ground for a twin. Shifting stones with his boot he exposed pale, tiny slugs and miniature worms. Putting his weight behind a boulder he rolled it from its ancient bed. Beneath lay the red he valued, the colour as rich as Japanese lacquer. On his haunches, he collected all he could.

With his jacket weighed down with samples, a sliver as green as jade amongst them, he walked the mare across the desolate moor, guiding her around the semi-hidden rocks in the long grass and over covert rabbit holes.

Although he looked calm, relaxed, walking with his favourite mare, his mind raced with exciting possibilities. He couldn't wait to get home to discover who owned the land.

Reaching the roadway he mounted. As he settled into the saddle the warm leather protested, creaking with his shifting weight. Looking back across the moor land, the long course grass moving like green water in a light breeze, he felt neither a kinship with the land or sensed the ancient, primordial harmony of its vast emptiness.

Turning the horse, nudging her flanks with the heels of

his boots, he steered her forward. Almost immediately he became preoccupied, the beat of the mare's hooves and the murmur of the countryside faded away as the quarry in his mind sprang to life.

Men were digging down, hacking out galleries as they went, blasting out slate, some red. Above the growing abyss the thick wire-rope of the Blondin stretched between two high towers. There were two great coaxial winding drums lifting the loads. In his imagination he heard Ruby reaping her rocky harvest. The sound of the machinery, the explosions, terrifying clatter of falling rock, the snarl of trucks on metal rails, men's shouts, overlaid with the metallic drone of wire-cable, thicker than a man's wrist, running through the drums. It was as though it was happening here and now. Bursting with excitement, he was alive to it all.

Ruby, for he had already named his quarry, would use advanced methods. There'd be a modern railway to take the slate to port. The trucks pulled by horses on tramways were becoming a thing of the past and had no place in his new kingdom.

There was plenty to think about on the return journey home, so he took his time and considered his moves, secretive and otherwise. Hardly aware of the horse beneath him, although his unseeing eyes were on the gentle rise and fall of the animal's head, he planned the financial raid on the Garddryn quarry assets. Pilfering his young son's inheritance was a necessity, if his new venture was to succeed.

The May sun was sinking behind the oaks in the park as he neared Plas Mawr. Approaching the majestic gates made the blood in his veins run faster. The ostentation was a daily reminder that he had accomplished all he set out to do so long ago. That the mansion with its fine trappings was now his home gave him an immense sense of pride and pleasure. The gates alone had cost the original owner a king's ransom, designed by the architect of the mansion to match the status of the house beyond, the black metal filigree worked so artistically that they were stately enough to impress any visitors, royal or otherwise. George the third and fourth were said to have stayed overnight. In the seven years of his sovereignty, William the fourth had enjoyed many weekends at Plas Mawr. Unfortunately, Victoria, the modern monarch, chose Penrhyn Castle when visiting Snowdonia.

Secretly he considered Plas Mawr superior to Penrhyn. Older by many generations, the house was built of honey coloured stone imported from the west of England. Both houses boasted fine parks, but Plas Mawr had a fine Italianate feature, staged terraces where visitors could enjoy the spectacular view of the ocean at sunset.

As he reached the gates, a liveried servant came out of the gatehouse and hurried towards him. Although the man was new to his employment, he was aware that the master could be difficult and demanding. Drawing the gate inwards, tipping his hat with his forefinger in the ageless gesture of servitude, he saw that Tommy Standish, as all the servants referred to him privately, a humble village boy after all, was in a fair humour.

With the gates open, Tommy had an uninterrupted view of the tree-lined avenue and the magnificent house beyond.

It was a relief to be back; tamping down his excitement was making him jittery. He was anxious to get to the library to take a look at the maps of the locality. Bertram Bellamy, his late father-in-law, had collected many over the years and had updated them as more information became available.

The mare lifted her head, snorting as they passed through the open gates. Tommy shifted in the saddle to give an order to the gateman, then turning back he gave a gentle nudge with his heels and the mare picked up her pace.

Behind him the gates clunked as the metal came together. The gateman's boots scrunched on the shingle as he slowly made his way back to the gatehouse.

As he neared the house, Tommy took a moment to admire the architectural splendour of the mansion. He gave a passing thought to the black slaves labouring under a hot sun that had brought the house to existence. The thought didn't rise out of sympathy, or gratitude, but for the absolute aptness of it all.

Eager to be indoors, he spurred the mare into a gallop and with her black mane and tail streaming, she sprinted towards home.

Coming to the house, Tommy slowed her to a trot.

Nostrils flaring she snorted; her gleaming coat quivering, tail lashing, she snorted again. Dismounting he patted her neck and she nuzzled into his chest. Stroking her long jaw he wondered how many months it had been since either of them had had so much pleasure. The ride out had been good, productive; the jaunt had lifted his spirits and the mare had benefited from the exercise too.

Rounding the corner of the house, a stable-boy hurried toward him. 'Master, I'll take her now.' Taking the bridle the lad stroked the animal's hot neck. 'She'll be ready for her rub down and a net of hay.'

Tommy looked serious. 'Mind you do a thorough job, Jones.'

Leading the horse away, the boy touched his hat. 'Yes, Master.'

Tommy watched as they disappeared around the side of the house making for the stable-block, before climbing the steps towards the front door.

Louise Bellamy, Henrietta's mother, came down the wide staircase as he stepped into the grand hall. She had lost weight since he had last seen her and now her face was hawk like, chiselled to the bone. There was no welcoming smile but he didn't expect there to be.

'There you are, Tommy, I expected you earlier.'

Her presence was annoying but he would not allow her to ruin his good humour. Feigning pleasure he walked to her and kissed the side of her creased face. 'How are you, Louise?'

She wasn't fooled and her thin lips twitched as he touched her. 'Henrietta is not well, but I suppose you know all about that.' Her tone left no doubt as to whom she blamed for her daughter's state of health.

Her arrogance irritated him intensely. His glance went to the footman hovering beside the still open door.

Turning back to Louise, he barked sharply, 'The hall is not the place to discuss my wife's health. The library if you please.' Turning on his heel he walked determinedly to the library door.

Sniffing, Louise glanced at the impassive face of the footman. The servant had belonged to her before Henrietta had chosen to marry. She gave a small dissatisfied huff, before following Tommy.

As he went through, he left the door open.

Louise followed, closing it behind her.

Barely moving from the door, she stood still, battling to remain calm, her hands small fists, the birdlike bones, ivory. 'How could you allow this thing to happen to Henrietta? You know that she is not strong ...'

He was incredulous. 'My fault is it? Enlighten me please. Your daughter chooses to become addicted to opium.'

He saw her eyes narrow and a supercilious curl come to her mouth. The desire to hurt her, bend her to his will, overtook any sympathy he had for the old lady.

Guessing that she knew only half of the truth, he delivered his poison; 'And an alcoholic. Let's not forget the drink.'

He saw her flinch and knew he'd been correct; she hadn't known about that.

Her face paled. Coming further into the room, she crumpled into a chair beside the large desk. 'How long has she been a ...?' her voice was barely a whisper.

Raising his dark satanic brows, he fixed his eyes upon

her. 'The opium addiction began before the birth of Edward. The sherry...' he snorted. 'Who knows? It could be years.' What he really wanted to say was that he didn't really care when it began, as he was tired of her being his wife.

Her voice weak, she whispered, 'My God. And I didn't notice.'

She was looking at the thin creased skin on the back of her hand, noting the light brown smudges that were beginning to blur together.

'I had no idea.' A tear trailed down her powdered face.

'Well, you know now.' His eyes fixed on her bent head. 'Why blame me for Henrietta's failure? That she can't manage her own life is surely more to do with you as a mother, than me as a late comer.'

Two tears dripped off Louise's jawbone. Bringing her hand up, she wiped the wetness off her cheek. Maybe he was right. Perhaps the blame did belong to her. The thought that she had damaged her child cut into her like a sharp knife. If the failure was hers, was she also culpable for George? That terrible night when he had begged her for money to pay off his debts and she had refused him; if she had succumbed to his entreaty would he not be the brain-damaged cripple that he now was? Did this tragedy also belong at her feet?

A ghost of a whisper passed her lips, 'Poor George.'

Standing, she went to the window and looked out onto the sunlit lawns, the edges studded with rose bushes, the reds already beginning to bloom. 'Do you believe that it is my fault?'

He had the grace to be embarrassed. Maybe he had gone too far. He coughed lightly. 'It doesn't all lie at your door. Henrietta has to be held accountable too. It was her decision to dose so often that she became obsessed with laudanum. Sensible people only take it to numb acute pain.' Exasperated he raised his hands running them through his thick hair.

Her eyes were on the trees in the avenue. She sighed.

'There's another sort of pain too, and it's much harder to kill.' What had Henrietta suffered that had brought the girl to this?

So the blame was coming back to him. Well, he wouldn't allow it. 'If you are referring to sentimental claptrap and the nonsense talked of emotions, this discussion is a waste of my time. I would understand it, if she had suffered a recent bereavement or something equally as catastrophic, but what has Henrietta got to be unhappy about?'

Arms akimbo he gestured to the rich opulence of the room. 'She has all this, and a small child.'

It wasn't lost on Louise that he didn't mention himself. Maybe Bertram, her late but still very dear husband, had been right when he suggested that Tommy wouldn't make Henrietta happy. She had ignored his misgivings and insisted that the marriage should go ahead. Had she heeded his words everything would be so different now. But Hen' had been pregnant, the wedding had to take place. The shame to the family would have been unendurable if it had not.

Turning to face him, she looked into his eyes for a glimmer of sympathy he might have for her daughter's plight. 'So what do you suggest we do?'

Going to bureau he took a bottle of brandy and poured a good measure into a glass. 'Do? Short of locking her up, I have no idea.' Drinking a mouthful, he topped the glass up, before putting the bottle down on the desktop.

Watching him, she thought of Bertram; it was what he used to do, keep a bottle of good brandy in the bureau. When she remonstrated with him, he would say there was no need to bother the servants for a little nip that he was able to get for himself. How often had she reminded him that he had a valet and a butler to do his bidding?

Bringing herself back to the moment, she said 'Locking her up, seems very harsh. Perhaps the doctor could suggest something?'

'He already has.'

'Oh, you didn't mention that you had consulted someone.'

He took another sip and then holding the glass in his two hands he warmed the brandy. 'I sought the advice from a doctor in Chester.'

Her brow lifted. 'Oh! Why not visit Griffith, the local surgeon?'

'Louise. How would it look if it got about that Henrietta's a drunk?' he said, feigning incredulity.

She flinched at his hard words. She felt nauseous but she wouldn't leave the room until she had a promise from him that something would be done to help her girl.

Although the day was warm, the sunless library was chill. A small fire burned in the Mona marble chimneypiece. Moving from the window, Louise went to it.

'Did this doctor make any proposal?'

Before answering he swallowed a mouthful of brandy. 'There was nothing he could recommend until he's seen her. But he said there was a hospital that specialises in treating addictions.'

Louise was enthusiastic. 'I'll tell Henrietta.'

He had already told Henrietta and to say that she had taken the news badly was an understatement. That his wife had not informed her mother of his intentions could only mean that she must be too drugged or too drunk to do so.

Although he was prepared to forbid her visiting Henrietta if necessary, he tried a gentler tack to secure her co-operation. 'I would prefer that you didn't mention it. I have told Henrietta and she agrees that it is the best thing to do. She's quite willing to try.'

Relief made her conciliatory. 'I'm sorry if I gave the impression that I blame you. Henrietta's welfare is dear to you, I know that. How long will it be before she can meet this doctor?'

Putting another inch of brandy into the glass, he swirled

the liquid. 'I'll make the necessary arrangements very soon. It'll take a week to finalise.'

She glanced at him, watching as he put aside the bottle. 'Then I'll stay until that time.'

Alarmed, Tommy backtracked. 'There's no need for you to do that. It might unsettle her you being here. In fact I would suggest that you should go home today without seeing her at all. Think of George; you know how distraught he gets when you are not with him.'

The tone of his voice and his demeanour were so unlike his usual behaviour, Louise was alerted that all was not quite as it should be. That he should consider it feasible for her to return home when she had arrived only a few hours ago after a tedious and tiring journey, was quite astonishing. Her daughter's happiness and health were at stake; what could possibly be more appropriate than that her mother should remain with her? Without giving him an inkling of what her intentions were, she made for the door.

A lock of hair fell from her normally immaculate coiffeur; absentmindedly she tucked it beneath the tortoiseshell comb in her hair. 'I really must go and tidy myself. Please excuse me.' There was a swish of taffeta as she went through the door.

A footman standing beside the front door, moved forward awaiting her instructions as she came out of the library.

For a moment, Tommy listened to their muted voices. The relief he felt at her imminent departure sweeping over him.

Imagining that at any moment Louise would instruct her maid to begin packing and the footman would arrange for the carriage to be brought round, he felt that he could examine the map of the land that held his interest, without further hindrance.

Slipping off his coat, he took another a sip of brandy from the almost empty glass. Putting the glass aside, he crossed the room to the cabinet, which had been specially made to house the map collection. It comprised of five drawers, made wide and deep enough to lay the maps flat to avoid unsightly creases. Several of the parchments were ancient. Many others were bespoke, drawn for Bertram's personal record.

Finding the one he needed, he took it to the large oak table at the far end of the room. Aligning it to the table edge, he followed the boundaries the Enclosure Act had created, until he came to the parcel of land that interested him. It was much larger than he had first thought. If the Snowdon Railway was built as planned and extra miles of track were laid, Ruby Slate Quarry would have perfects links to the port in Caernarvon.

Excitement mounting, he searched the glossary that Bertram had made, faded now, but the name was still legible.

The breath he was holding came out in a long sigh. 'Elias Parry! The old devil must be near eighty, if he's still alive.'

Tomorrow, he would call on his own solicitor, Madoc. It was imperative that he send a letter to Parry or his heirs and settle a price for the land.

Thoughtful, he sat in the hide armchair behind his desk, his head cushioned by the high-back; he began spinning ideas. It wasn't his intention to form an alliance with investors, unless it was impossible to achieve the enterprise without them. Ruby would be his, and his alone. Haulage would be his main problem. Initially trams would have to run on tracks; it would be the cheapest option. A few major quarries had switched to engines, but he wasn't ready to banish the horses just yet. The venture was too speculative to spend an astronomical amount of money on. When he was certain the harvest was good and would be improved with better cartage, then he'd start thinking about changing over.

Envisaging the future, his eyes shone with excitement. A new village would spring up around Ruby. The workers would need homes. If he was involved financially in the construction, there was no knowing how big the rewards might be. The possibilities were endless.

Smiling, he picked up his glass and sipped the expensive, mellow brandy.

The library door opened sharply. Startled, he nearly knocked the glass over. Cursing, brushing imaginary splashes from his trousers, he stood with the backs of his knees against the seat of the chair.

'Louise, I would prefer you to knock before barging in here.'

Her eyes sparked fire. 'I bet you would. Well, you can sit down again, because I have quite a lot to say to you.'

He remained standing. 'I'm sorry to hear that, because I was just about to leave the house. So whatever you wish to discuss with me, will have to wait.'

Crossing to the desk, her hands trembling with anger, her mouth a hard thin line, she spat words, 'So you want to put my daughter in a lunatic asylum. How dare you?'

The wide desk stood between them, preventing her slapping his insolent face. 'This family has done a great deal for you and how do you repay us? Propose to lock our daughter away? It's a pity that Bertram is not here to throw you out.'

His anger matched hers. He bellowed, 'Your darling daughter has only herself to blame. If she behaves like a lunatic, then she must be treated like one.'

His hands were clenched so tightly that the knuckles on his fists were bone white. 'If Henrietta continues to behave in such a fashion, she'll go to Denbigh Asylum at the first opportunity. If she learns to control her addictions, she will be treated by Doctor Rogers in Chester. Now I want you to leave. If you feel the journey to your home is too tiresome to make today, I suggest you put up in lodgings in Caernarvon.'

A pair of pale yellow kid gloves lay on the corner of the desk; picking them up sharply, his nails clicking on the wood, he donned them quickly.

His mouth was tight with anger. 'I will organise your carriage on my way out. It would be foolish to upset Henrietta more than is necessary, so please refrain from going to her room before you depart. If Henrietta becomes nervous, it upsets young Edward.'

His departure was noisy, his voice strident as he ordered a carriage and his horse to be brought immediately.

The fierce anger that had surged through her left Louise weak. Crumpling into the chair beside the fireplace, she looked around the familiar room. Once it had been her beloved Bertram's domain. In the past she would join him here and they would spend an hour or more chatting or reading companionably. Now it was a place she could be dismissed from by a man that had started life as the son of a quarrier, a village boy. How times change. His was the ascending star, whilst her family were in an emotional downward spiral.

There was hardly any heat from the fire. She thought to ring for a servant to stoke the embers but she couldn't summon the energy required to be polite to the servants.

Her eye caught the brandy bottle on the desk. There was still a small amount in it.

Going to the bureau, she took a glass and poured brandy into it. Tasting it, she was flung back into the past, to a cold winter's afternoon when she had come in after a brisk walk. Bertram had been behind the desk and he had risen as she entered. On touching her cold hands, he had poured a large measure of brandy for her. They had sat by a roaring fire, laughing at some mischief George and Henrietta had got into involving a runaway sled.

The memory was crystal clear. Rain like splinters of ice had hit the window-pane, and she'd been glad to be indoors with the warmth and crackle of the fire. Bertram was smoking a cigar and the fragrance of sweet tobacco was in the room. As he handed her the glass he touched her arm gently.

It was as though those moments were happening now and he was in the room beside her. Slowly, so as not to disrupt the impression, she crossed back to the chair beside the fireplace, her cold hand clutching the glass.

Sitting, she watched the small flames, finding comfort in the notion that he sat alongside her in the way he once did, patiently gauging every nuance of her mood.

'What shall I do, Bertram?' her voice was hardly above a whisper.

His familiar voice came into her mind. 'Do, my love? You will do what you must. Find a way to block him. There are people that you can turn to, friends and solicitors. Do it not only for Henrietta, but George too.'

'George!' Until this moment the idea had never occurred to her that Tommy might have something to do with the evil thing that had happened to George, her only son. If George had not been injured, he would have inherited everything and she and Henrietta would have been saved from this nightmare.

Agitated she rose. Pacing across to the window she looked out across the lawns. The rose trees were bending in the newly risen breeze.

Her thoughts clearing, she decided that she would leave Plas Mawr and stay in Caernarvon overnight. First thing tomorrow morning she would seek help; there were old friends of Bertram's that would be happy to give their assistance. She would start with Madoc, the family solicitor.

Tommy had taken the brown stallion from his comfortable stable and ridden away with little thought of where he was heading. It was too late to begin a journey to visit his old friend the Colonel. He would have liked to discuss his ideas regarding the new quarry with Edward, but he didn't relish turning up there after dark and without an invitation.

Of course he could call at the local hostelry. He was about to steer the horse in the direction of the Half-Way, when he thought better of it. The quarrymen that drank there were unlikely to make him welcome.

Aimless, he thought of his options. He could go back to Plas Mawr and face Louise or he could pay a visit to his parents' home. It had been a long time since he had seen his mother. He hadn't set eyes on her since the move into the new cottage his father and brother had built two years ago. Not that she'd hold that against him; she'd give him a hearty greeting if he turned up on her step.

If he went, there'd be a lecture from his father. Joe Standish was too much of a union man, bleating on about how a union was the only way forward in this modern world.

Providing for a quarry hospital had been his most recent bleat. Not to mention his ideas of benefits and sick pay. The bugger wanted benefits for widows and orphans too, ignoring entirely that the majority of fatal accidents at the Garddryn were caused by careless quarrymen. Why should the Garddryn get the blame if a man died of pneumonia weeks after tripping over something at the quarry, or falling off a terrace, getting knocked out by a plummeting stone? The trouble with the quarrier families today was that they considered themselves above parish handouts.

Some of the quarry owners were fools to themselves and they made it harder for everyone else to make a decent living. They gave the men too much when they began erecting hospitals, etcetera.

The brown stallion, fairly elderly and hardly used, was walking in the direction of his parents' cottage but he took little heed of it. Subconsciously he was listening out for Louise's carriage on the parallel road.

To restore his earlier good mood he turned his deliberation to his latest lover. Lady Isabelle was a perfect dalliance. The episode at Penrhyn had been delightful. They had spent two wonderful nights together. Lady Isabelle was capable of many unusual capers. If he'd had any sense, he would have been content with that. But to his embarrassment he'd made a bit of a fool of himself and had insisted on seeing her again. Because he'd persevered, they had met several times in Chester and London and he had become obsessed with the style of love making the lady demanded. How he hadn't marked her was a mystery to him. The whipping she'd directed should have scarred her. Now her husband was expected back and she could no longer risk seeing him. The enforced separation was playing havoc with his temper.

So much so that he was considering trying for Sadie again; she might have recovered her humour by now. Perhaps he should arrange an overnight visit to Penrhyn. Edward and he still hadn't discussed the quarry tramways. Tomorrow he'd send a note to discover if the Colonel was receiving guests. With a bit of judicious planning he could incorporate an appointment with his solicitor in Caernarvon.

Cheered by this decision, he spurred the horse in the direction of his parents' home.

Emily kneeling on an old sack, poking about with a garden fork in the border of flowers beneath the hedge, ignored the sound of hoof beats on the lane. It could be one of a dozen men riding out and she had little interest in the business that took them abroad during the evening. She was attempting to dig out the root of a particularly resilient dandelion that insisted on growing beneath the lavender bush.

She was listening for the sound of the tin bucket. Joe had taken the pig's feed to the pen and she expected him back at any moment. The pig could be an obstreperous bugger when he wanted to be, so she preferred Frank to feed him; his legs were a sight younger than Joe's.

Frank could scale the fence in a leap to avoid a smack from the porker's snout. He'd had them reeling with laughter on more than one occasion as he'd jumped, bucket in hand, over the fence and landed in the filthy ditch beneath the hedge, the angry pig in pursuit up to the last second. When his quarry was out of reach, Jake would waddle back to the trough in as dignified manner as he could manage.

It made her smile just thinking about it.

'What has you smiling, Mother?'

In surprise she dropped the fork, and rose slowly on knees that had begun to creak. 'Tommy! How lovely it is to see you.'

'I don't suppose Pater will think so.'

She grinned. 'Pater, is it? Whatever happened to plain old Da?'

Hating to be reminded of his humble origins, he flushed pink. Now he wished he hadn't made the excursion. Dismounting, he patted the stallion's neck affectionately and tied the reins to the gatepost.

Emily, wiping her dirty hand on her old linen pinafore, said 'How's Edward and Henrietta?'

'They're both very well,' he lied.

Standing aside from the gate, she ushered him in. 'Come on in, lad. Don't stand on ceremony. Father will be back any minute. He's gone to feed old Jake.'

'Jake?'

'The pig, his pen's at the bottom of the field. A lot's changed since we saw you last.' She tried to keep any trace of a reprimand from her voice.

Reaching the end of the path, Emily pushed open the front door that had stood ajar to let warm air into the cottage.

Tommy, taller than his father or Frank, had to duck his head under the lintel. This house had not been built with him in mind and it irked him to have proof of it. 'Where's Frank?'

Putting the kettle to the hot plate, Emily busied herself making tea. 'He's courting a young lady in the village. They'll have gone for a walk.'

Tommy was reminded of the time when he had courted Millie Barker, and the secret hours that they had spent together at the old mill.

Emily seemed to read his mind. 'Do you remember the lass you were walking out with, the one that was killed up at the old mill? What a terrible business that was. I see her mother occasionally in the village when I'm shopping at Maisy's. The poor woman has not been the same since her girl was murdered, and it broke her father's heart.'

Sighing, she scooped tealeaves into the pot.

Tommy remained silent, impassive. Millie Barker had deserved her fate. He felt no remorse at her untimely end. If she had kept her mouth shut ...

Reaching into a cupboard, Emily brought out a freshly baked apple pie. 'I must have known you were coming. I baked this for our tea.' She smiled up at him.

One thing his mother could do extremely well, was make pastry. It was her endless stews that he found so awful.

She was cutting into the pie with a long knife, releasing a sweet aroma. Without looking up, she said with a hint of pride, 'These apples are the first crop of a young tree our Frank planted a year ago.'

The kettle came to the boil saving him from saying anything favourable about his younger brother. Lifting it, he poured the water onto the leaves in the pot.

Joe was heard stamping mud off his boots as he came up the garden path, the empty bucket rattling.

Emily glanced at her elder boy, his head was half-turned from her and he looked so like Joe, the same firm jaw-line and high cheekbones.

They were both holding their breath waiting for the door to open. Tommy wishing that he hadn't given in to the whim that brought him to his parents' home. Emily praying that the encounter between the pair, at loggerheads at the quarry, would build bridges.

Dumping the bucket, Joe crossed the threshold. 'I wondered whose animal that was tied outside, as its not the vicar's; I guessed it might be you.'

He forced a smile, making the effort for Emily's sake. Knowing how much this visit would mean to her. He wished that he could feel an ounce of forgiveness in his soul for his first-born, but he'd be lying if he admitted to any such thing. Two years ago, Tommy broke his mother's heart. In Joe's book that was unforgivable.

Since boyhood, Tommy had ridden roughshod over everyone around him. When he was young it was easy to make excuses; as he grew and the cruelty in his character developed, it became more difficult.

Stalling, keeping the harsh words he would like to say in check, Joe wiped his feet thoroughly, inspecting the soles for dirt before he stepped off the doormat. 'So to what do we owe this pleasure?'

Under his father's roof, Tommy felt five-years-old. 'The cottage, I wondered how it was coming on.'

Emily missed Tommy's sharp intake of breath, before he answered his father. She was marvelling at the thorough cleaning Joe had given his boots, when a cursory swipe was the norm.

Dipping his head, Joe kissed Emily's cheek. 'That pie looks scrumptious.'

'I made it with the new apples. They've kept really well over winter.'

Joe's tone was cursory, 'So they should, they've had enough attention.'

Sitting in the frayed chair, he pulled off his work boots. 'Come on then, tell us all your news from home, our Tommy,' he said.

'There's not a lot to tell. Edward is well as is Henrietta. Louise Bellamy is here on a visit. Henrietta was really looking forward to spending some time with her. I expect that in a day or two they will go off on a shopping expedition.'

Joe busied himself pouring the tea.

Emily put a slice of pie onto one of her best plates, reserved for Christmas and the vicar's visits. Handing it to Tommy, she smiled a little smugly. 'So what do you think of our new home?'

Emily was proud that Frank and Joe had accomplished the incredible task of building the cottage. It had been more than a year of agonising labour and all done on top of a day's work. They had been full of enthusiasm when work started on digging the foundations. They had expected to complete the task quite quickly, but these hopes were dashed when they hit the boulders lying beneath the surface. Digging deep, they brought up enough stone to build the thick walls. Joe used explosive to blast the rocks that were too big to move. It had been like a tinker's wedding, huge booms and cracks splitting the air. The harvested rock completed the last layer of the walls.

What a day that had been. Joe had been up the ladder making a ceremony of planting the last stone, grinning enough to split his face in two. Below, Frank swiping at his eyes with the back of his gritty hand. Not that she'd been much better, drying her tears on her apron hem.

That night Frank tasted his first proper ale at the Half-Way. Counting his new calluses as he supped. He wore them like precious medals. Reckoned that the new house should be called Corn Cottage and the name stuck.

Less than a fortnight after the walls were finished, the timber to support the roof was on. Frank put the slates to it. It had been a real achievement.

She'd shed no tears at leaving Bryn Tirion, a draughty cold place, damp too. Corn Cottage was sound, drier than any she'd lived in and more comfortable. The living room was larger than most. The scullery, although freezing in the winter, was big enough for the dolly and tub. But more

70

importantly, Corn Cottage wasn't part of the family heartache. The spirit of her darling little daughter, Chloe was here, but not the heartbreak of her sudden passing away.

Emily waited for Tommy's answer and when she thought he hadn't heard her, she repeated the question. 'So what do you think of it?'

Tommy's eyes roved over the room, which was primitive when compared to any at Plas Mawr, and that included the scullery at the mansion. The walls of his beloved house were adorned with patterned brocades, curtains in corresponding shades falling from ceiling to floor in a waterfall of exquisite fabrics. The few pieces of furniture here were the simple items of his childhood and not remotely like the spindly furniture of exotic cherry, satin, or mahogany he was now familiar with. This rough Welsh oak was far too countrified, peasant.

His eyes went to the beamed ceiling. 'How long did it take to build?'

Joe saw that he was avoiding answering his mother's question. His jaw tightened with aggravation. He was about to make a sharp comment when Tommy answered.

'It looks very substantial, cosy too.'

Taking this as approval, Emily smiled happily. 'It took more than a year to do the job. Frank and your Father worked all the hours God sent. Up at the quarry all day, then back home for a bit of tea and out until bedtime, in all weathers. They worked like slaves.'

A tinge of haughtiness filtered into Tommy's voice. 'And is Frank as pleased with it, as you are?'

'Oh, yes.' Eager to impart the plans for the future, she went on, 'When he marries he'll build a room on the back. Later, God willing, another will go up if he should start a family. It will be nice to have a bairn or two about the place.'

'Seems you have everything organised.'

Aware that something had annoyed Tommy, jealousy

71

probably, Joe's words were clipped, 'Aye, and when we've popped our clogs, the house'll be his an' all.'

Emily thought that it had been a touch tactless to mention this and was keen to straighten Tommy's ruffled feathers. 'It's only fair that he should have it, as he did a lot of the work in its creation. And you have a lovely home with your wife and little one. There's nothing that you would want from our humble cott.'

Tommy's top lip lifted. 'Frank's welcome to it.'

Joe sighed.

A few minutes later, Tommy put aside the empty plate and making his excuses left the house, suddenly remembering that he had made a promise to call on a friend.

Emily stood at the garden gate, watching horse and rider until they were lost to the trees. When there was no hope of sighting them again, she listened to the faint beat of hooves.

Coming back into the house, despondent now, she closed the front door. 'Do you think he'll call again soon?'

Joe thought that there wasn't a cat in hell's chance of it, but seeing her crestfallen expression, he replied cheerfully 'I expect that he will.'

CHAPTER FOUR

Standing on the bluff of a hill, Mr Thomas Parker, a specialist in minerals surveyed the surrounding land. An Englishman, he had settled with his large family in South Wales where his expertise was much sought after for the detection of copper, tin, coal and other potentially lucrative mining commodities.

The majority of his work was sedentary; field expeditions he assigned to two younger men he employed for the task of hiking over fell and mountain. That Tommy Standish had inveigled him to this remote and barren acreage in North Wales was testimony to Tommy's reputation as a business-man, with immense wealth at his command.

Parker was short and rotund; at the slightest exertion his moon-face flushed unhealthily, the pinkness a great contrast to the white side-whiskers bushing on his cheeks. His mouth was full, the top lip partially veiled by a moustache fringed with yellow. Self-important, he was inclined to be pompous, a characteristic shown in plenty to fledgling entrepreneurs; affluent men of influence were treated with less pretension.

Parker chose to forget that he was self-taught in the mysteries of mineral science and the references he made to Trinity were not to Cambridge, but an inferior college in Glasgow.

Shielding his eyes against the July noonday sun, he looked to the far distance; the hills on the horizon were dark lavender, silhouetted against the pale sky. Making a slow turn, his unusually small feet taking tottering steps, he gazed towards the impressive Snowdonia range of mountains; at midday the peaks were almost colourless, disappearing into the blank sky.

A light breeze wafted across the moor-land and a long strand of hair that grew just above his right ear, arranged properly it was meant to disguise his baldpate, lifted and fell to one side.

Standing beside the man, Tommy's eyes were drawn to the thatch flying like a white pennant and wondered why Parker seemed oblivious to it.

Harrumphing, Parker rubbed the end of his nose with his forefinger. 'The lay of the land and the proximity of other quarries lead me to believe that you are correct to suppose this area could be productive for quarrying, Mr Standish.'

Having a high regard for the man's reputation, Tommy was euphoric. Weeks ago, when he had picked up the wedge of red slate he had known that Ruby, his own quarry, lay beneath the springy sod.

Hiding his elation, Tommy spoke calmly, 'Can we get proof?'

Parker smiled, chuckling. 'One can never be wholly certain until digging begins.'

With a sweep of his arm, Parker encompassed the vast acreage. 'We can take samples from over a wide area, but it will not tell us how deep the slate might run, but an indication of its quality can be ascertained from specimens.'

Linking his fingers across his pot belly, Parker smiled. 'But I'd stake my reputation that below here,' he patted the wiry grass with his shoe, 'there's slate and a goodly amount of it too.'

Trying to contain his happiness, not too smile too broadly or vulgarly, Tommy looked across the virgin land.

The two men spent the next hour collecting specimens of rock and slate. Parker stashed numerous samples in a canvas bag and, tying the cord to the saddle on his grazing mare, he patted her fat rump before mounting. It took him a moment to settle and regain his breath and he was reminded of his age and corpulence. Riding in a saddle was no longer a favoured mode of travel; his wife and age had converted him to horse-drawn vehicles. Looping the reins loosely over his wrist, he wiped the grime from his hands onto a grey handkerchief.

Tommy mounted easily and effortlessly, and Parker was consumed with yearning for his own lost youth and suppleness. The thought wasn't new to him; it invaded regularly, he had become adept at banishing it to the labyrinths of his mind and he did so now.

'Will you go ahead and purchase the land, Mr Standish?'

Throughout the afternoon Parker had played with the idea of selling the information about the site to the highest bidder in the mining field; he knew many men that would kill to get the opportunity to buy a piece of property with the scope of becoming as immense as the nearby Penrhyn and Garddryn quarries.

The warm leather of Tommy's saddle creaked as he half-turned towards Parker. With a self-congratulatory smile on his mouth, Tommy said, 'I already do own it, Mr Parker.'

Tommy had a high regard for Parker's ability to seek out minerals but that didn't mean he trusted the man. The information Parker had gathered today was valuable, very valuable indeed.

The acquisition of the land had been straightforward. Elias Parry had accepted Tommy's offer without argument. The financial reward gained by the sale was to help his grandchildren and great grandchildren, who having no interest in raising sheep on the land, had set up as shipwrights in Caernarvon.

Madoc, Tommy's solicitor, had hurried the signing of the relevant contract before speculators became wise to the transaction, monetary recompense above the usual fee being paid for his trouble. Equally anxious, Elias Parry had put his cross upon the documents before Tommy Standish had a change of heart.

Delighted that the transaction had gone without a hitch, before speculators discovered the potential of the land and inflated the price, Tommy organised the setting up of the company, assisted by Madoc.

Tommy believed that it was only a matter of a short time before the proposed railway that had been pledged by the railway company came into being. Until that happened Ruby slate would be taken to the nearest port in wagons pulled by horses on a tramway. The vast profits would come at a later stage, after the laying of the railway track.

The July evening was hot with no promise of respite come nightfall. The windows of the Half-Way were open and the flimsy curtains stained with smoke and ancient condensation hung limp at the old sash frames. Muted noise, like the hum of thousands of flying insects, spilled out onto the narrow lane. The stone walls oozed the day's heat. Tobacco smoke and the scent of ale lay on the hot, still air.

Thirsty, Joe approached the inn anticipating the first taste of ale. The day had been devoted to mending the fence around the pig pen and raking the weeds growing between the root vegetables on his patch of land.

As he was about to enter, he heard the high clear voice of a boy singing coming from the nearby chapel, pure and virginal. He was caught by the beauty and slowing his step he listened until the last innocent note died.

He was just moving on when two men walked out of the inn; passing him they gave a long glance, before turning to walk up the lane, their heads close together in conversation. Joe half-turned and watched them walking away. He knew that they were discussing him. One of the men glanced over his shoulder to look back and then he bumped his elbow into his comrade.

Stepping over the threshold, Joe entered the packed room

and silence fell almost instantly. It wasn't the first time he'd met hostility when walking into the tavern; it had happened many years ago when he was raw to rubbling, a novice worker in the quarry, an Englishman.

Without breaking his stride, Joe walked to the bar counter. The man there looked at him with cold eyes. 'Ale?'

In a firm voice, Joe answered, 'Aye, I'll have a quart of the stuff.'

Turning to a large wooden barrel, the barman poured ale into a glass and placed it on the counter before Joe. Their eyes met as he put a coin into the barman's wet palm.

Behind Joe, a strident voice demanded, 'So is it true then?'

As he wasn't being addressed by name, Joe ignored the enquiry. Taking a long swig from the glass he wiped his mouth with the back of his hand. Then issued a long satisfied sigh.

'Standish.'

Turning slowly, Joe looked to the inquisitive faces.

Davies, a man he knew by sight, fixed him with a penetrating stare. 'What do you know of this new quarry?'

'What quarry?' Joe was brusque.

A rustle of conversation swept over the room. From a dark corner, someone shouted 'The quarry that Tommy Standish has bought.'

Joe couldn't hide his surprise and his eyebrows lifted. 'I've heard nothing of it.'

The innkeeper added his own derisory comment. 'Oh, come on. Surely your own son keeps you informed of what he's planning. He'd hardly buy a bloody quarry without telling his *Pater*.'

Joe turned to face the men squarely. 'My son has seen fit to keep me in the dark about his marriage, the birth of his bairn, moving out of his home and into another. Why in God's name would he tell me his business arrangements?'

Frank came through the door. Glancing quickly at his

father, he spoke sharply, 'What's up?'

Morgan Sperret, a village busybody, a horseman on the tramway, gave Frank a truculent stare. 'Did you know what your brother's about? Buying a quarry and setting up for his self?'

Frank frowned. 'I never heard anything so daft. Did you, Da?'

Joe's lip curled. 'No, I bloody didn't. But where our Tommy's concerned, anything might have happened.'

Joe fixed his eyes on the man he thought had the most common sense. 'What quarry are we talking about, Hywel?

Relighting his pipe, Hywel drew in fragrant smoke. 'It's not a quarry yet, but Elias Parry has sold him a large piece of land a few miles from here; it borders on the mountains.'

Hywel pointed the stem of his pipe at Joe. 'If he's got that, and he has any success, he'll dig into the mountains for sure.'

Joe's thoughts flowed fast, instantly understanding the repercussions of this news; his answer was stark. 'At this point I'm not as worried for the mountains, as I am about us.'

Irate, the men muttered.

Someone voiced their collective opinion, 'Easy for you to say that as they are Welsh mountains and you an Englishman.'

Joe shot the man a venomous look. Raising his voice he spoke to all, 'Tommy's a hard case, but I don't need to tell that to the men that work for the bugger. If he has a crack at another quarry, the men at the Garddryn and the new quarry will suffer. He'd be the biggest employer in the district with a monopoly on wages,' he snorted. 'The pay would be as low as possible. The men's welfare not considered. It'd be a bad day for Garddryn village, if this information is true.'

The man who had made the offensive remark, turned his eyes from Joe.

Taking the opportunity to air the subject close to his heart, Joe raised his voice over the murmuring, 'If this news is accurate, the only thing that'll protect us is the formation of a quarrymen's union.'

Most agreed, but were too afraid of the consequences to make a comment. It was a moment to lift their ales and take a drink.

Nudging his father, Frank whispered 'There's a couple of tell-tales sitting in the corner. Take care, Da, or we'll find ourselves locked out of the quarry and barred from every other in the district.'

'Thanks, lad. I'll bide me time for now. But if it's true about our Tommy and this new perishing quarry, the union will be even more important to us.'

'Aye, I know.' Thoughtful, Frank picked up his ale and took a long swig.

Joe wondered if he should keep the news from Emily. How long would it be before it was all over the village and she overheard it in Maisy's shop? There was only one solution. Ask Tommy outright. It wasn't a meeting he would look forward to, but Tommy was his son. Men had a right to blame a father for the way he turned his bairns out into the world.

Finishing his ale, Frank gave Joe a sidelong glance. 'Want another?'

'Go on then, but I'll buy it.'

Emily was in bed when Joe and Frank arrived home. Although it was ten o'clock it was still light, the sun dropping into the sea painting a path of red-gold across the darkening ocean.

After sharing a pot of strong tea, Frank went to his room at the back of the cottage. Joe sat for a while thinking of Tommy and his early childhood. Eventually his mind turned to his beloved daughter. Chloe had been gone sixteen years. At times the pain was as fresh as that first day.

CHAPTER FIVE

Tommy was in the library poring over papers when the new footman, after a tentative knock, entered. Irritated by the interruption, Tommy looked up from the documents piled on his desk.

'What is it, Roberts?'

'I beg your pardon, sir.' The man gave a small bow. 'Mr Joseph Standish wishes to see you. He's waiting in the hall, sir.'

Tommy had expected his father to come sniffing around looking for information. The new quarry would be the talk of the district. Every quarryman and village peasant would be hungry for particulars of Ruby. There was no better man to send nosing than Joe Standish, father of the master, would-be *union* man.

Rudely abrupt, Tommy ordered, 'Let him wait ten minutes before sending him in.'

The servant withdrew.

As the heavy door clicked closed, Tommy glanced at the documents but his concentration had fled. Slapping the palm of his hand down on the topmost paper he cursed.

Rising, he pushed the heavy chair back from the desk and crossed to the bureau. His hand went to the bottle of brandy he kept there. Pouring a good measure into a crystal glass, he tipped it to his lips and swallowed a mouthful. The fire of the spirit burned a path to his belly, taking the edge off his temper.

Clutching the glass against his waistcoat, he thought of

his father waiting impatiently beyond the library door. The man could not abide standing still. The idea of Joe Standish simmering with indignation, brought a small smile to Tommy's mouth. He was glad the old man was cogitating in the opulent hall. In future he'd think twice about opposing the authority of his betters.

Topping up the glass, the lip of the bottle chinking on the rim made him aware that his hand was trembling. His temper flared at his weakness. It was entirely his father's fault; his visit was disconcerting.

'Bastard!' He spat the word like a blasphemy.

His father was a menace, baulking at every change that was made in the Garddryn. Refusing to accept that longer hours, and all-day Saturday labour, was a necessity if the quarry was to increase output.

It was a struggle to control his anger. Taking a deep draft from the glass, he held the fiery liquid on his tongue before swallowing.

His eyes went to the documents; there amidst the estimated figures, information and calculations lay his embryonic quarry, his vision. It was a dream his father had no part of. It was his alone.

Slightly more relaxed, he went behind his desk and sat in the leather chair. Picking up a legal deed, he breathed the scent of the aged parchment.

Left to kick his heels, Joe paced the area between the long arched windows, his work boots clacking on the mosaic floor. Angered by the shoddy reception meted out by his elder son, he wished to God that at some point in the past he had thrashed some manners into his lad. It was too late now. From his own loins he had created a man without scruple, shame, or compassion. Emily's part in the creation of Tommy Standish didn't enter Joe's thoughts.

Glancing along the hallway towards the library door, where no doubt his prodigal son amused himself with some new idea of how to make the *lot* of quarrymen more ill-starred, he snarled and turned in that direction.

Startled by the man's boldness, the footman came quickly from the sanctuary of the cloaks room.

'Allow me to show you into the library, sir.' Calling a workman 'sir' stuck in the servant's craw. Joe Standish was nothing but a quarryman, but it was prudent to be polite. Anger leached from the man.

As they entered the library, Joe shouldered passed the man, giving him a sidelong glance. 'There's no need for your ceremonials; the man here knows that I'm his father.'

The footman was careful not to catch the eye of his employer, as he backed out of the room.

Tommy didn't rise. 'And to what do we owe this pleasure?'

Joe's china blue eyes were flint hard. 'I don't think you'll consider my visit a pleasure when you know why I'm here.'

Tommy's top lip rose fractionally. 'Whatever it is, you had better tell me reasonably quickly; I have an appointment to keep at Penrhyn Castle.'

The beginning of the sneer wasn't lost on Joe, and his response was curt. 'I have no wish to detain you. The only reason I am here is to discover if the rumour that you are setting up a quarry in the district, is true.'

Tommy lifted the brandy glass to his mouth, before taking a draft he said, 'Yes, perfectly true.'

Joe was startled, the last thing he expected was a straight answer; evasions and down right lies was more Tommy's style. For a moment he was lost for words.

Tommy smirked. It was a long time since he had silenced the old man and it felt good to have bested him, however briefly. 'You seem surprised, I don't know why; it's not a secret that I have purchased the land that formerly belonged to Elias Parry. To be specific, it's the tract that runs seven miles north of Llandfydd and goes almost to the mountains to the west.'

Joe pictured the bleak terrain, vast, remote, virtually

inaccessible. 'It's a hell of a long way to cart slate from there to the port. To lay a tramway for wagons, or build a railway, would cost a king's ransom.'

Tommy smiled. 'But Father, I do possess a king's ransom. So I see no difficulties there.'

Accepting this reality, Joe's hope that the quarry wasn't viable faded fast. Tommy Standish as the biggest land and quarry owner would rule the lives of the quarrymen of the district. With the Garddryn and now a second quarry under his management his word would be law. The bastard would set wages low and risks high. A wave of hopelessness crept over Joe. He struggled to find the energy to continue the conversational brawl, but did so, for no other reason than to set doubts in Tommy's mind.

'You'll never haul enough slate to make it a profitable enterprise. However much your quarrymen blast out, there's no way that you could transport it to Caernarvon.'

Tommy's eyes twinkled. 'Ah, obviously you don't know everything, Father. Soon there will be a railway running from Snowdon to the coast. The railway company is already operational. I plan to invest money in it, along with dozens of other rich financiers.'

He grinned. 'I can't lose, can I? Railway, new quarry, quarrymen's houses, workers shops, loans for house building. Not forgetting the annual income for the rents from the smallholders and cotters on my land. The list for profitable enterprises is endless.'

Joe's eyes were dark, brooding. 'It all might seem *endless* now, but time will tell.'

Tommy rose. Extending his hand across the desk, he faked a smile. 'Well, goodbye, Father. I'm afraid I really must ask you to leave, as I should make tracks to Penrhyn Castle.'

Joe couldn't resist a verbal swipe, 'Penrhyn is it? I'd heard that you were tupping a wench there. It's the talk of the quarry and the village, but then the peasants must have something to laugh about. Wouldn't you say so, Son?'

Tommy withdrew his hand.

Brusquely, Joe turned to the door. Glancing over his shoulder, he was facetious, 'I'll give your mother your love, shall I?'

The library door was barely closed on his father, when it opened again on Henrietta and her mother making a feminine entrance in a whisper of silk and brocade. The dense black of Henrietta's gown drew Tommy's attention to her pale, translucent complexion. It was just another annoying reminder of her dependency on opium.

Glancing from wife to mother-in-law, Tommy scowled. 'Am I to be troubled further?'

Unaccustomed to being addressed impolitely, Louise bridled. 'That I can't answer, but I suppose it rather depends upon you.'

Downing the remainder of the brandy, he rose and gathered the papers on his desk together. 'Tell me quickly; I have an appointment to keep.'

Louise looked down her long, thin nose. 'We have no desire to detain you. All we need is a promise that you will not send poor Henrietta to Denbigh hospital as you have threatened to do, yet again. It is not two months since I had your promise via Madoc the solicitor that you would desist in taking this line with Henrietta.'

Tommy did remember; he had been mortified when calling on Madoc in connection with the purchase of the Ruby land, to be warned of the possible consequences if he were to put his wife away.

'The scandal alone would finish you.' Madoc had cautioned.

Unlocking the desk drawer, Tommy put the papers inside; relocking it, he pocketed the key.

His eyes were hard as he looked from Henrietta to her mother. 'Yes, Louise, I do recall the incident. I remember that it was you that brought embarrassment on the family by confiding our business to an outsider. Calling on Madoc at his office to discuss the state of my marriage, was unforgivable.'

Tommy came from around the desk. 'I have neither the inclination nor the time to discuss such matters. No doubt, Henrietta, if she hasn't already, will give you the details of our most recent debacle.'

Taking an envelope off the desk, he slipped it in the pocket of his frock coat. 'I am expected at Penrhyn Castle and must leave immediately.'

Trying to hide her enmity, Louise beseeched, 'Surely this matter is more important than any arrangement that you may have made with the Colonel.'

Tommy frowned. 'Why would you assume that?'

'Because, Tommy, we are discussing your wife's happiness.'

Tommy glanced to Henrietta and smirked. 'Oh! But my dear wife claims she relinquished happiness, the day she married me.'

Taking his silver topped stick from against the side of the desk, he stuck it in the crook of his arm. 'I expect to return tomorrow. If not, the following day.'

'But, Tommy.' Louise's entreaty sounded like a long sigh.

Listless, Henrietta flung herself into the overstuffed chair by the chimneypiece. 'Oh, let him go, Mother. He only does what he wants to do. There no keeping him against his will.'

Sounding tired and dispirited, Henrietta looked into the grate. 'If it's not Lady Isabelle's company he seeks, it'll be that of the kitchen maid, Sadie Pearson.'

Tommy hid his shock well. That his infidelity was known to his wife shook him and for a moment he felt vulnerable. If Henrietta were to divorce him, how secure would his position within Plas Mawr and the Garddryn be? Rallying his wits, he reasoned that no judge would give precedence to a wife over her husband regarding property and land. And certainly not a woman reliant on opium and alcohol, with the added taint of indulging in sexual intercourse before marriage. Henrietta, or at least her mother, had too much sense to bring that calamity down on their heads. Louise would never sanction a divorce. She had arranged their hurried marriage when the scandal of Henrietta's pregnancy threatened to become public knowledge. There was also young Edward's future to consider; what chance did he have within society if his mother was branded a harlot and a drunk? He, as master of the household and the Garddryn, had nothing to fear from the two women. Louise would rather die than see her family made a mockery of.

Laughing off the accusation of adultery, he was patronising, 'Henrietta dear, you're having delusions again.'

Tilting her sullen face to his, he smiled. 'I told you that no good would come of over indulging on laudanum. The medicine puts silly, extravagant ideas into your head.'

Turning to Louise, the fixed smile still on his mouth, he was mocking, 'Please explain to Henrietta that it's the opium that does this to her.'

Louise started to reply, but he rudely spoke over her voice.

Sounding as though frustrated beyond endurance, he said, 'Louise, I suggested that Hen' saw the doctor in Chester. But you must reject everything I recommend. Even though it's Henrietta that will suffer in the long run.'

Louise didn't state the obvious, that it was the particular doctor that Tommy had suggested, attached as he was to the Denbigh asylum, who would have locked poor Henrietta up for God knows how long, that she objected to.

With enormous difficulty, Louise kept a tight hold on her temper. 'I have no intention of getting into an argument with you, Tommy. Can we not calm down and discuss this matter with decorum?'

Tommy laughed loudly. 'Decorum? when did your daughter show any of that?'

With an air of resignation, Henrietta said, 'Let him go, Mother.'

Tommy didn't bother to reply. Turning, he made for the door, and without a backward glance he went through into the hallway, calling for Miles the butler.

The two women in the library listened to his muted voice, each with her own unwholesome thoughts of Tommy Standish, the interloper.

On the doorstep, shunning the carriage, Tommy ordered that his favourite mare be brought round by the groom.

Minutes later he rode down the long avenue, the late afternoon sun warm on his back. The ride gave him time to consider Henrietta's knowledge of his lovers, Lady Isabelle and Sadie Pearson. The denouncement had been a close call. The surprise left him fumbling for an apt reply. Thank God he'd had plenty of practice at showing no emotion. Perhaps he should take up poker? Then remembering George's downfall, brought about by his gambling, he laughed out loud. It didn't cross his mind to blame himself as the cause of George's catastrophe.

Henrietta listened to the mare's hooves on the gravel. The sound was drowned by the swish of her mother's skirt, as she crossed to the fireplace to tug the bell rope to summon a servant.

Leaving her mother to the tea she ordered, Henrietta feigning a headache, retired to her room. There, opening the drawer which held her undergarments, she drew out a medicine bottle. Pouring a large measure of the liquid into a glass she carried it back to her bed. Lying on the satin coverlet, she drank the nectar that would bring peace, the banishment of Tommy Standish. As she sipped, so he receded, until he was little more than a speck on the patterned wallpaper, a speck without voice, a silent harmless dot.

The glass slipped from her hand as she fell into unconsciousness.

Finishing her tea, Louise went into the garden to enjoy the last of the sunshine. As she crossed the lawn, her long skirt stirred the scent of the warm grass, rousing memories of Bertram her late husband, soul mate and lover. How he enjoyed the smell of mown lawns. At this time of day they used to sit in the Italianate garden, silent companions, watching the sun, a blazing orange orb, slipping into the ocean.

Shielding her eyes, Louise looked up into the clear sky, the sun had begun its descending arc in the cerulean plain, the calm sea beckoning. Its journey was too beautiful, too spectacular to miss; crossing the terrace she made her way to the wide narrow steps that led to the gardens, to the ornate grey metal bench where she and Bertram had rested together so often.

Sitting, the grey taffeta skirt of her gown almost covering the seat, she watched the sky, the seabirds gliding, ethereal and fascinating, creating an avian ballet on the hot thermals.

Behind her, blades of grass as though trodden on by light feet stirred. She felt the reassuring presence of Bertram. Her hand reached for his and they sat together watching the birds until the sun, completing its descent touched the sea. Blazing red rays spread across the darkening sky. Then it was gone.

Rising with Bertram, Louise walked towards the fine red line marking the horizon, where sea meets sky.

When Louise Bellamy failed to appear for dinner and could not be found in her room, the servants began an indoor search. An hour later the exploration began in earnest, the staff sent in all directions to look in the gardens and parkland.

Henrietta, roused from her deep sleep, could throw no light on the whereabouts of her mother.

It was Gideon, the gardener, an ancient retainer, who found Louise lying on her favourite bench. She had been dead for sometime; the body had grown cold and stiff in the night air. Two younger gardeners brought her back to the house and she was laid in her bedroom to await the local surgeon.

It was late when the head groom was despatched to Penrhyn Castle to inform Tommy of his mother-in-law's demise.

The night was dense, without moonlight or star shine to aid the lone rider; his progress was slow on the rutted road. In the small hours he approached the castle. Dismounting, opening one of the gates, he walked the horse through, then mounted again.

The mile long avenue was flanked by high trees, black and eerie against the ink sky. He wasn't a particularly imaginative man, but the night had been long and solitary, the darkness virtually impenetrable. His nerves started to play tricks and he thought of the thousands of black beady eyes in the undergrowth watching his progress. His eyes were drawn to the pools of darkness beneath the trees, where crouching ghosts lay in wait. Commonsense told him that the humps were nothing more than bushes rustling in the tiny breeze, but still he kept his eyes to them.

A large bird swept beneath the canopy startling the horse; skittish the young animal neighed in alarm, dancing in a tight circle. The groom's heart raced, tripping sickeningly. His arm came up to protect his head. He gave a short sharp cry as the bird flew overhead, the under feathers of the wingspan showing eerily white against the blackness of the night.

Smiling at his own stupidity, acting like a young maid out at night for the first time, he leaned forward and patted the side of the animal's large head, bringing the mare under control, with his gentle voice. He continued the ride along the avenue at an easier pace, the slower beat of the hooves less likely to alarm resting birds.

Tommy was sleeping deeply, lying on the debris that was

Sadie Pearson's discarded shift, when a hurried knock sounded on the bedroom door. Urgent voices came from the hallway.

He came up fast. The light in the room was grey. The oil lamp had been left burning, turned down to a meagre flame to illuminate their love play and it had glowed feebly throughout the night whilst they slept.

The first thought that came to him was, fire. Moving quickly, he donned his breeches before throwing the bedclothes over the kitchen maid. Sadie, half-asleep began to protest and came up for air.

Tommy put his finger to his lips, frowning. 'Shush!'

Sadie's eyes flew to the closed door. Drawing the bed-covers over her body she shivered with fear; her escapade had surely been discovered and the housekeeper was banging the door to gain entrance to humiliate her before evicting her from the castle.

Strands of her hair were still visible and Tommy threw the counterpane over the pillow to hide her completely.

There came a more urgent knock.

Annoyed, Tommy shouted, 'Just wait a minute.'

A moment later he had the door partially open. 'What is it, for God sake? You will wake the dead.'

A tired and hastily dressed footman stood on the threshold, a lit lamp in his hand, the flickering flame making his lined and elderly face an ugly gargoyle.

Somewhat startled, Tommy shouted, 'What is it, man?'

The footman dipped his head, his grey shaggy hair falling dangerously near to the hot glass of the lamp. 'I am sorry to disturb you, sir, but there is a messenger from Plas Mawr. He has been escorted into the library to await you.'

It could only mean serious trouble. In his mind he saw his beloved mansion enveloped by flames, thick smoke climbing towards the dark sky.

A sudden cramping of his bowels shot a sickening pain through his belly. 'I'll come down at once.'

'I'll bring tea to you, sir.'

Without acknowledging the man, Tommy closed the door. Grabbing his clothes off the chair where he had abandoned them a few hours ago, he tried to dress quickly. Too hasty he thrust an arm into a sleeve of his fine cotton shirt and was stopped by the fastening on the wide cuff. He spat a curse. Slowing down, he undid the cuff, donned the garment.

From the shadows of the bed, Sadie whispered, 'What's wrong?'

Glancing over his shoulder, matching her quiet voice, he said, 'I don't know. A messenger has arrived from Plas Mawr. He's in the library.'

'It wasn't the housekeeper come to chuck me out?'

Sitting on the side of the bed, Tommy pulled on a shoe, grunting as his foot settled into the soft leather.

With a hint of a smile, he said, 'No, she hasn't yet discovered what a trollop you are.'

'Shall I wait here for you?' Sadie was worried. She might not see him again for weeks.

'No, don't bother. You get about your business. It'll not be long before you need to be up and about anyway.'

She tried hard not to let her disappointment show. Robbed of two hours of his presence brought her close to tears. 'Perhaps I'll see you later?' she said hopefully.

He didn't answer, or look back. Opening the door, he went out.

Sadie lay for few moments looking at the intricate ceiling, feeling sad.

On closing the door, Tommy felt the draughts of the long hallway, cold air sweeping up the wide staircase from the grand hall, funnelling into the stone walled corridor.

The footman had thought to wait at the top of the stairs with the lamp to light his way and Tommy was grateful. Getting to the library in the dark would be a nightmare.

The footman was buttoning his coat one-handed.

Giving the man a sidelong glance, Tommy muttered a few

words. It was as near to a thank you as the servant would get.

Descending the stone steps, the footman held the lamp for Tommy's benefit. The dancing light cast elongated shadows on the walls and illuminated the sinister carvings.

Entering the library ahead of the servant, Tommy saw that the fire had been stoked and the Plas Mawr servant was warming his back at it. On seeing the master, the man stepped aside.

It was impossible to contain his anxiety and Tommy blurted, 'What news have you brought? Out with it man.'

The groom gave a deep bow, on rising his expression was sorrowful. 'I'm afraid the mistress has been found dead in the garden, Master.'

Tommy shouted, 'Henrietta's dead.' His heart soared. The terrible marriage was at an end. Henrietta could not snatch Plas Mawr from him; she was dead. The grand mansion had become his after all.

Mortified by his mistake, the groom flushed red. 'Begging your pardon. I meant Mrs Louise Bellamy, the former mistress, sir.'

'Louise!' Tommy's spirit fell and tears of frustration filled his eyes.

'I'm so sorry, Master. I didn't mean to...'

Tommy interrupted, 'How did it happen?'

The groom dipped his head. 'Nobody knows yet, sir. We found her lying on the bench in the Italian garden. She was quite chilled, so she may have been there for a little while.'

Tommy closed his eyes for a moment, not out of pity for Louise but for his own bitter disappointment.

Taking a deep breath, he tried to pull himself together. 'Get to the kitchen, Price. There's sure to be someone there to find you something to eat and drink. Rest the horse before you return to Plas Mawr. It's a long ride.'

The groom retreated quickly.

Tommy walked to an arched window and looked out over

the mountains, the heights colourless in the early grey dawn. So Louise was gone, he thought, watching a sea bird circling in the misty sky. What difference would her passing make? The house in Chester, her main residence since Bertram's death, would now go to Henrietta. George, the idiot son, wouldn't inherit the property. But he did live there. That problem could easily be overcome. Henrietta would be too inebriated for the foreseeable future to be aware of any changes in her brother's circumstances. The loss of her mother was sure to send her hastening for one bottle or another.

Chilled he turned from the window. The heat of the fire beckoned, but deciding that the sooner he made tracks home the sooner he would know how the land lay, he forfeited the small pleasure of it. Purposefully he strode towards the door, his steps hardly making a sound on the thick carpet.

In the foyer he expected to see minions going about their duties. As there was no one there he realised that the hour must be earlier than he had first supposed.

Sadie came to mind; he wondered if she was still in his room. With thoughts of the pearl lustre of her ample flesh and the girl's rather unique willingness to satisfy his most pressing desires stirring his ardour, he hurried up the stairs. If she was there, he would delay his departure. Plas Mawr could wait for his return. There was nothing to gain by hurrying back. So why risk breaking his neck in the half-light of a false dawn? With luck there would be time for another game with the wench before he left. After a satisfying encounter, what better than a hearty breakfast before his ride home?

The grey daylight hadn't penetrated the long, vaulted corridor and the air was chill on his face as he strode towards the bedroom. Reaching the oak panelled door, his hand covering the handle, he felt a frisson of excitement at the prospect of Sadie.

Stepping inside, he took in the room; the lamp was still

burning, the bedclothes piled onto the four-poster bed in an untidy heap. On the top of the highly polished chest of drawers his belongings were laid out, arranged neatly by an underling yesterday.

The bedroom was too large for the air to grow stale overnight but he detected a faint scent of sex and he wondered if he imagined it, or was it because he knew what had taken place?

During the last few months he had learned many tricks from Lady Isabelle and last night, Sadie had been a willing partner for his unusual requests.

For a moment he supposed that Sadie was where he had left her, under the pile of bedclothes. Crossing to the bed, discovering it empty, he wasn't particularly disappointed, as suddenly he felt quite tired. The bed still vaguely warm was inviting.

After using the commode to relieve himself, his fear for Plas Mawr had been too great to do so earlier, he went to the small table where a decanter stood on a silver tray. Pouring a large brandy, a stiffener before breakfast, he swallowed a mouthful. The amber liquid warming his empty belly.

Slipping off his shoes, he stretched out on the bed, giving a small sigh as his head sank into the soft pillow.

So Louise was gone, he thought, staring at the ceiling, noting the recently applied gilding on the bosses. Gone for good and she wouldn't be coming back. The idea brought a small smile to his mouth, a slight creasing of the skin around his penetrating eyes.

Remembering the brandy he rolled onto his side; propped up on his elbow, his head cupped in the palm of his hand, he reached for the glass. Sniffing the heady fragrance he savoured the pleasure of the excellent brandy before taking a sip. He was warmed instantly; it had been cold in the library and on the stairs.

The bedroom wasn't too unpleasant, the fire in the chimneypiece had burned for most of the night and now small pink nuggets, like the eyes of albino rodents, lay in the ash. If he could bring himself to move he would throw wood from the basket onto it, the new flames would extinguish the curious eyeballs.

Rolling onto his back, holding the glass to his chest, he sighed then yawned and sighed again. He would close his eyes for just a moment, then get up and build the fire.

An image of Louise came to him. The first time he had seen her she had swept into the breakfast room. She'd been heavy then and her gown, a great splash of lavender trimmed with frivolous ribbons and flounces rustled as she crossed the room. What a tartar she'd been back then; she'd mellowed with age. Bertram's sudden death had hit her hard, drawing all the mettle out of her. Lately the weight had dropped off until she was skin and bones; he wondered if that had something to do with her unexpected and so far unexplained death. Whatever the cause, she was gone and there was nothing to think about but the Will.

Still clutching the glass, he dropped into a peaceful sleep.

Louise's funeral was a quiet affair, the service held in the small chapel on the estate. She was laid to rest beside her late husband in the stone vault erected by the original owners of Plas Mawr.

The mausoleum was large and grand, proof that the earlier sugar plantation proprietors believed that the house, family and wealth would endure. It was the final resting place for the Bellamy family fortunate enough to have returned home from Jamaica before their demise.

Throughout the service Henrietta sobbed quietly behind her black lace veil. Tommy looking stoic stood beside her, wondering how long it would be before she followed her mother. Grey and lifeless, hardly sober during the past days, Henrietta did not look long for this world.

The service came to an end and the small procession walked towards the house with Tommy and Henrietta leading. On reaching the lawns, the woods surrounding the burial chamber far behind them, Tommy looked over his shoulder to the few guests that had attended. The solicitor was amongst them.

Giving an affectionate pat to Henrietta's limp arm, he could afford to be magnanimous with the time of the reading of the Will drawing close. Within an hour the house in Chester and Louise's private fortune would be in his control.

Bellamy's Will had been a travesty. The corner of Tommy's lip curled at the memory of that dreadful day. A repeat didn't bear thinking about and he wouldn't ruin his day giving it credence.

Banishing Bellamy from his thoughts he led the funeral party into the house. Henrietta tried to make her excuses and retreat to her room but Tommy held her firmly.

Gripping her arm tight, his voice was harsh as he whispered, 'It's your duty to remain with our guests. These people were friends of your mother's. At least treat them with some respect, even if you are unable to extend the same privilege to me.'

Eyes wet with tears, Henrietta said hopefully, 'I'll go just for a moment.'

'No! Stay,' he barked close to her ear.

A footman came alongside Tommy. 'Everything is ready, sir. Would you like me to lead the guests into the music room?'

'Yes, Roberts. Do it at once.'

Beethoven's Piano Sonata, played expertly on the pianoforte, greeted the company. The music a favourite of Louise had been chosen by a close and lifetime friend. The house servants, under the close eye of Miles the butler, attended, serving champagne to the ladies and whisky or brandy to the gentlemen.

The moment that Tommy's eyes were not on her, Henrietta escaped into the garden, her personal maid following a few moments later on the pretext of bringing a shawl to her mistress. Hidden in the maid's apron pocket was the small bottle of laudanum that Henrietta had begged her to bring out to her.

Covertly, her back to the house, the maid tipped the contents into the nearly empty champagne glass that Henrietta was clutching to the bodice of her black dress. Henrietta shivering, her cold hands trembling, drank the liquid down. With hurried, nervous thanks, she dismissed the girl kindly. Watching as she made her way to the back of the house.

As the medicine worked its magic, the heartbreaking sadness eased. Henrietta walked across the lawn, her hands steadier, her heart settled into a more even beat.

With her strength returning she noticed that the red roses were closing, the fragile petals enfolding the vulnerable stamens.

Glancing towards the house, she saw Tommy at the window looking out, watching.

The reading of the Will would take place in the library soon. If her mother had left her the house in Chester would she have the courage to move her young son out of Plas Mawr and take him to live there? Could she manage the finances? Such things had never been explained to her. Father, and then Tommy, had taken care of all things financial. She glanced back to the window, but Tommy was no longer standing there. Slowly, reluctantly, Henrietta made her way back indoors.

Leaving the funeral guests in the music room, the solicitor, Tommy and Henrietta retired to the library. Madoc, on settling himself behind Tommy's desk, broke the seal of the Last Will and Testament of Louise Anne Bellamy.

Louise left the Chester house and most of her money to Henrietta. There were a few minor bequests to her servants in Chester and Plas Mawr. A painting by the Spanish modern artist Goya, which had been a wedding present, was to be delivered to her close friend Miriam, as she had always admired the picture in Louise's bedroom.

Tommy was pleased with the outcome. Louise hadn't been so foolish as to have bequeathed the servants enough money to change their habits. They would still depend upon Plas Mawr for their living. The painting he could well do without; it was fussy and feminine and Miriam was welcome to it. Inwardly he smiled at Louise's attempts to keep George in the Chester house. The house now belonged to Henrietta, which meant that legally it came to him as her husband. The same applied to the thousands the old biddy had hoarded.

Henrietta rose and edged around Tommy. 'I am going to my room,' she said.

Standing, he stepped back to allow her skirt to sweep by him. 'Henrietta dear, you deserve a rest. Maybe I'll see you later.' He placed an ineffectual kiss on the side of her face.

Henrietta turned to the solicitor, tears not far from her eyes. 'Mr Madoc, thank you for attending to my mother's wishes with such kindness.'

Standing, Madoc gave a slight bow from the waist. 'I was happy to be of service to your mother, a most charming lady.'

Climbing the stairs, Henrietta silently thanked her mother for the house and the money. Now she had the opportunity to escape from her soulless marriage. The chance of moving into the Chester house with George was possible. Tomorrow she would consult with Madoc privately. It struck her as odd that she did not know his Christian name, although he had been the family solicitor since Mr Wythenshawe the heavily whiskered, doughty old man had passed away.

How would Tommy react when he realised that their marriage was finally at an end? Would he see her plan to move into the house in Chester with young Edward as a betrayal?

Fortunately her mother had made the necessary

financial arrangements for George to remain there with a nurse and small staff.

Madoc had explained everything in such a complicated way that it was difficult to follow but he had been most reassuring when she tried to question him. Very soon she would begin taking care of her broken brother.

Tears welled in her eyes. Was it really true that her mother was gone for ever? And she would never again be consoled by her kind words or loving caresses. A desert of loneliness was before her, barren of love, comfort or company.

She made it to her bedroom before the deluge of tears began again.

His face empty of expression, Tommy went to the bureau and replenished his glass from the brandy bottle.

Glancing at the solicitor, he said, 'Want a fill up?'

A sigh escaped Madoc as he stretched across the desk and handed Tommy his almost empty glass.

Pouring the amber liquid into it, Tommy passed it back. 'That went well.'

Madoc put the glass to his lips, sipped and then said, 'Yes. No hitches.'

'I don't expect hitches when I'm paying you the amount I am.' Tommy said, smiling sardonically.

Withdrawing a package from the inside pocket of his coat, he handed it across the desk to Madoc. 'You'll find it all there.'

Slipping it into his own pocket, Madoc smiled. 'Nice doing business with you, Mr Standish.'

Tommy's voice took on a hard edge. 'Remember, Madoc, the job's not finished until you've discreetly sold the house and contents. Convincing Louise that George would be better off staying in Chester with his nurses wasn't the end of the assignment.'

Madoc's right eyebrow arched quizzically. 'When will George go?'

A shadow of a smile crossed Tommy's face. 'He leaves for Denbigh Asylum tomorrow.'

In her room Henrietta gave into her grief. Eventually she fell into a disturbed sleep. In the early hours she awoke with a splitting headache, her nose blocked from crying. She lay for long moments going over the dreadful day.

Her thoughts turned to Tommy and their imminent parting and she was torn between relief and sadness, relief that at last the torment was finally coming to an end and bitter sadness recalling the early heady days of their love. Or had she been the only one in love when they started out? Was it true, as she had suspected for some while now, that he had married her for the status and monetary gain? If this were so, the betrayal was terrible. It proved once and for all that she was worthless, incapable of distinguishing truth from lies. If that were so, she was as vulnerable as a woman can be.

The endless questions were confusing and however long the problems circled in her mind she never came up with an answer, only more questions.

Her headache was unbearable; she rose from the bed. At the dressing table she took a dose of opium from the drawer. At last she rested, dreaming of George, a lively boy of ten chasing her through the ten-acre wood hazed with bluebells.

The following morning, Henrietta slept late. Dressing with the help of her maid, she prepared to join Tommy at the midday meal. On learning that he had left the house early and would not return today, she dismissed the servant and moved to her personal sitting room.

The feminine room was light and airy, the window thrown open to catch the slight breeze of the late August day. The lace curtains fluttering gently, drawing in the perfume of the white roses climbing to the first casement. At the window she stood for a moment looking out, watching Gideon the gardener dead-heading the pink geraniums in the stone urns.

Sinking gently down onto the window seat, she watched the daily rituals of the garden, a young man hoeing and another raking the first fallen leaves. The rhythm of life, she thought sadly, and I am no longer a part of it.

Even her plans to rise early and take the carriage into town had come to nothing and there was no one to blame but herself. Had she not given in to her craving last night she would now be on her way to the solicitor's office and then onto Chester. Little Edward probably asleep in his bassinet, unaware that he was beginning a new era in his young life.

The tinkling chimes of the clock on the marble mantelpiece heralded noon.

Her eyes went to it and she muttered, 'Too late to do anything about it today.' Disconsolate she rose. Automatically she walked to the dressing room. Opening the drawer of the dressing table, she took out the opium.

In her bedroom she loosened her skirt and bodice, then slipped onto the neatly made bed. Peace would come. Peace and self forgiveness.

Tommy had risen very early and taking his carriage, Owen Roberts in the driving seat, he made his way to Caernarvon to the railway branch line that would take him onto Bangor station.

Before noon he was at Doctor Rogers's comfortable rooms in central Chester.

The doctor greeted him affably, 'Well, Mr Standish, so you have come to complete our arrangements?'

Tommy slipped his hand inside his coat pocket and withdrew a brown paper package. The week was proving to be expensive in the short term but he would reap financial rewards when the job in hand was completed.

Pushing the packet across the desk, he said, 'You'll find everything in order, Doctor. The agreed amount is there in full. The annual payment will of course fall due this day twelve months hence.'

101

Picking up the packet the doctor slipped it inside his desk drawer, locking it he pocketed the key in his frockcoat pocket. 'I'm ready if you are. My carriage is waiting at the front door. The other carriage will be waiting at your late mother-in-law's house by now. So let's go.'

Tommy followed the man along the corridor. At the doorstep, the doctor came to a standstill to give instruction to an underling. Tommy carried on down the front steps to the pavement. The air outdoors smelled of city dust and industrial chimneys belching smoke.

A carriage, with two impatient mares shifting their hooves restlessly, was aligned to the pavement. The coachman was wearing a messy livery, Tommy immediately marked him down as a hireling probably employed by the day. The equipage although clean was dated by at least a decade. The whole ensemble was probably hired. Maybe the good doctor was not as well-off financially as he liked to pretend.

Tommy was considering that he might have got away with offering him less for his services, when his line of thought was interrupted by the doctor descending to the pavement.

'All set?' the doctor asked jovially.

Tommy faked a smile. 'Ready when you are.'

As Tommy was not in the habit of acknowledging lackeys, he was oblivious to the footman's assistance as he climbed aboard with the doctor following.

They were almost settled when a young maid came rushing down the steps. 'Doctor Rogers, sir. Cook has sent a basket of refreshments.'

Flustered, the girl bobbed a curtsy, holding onto her cap. 'Beg pardon, sir.'

Taking the basket from her, the footman placed it near to the doctor's shoes. With a slight bow from the waist the servant closed the carriage door, giving the painted wood a light rap with his knuckles.

The carriage moved forward filtering into the procession of gigs on the fairly busy road. Passing the park, Tommy admired the young ladies escorted by their mammas or elegant gentlemen.

Glancing out, the doctor chortled. 'Fine feathers are no protection from the present miasma.'

Tommy had been thinking of the fashionable habit of naming girls after flowers, Daisy, Rose, Iris, Violet ...

The doctor's words ended the list of floral names he was compiling in his head. 'There's contagion?'

Taking a pouch from his coat pocket the doctor put a pinch of snuff to his nostrils, sniffing noisily. 'There's always something or another.'

Glancing out on the feminine strollers, Tommy decided that his trip had been foolhardy. He could quite easily have told Madoc to come in his place. Money would have guaranteed the solicitor's co-operation. But foolishly he had allowed his overpowering need to see that George was still incapable of naming him as his assailant on that night so long ago.

'So what infection is it now, Doctor?

Pulling a linen handkerchief out of his pocket the doctor blew his nose, wiping it fastidiously. 'The pox is always there but scarlet fever is the threat right now. Dropping like flies, specially the children.'

Tommy started to say, 'How contagious is it...' when the carriage lurched to a halt outside Louise's former home.

The doctor bent to pick up the basket, lifting it onto the seat opposite. Darts of pain shot through his limbs as he leaned forward to release the door catch. With thoughts of a glass of brandy, an excellent painkiller, he climbed down to the pavement slowly. The carriage rocked with the change of weight, throwing Tommy off balance, stooped as he was to alight himself.

The coachman's wages didn't run to attending to his passengers on reaching their destination. Remaining in his seat, looking ahead, he ignored both men as they climbed the steps to the front door.

The doctor was peeved that his rheumatics should choose today of all days to set his bones singing. Ill-tempered he yanked the bell rod and listened for sounds from within the large Georgian townhouse.

Tommy stood on the lower step, clutching his silver-topped ebony stick. He was nervous, his stomach airy and light, for in a moment he would be confronted with George, a man he hadn't laid eyes on since he was brought to this house to live in seclusion. His belly fluttered at the door opened.

George's nurse looked bewildered to see the two men, obviously officials, standing on the steps. 'Yes. What can I do for you, gentlemen?'

The job of opening the door had never fallen to her before, but as the footmen and butler had been dismissed by solicitor's letter a few days previously, there was no servant to attend.

The doctor was brusque, saying sharply, 'We have come to take Mr George Bellamy to a nursing home.'

There was just time for the woman's mouth to become a surprised 'O' before the doctor brushed passed her.

Standing in the centre of the large hall, his back stiff with self-importance, the doctor spoke haughtily, 'A carriage with two male attendants is waiting to escort him.'

The woman looked perplexed, her face vacant. 'I know nothing of this.'

'And why should you?' Doctor Rogers answered rudely. 'You're not a member of the family, are you?'

She looked down at the toecaps of her brown boots. 'No, of course not, sir.'

'Then it won't concern you. I have the brother-in-law of the patient here with me, Mr Tommy Standish of Plas Mawr.'

The nurse had heard all about Mr Tommy Standish from her late employer; Mrs Louise Bellamy had abhorred the man. Many a night, her ladyship would sit beside her son's bed and talk of the time when George was a young and lively boy, heir to Plas Mawr and all that went with it. Tommy Standish had all that now. Louise Bellamy had never been happy about the rising star of Standish, as she would refer to him when out of his hearing.

'Is there no letter or anything?' Her eyes moved to the open door where two men in coarse black uniforms were climbing up the steps.

'What letter?' Doctor Rogers snapped. 'From whom do you require authority? The man in charge is standing before you.'

Tears filmed the nurse's eyes. 'I'm sorry, sir. It was just a shock, that's all, you turning up out of the blue.'

Doctor Rogers harrumphed. 'We don't need to inform all and sundry. Stand aside and let us get on with the job in hand.'

Powerless, the nurse watched Doctor Rogers and Mr Standish climb the stairs. The two attendants had come in uninvited and were following the pair up the wide staircase.

As they reached the landing, Tommy looked from left to right for the location of George's room. He was saved from a search by a young maid hurrying towards the back stairs.

Tommy called to her, 'Show us George Bellamy's room.'

She hesitated for a moment seeing the strangers, but then catching Tommy's eye, the best looking man she had seen in an age, she hurried forward. 'Mr George is at the end of the corridor, the last door; shall I show you to it, sir?'

'There's no need. Get back to your work.'

George stared in terror as the four men entered his bedroom. Crying out in distress, he clutched the blankets attempting to hide.

The nurse standing in the open doorway saw the men

advance on George. Rushing in she tried to pacify the sick man. 'George, it's all right.'

The two men began to haul him out of the bed.

Grabbing the sleeve of one, she yelled, 'Where are you taking him?'

Doctor Rogers yanked her hand away. 'This is no concern of yours. You have done your duty and you will be rewarded for that. Now stand aside.'

She stood at the foot of the bed, in tears. Then realizing that she still could be of use to George, she began to pack his personal possessions into a bag.

The two attendants got George standing limply between them.

Exasperated, the taller of the two tried to pull off George's dressing gown.

Unused to such rough handling, George began to cry.

Tommy watched for a moment, then turning he left the room. There was no sense staying in the stuffy atmosphere, witnessing a messy scene. He had observed all he needed to. George hadn't even known that he was present. There was no chance this side of heaven that George Bellamy could name him as his would-be murderer.

If the unthinkable had occurred and they had found George lucid and only too happy to bawl out the truth, he could have bought the doctor's silence and that of his two henchmen. It might have been necessary to deal differently with the nurse.

Pleased with himself, everything so far had gone according to plan. Henrietta was at home oblivious of today's events. Within minutes George would be on his way to Denbigh asylum where he would spend the rest of his days.

With only one small task left to perform, he opened a bedroom door hoping it was Louise's old room. At the third try, he walked into a pale blue room delicately furnished. It wasn't to his taste but he saw that it must have been very costly. Louise never did stint herself.

With his ear cocked for sounds from the corridor, he went to the dressing table. In the top drawer amongst feminine furbelows he found what he was looking for, the silver jewellery box that Louise had used when travelling. On her last trip to Plas Mawr the silver case had been omitted from her luggage, an oversight of the maid.

Earlier, on the train from Bangor he had recalled the fuss Louise had made shortly after her arrival at the mansion. It had taken a considerable effort by Henrietta to calm the old lady.

A noise of shuffling feet and a sharp cry came from the direction of the corridor. Tommy glanced at the door. In his mind's eye, he saw George being bundled towards the stairs.

Unperturbed he took the jewellery box out of the nest of lace. At a glance he saw that the elaborate chasing on the lid had been done by a fine silversmith. Reverently he passed the palm of his hand over it before opening the box. He wasn't disappointed with the contents; there were several worthwhile pieces lying on a red silk covered pad. These had been Louise's prize possessions, the jewellery that she had planned to wear on the visit to Plas Mawr that proved to be her last.

Putting the box aside for a moment, he searched in a lower drawer for something to put it into. It wouldn't do to be seen leaving the house with the silver box under his arm. Finding a small leather bag, he placed it inside. Thinking quickly, Louise's silver box would raise questions if found at Plas Mawr, he tipped the contents into the bag and placed the box back on the Nottingham lace.

Searching methodically through the other drawers, he found little of value that he could carry easily. Satisfied with his ten minute labour, he closed the bag and left the room. Stepping into the corridor, he didn't notice the nurse closing the door of George's bedroom.

Though her eyes were filled with tears, Mary noticed Louise's bag tucked under his arm.

The swish of her skirt alerted Tommy to her presence.

Caught wrong footed, he spoke sharply, 'I want all the staff in the sitting room immediately.'

'Yes, sir.'

Standing at the top landing, the nurse watched him trip down the stairs. Arriving at the bottom he turned towards the library. She heard the familiar clunk of the heavy door as it closed behind him.

Turning away she made for the backstairs, her thoughts bleak. In a moment she would be dismissed of that she was certain. With poor George gone, there was no need to keep a nurse or the household staff.

Tessa the upstairs maid and Mildred the cook were standing at the back door getting a breath of air as she came into the large kitchen. The old bread oven fire had been lit since morning; the fragrance of newly baked bread still hung in the room, as did the heat from the coals.

Cook, leaning against the doorjamb, glanced at the slightly dishevelled nurse. 'Tessa says that visitors came and took poor old George away. It can't be true. Can it?' Her head to one side she waited for confirmation of the young maid's lies.

Mary O'Donnell, nurse to George for more than two years, nodded. 'I'm afraid it is true.' Tears welled in her eyes and she wiped them with the hem of her apron.

Cook eased her bulk off the doorpost and came into the room. Coming alongside Mary she put an arm around the distressed nurse.

A great sadness washed over Mary. 'I don't even know where they have taken him,' she cried.

Stunned, Cook looked into the woman's face. 'Wouldn't they tell you?'

Mary pulled a handkerchief from her uniform pocket and dabbed her nose, sniffing. 'No. They said nothing at all.'

Tears caught on her eyelashes. 'They just bundled poor George up like a sack of old washing.'

She sniffed again. 'I've been sent to tell you we are wanted in the sitting room.'

Confused by the speed of events, Tessa's mouth dropped open. 'Why?'

Exasperated, Cook clicked her tongue. 'Tess, you are the silliest of wenches.'

Huffing, the elder woman moved from the door. Putting the full kettle on the hob, she kept her back to the two women, to hide her tears.

Tessa, oblivious to the cook's distress, turned towards Mary. 'I only asked.'

Mary looked kindly at the maid. 'Tessa, with George gone, there's no need to keep us on. Mr Standish has come to pay us off. We are to be let go.'

Instant tears welled in Tessa's eyes. 'Me father will create summat terrible when he hears this. He'll give me a clout for losing me place.'

Mary hugged her. 'It's not your fault. You must tell him that the house is to be closed down.'

Wiping the end of her nose on the back of her hand, Tessa gave a weak smile. 'I can't tell 'im that, he'd come and rob the place.'

'Tess, you have to explain it to him.'

Glancing at cook, Mary tried to hurry her. 'We must go. Mr Standish will lose his temper if we dally too long.'

Sighing, Cook was philosophical. 'What does it matter if he loses it? It can't make much difference to us now.'

Mary managed a half-smile. 'Best to depart on a good note though, Cook.'

In the sitting room, the three women waited for more than five minutes for Tommy Standish to appear.

Mary O'Donnell, standing with her back to the empty fireplace, was sick with worry, wondering where George was at that moment, and his state of mind. The poor man snatched from his comfortable room, reduced to tears, with no one to explain matters to him. Where might they have taken him? Who could she ask for help? Not Tommy Standish or Doctor Rogers. If she were to find him, it would be by her own intelligence. Vowing that she would do everything in her power to discover his whereabouts and make sure no further harm befall the man, she waited for Tommy Standish, the interloper.

Footsteps on the mosaic floor brought her back to the problem of the moment. She was about to be let go. How was she going to take care of her family? Four young fatherless children, fostered out to her mother-in-law who hadn't a bean to her name.

Tommy had watched the departure of the Denbigh Asylum carriage from the comfort of the library; when the equipage had disappeared around the bend in the road, he walked across to the desk and placed the leather bag and his cane on the top. Taking a small silver canteen from his frockcoat pocket, he helped himself to a snifter of brandy.

Minutes later, satisfied all had gone according to plan, he made his way to the sitting room. Passing the long-case clock he saw that he would not make the late train. It would be necessary to put up at a hotel for the night. The thought brought a smile to his face. There was a chance of a little sport when staying in a town hotel. Female thighs came to his mind and with this arousing thought he entered the sitting room.

His glance fell on Tessa, but his erotic vision of her naked body vanished as she sniffed and brushed her nose with the back of her hand. Unable to meet the nurse's eyes, the woman had seen too much, he let his gaze fall on the heavy and none to clean cook. What had Louise been thinking of employing such rabble?

Tommy's eyes went over the three. 'As you are aware, Mr George has been taken to a nursing home. So I am afraid it falls to me to pay your wages to date. It's fortunate that your late mistress saw fit to leave you all a little money in her Will. This will assist you until such time as you find other employment. '

Mary O'Donnell wasn't listening to his words; her thoughts were entirely with George. She wondered how she might help the crippled man she'd grown fond of.

She was brought back to the moment as her hand inadvertently touched Tommy Standish's as he handed her an envelope containing a reference and wages.

The task over, Tommy strode out of the room.

Doctor Rogers was standing in the hallway as Tommy came through the sitting room door.

His patient disposed of, he was hearty. 'There you are, Mr Standish. Everything is in order. George Bellamy has departed for the nursing home.'

Tommy smiled. 'Good. It was an admirable job well done. Now that everything is taken care of, would you take a glass of brandy or port with me? Louise kept an excellent bottle of port-wine in the drawing room. '

'I don't mind if I do,' the doctor chortled. 'It's thirsty work despatching people to a better life.'

The drawing room door was closing as the three women came out of the sitting room. Cook and Tessa made their way back to the kitchen for a final cup of tea before their departure. Packing their belongings would take little more than five minutes.

Mary O'Donnell was fired up by the ignominy of it all and as she passed the drawing room door and heard the muted voices from within she saw her chance of personal justice. If she stopped to consider her actions, the moment would be lost. With this thought, she hurried towards the library.

Her heart was in her mouth as she approached the room. With a quick nervous glance over her shoulder, she pulled the heavy oak door open and slipped in. With her back against the door she looked across to the desk. She hadn't been wrong; Louise's bag was here as was his ebony stick.

Taking the four steps to the desk, ears cocked for the slightest sound from the hallway, she snatched up the bag. Releasing the catch she wasn't surprised to see Louise Bellamy's precious sapphire necklace, three strands of pearls and an assortment of costly gems jumbled together. Taking the necklace, she slipped it into her coat pocket. A diamond brooch was too much of a temptation and she took it quickly. The pearls she left, they gave weight to the bag. Tommy Standish's suspicions would be aroused if the bag felt light when he picked it up.

If the gems were found on her it would mean years of incarceration, separated from her children. For an instant she thought to put the booty back, for the penalty of her actions could mean the end of her life; prisons were notorious for doing the executioner's job for him.

Blood pounded in her head as the consequences were laid bare in her imagination.

But there was no point torturing herself; it was done. The jewels were in her pocket. The reasons for the theft were the right ones, albeit done on impulse.

The thought gave her courage and she crossed to the door quickly. Putting her ear against the wood she listened for sounds in the hallway but there was only the noise of blood pulsing in her ears.

Turning the brass knob slowly, she opened the door a fraction and looked out. The hallway was empty. Slipping out, she cast a nervous glance in the direction of the drawing-room. Muted voices came from that direction, just audible through the panelled door.

A moment later she heard footsteps on the wooden surround near the drawing room door and her heart lurched so violently that she thought she might vomit.

Her eyes flashed to the closed front door, three strides away. In the time it would take to make those steps, either Tommy Standish or the doctor would come out of the room and discover her.

Fear robbed her of her wits and for a heart stopping moment she stood rock still waiting for someone to snatch her shoulder.

The footfalls were ridiculously loud, terrifying. With every ounce of her willpower she took two strides and pulled open the front door.

The warm air of the late afternoon came as a shock. People were going about their business, carriages passing by, everything was so unbelievably normal. Walking quickly, distancing herself from the house as quickly as possible without drawing attention, she made it along the Row to her children.

CHAPTER SIX

It was a wet Saturday afternoon when serious trouble erupted at the Garddryn Quarry. The quarrymen were finishing for the day when the steward informed them that they must work until four o'clock. The orders for the extra hours came from the top, Tommy Standish.

Although the steward had little sympathy for the men generally, on this occasion he thought that Tommy Standish had gone too far. The Garddryn had been a simmering cauldron threatening to boil over since the New Year began. Tommy Standish had given no quarter to the men and their grievances had multiplied with every passing month.

There had been three fatal accidents since October. Shamus O'Flaherty, a well liked Irishman, had fallen beneath a wagon and lost a leg. He died from loss of blood before the day was over. The quarrymen blamed the lack of a quarry hospital for Shamus's demise. Other quarries in the district had small hospitals near to the workings.

Three weeks later it was the turn of Cadoc Preece, catching his foot beneath a rock as he scrambled away from a primed explosive; he was blown to smithereens. His young widow and flock of small children were now living with the threat of the workhouse hanging over them.

A rock fall had claimed the third victim. It had happened on the last afternoon before Christmas. It was an accident waiting to happen, or so the quarrymen reckoned. A dangerous overhang, which would have been removed had there been time to do it and permission granted by management;

the spit of unstable slate had collapsed, killing John Jenkins working beneath it. There was a chance that the management could be held responsible in this case; if so, compensation would go to the Jenkins family.

The steward was swearing that he had told Jenkins that under no circumstances was he to work in the vicinity of the danger.

The steward had been vilified for his actions, but with Tommy Standish pulling the strings, Rees Roberts would agree to anything that the master dictated.

On the fateful Saturday afternoon, the quarrymen were packing up, gathering their tools together before taking the track to home when they saw the steward approaching. During the winter months Rees Roberts had put on a stone or more of weight which didn't sit well on his short body.

Full of his own self-importance, Roberts strode towards the workers shouting belligerently, 'Aye, you men, what the hell do you think you're doing?'

The eldest amongst the quarrymen didn't bother to meet the steward's eye. 'What does it look like we're bloody doing? We're going home.'

Roberts fixed the quarryman with a withering stare. 'Not at this time of day, you're not. The Master wants you all to work until the light fails.'

Billy Williams the youngster of the group had an arrangement to meet a girl. He'd thought of little else all day. Seeing his fun snatched away, he whined sulkily, 'It's Saturday. Four months ago we finished at noon on a Saturday. That was changed, so now we work until two o'clock. So what's this, are we to work a normal day from now on?'

Jabbing the lad painfully in the chest with his dirty finger, Roberts punctuated his words with fierce little stabs, 'You'll ... do ... as ... you're ... told ... or ... face ... the ... consequences.' His top lip curled in a snarl. 'If you don't like it, you know what to do. There's plenty more who'd be glad of your job. So stop snivelling, pipsqueak.'

The bullying was enough to spark the simmering anger and the mood of the crowd turned from merely dissatisfied to threatening. Someone cursed the name of Tommy Standish. There was a ripple of angry agreement. A few shouted oaths. An ugly expletive directed personally at the steward was bawled in English. There was a murmur of agreement and the men still clutching their work picks and shovels closed in on Roberts.

They came close, close enough for him to smell the day's toil on their clothes, the wet clay of slate-dust and sweat. They looked like madmen with their necks sunk into the collars of dirty fustian coats and their shoulders hunched against the vicious wind.

The sheer drop of the cliff-face was at his back and it took all his will-power to summon a voice of authority. 'Let me pass. I'll go to the office and have another word with Mr Standish.'

The men didn't budge. For once they held the upper hand and they were not prepared to relinquish it in a hurry. The satisfaction of seeing Roberts sweat for a change was too good to surrender. Most of them had a vision of him sprawled at the foot of the quarry.

Roberts knew without a doubt what was in their minds and his bowels quivered. It was his worse nightmare; quarrymen wreaking vengeance for past wrongs, the unfair bargain, unpaid compensation, erroneous death certificates and costly bribes. Were his sins coming home to roost today? Blind fool! To skirt the quarry edge unaccompanied was only for madmen or saints. He scanned the crowd for a sympathiser but only angry faces looked back.

A moment passed, but it seemed a lifetime before Roberts heard other men coming down the track. His instinctive reaction was to holler for help but the shout died on his lips; the new arrivals could just as easily join the fracas and hurry his exit out of this world, as rush to his rescue. His wits sharp to every nuance and movement of the men bent on his destruction, he watched their faces for signs that they were aware that others approached. But no eyes flicked to the sound; they were too intent on collective violence.

The quarrymen heading down the track crossed the small isthmus bridging the twin waste dumps and came in sight of the scene being played out at the cliff-edge.

The man at the forefront of the group raised his arms halting the men behind him. 'What's going on there?'

As heads turned towards the speaker, Rees Roberts snatched the opportunity to take a step away from the dangerous drop.

Billy Williams pointed at the steward, and he yelled resentfully, 'Roberts says we've got to work a full day. We were just explaining to him that it ain't safe. The light is already fading.'

The new arrival guessed there'd been a lot more than this simple explanation going on, but held his tongue.

Rees Roberts took another step forward, further distancing himself from the rock face. The terrifying skirmish had robbed him of bluster and with unusual politeness he explained that it was Tommy Standish who had made the suggestion of working the extra time.

Joe Standish was the last man to come on the scene. Earlier he'd left a broken shovel on Bethlehem gallery; the handle had snapped and in anger he'd flung it aside. Later, climbing to the cabanod he'd found an ancient shank that could be made to fit the blade and had gone back to Bethlehem to retrieve the abandoned tool.

The steward couldn't abide Joe. As father of the master and a quarryman he regarded him as neither fish nor foul. Watching the elder Standish approach, shovel handle parked on his shoulder, Rees Roberts's eyes narrowed spitefully.

Joe caught the tail end of the, 'ain't safe,' as he came alongside and he laughed mirthlessly. 'When did safety matter to Garddryn management?'

As though ignorant of the dangerous atmosphere, Joe looked from the men to the wet clouds overhead. 'No point standing in this drizzle arguing the toss over it. There's ale in the Half-Way to be supped and a blazing fire to drive out the damp. If you men are in need of a chin-wag, at least do it in comfort.'

Resettling the shovel handle, clamping his rough hand around it, Joe turned, walking away.

Joe's commonplace words brought sense back to the men. The madness evaporated and the crowd opened up.

Relief washed over the steward. Anxious to be away from the vicinity of the quarry edge, he spoke hurriedly, 'I'll go and have another word with the Master. Just let me pass through.'

Someone sighed. 'Go, for God sake. You're no use here.'

Fleeing, Rees Roberts admitted to himself that the episode had scared him. When his back had been to the cliff-edge his imagination had turned his bowels to water and now there was a fierce cramp in his belly. But he wouldn't let the quarrymen see him with a bend in his middle against the discomfort; the buggers would guess that he was making a dash for the privy and he'd never hear the last of it.

As soon as he was out of sight of the men, he trotted up the alley to the small red-brick shed housing the six-hole privy. The force of his entry sent the door banging back against the wall startling the lone occupant. The man left fairly smartly as Roberts dropped his moleskin trousers. A great sigh of relief escaping him as his buttocks hit the privy seat.

A thick drizzle was falling as Roberts came out. For a moment he stood in the shelter of the doorway gauging the weather; then pulling up his coat collar he made his way along the narrow alley avoiding the overgrown hedge dripping fat drops of water.

A cold splash fell onto his head trickling down his neck. Belligerently he glanced up to the rusty guttering oozing brown dirty water. Everything was sodden, an incessant drip, drip, drip of water.

Reaching the end of the alleyway, Roberts glanced towards the working. The quarry was silent, veiled in rain. That his orders had been ignored plunged him into a dour mood and making a mental list of the names of the men caught up in the fracas, Roberts vowed to have the jobs of everyone involved.

The rainfall increased; hunching his shoulders against it, he skirted the old outhouses. Beyond the buildings he could get a good view of the track; if the men were still on it, he would insist they return to work at once. It did not improve his sour mood to find the pathway deserted, flitting sparrows in the straggly mountain ash the only sign of life. He stood for a moment, staring through the rain, blaspheming, cursing every quarryman in Christendom.

As the inevitable could no longer be put off, Oakley, the quarry manager, had to be informed that the workers had ignored orders and fled the quarry. Retracing his step Roberts braced himself for an ugly scene. The biggest fear was that Oakley would sack him for failing to control the men. A feeling of despair swept over him.

Oakley's underling, Elias Hubbard, a gangling young man who looked as though he hadn't had a decent dinner since Whitsuntide, was perched on a stool at a high desk as Rees Roberts entered. Inching his skinny bottom off the seat the youth stepped down. The young assistant was exceptionally nervous, terrified of Roberts loutish manner.

The boy's light brown eyes flicked over the steward's face. 'Mr Roberts, what can I do for you?'

The steward offered no polite preliminaries. Sullen, he said, 'Where's Oakley?'

The boy sniffed, a nervous tick pulling at his right eye. 'Mr Oakley has left for the day. Can I be of any help?'

Robert Rees didn't trouble to answer. Instead he glanced at Tommy Standish's closed office door.

Following the steward's line of sight, the boy blanched. He hoped to God that he wasn't expected to interrupt Mr Standish. He tried drawing the steward's attention away from the panelled door. 'Exactly what is it that I can help you with?'

The steward raised his eyes in exasperation and gave an aggrieved sigh. 'You can start by telling Mr Standish that I'd like a word with him.'

The boy retreated, stepping back from the reception counter. 'I'd prefer not to disturb him if you don't mind.'

Roberts muttered an obscenity. The day was becoming more irritating by the moment; incessant rain, obnoxious quarrymen, and now this blithering idiot behaving like a petrified rabbit in the light of a lantern. Stomping across the room Roberts knocked on the door sharply.

'Who is it?' Tommy Standish roared.

Roberts shouted his name before opening the door.

Tommy's office was fuggy with cigar smoke; earlier there had been a meeting with Madoc and finishing their business regarding Ruby Quarry, they had both smoked a Havana and drunk several large whiskies.

Sitting behind the large desk, a pile of paper before him, Tommy looked up. 'What is it, Roberts?'

Faced with the Master, Roberts was yielding. There was a trace of a whine in his voice, as he explained, 'I passed your orders onto the men but they refused to work the extra time, Mr Standish.'

The consumed whisky flawed Tommy's judgment. Rising violently, almost knocking over the chair, he bawled, 'You can tell the louts if they quit now there'll be no work on Monday morning. See how the bastards like that!'

Startled, Roberts took a step back. 'I think they'll take umbrage.'

'Umbrage! I don't care what the buggers take. For all I care they can take their wages now and not come back next week.'

Coming around the desk, Tommy brushed roughly passed the man, causing the steward to step back to keep his balance.

Tommy went through the door, hastening to the outer office, Rees Roberts only a pace behind him.

Elias Hubbard was sitting on the high stool, watching several men congregating outside. He turned from the window guiltily as the two men approached.

Tommy roared, 'Get me Oakley, immediately.'

'Mr Oakley isn't here this afternoon, sir.'

The absence of the manager had completely slipped Tommy's mind; he took this added irritation out on the boy. 'I don't care where he is, find him. Or I will dispense with your inadequate services.'

Rees Roberts, keeping a safe distance behind Tommy, wished that he hadn't stirred up this hornet's nest. If he hadn't been frightened out of his wits at the cliff-face he could have dealt with the men himself. A catastrophe was in the making and his bonus, if not his job, would probably be an early casualty.

Without waiting for the office boy to respond, Tommy marched outside. Rees Roberts trailing him hid his surprise at seeing a contingent of men huddled in the rain; Joe Standish was amongst them.

Glancing into Standish's eyes he muttered under his breath, 'What skulduggery has brought that bastard back?'

Joe was at the forefront of the group, the shovel handle on his shoulder, the blade with the snapped shaft clutched in his dirty hand.

Tommy took in every detail of his father. His familiar face was as intractable and determined as ever. Other men were stamping their feet against the cold, huddling together to gain some meagre protection, but not his father, he stood alone, aloof, resolute. His father's indomitable spirit angered Tommy beyond reason.

From the small crowd a lad, a novice to the Garddryn,

shouted, 'It's not right that we have to work all Saturday afternoon.'

Tommy's eyes flashed to the boy, then back to Joe Standish looking for a response but the old man's expression was fathomless.

Tommy's eyes came back to the boy. 'Take your tools and get off my property. You're sacked.'

An old man endeavouring to take the heat off the youngster, stepped forward. 'You can't do that. The lad was only saying ...'

Tommy jabbed the man with his forefinger. 'And you, you old bugger, can follow him out of the quarry gates. I'll not be answered back to by quarry louts. Bugger off, before I really lose my temper.'

The old man's eyes filmed with tears. Five small children and their mother, his son's wife and orphans were relying on him. Without his wages and protection they would be in the workhouse almost immediately.

There was angry muttering in the group but no one spoke out hastily.

Twm Tomos, the recently elected president of the cabanod, elbowed his way forward to speak for the men. Outlining the difficulty, he said, 'Mr Standish, if you let these two go then you might as well let us all go. It wouldn't be right if we were to cut slate whilst two of our number struggled to survive without work. Until they're reinstated, we must withdraw our labour.'

A murmur of assent rippled through the crowd. Those less brave looked from one to another but respecting the speaker they kept silent.

Tommy's eyes blazed. 'Let's put your solidarity to the bloody test, shall we? The old man and the boy will not work in the Garddryn again. So make your choice. Work or starve.'

Twm Tomos felt a distinct lurch in the region of his heart. There was no going back on his word, but in trying to help

122

two workers he'd put the livelihood of all the other men at risk. The men waited for his response but words failed him.

Tommy's eyes roved over the crowd and he smirked. 'Come on then, make up your bloody minds, stay or go the choice is yours. Or is the thought of starvation too hard to bear?'

Joe Standish's strong voice carried across the quadrangle. 'So the choice is either to starve our souls or our bellies.'

All eyes turned to Joe.

Sneering, Tommy shouted, 'Souls don't need feeding, bellies do.' Pleased with this reply, he laughed.

Joe's voice rang out, 'The souls of right thinking men are nourished with love, compassion and benevolence. But you Tommy Standish, may God forgive me if I was at fault, never grasped that simple lesson.'

Joe had never before censured Tommy in the presence of another man. It was a turning point in their relationship, probably the last corner to be rounded before communication withered between them. Joe's heart was heavy. Two of his children were now lost to him, his beloved daughter Chloe and young Tommy.

Frank, in the centre of the crowd, knew how much the words cost the old man. His gaze went to his elder brother and he was pleased to see that the sanctimonious grin was off his face. Tommy was angry, probably angrier than he had ever been. Frank had lived through many of his brother's rages but there was nothing in the past that matched the look that was now in his eyes.

Turning on his heel, Tommy walked back to the office building.

Joe slept fitfully on the night following the fracas at the quarry. Last night, Sunday, had been no better, tossing and turning through the dark hours and when he did drop off his sleep was ruined by vivid dreams. Tired, feeling his age, he rose from his bed leaving Emily sleeping.

Frank was shaving in the scullery when he heard his father moving about in the kitchen-cum-living room. Through the partially open door, he called, 'Morning, Da. It's perishing cold this morning.'

'Aye, it's bloody parky all right.' Shivering in his combinations, Joe threw a dry log on the splinters of wood that Frank had piled onto last night's embers.

Frank came in drying his face. 'Are you all right, Da? You look a bit pasty.'

Joe sighed. 'I'm just a bit tired, it's nowt more than that.'

Frank draped the small towel around the back of his neck. 'Not worried are you, Da?'

Joe looked up quickly. 'About what?'

'I just thought you might be thinking about the trouble at the quarry and wondering what our Tommy will do next.'

Joe sighed. He'd thought of little else since the debacle on Saturday afternoon. 'What can he do? He can't shut the bloody place. How would he live in the style he's fast become accustomed to without the quarry profits to pay the expenses?'

Frank frowned. 'His face was evil last Saturday.' Frank couldn't abide discontent. His mother reckoned he'd walk a dozen miles to avoid an argument.

Joe grinned. 'Aye and mine will be evil if I don't get time for a shave. Stop jawing lad and get on with making a brew while I get sorted.'

Pulling his trousers off the fireguard where they had been left to air overnight, Joe shucked his legs into them. The leather belt was curled on the chair; taking it he threaded it through the trouser loops and fastened the buckle. As he slumped into the chair to pull on his socks and boots he gave a small grunt and wondered when he had begun to do that. He was getting old, perhaps too old for the hard life of a quarryman. But there were men a lot older than him breaking slate. Geraint Pugh was seventy if he was a day and Evan Humphrey's seventieth was in the past.

The old men that had survived weren't in the majority. The quarry had seen a lot of Geraint's and Evans's fellow workers off. You had to have luck to survive decades as a quarrier. Most at the Garddryn today were young men and boys, or did they just look like boys now he was getting old? Bending forward to tie his boot laces he grunted again and gave a small private smile.

Rising slowly, he stamped his feet into the boots. Now he was ready to face his early morning shave. The slate floor in the scullery was murderously cold to bare feet. It was as well to prepare beforehand, half dressing and donning socks and boots before facing the freezing temperature.

It was Joe's prerogative to use the scullery after Frank; it gave him an extra ten minutes in bed whilst Frank washed and shaved. Not that the lad's earlier presence warmed the room in the slightest.

Ready for work, Frank came into the living room to put the pan of oatmeal soaking beside the fire onto the hob.

Looking over his shoulder, he called to Joe, 'You'll find hot water in the pan on the drainer for your shave, Da.'

'Thanks lad.' Joe smiled. Like chalk and cheese his two lads. Frank couldn't wait to do a good turn, whilst the other couldn't wait to ...

Frank stood in the open doorway. 'What about the two chaps Tommy sacked? What'll happen to them?'

Lathering his chin, Joe peered into the small looking-glass propped on the kitchen shelf. 'I'm hoping that Twm Tomos has had a word with our Tommy about that.'

Frank's face creased in a worried frown. 'Not much point trying to talk to Tommy.'

There was a momentary pause before Joe answered. His open razor needed sharpening and he'd nicked his chin. Dabbing at the bead of blood, he murmured, 'Aye, but all we can do is try.'

'I do hope everything's going to be all right, Da.'

Turning his head, Joe glanced at Frank. 'Of course it'll be

all right. Go and throw last night's scraping to the pigs and give the hens a handful of summat. There's a good lad.'

As the outside door opened, Joe shouted, 'And put your perishing coat on, Frank!'

Emily, an old shawl thrown over her cotton nightdress, came from the bedroom to stand beside the fire.

Drying his hands, Joe came into the room. 'You're up early, sweetheart?'

'With the racket that's going on this morning, it's no surprise that I'm up. '

Slightly belligerent, her hair a tangled web and her bare feet buried in the rag rug, he thought her as lovely as ever. Folding her in his arms, he hugged her close, kissing her cheek.

'Will everything be all right this morning, Joe?'

'My guess is as good as yours, sweetheart. There's no knowing with our Tommy.'

Emily fingered the narrow hem on the neck of his combinations. 'If it's not all right and he starts making more trouble, I'm going up to that house of his and giving him a piece of my mind.'

Joe chuckled. 'That should do it. There's nowt like the rough edge of a mother's tongue to bring a lad back into line.'

The kettle began to sing. Releasing her, Joe poured boiling water onto the tealeaves in the pot. Whilst it brewed he prepared two bottles, dropping a spoonful of sugar into each, topping them up with steaming tea.

Emily stood at the table conducting an imaginary conversation with her eldest son, as she dosed doorsteps of bread with dripping.

Frank came in bringing the freezing air with him. 'Jake's getting old.' He grinned. 'He didn't want to come out of the sty this morning. Daisy snaffled his breakfast.'

Abandoning the conversation going on in her head, Emily turned to Frank. 'Did you give the hens summat?'

'Aye, I gave them last night's parings and a handful of dandelion leaves from under the hedge.'

'Good lad.'

Frank slipped the bottle of tea and the tin holding the bread into his satchel and put the strap over his shoulder.

Joe took up the other. It was the bag he'd carried since his days as a Lancashire miner. A keepsake in memory of the other Frank, his mate killed in the Galloway pit so long ago. There were times when delving into the old bag he could be transported back in time to the Galloway and the back streets of Manchester. This morning he wasn't thinking of the other Frank; his thoughts were taken entirely with his son, master of the Garddryn Quarry.

'Ready, Da?'

'As ready as I'll ever be.' Joe sighed.

A cold blast of air straight off the snow-capped mountains blew into the room as Frank opened the front door.

Pulling her shawl tight, Emily shivered.

Standing beside her, Joe dipped his head. 'Give us a kiss then.'

Emily pecked his cheek.

He gave a long suffering sigh. 'Suppose that'll have to suffice.'

Emily found it impossible not to smile. 'Away with you, Joe Standish, it's too perishing cold to stand kissing in the open doorway.'

Frank was on the doorstep, fidgeting. 'Come on, Da. We'll be late.'

'I'm coming now.'

As Emily closed the door, Joe gave her a wave. Standing at the window she watched them cross the small field to the gate, half hoping that Joe would turn to wave again. A moment later they were behind the evergreen hedge. She caught a brief glimpse of them passing the blackthorn, then they were gone.

The chill leaching through the window pane sent her

back to the fire. In the quietness the tick of the mantel clock and the fire falling in on itself was suddenly noticeable. Every morning it took her a moment to adjust to the solitude. It was the time she thought about her day, planning it out in her mind. If there was an hour to spare she'd visit her friend now living in Bryn Tirion, the old house that she and Joe had rented when they arrived in Garddryn.

Tommy had been three-years-old when they moved in. Darling Chloe had been born in Bryn Tirion. Emily's heart gave a familiar lurch as her daughter came to her mind.

Frank had been born in the same bed, in the same room, as the sister he never knew.

What a blessing Frank was, she wouldn't be without him for all the tea in China. Tommy was a different kettle of fish. It wasn't that she didn't love Tommy, she did, and because she was his mother she always would.

Sighing, she thought of the visit she may be forced to pay on that young man today. What had it come to when she must go hat in hand to her first born to beg for the jobs of two of his workers? Perhaps there'd be no time to call on Maud today. Pity, she wanted to take her a pot of blackberry jam and a bottle of rosehip syrup for her youngest who suffered from a perpetual cough.

The tea in her mug was cold. Reaching for the kettle she put it back on the hob to make another brew. 'That's what comes of daydreaming instead of getting on,' she muttered.

Taking her heavy green cape from the back of the door she put it over her nightdress and went out to the privy. It was a lot colder outside than she had thought; the wind was rising and there was a scent of snow on the air.

Hurrying, the hem of her nightdress furling around her ankles, she crossed the tiny backyard and dashed into the small wooden building. Inside, bolting the door, she gave a quick glance at the swirling water beneath the round hole in the stout plank.

The stream was full, swollen with melted snow and rain running off the mountains, the turbulent water rushing over the half submerged rocks.

Quickly, it was too cold to linger, she lifted the hem of her nightgown.

Back indoors she took a moment to thaw through beside the fire before getting her grey merino skirt from the press. Whilst in the privy, she had planned what she'd say to her eldest if she were forced to pay a visit.

Walking towards the Garddryn Quarry, Joe was too disturbed to notice the early morning splendour of the mountains white with snow, or the hoar frost silvering the black branches and crisping the blades of grass with shades of platinum. Hundreds of men were walking with him, their boots beating a tattoo to the percussion of clinking hobnails.

Frank was beside him, silent, keeping his own counsel. It didn't take a psychic to know what was in the young man's head, for similar thoughts were rattling around his own brain. If two quarrymen could be sacked so easily, so could they. What awaited them at the Garddryn? A degrading scene, the two men involved begging for their jobs at the gates? It would be impossible to ignore a fellow worker's plight. Would management put on a display of misplaced authority, a show of strength and unity? Wipe their highly polished boots on the workers pride?

His face set in a grimace, Frank mentally beat his elder brother until he begged for mercy. Tommy was on his knees in the dirt, begging for forgiveness, promising that from now on he would be a loyal brother, a loving son, and a credit to the quarry. Lifting Tommy from the dirt, Frank ended the daydream.

Glancing sideways, Frank saw his father's pensive profile, the hard-tight line of his jaw, and wondered if mentally he was also giving Tommy a thrashing. If he was, he hoped he was doing a better job than he'd done himself. With a touch of scorn, he thought, *lifting him from the dirt indeed, it was where the bugger belonged.* It was the two quarrymen that he should be thinking about, not that bugger Tommy. At midday, if the worst came to the worst, he'd start a collection; with a bit of luck he might raise enough money to help with necessities.

The first men arrived at the Garddryn gates and a dozen or more voices shouted,

'Gate's shut!'

The words took Joe hurtling back in time, to that morning long ago when a similar cry went out. 'Pit's shut!' It was like a cold breath on the back of his neck. 'Pit's shut.' Two words full of foreboding. Shouted when he was still reeling from the ordeal of passing the house where his best mate lay dead, laid out in his mother-in-law's parlour.

He could remember with perfect clarity the icy tentacles of fear that had crawled through his belly on that day long ago when he was thrust on the slag heap of unemployed humanity. His baby son, Tommy, only days away from feeling the first pinch of hunger.

A vicious dig from an elbow brought Joe back to the moment. Men were shoving, trying to get closer to the gates. It was a physical effort not to be carried along with them.

'Gates shut!' roared again.

Joe came face to face with the reality that the men were locked out of their livelihood and it was his son's doing. Although he had prayed that Tommy would not bring his workforce to financial famine, ultimately he had chosen to do it. Joe's vision blurred with tears. Tommy was the boy he had nurtured, loved and strived for; how could he contemplate creating mayhem here at the Garddryn? Tommy's actions risked bringing the community to its knees, as the closing of the Galloway brought ruin and starvation to the streets of Lancashire. Tears filled Joe's eyes. God in heaven, the lad had been a victim of that travesty. How could he ...

Noticing that his father had turned the colour of alabaster, Frank shouted over the din, his voice cracking, 'Da, you all right?'

Hanging onto Joe's coat sleeve, Frank shook him in panic. 'Da, answer me for God sake, answer me!'

The lad's voice was lost to Joe: his entire mind was directed towards Tommy, walking steadily towards the angry crowd.

The men against the gates were clinging to the sturdy metal shafts, shaking them viciously. The noise was incredible and adding to the clatter were hundreds of angry voices.

Coming calmly towards them, Tommy appeared oblivious to the commotion.

Rees Roberts following a few feet behind him looked less confident, less sanctimonious. A dozen men, strangers, trailed behind the steward.

From within the crowd someone shouted, 'Good God, Standish has hired henchmen.'

Tommy's voice silenced the racket. 'The Garddryn stays closed until you all agree to the new hours of work. From now on, Saturday will be worked as a normal day. Select a man to speak for you and send him to the office when you have all agreed to the terms.'

Caleb Holmes, a wagon man for more than a decade at the Garddryn, shouted, 'You can't do that.'

Tommy's face was stony. 'I can do what I bloody like. So I'll start by sacking you. Get off my property.'

Outraged, the man standing beside Caleb, called out, 'You'd better sack me an' all. I'll not be forced to work all day Saturday.'

Someone bawled, 'How do you expect us to get home to Anglesey and back again for Sunday night?'

'It's not my problem,' Tommy said, turning away. His voice lost on the uproar.

Joe's eyes were on Tommy and angry words he'd spoken

131

long ago came back to him. *I'd have rather dropped you in the gutter as we were leaving Manchester ...*

The men at the rear, unable to hear what was going on, pressed forward forcing the crowd together. Within seconds hundreds of bodies were packed close and those in the heart and at the front, started to panic. The men at the gates were forced onto the unyielding metal, driving the air out of their lungs.

Several voices yelled, 'Stop it, you fools. Stop shoving. Stop pushing.'

Disaster was imminent. A man lost his footing and disappeared from sight.

With the instincts of a father, knowing that his lad hadn't the weight to stay upright in the crush, Joe drove Frank towards the verge in an effort to save him. 'Stay upright, lad. Stay upright.'

It was almost impossible for Joe to speak, bodies were packed so close around him, crushing the breath out of him, his lungs were on fire and there was a severe pain in his chest threatening to bring him down. The muscles in his thighs were burning with the force it took to keep his footing, pushing his youngest through the men fighting for their lives.

Frank broke free and turning fast, he grabbed Joe's arm. For a terrible moment he thought that he had lost his father as a quarrier came between them almost sweeping Joe aside. With all his young strength, he held on, desperately trying to haul his father from the quagmire of humanity.

Caleb Holmes was blocking Joe's escape. Caleb tripped and was swept away on a tide of bodies. For a split second Joe's exit was clear and Frank pulled with all the strength left in his arms. Joe came free like a drowning man, gasping for air, racked with choking spasms.

Terrified, Frank frantically towed him up the verge, away from flying feet. Scrambling up the bank, careless of the limbs they stood on, they made it to the hawthorn hedge and clung to the first handhold they could.

Joe was hunched, struggling to take in air. Beside him, feeling totally useless, Frank waited for his father's last breath to rattle in his throat.

'I'll kill that bugger of mine,' Joe said when he could breathe again.

Placing his arms around Frank's shoulder, Joe pulled him close, smelling household soap and warm flannel. Thanking God that his boy was safe, he pulled him closer still, burying his wet eyes in the shoulder of the boy's fustian coat.

The bedlam began to die down. Men scrambling out of the melee climbed onto the steep verges and were clinging to the hedgerow and the young trees. Those that had no handhold dug their nails into sods of grass, to keep their footing. Their escape gave breathing space to those on the track and the men there began hauling the injured to their feet. Several remained down, unmoving.

Tommy didn't glance back as he retreated to the imposing granite building that housed his office. The last thing he needed was a second look at his father's face, he had seen in the flint blue eyes, that he judged and condemned.

His lip curling in a snarl, Tommy spoke his thoughts aloud, 'The supercilious bugger thinks he knows everything. Well, he, Tommy Standish, master of all he surveyed, was prepared to show the old man just how wrong he was, the same went for the rabble standing with him.'

Kicking up stones in his hurry, his heart beating faster than was healthy, face white with rage, Tommy crossed the carriage-turning circle. His uneasy entourage following a few yards behind him.

Rees Roberts was bringing up the rear, keeping as far away from the master as possible. Anyone that came in striking distance, not only risked losing his livelihood, but was quite likely to get kicked like a dog into the bargain.

Tommy's mind was racing over the sequence of events. How had everything gone so terribly wrong? His plan had been a temporary lock-out to teach those quarrymen that had refused to work on Saturday a lesson. That it had backfired the moment he had put it into action, was infuriating. The threat had not cowed the men into submission as anticipated, but some alchemy working between them had strengthened their resolve not to accept the extra hours added to a Saturday shift.

Heavy spots of rain fell and he glanced at the sky; slate-grey voluminous clouds were sweeping in across the ocean, threatening a storm. If it broke soon, it would catch the idle workforce lazing outside the gates; they deserved a drenching. Hurrying he reached the steps of the building.

Roberts came up beside him, forced to trot to catch up; he was slightly out of breath, his cheeks red and wet with rain.

Ignoring the man blustering beside him, Tommy flung the front door wide. Flying back it banged into the wall making a small crater in the wallpaper and plaster.

Elias Hubbard, the office underling, jumped, giving a pathetic cry as the door ricocheted off the wall. Before the door swung back, Roberts charged through.

Oblivious to the steward following after him, Tommy strode down the short hallway. Reaching his office, he opened the door and went in, slamming it closed.

Rees Roberts gave Elias a nasty look. 'What you staring at?'

'Nothing.'

'Stare at *nothing* somewhere else.'

Advancing on Tommy's door, Roberts knocked and without pausing opened it.

'Get out!' Tommy roared. 'Get the hell out, you useless bastard. '

Flushing with embarrassment, Roberts yelled at Elias, 'You still bloody staring? Get on with some work, or follow the rest of the work-shy off the property.'

It was impossible to stay in the outer office with Elias creeping around passing furtive glances, so Roberts stomped outdoors.

The edge of the storm was skirting the Garddryn. Cursing the day and the weather, Roberts hunted in his coat pocket for his pipe; finding it he jammed it between his teeth. Putting a light to the tobacco, he threw the spent Lucifer into the wet grass; landing on a wet dandelion leaf it fizzled out. Sucking in a mouthful of smoke, he cursed his bad luck. He was standing in the rain, when he should have been indoors, dry and comfortable, a mug of tea in his hand.

With nothing better to do, Roberts made his way to the privy. The place was empty, but for the stench of the last occupant, and stink of effluent lying below the six-holer. Puffing clouds of sweet tobacco smoke, he made a brave attempt to override the reek. The atmosphere was still better here, than in the main office.

Tommy wasn't surprised to see his hands shaking as he opened the bow-fronted door of the new yew-wood cabinet. Taking out a heavy decanter he poured a good measure of brandy into a glass, his front teeth chattering against the rim as he put it to his lips. Taking a mouthful, he swallowed quickly, feeling the nectar warming his gullet, leaching into his bloodstream, calming his nerves. Slightly less shaky, he made his way around his desk and sat on the edge of his comfortable green leather chair.

Although his eyes were fixed on the desk-top, instead of seeing the tooled leather, he was re-living the fracas. In the pack of bodies he'd caught sight of his father's face; his expression had been of disgust. Frank's had been no better, loathing had been written plain across his simple phizog. The boy had got above himself. Well, he could still cook the young lout's goose for him.

He took another mouthful of brandy, holding it on his tongue, savouring the slight abrasive quality of the alcohol before swallowing. Almost instantly it began to work its magic, harnessing the raging anger, the red mist.

The tremor left him and he relaxed. With his long legs stretched beneath the desk and head against the high back of the chair, he held the glass closely against his chest.

As his brain cleared, brutal ideas took shape; for long moments he allowed himself the luxury of developing scenarios that would bring devastation to the quarrymen, his father and brother included. A picture of his mother came into his mind and he dismissed her; she too could suffer. Hadn't he suffered consuming her interminable stews? Enduring the smacks handed out for his cheek and lies.

It was twilight when Tommy left the office. He had sat without lighting the lamp until it was too dark to see across the room; at that point he rose to leave for home. Slightly clumsy after several brandies, he came into the outer office.

Elias Hubbard was standing behind the sanctuary of the counter. His heart quaked in his chest as he prepared to address the master. With a break in his voice, he said, 'Mr Roberts asked me to give you a message.'

'Why couldn't he give it to me himself?' Tommy's words were a little slurred.

Elias felt a tightening in his bowels. 'He went to help with the injured.'

'Injured? What injured?'

Elias would have preferred to be anywhere but where he stood, the bearer of portentous news. 'There were three fatalities at the gates, sir. Many were hurt, some have broken bones.'

Placing his hat on his head, Tommy swayed slightly. 'If they will fight, what do they expect?'

'Oh they weren't figh ...' Elias knew when not to upset the master, so stopped mid flow in his explanation.

Tommy hadn't heard the boy. Buttoning his coat, he

barked an order, 'Get me my carriage. I'll not ride to Plas Mawr in this wet.'

'Yes, Mr Standish.' Elias fled to the comparative safety of the stables to alert the servants that the master was ready to leave for his mansion.

Afraid to return to the office, Elias wasted five minutes sheltering from the worst of the weather under the overhang of the building until he heard the beat of hooves and the rattle of wheels on the cobbles. The cab was lit by two lanterns, giving twin circles of yellow light as it emerged out of the darkness of the stable yard.

From the shadows, he watched the master climb in. Almost at once the vehicle drew away from the building, disappearing as it turned out of the main office gate. He listened for a moment until the drum of the wheels and clatter of hooves diminished before he moved.

Glancing around, Elias wasn't sure that the hired heavies had departed. His stomach wouldn't cope with a sudden encounter. By some unconscious process his guts gave a long growl. Although reluctant to scoot across the open space, he made a dash for the front door.

Joe and Frank had come through virtually unscathed; the few cuts and bruises they had gathered in the melee would heal fairly soon.

The surgeon was on the scene quickly. As the incident had happened before his breakfast time, he was found at home. On seeing the carnage, he demanded that several men remain at the gates to help the injured. Joe had volunteered to stay and work had been found for him assisting the local barber.

Frank had remained with his father, until he was roped in to cart the three dead to the Half-Way, before their wives and children came upon the atrocity. These poor men were now lodged in the cold cellar beneath the inn, waiting for the special constable to view their bodies and apportion blame, if culprits could be named.

Emily had hardly finishing dressing when her friend, Maud Jones, came rushing through the unlocked front door. Almost incoherent the young woman blurted out the news of the calamity.

Emily paled as an image of Frank and Joe lying injured flashed into her mind. Flummoxed she couldn't gather her wits and remember where she had left her boots.

'What are you searching for, Emily?'

'Me boots! Me boots!' she cried in a panic.

Stooping, Maud brought them from under the table where Emily had abandoned them the previous night.

Subsiding into the chair, Emily donned them quickly, fastening less than half of the little black buttons in her haste. Standing, she caught a glimpse of her reflection in the mirror over the mantel; her hair was falling loose to her shoulders but there wasn't time to tie it back. Rushing across to the door, she grabbed a cloak off the peg and threw it over her shoulders. She said something before she dashed through the door but the words were lost to Maud.

Running as quickly as the conditions underfoot would allow, Emily crossed the small field; opening the gate she rushed through. Closing it was more of a reflex action than a thought. Out on the lane, she ran. Unfit and unaccustomed to vigorous exercise she was ungainly and not as fast as she would have wished. In a moment she had a stitch in her side, her breathing was jagged and noisy and with every stride a burning pain shot through her calves. Only the tormenting picture of Frank and Joe lying injured kept her hastening on.

She had covered half the distance to the Garddryn when Maisy Lloyd, the local shop keeper, waved her down. 'Emily, I've just seen your Joe and Frank and they are fine. So stop rushing, you'll give yourself an attack of summat or another.'

Tears sprung to Emily's eyes. 'Oh, thank the Lord.'

Backing up to a low stone wall, she sat down to catch her breath.

'Emily, they're both fine. Stop panicking and get your breath back,' Maisy said kindly.

Emily wheezed, coughing. 'I was so frightened that something terrible had happened to them.'

Retying the ribbons on her bonnet, Maisy fluffed the bow under her double chin. 'They're perfectly all right, not a scratch between them.' She gave a meaningful sniff. 'It's the other one, you should be worrying about.'

'Tommy?' Rising quickly, Emily glanced in the direction of the quarry track. 'Is he hurt?'

Pursing her lips, horizontal creases deepened above Maisy's top lip. 'No, indeed he isn't. But he'll not make himself popular locking the quarrymen out of the Garddryn.'

Emily's jaw dropped. 'He never has?'

'I'm afraid that is exactly what he has done.'

Maisy was well aware of the impact a lock-out or a strike would have on her business but this wasn't the time to begin shouting the odds. Poor Emily would have enough to bear if the quarry families starved because of her son.

Emily gathered the front of her cape in her hands. 'I must go. I have to find out what's going on.'

It took her several minutes to reach the entrance of the track. It came as no surprise that hundreds of quarrymen had gathered together there. Women were approaching, some with children.

A tall, rake-thin man, a friend of Joe's, was standing on the edge of the crowd. He was pale with shock and his coat sleeve was torn, his trousers muddied. A large bruise was darkening on his forehead and a cut on his bony cheekbone needed cleaning.

Seeing Emily, he broke away from the men. 'Emily, you'll find Joe up near the gates.'

'Are they both all right?' Emily's voice was unsteady.

'Oh yes. Joe's still there because he's a good chap to have around in a crisis. Not for any other reason. Frank was with him but he's taken someone back to the village.'

He didn't think it necessary to elaborate, to say that Frank had volunteered to stretcher-bear one of the fatalities to the Half-Way cellar.

Trying to give a reassuring smile, he went on, 'Joe got roped in to help with the injured. They've started to stretcher some of them down to the infirmary.'

'How many were hurt?' she was afraid to ask.

His voice dropped a notch, 'They reckon about thirty at a rough guess.'

Emily hand flew to her mouth. 'Oh Lord, that's terrible.'

'Aye it is, but I suppose it could have been worse.'

Glancing down the track, to the bend that curved around a waste mountain, she said, 'I'll go and see if I can help.'

His eyes flicked in the same direction. 'A crowd of us offered, but there were too many already there. It only adds to the confusion, everyone milling around. Things will have calmed down now. It's at times like this that you really feel bloody useless.'

She took two steps. 'I must go and find Joe and Frank. You need someone to see to that cut on your face.'

His dirty hand came up to his jaw. 'It's only a bit of a scratch. It can wait.'

The delay cost her a minute; trotting she tried to make up the lost time. The nearer she got to the gates the more dreadful the destruction. It was easy to imagine the scene. Men fighting for their lives to get out of the crush. The verges, hedgerows and sapling trees were destroyed, as though a ruthless giant had charged with a great weapon, scything his way to the quarry.

That Joe and Frank had been caught up in it was terrifying. Awful to think that she had been at home, brewing a pot of tea, preparing to visit her eldest son, unaware of the trauma that Joe and Frank were living through.

A broken mountain ash lay across her path, the berries hanging in bright clusters still scarlet, but come tomorrow they would be darkened and limp. There were times, like this, that she was reminded just how fleeting and precious life was.

Men were coming down the track. She heard their voices moments before they appeared. The noise disturbed a pair of pigeons; flying from a bare branch they scattered an assortment of small brown birds. Four men came around the bend they were carrying an injured man on an old door. They gave her a sidelong glance as they passed and she mouthed, bore da, although it was far from being a good morning.

Progress was slower the further she went. The muddy surface had been raked up in the riot. Sapling trees, broken branches, small personal belongings, spectacles, pipes, tobacco pouches, snuff boxes, littered the roadway. Canvas wallets, coats, hats, mufflers and gloves lay trampled into the sodden mess.

Coming in sight of the closed gates, seeing several men tending to the injured, it hit her that it was Tommy's evil deeds, his dreadful lock-out, that had created this terrible ruin. The thought made her want to cry.

Tears were filming her eyes as she walked towards Joe. On his knees, he was holding a man's broken leg whilst wooden splints were strapped on by the local bonesetter. The surgeon had departed to the small infirmary to administer to his patients there.

My son did this, she thought, looking at a covered corpse lying at the foot of the gate.

The afternoon twilight was turning to darkness as Joe, Emily and Frank walked up the lane to Corn Cottage. Conversation was at a premium. The deaths were too new to talk affectionately of the dead. The injured, although they

141

had their sympathy, were considered to be amongst the fortunate when measured against the three fatalities.

They were afraid to speak of Tommy; individually they had accepted that the blame lay with him, but to discuss it brought the shame out in the open. To Joe, his son's name was a blasphemy and he was thankful that neither Emily nor Frank spoke of him.

Reaching the cottage, Joe rooted in his coat pocket for his front door key, pushing it into the big lock he discovered the door unlocked. Too tired to wonder why, or worry about it, he pushed the door open.

The living room was cold and dark. The morning fire had burned out long ago. Joe took a Lucifer from his pocket and lit the lamp on the table.

Keeping her cape on, she was perished through, Emily began to rake out the cold ashes from the grate.

Joe glanced at her. 'Leave that, Emily. I'll fix it. Get yourself washed.'

Mud streaked her face and there was a smudge of blood above her left eyebrow. Her hands were filthy as were her clothes. She didn't answer; she was far too tired for words. Going into the scullery, she washed in cold water.

Subdued, Frank emptied his canvas satchel onto the table. The tin, holding the bread and dripping that should have been his midday meal, was dented. The bottle holding the tea smashed, staining the white material. It was a miracle that the satchel had remained on his shoulder and survived the crush. The tea stain might boil out.

Wrapping the broken glass into an old newspaper, he went over the meeting that the quarrymen had held outside the Half-Way. The men had decided that they wouldn't go to the Garddryn tomorrow, for more of the same from Tommy Standish. They would send a couple of men to the gates. If they were open, all well and good. Negotiations could start about the reinstatement of the sacked men.

He thought the men great optimists. Tommy wasn't going

to buckle that quickly or easily. The lock-out was a terrible reality to be faced. Next week there'd be no money coming into the house.

Throwing the paper that the bread and dripping had been wrapped in into the fire, Frank watched the grease flame. Thank God, he thought, watching the blackened paper curl, that he had never experienced a day like this one, nor did he ever want another. Lifting a dead comrade onto a make-do stretcher, and hauling him to the place where he had expected to share ale with him at the end of the day, had been heartrending. Keening women had followed the small entourage, wailing children hanging onto his coat. He had tried desperately hard not to falter in his step and tip the poor sod into the gutter, a final indignity.

Sniffing back tears, he wiped the end of his nose on the back of his hand. 'I'll get the hens some food and lock 'em in for the night. The last thing we need is the fox to make a meal of the poor devils. I'll find summat to give the pigs and see that they're safe in too.'

Joe looked up from sorting rubbish he'd hauled out of his pockets. 'Good lad, Frank. Take the lantern with you, it's pitch black out there.'

'Don't need it, Da. I'll see all right.' He desperately needed to be alone, to have a good blubber.

As the door closed behind him, Emily came back into the room. 'Do you think he's all right, Joe? He's very quiet, and pale.'

'He's as well as any of us. The day's events have been a terrible shock. The lad just needs to be alone for a while. Leave him be. He'll be better when he comes back in. You'll see.'

Her eyes went to the dark window. 'I hope you're right. I hate to think of him alone and upset.'

Folding her in his arms, Joe spoke gently, 'It's a rite of passage. He can't become a man until he's weathered knocks.'

'Aye, I know that. But it's hard watching a lad such as Frank get through a day like today.'

He kissed her forehead lightly. 'When he comes in, you can pet him a bit. Give him summat to eat.'

She gave a weak smile. 'I suppose that's what you'd like too?'

'It wouldn't go amiss, girl.'

The following morning Frank and Joe rose and prepared for work. It had been arranged that the quarrymen would meet on the village common half-an-hour before normal work-time. Two men would walk down the track to the Garddryn gates. If they were open, then they would return to work and meet Rees Roberts to discuss the reinstatement of the sacked men.

The morning was cold and grey, the sun hardly over the horizon as the men began to congregate. The common was a safer meeting place, out in the open. The high banks bordering the quarry track and the twelve-foot metal gates had proved to be a death trap yesterday.

When several hundreds had gathered and the time for beginning work was upon them, two men were selected for the errand. Twm Tomos, president of the caban, a respected man, was well known for his cool head and common sense. Joe Standish was chosen for no other reason, the men explained, than he was the father of the miscreant of the disaster, so it was his prerogative and duty to put matters right and bring his son in line.

Joe understood why they thought he might succeed, but he had no delusions. The chance of getting anywhere with Tommy, when he'd dug his heels in, was virtually nil. Face to face with the bugger, he was more likely to murder him, than talk. But because there was a slender chance, perhaps he'd had time to come to his senses and realise the damage he would do to the business if he held firm on this lock-out, he agreed to try.

As Joe stepped out of the crowd, Twm Tomos at his side,

Frank strode forward and came alongside his father.

'I'm coming too, Da,' he said firmly.

Frank was afraid of what might happen if his father and Tommy came face to face, the events of yesterday still raw.

There was an awful sense of déjà vu walking back up the track. The noise, the terrible shouts and screams of the men crushed and trampled was in the mind of all three. They were silent but for their boots striking slivers of slate, hobnails grinding yesterday's lost property into the mud.

Rees Roberts was at the gates, with twelve hired henchmen standing behind him.

Twm Tomos stood firm. 'So are these gates to remain closed?'

A sanctimonious smile spread across Roberts face. 'My orders are to keep them closed today. Who knows what might happen tomorrow?'

Even as he spoke, he didn't doubt the gates would open tomorrow and the men would file through and his job would be secure. Going twenty-four-hours without work, would teach them a lesson. Every man's pay packet would have less money in it at Saturday Reckoning.

Outwardly, Twm remained calm. 'Do these orders come from Mr Standish?'

Joe couldn't match Twm's composure, his fingers itched to get around Rees Roberts throat to strangle the self-important bugger. His boots raked the splinters of slate as he moved a step closer to the gates.

Twm struggling to remain calm, gave a slight smile. 'Is Tommy Standish on the property? If he is, we would like a word with him.'

Rees Roberts's eyes didn't get passed Joe Standish's face. He couldn't stand the man, enjoyed harrying the English incomer. 'Mr Standish is away at the moment. Penrhyn Castle, I think. Or he may be visiting the Assheton-Smiths in Port Dinorwic.' He gave a ridiculous grin. 'He was very particular about letting no one in today. No one! Regardless,' he said turning away. The henchmen following him.

Throughout the verbal encounter, Frank's teeth were so firmly clenched, his jaw ached.

With nothing to gain by remaining, the three turned away and walked back to the village green.

Twm looking sideways at Joe, said 'What do you think the chances are that the problem will be resolved tomorrow?'

'Slight,' Joe answered, pulling his pipe out of his pocket.

Twm sighed. 'I fear you may be right. But why the cat and mouse?'

'Because the bugger can,' Joe answered simply.

Not trusting his temper, Frank plunged his hands into his pockets and kept his head down.

The quarriers on the common fell silent as the three approached.

'I am afraid that the gates are locked,' Twm explained. 'But Rees Roberts thinks they will open tomorrow.' He tried to smile, though in his heart he knew the situation was dire. 'Why not enjoy a free day? Or get the chores your wives have been nagging about done?'

Someone from within the crowd shouted, 'What are the chances of that happening?'

A man shouted a reply, 'What, the day off, or doing the chores?'

'Don't be daft man. Work! Are we likely to get back tomorrow? I've several kiddies at home. I have no money to fall back on. With no work, my family will be in Queer Street by the end of the week.'

These words sobered the men.

Horas Jones, Joe's next door neighbour, shouted, 'My lot will be in the same boat. We've no savings. Food goes on the table when I'm paid. We have to get back tomorrow, come hell or high water.'

Twm waved for silence. 'It's no use going over what might happen. Let's wait until tomorrow and see what turns up. We're probably worrying about nothing. The gates could be

146

wide in the morning. Meet here, at the same time. Joe and Frank Standish will go up and find out.'

'Why send that English bugger? It's his son that's caused all this. He'll probably side with him; families stick together. It's the Standish clan that's sent our workmates to their graves.'

Since yesterday, Joe had wondered how long it would be before someone voiced this opinion.

Angry, Twm's face turned red. 'I've never heard so much bloody rubbish in my life; shame on you Woody Pritchard! Joe Standish stands shoulder to shoulder with us. He's one of us, a quarryman. Anymore of this nonsense and I'll speak to the minister of Salem chapel, ask him to have a strong word with you about your Christian duty. Now bugger off home. I'll hear no more of your drivel today.'

That Twm using expletives was a measure of his anger. An advocate of a pure language, he abhorred the pollution of slang and profanities.

The men dispersed, Joe and Frank aware that they were watched as they walked towards Corn Cottage.

The following morning, the men gathered on the village common again.

From the edge of the crowd, Woody Pritchard glanced hostilely at Joe.

Seeing the man's murderous expression, Joe was afraid for his family. Frank went about the village without considering someone with a grudge may wish to harm him. If they didn't get back to work today, he must take precaution to protect the boy.

Glancing at the leaden sky, Joe prayed that they would get back into the Garddryn, today.

The walk up the track was repeated. On the last stretch, it was obvious the gates were shut. Rees Roberts stood behind the barred metal. A dozen henchmen behind him.

Twm opened the conversation. 'Mr Roberts, we expected the gates to be open today.'

'Not today, Tomos.'

Twm's grey eyebrows rose. 'And why would that be. Mr Standish has returned to Plas Mawr? Why hasn't he given the order for the men to return to work?'

'The master is taking a well earned rest. He's taking a few days off to decide what to do about the renegade workforce.'

'Renegade!'

Enjoying the moment of control, Rees Roberts repeated a conversation he'd overheard between Mr Oakley and the master. 'Mr Standish has Ruby quarry to consider. He will soon need a workforce there. He's considering training itinerant Irish in the Garddryn, before moving them to Ruby.'

Unable to hide his fury a moment longer, Joe grabbed the metal struts on the gates. 'Over my dead body,' he roared.

Roberts snorted. 'I think you'll find he can do whatever he wants; the Garddryn is his property.'

Frank shook with rage. 'That's where you are wrong. This quarry belongs to his son, Edward Standish.'

Rees Roberts laughed. 'But the boy is a child. What can he do?'

Frank's face was mutinous. 'We'll find out, what can be done.'

Joe put a restraining hand on his arm. 'Say nowt, lad. Let's keep our powder dry.'

The men on the common fell silent seeing the three approach. It was obvious from their expressions that all was not well. There would be no work today.

Twm's voice was low, as he explained, 'We have very bad news. It seems that the Garddryn is to remain closed.'

'For how long?'

Twm raised his two arms in the air, then let them fall to his side. 'I don't know. There's talk of bringing in Irish to fill our places.'

The men's voices were as one as they hollered, 'Irish!'

Someone shouted, 'They can't do that.'

Twm sounded defeated. 'We may not be able to stop them.'

Joe stepped forward. Loud enough for all to hear, he bellowed, 'We can stop them, if we organise ourselves properly. We can barricade the track so the buggers can't pass us.'

'What with?' someone shouted.

Determined to fight, and make the men fight with him, Joe shouted loudly, 'Our bodies, quarrymen's bodies, that's what with.'

Most of the men cheered.

Joe had their attention. 'Everyday, all day, until it's too dark to work, we form a human barrier across the track, let no man pass. We'll have a twenty-four-hour rota, with enough men; we can stop the Irish coming in under the cover of darkness.'

Woody Pritchard shouted, 'What about the fields, there are so many ways to get into the place?'

Joe was positive, determined to try anything and everything, to thwart Tommy.

'Then we'll block those too,' he shouted. 'Every man must play his part. The Garddryn stays shut until we say it opens.'

Men cheered.

Joe caught the eyes of Horas, his neighbour, and saw his fear.

It wasn't going to be easy, Joe thought, but the alternative was worse. If they did nowt, they'd be trodden into the muck with no say, no rights, and poor pay. If the Irish workers got into the Garddryn, quarrymen here would be finished. There was no other work in the district. It would mean upping sticks and moving. He was too old to seek employment in the mines of Merthyr. His reckoning was simple; if the Garddryn stayed closed for weeks, the workers would be faced with two options, starvation or a flit.

CHAPTER SEVEN

Joe heard the gallop of a solitary horse as he turned into the gates of Plas Mawr. Horse and rider were approaching, travelling swiftly down the tree-lined avenue towards him. Almost at once he recognised his son, the arrogant posture of his first born. As he wouldn't give the young whelp the satisfaction of seeing him stand aside, Joe remained rooted, the gravel beneath his boots scrunching as he physically dug in his heels.

Tommy's eyes narrowed viciously seeing his father standing there. His fury erupted and lowering his head, using the animal as a weapon, he ran full tilt at Joe.

To trample was against the beast's nature and the black mare gave a high pitched keening wail as she fought against the reins and hurled aside. Terrified, she reared, almost throwing her rider.

Swearing fiercely, Tommy struggled to remain in the saddle, his boots clenched to the mare's flanks.

Joe's face was murderous. 'Young hound!'

The mare under control, Tommy glared at his father. 'You're trespassing. You have no right to be on the property.'

Furious, Joe roared, 'And is that what you'd tell the judge and jury? I killed my father as he walked towards my home because he was trespassing.'

Joe's words were sobering. Tommy saw the stupidity of his actions. He'd brought himself close to a hangman's noose, and not for the first time. In a fit of emotion he had risked losing everything, the mansion, his status and freedom. But worst of all he had betrayed the burning contempt he fostered for his parents' pride.

Surly, he barked, 'What do you want here anyway? You're wasting your time if you've come to beg me to open the Garddryn gates and let the motley crew you call friends, back in. I'll hire Irish, before I allow the scoundrels to return.'

Incapable of controlling his anger, Joe gripped Tommy's coat toppling him from the horse's back. The air whumphed out of his lungs as he landed at Joe's feet with a dull thud.

Smacked by Tommy's boots, the mare panicked. Side-stepping, her hooves came precariously close to Tommy's chest. Raising his arm, he clouted her back leg and the animal gave a whinnying cry and cantered back to her stable.

Joe hauled Tommy to his feet. His voice thundering, he shouted, 'I'll not thump the living daylights out of you whilst you're down. Up! You bugger.'

Caught in Joe's fierce grasp, breath knocked from his lungs, Tommy staggered. He was almost upright as Joe clouted his jaw. The blow was vicious, sending him hurtling back to the ground.

Grabbing the front of Tommy's embroidered shirt, catching the silk lavender necktie in his rough hand, Joe dragged him up, clouting him again.

Holding him at arms length, punctuating his words with blows, Joe spat contempt, 'I ... wish ... to ... God ... I ... had ... never ... set ... eyes ... on ... you! Do ... you ... hear ... me, you bastard?'

Reeling, Tommy threw an ineffectual punch, skimming Joe's chin.

Joe was too enraged to feel the contact and giving a savage grunt, he flung Tommy aside. 'You're bloody useless! The soft life has made you soft yoursen.'

Joe turned away in disgust, leaving Tommy sprawled on

the damp gravel. Appearing hardly winded, Joe strode towards the gates.

Regaining his feet, swaying, Tommy called feebly, 'I'll get you.'

Pride in tatters, as was his coat, he ran his hand over the damaged cloth. The new coat delivered only yesterday was beyond repair; every button had been torn loose taking a piece of grey merino wool with it.

His necktie was tight against his throat. Lifting his bruised and trembling hand, he slackened it, smearing blood onto the silk.

Joe was nearing the gates.

Tommy called after him, 'You'll pay dearly for this,' his words slurred. One of his front teeth had come loose and his lip was cut. The metallic taste of blood was on his tongue.

His eyes still on his father's back, he pulled a white silk handkerchief out of his pocket and gently dabbed the wounds on his face.

Horseless, he started to make his way back to the mansion. With every painful step he swore revenge, on his father and his so-called friends. The moment he arrived back at the house, he would send for Oakley, and despatch him to hire the Irish tinkers immediately.

Striding down the lane, his mood bleak, Joe cursed the day he'd sired the lout. Tommy Standish cast a black shadow. His avarice had torn the heart out of the neighbourhood, ruining what security and harmony existed. For him to rise others must fall. For some God forsaken reason, Tommy never appreciated that he could be part of a family and community, not separate from them.

Delving into his coat pocket, Joe drew out a red-check handkerchief and wiped the sweat off his brow, before dabbing his eyes.

Reaching the gates, he passed under the ornate arch. Stepping onto the roadway, he was glad to be off the property and away from the temptation of having another swipe at Tommy.

He hadn't gone far when he heard the sound of fast flowing water rushing over stones. Anxious to get cleaned up before he faced Emily, he crossed the grass verge and went through a gap in the hedge. The pathway to the stream was rutted by cart wheels, imprinted with crescent horseshoes. Stepping around the muddier places, he came to the water's edge and kneeling on the mossy bank, he cupped his hands to throw icy water on his hot face. Fresh blood from his scuffed knuckles ran in pink rivulets to his wrists, as pale as pigeon blood; the fat drops fell into the beck.

The fight had shaken him, his guts were trembling and he felt nauseous and weak. Never before had he laid hands on his children. Smacking, he'd left to Emily; her touch had always been controlled. There had been times in young Tommy's life that he had come close to thrashing the boy, but he had stayed his hand, afraid that he'd fail to hold his temper in check and murder the little bugger. Perhaps that's where he had gone wrong; maybe he should have leathered the lad, knocked some sense into him years ago.

Tears were on his wet face, mingling with cold mountain water, tears for little Tommy, the chap that had sometimes made him laugh. The boy he'd helped make Christmas lanterns. Tracked rabbits in the snow, and walked the miles around the Garddryn on Saturday afternoons.

When he felt that he had recovered as much as he was likely too, he rose slowly. Sighing, he drew the palms of his wet hands across his trousers to dry them. Inspecting the damage on his knuckles, scraped and red raw, he saw that there was no way he could hide the injury from Emily and he sighed again.

Making for home, he walked back to the pathway. Unaware as he trekked over the short mossy grass, that this was the place Tommy had run to, desperate and terrified, to burn the evidence of the attack on George.

The distance between Plas Mawr and Corn Cottage was three miles. The route was not overly familiar. Joe normally shied away from walking towards the mansion. Other tracks had more appeal if he was taking a constitutional. The path he trod most often was to the tiny graveyard on the mountainside, where his little Chloe lay in perpetual childhood. Her baby face came into his mind and he banished the thought, afraid that today of all days he would weep bitterly if he dwelt on his sweet innocent child.

Plagued with memories, he walked steadily home, grateful that he met no one on the lanes. Anyone associated with the Garddryn would have applauded him for leathering Tommy, but he viewed the debacle differently. The Standish family were not the sort of folk to wash their dirty linen in public, for the amusement of their neighbours.

Corn cottage came into view. Joe gave his knuckles a quick glance; nothing had improved. If anything the broken skin appeared worse; the bruises were beginning to show a livid red-purple.

Opening the gate, he made his way up the path. With a gentle sigh, he opened the front door.

The fragrance of warm yeast, dough, and mutton stewing greeted him as he came in.

Emily was standing at the far end of the kitchen table, rolling out pastry, the topping for a mutton and potato pie. Nearer the fire, at the other end of the board, dough was rising in a brown bowl.

As he entered, she glanced round with a ready smile on her lips, which faded quickly at the sight of him. 'Whatever's happened? Joe, you look terrible,' she cried in alarm.

Quickly, rubbing her hands together to shed flour, wiping the remainder onto her apron, she rushed to his side.

Shoulders hunched, his face grey, he looked ten-years-older than he should. His voice dull, he said unconvincingly, 'Don't fret, Emily. I am all right, really.'

'But, Joe, what happened?'

As he slumped heavily into the chair at the fireside, he accidentally kicked the fender with his mud rimed boots.

Blind to the mud he'd traipsed in, Emily knelt at his feet, her skirt making a green circle on the rag rug. Taking one of his injured hands in hers, she held it gently. 'Was this something to do with the quarry?'

An image of the quarry track, the injured and dying lying side by side, flashed into her mind. 'There's not been another catastrophe like the last one? A week's hardly passed since we buried the unfortunates from that,' she said horrified.

He was quick to dispel her fear. 'No. It's not as bad as that, lass. But it's not good. It's our Tommy. I gave the lad a right thrashing.'

Shocked, she let go of his hand and covered her mouth with it. 'Joe, is he all right?'

'Course he's all right. If I had meant to kill the bugger, I would have done so,' he said sharply.

Rising from the chair, he crossed to the dresser and from the bottom cupboard took out a bottle of whisky, pouring a generous measure into a glass.

Coming back to the seat, he caught his reflection in the looking glass over the mantel and was surprised to see that his face was virtually unscathed, if he didn't count the haggard lines and the sadness in his eyes.

He took a mouthful of the cheap whisky. Fiery, it slid into his gut, killing the nausea. He swallowed another mouthful quickly, it was too harsh to hold on his tongue. Clutching the glass, he sat heavily.

On her haunches, her eyes beseeching, she said urgently, 'Tell me, Joe.' Her breath stilled in her lungs.

For a split second he closed his eyes, gathering the sequence of events together. 'I went to ask him to think again, consider the hardship he was bringing to the quarrymen and their families. As I arrived at the gates, the bugger was galloping along the avenue.' He kept the information, that their eldest had seen fit to try to trample his own father, to himself.

'The lout wouldn't listen, so I pulled him off his fancy horse and gave him something to think about.' His eyes flashed to hers.

The colour faded from her cheeks. 'So how hard did you hit him?'

'It was hard enough for him to remember it awhile. I don't expect you to understand, Emily...'

Her fingers clasped his knees tightly. 'I do understand, Joe. I understand what our Tommy has put the men at the Garddryn through. Don't think just because I love the lad, that I'm not mortifyingly embarrassed by him. It's right that you've pulled him up by his bootstraps. If you hadn't done it, I might have had to do the job meself.'

He smiled weakly. 'Our Emily, you never fail to amaze me.'

Rising clumsily, she straightened her skirt. Taking the kettle from the hearth, she set in on the hob.

Turning back to him, her head bent, she said quietly, 'That's the way it's supposed to be, Joe. Who'd want to live with someone that's always predictable?'

Watching as she put tealeaves into the pot, he said sadly, 'You could never say that Tommy was predictable, and look what's happened there.'

Closing the lid of the caddy, she glanced at him. 'I think you're wrong, Joe. Tommy is predictable. That's the sadness of it. What he does today, he'll do again tomorrow, however bad.'

He wondered how hard, and for how long, she had pondered on this before coming to such a heartbreaking conclusion. Accepting that her first child was flawed was probably one of the hardest things she had ever done.

A picture of Chloe drifted into his mind; he thought, Emily had accepted some terrible things in her life. She was strong, stronger than he was, for all he wanted to do was weep for his lost children.

Tommy arrived back into Plas Mawr and as there was no footman on duty to open the door, he barged in, flinging the heavy door back so fiercely that it rocked a small table. An ancient oriental vase toppled, smashing to smithereens on the mosaic floor.

The first and second footmen came running.

'Where the hell have you two been? You're paid to be on duty. Your place is in this hall until I say otherwise. Do you understand?'

Although the men nodded in agreement, their eyes were rooted to the injuries on the master's face. Obviously someone had seen fit to give Tommy Standish a thrashing.

Whatever their thoughts, they kept them carefully hidden. Showing the master a bland expression, they apologised quickly, adding an excuse.

Tommy wasn't listening; roaring at the shorter of the two, he never could remember the man's name, he barked, 'Get to the stables and send the head-groom to me. Now! Don't stand there dithering, you buffoon. Go!'

As the man disappeared, the first footman gave a small bow. 'Is there anything I can do for you, sir?'

'Yes!' Tommy roared, 'Mind your own blasted business!'

Silent, the man bowed again.

Ignoring the ruined vase, Tommy strode towards his study. As he opened the panelled door, he glanced over his shoulder; the footman was crouching over the shards, holding a dustpan for a maid sweeping pieces into it.

Tommy shouted, 'Leave that. Send someone for Oakley. He'll be at the quarry office. Get him here at once.'

The man straightened. 'I'll send a man immediately, sir.'

Disturbed by the commotion, Henrietta came out of the drawing room; seeing Tommy standing in the study doorway, she walked towards him. Although his eyes met hers, he withdrew immediately, closing the study door with a bang.

His wounds were too interesting to ignore, and increasing her step, Henrietta entered the study without knocking.

Tommy was at the bureau, pouring brandy into a glass. Looking up as she entered, he was sarcastic, 'I didn't hear you knock.'

Henrietta had ceased to care for Tommy Standish. Recently she had learned that he had sold the house her mother had bequeathed to her. The house had been home to her poor crippled brother, George.

Heartlessly, Tommy had removed George and locked him away in Denbigh Asylum. She had beseeched Madoc, the family solicitor, to secure George's release but Tommy had certified him as an imbecile and Madoc said he was powerless to reverse the order. Although he had tried to reassure her with platitudes and had promised that in time, if George showed improvement, he might be liberated.

The words hadn't brought her much comfort. With the sale of the house, all her plans for a better life evaporated. What wouldn't she give to have those few days following her mother's funeral back again? Had she been brave and not succumbed to large doses of opium, she could have fled Plas Mawr with her young son. They would now be living in Chester, and she would be taking care of George in his rightful home. A night didn't pass that she didn't weep bitter tears for her lost opportunity.

Looking into her husband's wounded face, she felt the new but already familiar feeling of distaste for him.

'Fall from a mare.' He indicated his injuries with his forefinger, before lifting his glass and taking another mouthful of brandy.

She raised one eyebrow. 'Oh! Not like you to fall off.'

He was unused to this braver front that she had come to display recently. It irked him that she no longer trembled, either in passion or fear, at his presence. Given the chance he would swipe this new confident look off her face.

Looking over the rim of the glass, he lied, 'Fox leapt out of the bushes. The mare reared. There's no mystery.' He took a long swallow of the settling alcohol.

It appeared to Henrietta that he had been in a fight. She wasn't surprised; there were many who wanted to harm him, since the lock-out at the quarry. It would never have come to this had her father still been in charge. Bertram Bellamy had too much respect for the quarrymen, to starve them into submission. Tommy Standish hadn't her father's dignity.

Hardly disguising a small yawn, Henrietta glanced at the mantel clock. 'I'll send someone for the surgeon.'

Moving across to the door, sweeping the hem of her skirt off the floor, she turned to face him. 'I wasn't aware that the grounds of Plas Mawr harboured foxes.'

There was no mistaking the facetiousness of the remark. His eyes narrowed spitefully. The gamekeeper had been a favourite of Henrietta's father and she often visited his cottage to call on the man's sickly wife.

Wishing to wipe the half-smile from her face, Tommy gave a veiled threat, 'If the gamekeeper did his job properly we would be clear of vermin. Perhaps it's time he and his brood moved on.'

His remark touched a nerve. But as she had used her new heroin medicine on hearing that Tommy had returned to the house, she successfully remained passive. How much easier it was to deal with him when she had taken her medication.

Before passing through the door, her hand around the brass knob, she said calmly, 'I'll ask Miles to send a maid with hot water.'

After she had gone, Tommy's eyes remained on the closed door. Henrietta had been acting very differently since Griffith, the surgeon, had suggested this new cure for her opium and alcohol addiction. He wasn't sure if it didn't suit him better, to have her over-anxious and more biddable.

Hearing a carriage on the avenue, he put down his glass and went to the window. Oakley's equipage, pulled by a dapple-grey, came to a standstill at the wide steps leading to the front door. The office manager, on the threshold of his sixtieth birthday, climbed down stiffly. He had words with the driver, and walking with the support of an ebony stick, he approached the door.

The footman attended to the visitor, taking his black silk hat and gloves from him; he escorted him towards the study.

Tommy crossed to the bureau and refilled his glass. He was standing behind his desk, Henrietta and her medical problems forgotten, as the man was shown into the study.

Oakley hardly contained his surprise seeing Tommy's injured face. The handiwork of deposed quarrymen, was his first thought.

Tommy hurried to explain. The last thing he needed was rumours to run amok that he had been beaten by one of his workers or his own father.

Repeating his lie, he said with a tight smile on his now sore lip, 'Fox ran out of the bushes; the mare reared.'

'Bad show!' Oakley was genuinely concerned. 'Has the surgeon visited?'

Tommy tipped the glass to his mouth. 'The man's on his way.' He took a long pull at the brandy, to deaden the pain in his jaw and cheekbone.

'Oakley, I want you to organise the Irish workers to start immediately.'

The manager was flummoxed. Surely Tommy didn't envisage keeping the Garddryn men out indefinitely? 'I thought you had decided to use the itinerants only as a threat, until the quarrymen accept that the sacked men cannot come back to the quarry. That it is in their interest to return to work, and accept the longer working hours.'

'I have changed my mind. I want the Irish to take over. If there are not sufficient numbers of them already in Caernarvonshire waiting for the call to work, there are plenty of others to choose from; those on the blacklists from the mines in the south, immigrants from Liverpool, Amlwch copper men. Do what is necessary.'

'But surely ...' Oakley began to reason.

Interrupting him, Tommy slammed the glass down on the desk-top, splashing brandy onto the tooled leather. 'I will not argue on this, Oakley. The decision is mine. I demand that the Garddryn men are kept out, and others move in.'

'But!'

'No buts, Oakley. That is unless you wish to join the men on the other side of the Garddryn gates.'

Oakley sighed inwardly. This was turning into a very bad business indeed. 'I'll send someone to alert the Irish workers immediately, sir.'

'No!' Tommy snapped. 'I want you to go. The fewer people that know of our plans the better. I don't want to alert the quarrymen and have a battle royal on our hands. Get the itinerants moved in during the early hours of Sunday morning. They'll have started work, before the Garddryn men discover they're on site.'

Oakley looked aghast; the idea was seriously flawed. The quarrymen would cause a riot. The outcome would be catastrophic. Floundering, he tried to think of a way to put a stop to the madness. 'Catholics might not want to work on Sunday.'

Tommy's eyes narrowed menacingly. 'Then they'll starve too. If the buggers want to work, they'll be at the Garddryn in the early hours. Those that refuse because of their religious ethics, can ask the bloody angels to feed 'em.'

A great sense of defeat washed over Oakley. 'I'll do as you wish, sir.' His thoughts were with his son, Sam, working as a clerk in the quarry office. Sam had become an ardent reformer since hearing the men spouting *Union* in the Half-Way. How to keep this palaver quiet ...

Tommy interrupted Oakley's depressing thoughts. For some time he had suspected that Sam was being encouraged to report office business to the agitators. With shrewd manipulation the young man could be used to feed back inaccurate information to the rabble.

Pleased with this stratagem, Tommy gave a slight smile. 'Tell that boy of yours to come to Plas Mawr, first thing in the morning. I'm moving him from the clerks' pound, up to management. As from tomorrow, he can oversee the Ruby explorations.'

A weight lifted from Oakley's shoulders. It was difficult not to give a sigh of relief. The boy would not only be away from the dissenters, but he'd also have advancement. Suppressing an urge to smile, it would be inappropriate considering the master's injuries, he said gratefully, 'He will not let you down, Mr Standish. You have my word on that.'

It was gratifying to have the old man fawn. After this, Oakley would be completely in his pocket, the boy too. Enjoying his superiority, Tommy spoke sharply, 'See that he doesn't.'

Emily was brewing a second pot of tea for the six quarrymen that had arrived after dark for a discussion with Joe. She would have liked to go next door to Bryn Tirion to visit with Maud Jones. Maud's eldest, Cyril, was recovering from scarletina. She had a bottle of rosehip syrup for him. With unexpected visitors, she felt she should stay to make tea and keep some sort of order in her living room.

The milk, what was left of it, was in the cold scullery. Taking the empty kettle with her, she went to fetch the jug.

Emily passed the table, crowded, with five men around it. Joe was at the head, writing out a timetable. Tudor Williams, Tom Hughes, Woody Pritchard and Fergus Holmes watching him. She wondered if someone would offer to fill the kettle.

Dick Lord, perching on the edge of the chair besides the dresser, shifted his legs to let her pass. She noted the mud encrusted on the soles of his boots, and the floor only mopped today.

Arfon, engrossed in making a list of the men most likely to help guard the Garddryn, didn't notice her stepping over his big feet.

In the scullery, she filled the kettle from the bucket of water by the back door. Spilling water down the front of her skirt, she muttered under her breath, 'Men!'

Carrying the kettle and jug, she used her rear to bump open the scullery door. In the living room, she negotiated her way over Arfon's feet. Skirting Dick Lord's legs, she got another daft grin from the lummox.

Stifling a sigh, she put the kettle back to the fire and poured the tea, eking milk and sugar in each mug. She thought to offer around a piece of speckled bread, but the bara brith was meant to last the week, so decided against it. The men's dirty boots and dusty clothes would create enough work for her, without baking again before Saturday.

Arfon took a mug of tea without acknowledging her. Looking towards the men at the table, he said 'What about Jack Dickens? Should I put him on?'

Fergus grinned. 'He's a bit old for it.'

Joe chuckled. 'He's the same age as me, you cheeky bugger. Put him on. He's always did like a bit of a scrap.'

Taking a mug from Emily's hand, Joe's eyes caught hers and he winked. Emily raised one eyebrow, sardonically.

Arfon blew noisily on the hot tea. 'But he's all bluster, these days.'

Joe took a sip. 'Nowt wrong with that. Put him on.'

A fleeting image of Jack Dickens came to Emily's mind. The man had been Joe's first boss. A nastier piece of work it would be hard to find. Mentally she listed his faults, wife beater, bully and cheat.

The front door opened, bringing in a gust of cold air. Shutting it quickly, Frank wiped his boots thoroughly on the doormat.

Before Frank had a chance to say good evening to anyone, Arfon shouted across to him, 'Frank, do you want to be with the late crowd, watching through the night, or do you prefer mornings?'

'He'll be with me,' Joe spoke quickly. It wasn't his intention that Frank should be on Garddryn property without himself alongside. If things got ugly, he wanted to be looking out for the lad.

Emily glanced at Frank. 'Do you want a cuppa, Frank? I reckon I can squeeze one more out of the pot.'

'I'd love a cup, Mam.'

Turning towards his father, he frowned. 'What's going on? What's this watching through the night? What are you lot up to?'

'I'll tell you later, son,' Joe said, without looking up from the paper he was writing on.

Frank crossed to the fire, warming his hands to the blaze.

'You'll get chilblains, our Frank,' Emily warned.

The kettle came to the boil; lifting it, Frank poured water over the tepid dregs in the pot.

Joe leaned back in the chair, hands linked behind his head. 'I think that just about covers it. Working to this timetable means that there'll be men at the gates around the clock. It will take dozens to guard the other obvious ways in. The biggest problem will be watching the boundaries. The fences and hedgerows stretch for miles, and they are not all in good repair. It'll be easier to watch the roads.'

Sighing, Tudor aired his misgivings, 'The specials will not allow us to do that, surely. We'd be rounded up and thrown in the clink in no time.'

Although the thought of gaol was terrifying, Emily remained silent. It wasn't her place to voice an opinion, and embarrass Joe.

Joe purposely didn't glance her way. He might welcome her suggestions, but the men at the table would not. Wives to them were like furniture, hardly noticed until absent.

Joe brought his thoughts back to the matter-in-hand. 'The specials will have to catch us first. If we posted a couple of strong young men on the road into the village, they could run and warn us that the specials were about.'

Tom Hughes, team leader at the quarry, shrugged into his coat. 'I reckon I know two men that are robust and reliable enough to do just that.' Wrapping a muffler around his collar, he said, 'I'll call on them, before they go supping ale. They'll be watching the road at first light.'

Joe rose off the chair, stretching his cramped back. 'I think we've covered everything? Fergus and Dick, you arrange the first shift for the gates. Go carefully, we don't want to alert the special constables, or quarry management of our plans. Tell the men that we need them there at five-thirty. It's early, but the Irish will try to get in before first light. They might think as we've no work to go to, we'll lie abed in the morning.'

Getting ready to leave, Fergus pulled up the collar of his dark coat. 'No problem Joe. We'll get everyone organised.'

Tudor stuffed a battered tobacco box into his pocket. Then swallowing a mouthful of cold tea, he put the almost full mug back onto the table.

Woody Pritchard had lost the sheepish look he'd had when he arrived. The day following the disaster, he'd spoken against the Standish family, more in temper than any real malice. Joe had made a point of inviting him this evening. Better the devil you know, was a good maxim, worth remembering with trouble brewing.

Frank put his coat back on. 'I'll check on the pigs.'

Joe reached for the pipe he'd left on the mantel. 'Good lad. See that the hen house is secure too.'

As the men filed out of the cottage, Emily collected the mugs, carrying them into the scullery. Coming back from the cold room she straightened the rucked rug in front of the hearth.

'Joe, how long do you think all this'll go on for?'

Distracted, he looked up from the timetable in his hand. 'It's impossible to say. We can only hope that it's over quickly, so we can get back to some sort of normality.'

Frowning, Emily chewed her bottom lip. 'Money is going to be tight if it lasts any time at all.'

'That's for sure.'

She hesitated for a second or two and then said, 'It's too early to have vegetables from the field. There's still food in the store cupboard. I picked and pickled a lot last year, but it's not much to live on. I was just wondering what else I might do to help.'

'There's no need to panic just yet, Emily. Let's hope that it's over by this time next week. If not, then we'll come up with some idea. Everyone's in the same boat ...'

She was slightly exasperated by this reply. 'I know that, Joe. It's just that I like to be prepared, and plan a bit ahead.'

Joe frowned. 'We've got a bit of money put aside. We'll manage summat. I can do odd jobs, chopping wood, clearing stones off fields, whatever it takes.' He grinned 'Poaching won't go amiss.'

Her eyes flew open. 'Joe, you wouldn't!'

The idea was amusing and he chuckled. 'Oh yes, I would. I just might take meself to the grounds of Plas Mawr and bag a rabbit or two.'

'Joe, you wouldn't poach off our Tommy?'

He grinned. 'Emily darling, I'd snatch the horse from under his bum, if we needed to cook it.'

The picture that came into her mind made her giggle.

Putting his arms around her, he said softly against her hair, 'Stop fretting. We're not going to starve. Now, be a good lass and get me supper, I'm famished.'

She chuckled. 'Will a dish of our Tommy's old stallion do you?'

'It'll do as a last resort. But a bit of that left-over meat and potato pie, would do better.'

Lying in his bed, Emily sleeping restlessly beside him,

Joe thanked the Lord that they did not have children to feed. Many of the quarrymen would already be worrying about putting food on the table next week. There were rents to pay, school pennies to find, besides all the other necessities, candles, oil, and wood for the fire. The call on a man's wages was long.

Fitful, his mind dwelling on the Garddryn men out watching the roads on this damp and miserable night, whilst others kept watch at the quarry boundaries, listening for the tramp of the dreaded Irish, come to take their work.

Earlier, he'd stretched his legs, walking around the village after dark. The cottage windows already appeared less bright as cautious housewives rationed candles and lamp oil. The fires would be burning low in the grates, with chairs pulled close to the meagre flames.

The night was unusually peaceful, the lanes devoid of pedestrians; everyone had stayed home, saving pennies. His route had taken him passed the Half-Way; the inn had been empty. The quarrymen, he supposed, had gathered with their families to discuss the lock-out and the inevitable consequences.

Some homes had taken in the barrack men. The weekly boarders had been evicted from their shelter, their few possessions thrown in the dirt by Oakley's hired enforcers.

Bitterness had already taken hold in Garddryn village. If the Irish should come, there'd be a bloodbath.

Ambling home, he had let himself back into the cottage quietly. Emily had already gone to bed. Thoughtful, he had sat by the dying fire thinking of Frank, his old collier mate in the Galloway pit.

Five o'clock next morning, Joe roused his son. 'Come on lad; if we're to be at the track before daybreak, we'll have to get a move on. I'll dish the porridge, whilst you sort yourself out.'

'All right, Da. Give me a minute.'

From the doorway, Joe looked back to the untidy bed. 'Look lively, lad. Don't go back to sleep.'

'I won't.' Flinging aside the grey blanket, Frank swung his legs over the edge of the bed, his bare feet landing on the rag rug. Sighing tiredly, he rose. Scraping his hands through his tousled hair, he yawned noisily.

Joe cut doorsteps of bread, spreading dripping and sprinkling salt on each piece. Two bottles of sweetened tea, were on the table. He wondered how long it would be before they had to drink tea without the luxury of sugar. Their supply was running low and sugar was expensive.

Frank swilled his face in cold water in the scullery, and then paid a rapid visit to the outdoor privy. He came into the living room bemoaning the weather.

Coming to the table, he watched his father dollop porridge into two crock basins, sprinkling both with salt. They ate in silence, thinking of the day ahead.

Outdoors a cold wind was blowing off the ocean. Joe looked down to the sea; precipitation was travelling towards land, it was either hail or rain. Whichever, it was likely to catch them before they reached the quarry.

Other quarriers soon joined them on the roadway. When they reached the track, they were sixty strong, walking shoulder to shoulder, towards the gates. Many other men were coming up behind them.

A large group stopped at the quarry gates. The men that had watched throughout the night, greeted them cheerfully. There was nothing to report, no sighting of itinerant Irish, but rumours were rife. Foreign looking men had been spotted in Caernarvon and in Bangor. Dozens had supposedly bivouacked in outlying farms. Someone swore that several Garddryn quarriers had been questioned by the constables and told not to gather in group of more than four men, otherwise summary arrests would be made. Joe thought this was possibly the only rumour that had any truth in it.

The time came for the start of a new working day and the men fell silent. Although no one really expected Rees Roberts to appear and open the gates, their eyes turned to the direction of the quarry office.

The rain came as fine drizzle, veiling the stark lines of the terraces, obscuring the mountain peaks. The wait was wet and miserable, and they cursed the name of Tommy Standish.

The cold damp seemed to creep into Joe's flesh as he stood there, ashamed to call his son his own.

Someone shouted angrily, 'So the bastard has decided to let us starve.'

'What did you expect from jumped up gentry?' an elderly voice hollered from the centre of the crowd.

'What you going to do about it, Standish? He is your son.'

Frank's face reddened with anger. 'Why blame my father? It's nowt to do with him. This is Tommy's doing. You want someone to curse, curse that bugger.'

Joe put a restraining arm on Frank's sleeve. 'Leave it, lad.'

Tears of frustration shone in Frank's eyes. 'It's not right, Da. Why blame you for our Tommy's actions?'

Raising his voice so all could hear, Joe shouted, 'I wish I had influence with my elder son, if I had, I wouldn't rest until I had put this savage lock-out behind us. But I'm afraid Tommy Standish does as he wants and however flawed his thinking, I have no power to change it.'

'There must be something you could do,' a man bawled.

Joe snapped, 'Short of murdering the bugger ...'

'That'd be a start,' another shouted.

A ripple of laughter followed the man's words.

There was nothing to be achieved by waiting and most of the men started to walk away, many to regroup on the common land. Those elected to watch the boundaries paired off, heading towards the borders enclosing the quarry.

Frank and Joe started a long hard slog, steadily climbing

towards the highest point, from there they would see into the heart of the quarry, view the long straggling boundaries enclosing it. The ascent was hard going, but within an hour they made it to the winter snowline; here the land was treeless, barren but for short springy grass sprouting from the thin layer of peaty soil covering the slate mantle. Large boulders littered the mountainside, carried on ice-age flows, or tumbled from the peak through the millenniums.

Standing stones, erected by Druids from an ancient age, cast a dark Celtic mystery over the bleak terrain. On the wet and windswept mountainside, it was easy to imagine the spiritual essence of past sacrifices seeping from the giant megaliths.

Both wrapped in their own thoughts, they climbed on silently, needing all the breath they could draw into their lungs.

The rain eased and then stopped. The sky lightened as the clouds thinned and wraithlike patches of blue appeared.

Taking a breather, Joe sat on a wet boulder. Pulling the bottle of sweet tea from his pocket, he tipped it to his mouth and drank.

'Grand view, Da,' Frank said, drawing alongside.

'Aye, it is that.'

Joe glanced towards the peak. 'We've still a way to go though.'

Sitting beside his father, Frank pulled a tin from his satchel. 'Aye, we have. But I'm stopping here and eating me bit of snap before I take another step.'

Joe thought Frank sounded nine-years-old, and he smiled. 'Good idea. I'm famished an' all.'

'I wonder if Mam can see us,' Frank said, putting the tin on his lap and waving both his arms.

Joe grinned. 'I hope she's indoors, cooking the mutton for the lobscouse she promised us for our supper.'

'Smashing,' Frank said grinning. 'It's one of me favourites.'

They ate in virtual silence, looking down to the green and brown patchwork quilt that was the neighbouring villages and the surrounding farms.

The going was rougher as they moved on, the ground strewn with small boulders, stones and shards of slate. With their heads down against the cold wind, their breath hard in their lungs, they climbed to the highest point.

The wind across the peak was blustery, fierce short sharp gusts whipping their hair and booming in their ears.

Joe's eyes started to water; sniffing, he swiped at the tears with his gloved hand.

With Frank standing beside him, Joe scanned the valley. He pointed to a thin ribbon running between the dark borders that were the hedgerows and dry-stone walls.

'That's the road that links Caernarvon with Garddryn village,' he said, the wind whipping away his words. 'If the tinkers come from the port, that's the way they must travel. If they come from Porthmadoc, they have to come along that way there.' Turning slightly, he indicated the thin trail to the south. 'Do you see the road? It's not very distinct.'

Frank's coat was billowing, flapping around his knees. 'We'd be lucky to see anyone, unless they were quite close. Then it might be too late.'

Joe's eyes turned to Frank. 'It might not look very far-away, but that hillock on the Caernarvon road is at least eight miles distant. If we saw men on the move, we would have plenty of time to warn the Garddryn chaps.'

Stepping back to a boulder, Frank sat on it. 'As there's no one there, and that's eight miles away, I've got time to finish me bread and dripping.'

'Good idea, son.'

Perched on a low rock, legs outstretched, Joe drank the remainder of his tea.

Finishing the bread, Frank sat on the ground with his back to the boulder. He was asleep almost at once.

Solitarily, Joe watched the road from Caernarvon.

Occasionally he rose to check the Porthmadoc route. As there was no sign of activity, he went back to the low rock.

Glancing at Frank he marvelled at the lad's ability to sleep anywhere, a damp windswept mountainside as comfortable as his bed in Corn Cottage.

Taking his eyes from his son, he turned his head to the seabirds gliding effortlessly on the air currents, so graceful in their natural environment. When he could look up no longer, it was disorientating looking at the sky with clouds sweeping quickly across it, he watched the nearby sheep; several were gnawing their way through the sparse vegetation. Eventually, the woolly beasts turned, presenting dirty rumps. Joe redirected his gaze to the land.

The watery sun beamed through a rent in the low cloud. The wet air made the mountains in the distance seem incredibly close and clear. The lower slopes a patchwork of a thousand hues of green, dark as ink to lush spring green. Small stone buildings were distinct from the rock, carved of the same but separate, hard edged and brilliant. A cloud obscured the sun and the cottages vanished, camouflaged into the distant slopes. The emeralds faded, fusing into a darkened mass of mossy green.

The countryside of Wales never failed to astound him, and it was impossible to say which scene he preferred, the mists that cloaked the mountains and lay ethereal in the valley, or the winter sunrises with the mountains snow-peaked and bitten with frost. The mist gave mystery to the land, whilst winter dawn had a hard, brittle beauty. But it was hard to beat those long afternoons, when the air was still and bees laboured amongst the blooms. On such days there were sunsets that deserved nothing less that a fanfare of golden trumpets to herald the glorious red orb, sinking into the serene ocean. The beauty of the landscape had the power to awaken his soul and silence the inner devils reminding him of the hardships and bone-tiring work of wet drenching days which were best forgotten.

He wasn't sure if he had fallen into a doze for a time. Chilled, his back stiff from leaning up against the boulder, he sat for a long moment. Sighing, he rose slowly, ignoring the ominous creaking in the bones of his knees.

Looking down into the valley, he checked the roadway. There was no movement but he fixed his gaze on the dark ribbon running through the hedgerows, until his eyes began to play tricks.

Stooping, he touched Frank's shoulder.

Frank came awake slowly, rubbing his eyes. For a moment he was confused by the surroundings.

Joe clicked his tongue. 'I never knew anyone that could sleep like you, our Frank.' As he said this he had a pang of guilt. Hadn't he done the very same thing? Sleeping whilst on watch was a hanging offence for a chap serving in the army.

Yawning, his face pale from sleep, Frank stood. Chilled he stood hunched, looking down at the damp, green vale. 'So the Irish stayed away,' he said, yawning again.

Joe followed the boy's line of sight. 'Aye, for now, but let's not underestimate that brother of yours. Only the devil knows what's in that young bugger's mind.'

Frank gathered their few possessions together, shoving them into his canvas satchel. Slinging it over his shoulder, he was ready.

In the gathering darkness, they began the hard walk down.

Coming again to the Druids' standing stones, unearthly and eerie in the gloaming, they drew their eyes away from the giant megaliths.

Frank glanced at his father. 'Has anyone mentioned when the funerals will be?'

Joe's breath was husky from the effort of the downward walk. 'Day after tomorrow, I expect. The Coroner will have his say tomorrow. The families can go ahead with the burials after that. It's a terrible waste of life. To think that men go

to work every perishing day to work in dangerous conditions, especially at the Garddryn, then get crushed at the
very gates the poor buggers walked through six days a week
for years. It's not right. One day lad, the unions will put a
stop to all this injustice. Men will work in safety, and for a
fair bloody wage.'

Frank spoke quietly. 'It's a long time coming, Da.'

'Aye but it'll come, Frank. It'll come.'

They trekked on in silence.

Frank's thoughts were of the three men, their funerals
and the outcome of the coroner's verdict. He wondered if the
man was fair-minded and would place the blame where it
belonged, on the quarry management for keeping the gates
locked.

Joe was thinking ahead to Wednesday night, to the secret
meeting that would take place at Corn Cottage. Six men,
committed to bettering the lot of quarrymen, would come
together. Contemplating the formation of a society for
quarrymen, made his blood tingle. Trade unionism was
coming, and however hard the dictatorial quarry owners
might fight to stop it, they would ultimately lose the battle.
The strikes happening in England would be mirrored in the
Welsh mountains.

The following day, five minutes after the court convened,
the coroner delivered his verdict on the untimely death of
three Garddryn quarrymen. To a hushed assembly he stated
that it was his opinion that the men had lost their lives in
an unforeseeable, therefore unavoidable accident. Had the
men not been part of an unruly crowd of agitators, they
would be alive today. He gave permission for them to be
buried tomorrow.

In the near silent room, a woman began to weep quietly.

'Is that what you call justice?' a man bawled.

Rising, the coroner swept from the room.

Intent on keeping order, outnumbered by ten to one,

several constables moved aggressively towards the restive crowd.

'Justice! It's a joke!' the father of one of the fallen, cried out.

A constable bundled two men towards the door. 'Quiet now! Leave in an orderly fashion or face the consequences of gaol.'

'The court was in uproar, there was nearly a riot,' Joe said to Emily, when he reached home after the verdict had been announced to a shocked crowd.

'So the burials will go ahead tomorrow?' Emily placed a mug of tea in front of him.

'Aye, it's all arranged.'

Despondent, Emily slumped into a straight-backed chair at the table. 'I feel so sorry for the families. What the coroner said, wasn't right, Joe. It wasn't the quarrymen's fault that they were crushed. The gates shouldn't have been locked.'

Joe sighed. 'Aye, I know that, lass. And it all comes back to our Tommy. It was no one's fault but his. Yet again, he comes up smelling as sweet as ever.' He sighed again. 'So there's to be no blame attached to the bugger at all.'

Cupping her hands around a hot mug, Emily kept her eyes to the table top. 'If I'm honest, I have to say that I'm thankful for that. No one wants to see their son blamed for the death of three men. But it does seem shocking…'

Lines scored Joe's brow. 'Aye, it's shocking. What I wouldn't give to put the clock back to the day that the little sod stood before me, looking like butter wouldn't melt, and him saying he wanted to go to Plas Mawr for his lessons. Emily, if I had me time over again, I would slap him and send him upstairs with no supper, as punishment for bringing such a daft notion into the house.'

Lifting tearful eyes, she looked into his face. 'Joe, you were never a hard man like that; it wasn't in you to be anything but fair. You treated all our children with love and compassion.'

Standing, he reached for his pipe on the mantelpiece. 'And look where it's got me. I have a son living in grand style in a mansion, treating his workers like dog muck. Somehow, he manages to avoid the blame for the killing of three young men and orphaning children. And what about all the other poor buggers that have died, or been maimed at the Garddryn, during his bloody regime?'

Emily held her hand out to touch his arm. 'Joe, sweetheart. It's not your fault.'

He was near to tears. 'I fathered the bugger.'

Putting his unlit pipe in his pocket, he turned towards the door. 'I need a few ales to get the stink of my son from my nostrils.'

He went out quickly, without a backward glance.

Emily had not seen him in such a state since that terrible night, long ago, when he had revealed his true feelings about the loss of their beautiful daughter. His words spoken then still had the power to haunt her on dark sleepless nights.

Joe's grief following little Chloe's death had been a solitary agony; he had retreated to a dark place and she had been powerless to reach him. The raw emotions had been exposed when she told him they were to have another child.

Joe was devastated, saying that he couldn't risk losing another baby. She had tried to explain that Chloe had been a blessing from God.

In a voice she hardly recognised, he had cried out, 'If all this pain is a blessing from God, I would prefer that he turned his eyes from me and mine.'

Staggered, she had tried to reason with him, saying, that he didn't mean what he said.

'*Mean it!*' he'd replied. 'A day doesn't go by that I don't curse God.'

She had been fighting for her unformed child. Joe was lost in his grief for his little daughter. The memory of that night had the power to raise the fine hairs on her flesh and leave her anxious for Joe.

For several days and nights the men of the Garddryn guarded their territory. Tired and dispirited and no nearer to finding a solution to the lock-out, they were beginning to believe that the threat of the Irish had been nothing but a rumour put about by management.

Twelve miles away in Caernarvon, the Irish labourers were congregating. Forced into itinerancy during the last potato famine, they had arrived on the shores of Caernarvon seeking employment, a non-existent luxury across the breadth of Ireland. On the last ship load to dock, there were a hundred or more, desperate and near starved men, some travelling with their families. To camouflage their numbers, they divided into small groups and dissolved into the coastal community.

Shaun O'Leary, self-appointed leader, based himself at the Black Boy Inn within the town's walls, alert to local gossip. The news of the unrest at the Garddryn quarry reached him and he saw the chance of placing the migrants in blackleg jobs.

It was to the Black Boy Inn, that Mr Oakley travelled, to discuss strike-breaking at the Garddryn quarry.

On Saturday night the Half-Way filled with customers, spilling out onto the roadway. Although the inn keeper was pleased to see his trade return, the inn had been pitifully empty throughout the week, he could have held the takings in the palm of one hand. The men might be there, but they were not spending. Rationing was the norm and most didn't drink more than one glass of ale the entire evening. The reason they gathered was for news and comradeship.

Midnight saw the customers making for their homes. Most didn't believe that Irishmen would suspend their religious scruples and work on the Sabbath.

Throughout the evening, Joe had argued that the Irish were a desperate race. Famine had stalked the country for too many years for it to be otherwise. Given the chance, they would come in the early hours, and begin work at first light.

Many disagreed.

Eventually the inn was locked for the night and Joe, Frank, Tudor, Woody, Fergus Holmes and Tom Hughes remained at the closed door, watching the other customers saunter off to their homes. The last of the strollers disappeared at the bend of the road.

The lights in the inn were doused. The six men were plunged into blackness, as neither star nor moon glimmered through the heavy cloud.

The men were in a quandary; their number was too small to be of use if the Irish came in their droves, but to return home and ignore their misgiving, would be admitting defeat. It was as good as inviting the Irish to take over.

Woody broke the silence. 'So, what do we do now?'

Joe pulled his pipe out of his coat pocket. He knew that Frank's eyes were on him; the lad was expecting him to come up with an idea.

Stuffing a wad of tobacco into the bowl, Joe said calmly, 'We have two alternatives. We can go home and sleep safe in our beds, or we can walk to the track and do the best we can.'

No one answered and he went on, 'I don't expect the Irish will listen to reason if they do come. If we guard the Garddryn all night, we won't save our jobs. But we wouldn't have lain down and let it happen.'

Woody Pritchard grumbled, muttering 'We might break a few heads. Stop some of the bastards in their tracks.'

Joe smiled. 'There is that. But we would be woefully outnumbered.' He put the flame of a Lucifer to the tobacco.

Frank's eyes were on his father and the tiny flickering flame. 'I reckon we should stand our ground. We won't stop them, but they will see the faces of the men they are robbing.'

Woody was itching to get his knuckles bloodied. 'You're right, Frank.'

Fergus looked to Joe for confirmation. 'Is that what we should do, thrash the buggers?'

Rubbing his hands together, he grinned. 'Yeah, let's show the bastards our faces, and break a few beaks in the process.'

Tom said sensibly, 'Let's not get carried away, lads. There are six of us. If the Irish do come, there'll be a bloody sight more than six tramping down that road. I have kids to consider, plus me wife. I do not intend making a widow of her just to save face.'

Joe took his pipe from between his lips. 'He's right. Slow down chaps. Making kids orphans isn't what we are about. With the best will in the world, we can't change much. I suggest we get off home, and hope the buggers don't come tonight.'

Frank saw the sense in what he said. 'You're right, Da.' He smiled weakly. 'Mam would be furious if we got ourselves killed.'

Amused, Joe gave a half-smile. 'Aye, she would. I'd not be too happy about it either. Come on, lads, let's make tracks.'

Muttering, the men finally agreed, and a few moments later they separated making their way back to their homes.

It was almost one o'clock when Frank and Joe arrived back at Corn Cottage.

Coming into the living room, Joe kept his voice low so as not to disturb Emily. 'I'm off to me bed. I'm tuckered out.'

'Right, Da, see you in the morning.' Frank grinned. 'Sleep tight. Mind the bed bugs don't bite.'

Joe smiled. 'Aye, you an' all.'

Climbing in beside Emily, bringing the cold night air with him, afraid to snuggle up to her warmth for fear of disturbing her, he lay on his side of the bed thinking about the threat to the Garddryn jobs. Uneasy that the quarry had been left unguarded, he fell into a troubled sleep.

Before first light, he guessed that it was about four-thirty, he woke suddenly. Lying still, staring into the blackness, he listened for the sound that had woken him to be repeated. There it was, like the buzzing of summer insects. Alert now, he strained to identify it. Several moments passed before it came to him that it was voices, men's voices.

Fully awake, he slithered from beneath the blankets. Barefoot, he stood at the window. The night was pitch-black, windless. Carefully, the frame was tight, he eased the window open. On the still air, from far off, he heard voices, many of them.

Closing the window, the night was cold, he shivered in his nightshirt. Staring through the pane, he kept vigil. Weak moonlight illuminated the mountainside and he saw tiny figures climbing to the Garddryn boundary. Many more were crossing the fields, heading for the path that joined the quarry track. He could have wept. The last figure vanished into the blackness and there was silence, but for the drumming of blood in his ears. The quarrymen had lost.

He thought of waking Frank, but the lad would only want to go out and confront the interlopers; it would be safer if he knew nothing until full morning. His son's life was too precious to be wasted by the shameful actions of his elder brother.

There was no sleep left in him and he decided to sit with a brew and consider what was to be done next.

Scooping his clothes off the chair in the corner, he glanced back at the bed, wondering how long it might be before Emily slept so peacefully again. She would find it hard to live with her neighbours, with the shadow of her son's dishonour falling on Corn Cottage.

Dressed, he sat beside the emerging fire in the kitchen-cum-parlour waiting for the water in the kettle to boil. Going over the devastating turn of events, a fierce anger swept over him, a red rage directed at Tommy. It was a supreme act of will that kept him rooted in the cottage and not tearing through the lanes to Plas Mawr to haul the bastard from his clean comfortable bed.

Eventually, the kettle sang and he poured the boiling water into the pot and made the brew. Refilling the old kettle from the bucket in the scullery, he put it back on the flames.

Sitting again, sipping from a steaming mug, he went over every possible solution to the family's problem. Uprooting and going south to look for work, abandoning Corn Cottage and destroying Emily's dream of her own home, he couldn't countenance. Nor could he leave his darling child to her cold grave on the mountain. The idea of crossing to Anglesey and taking the punishing and dangerous labour offered in Parys copper workings occurred to him. He'd be home one day a week. It seemed a hard route to take. Short of murdering Tommy, there seemed no real solution at all.

The fire had been burning for more than two hours when Frank walked in from his bedroom and found his father sitting in the fireside chair looking into the hot coals.

'Is summat wrong, Da?'

Joe's soft words were a sigh, 'They came, lad. They came.'

Frank dropped onto a chair, the air knocked out of him. 'When?'

'At about four o'clock this morning.' Rising slowly, Joe lifted the kettle, pouring hot water on the stewed remains in the pot.

Frank's narrowed eyes were on him. 'Why didn't you wake me?'

The teapot lid clinked into place. 'What was the point? What could we do?'

Frank had no reply.

Taking another mug from the cupboard, Joe put it besides his used one. 'Short of going around the village and spreading the news, I'm at a loss to know what to do for the best.'

Reaching out, Frank took the full mug from Joe's hand.

'Well, that's what we'll do. The men have to be told what's going on.'

Joe gave a long sigh. 'There'll be ructions.'

'I'm up for a fight,' Frank said with determination.

Joe's eyes were on him. 'It's not like you to relish a scrap, lad.'

'This is different.'

'Aye, you can say that again.'

The red coal in the grate fell in on itself. Taking a large log from the hearth where it had been drying, Joe threw it onto the smouldering ash.

He glanced at Frank. 'Whilst you sort yourself out, I'll go round next door and have a word with Horas. He's worried sick over this business. This news won't make him feel any better either.'

'I'll just have a quick wash, then I'll be with you, Da.'

Joe shrugged into his old coat. 'I should be back in a few minutes.'

Opening the door on the cold morning, he looked skywards. The day was brightening, promising to be fine. Thankful for small mercies, he went down the narrow path to the wooden gate.

Bryn Tirion, the home of the Jones family, was less than a hundred yards from Corn Cottage. Joe found it odd walking up the short path and knocking on the front door of his old home.

Horas, with a child in his arms, opened the door at the first clatter of the wooden knocker. Only quarry business would have brought Joe Standish to his door, and fearing the worst, his face paled. 'Joe, what's up?'

Joe was reluctant to discuss the problem on the doorstep, but the noise from within the house was deafening with children shouting and crying; the racket kept him rooted to the spot. 'I'm afraid I have some disturbing news, Horas.'

Horas stood back from the threshold. 'Come in, man, come in.'

Joe got a glimpse of the room in chaos. 'No, it's all right. I can't stop. I just wanted to tell you that the Irish immigrants invaded the Garddryn this morning.'

Horas lowered the child to the ground. 'Mildred, go and find your mam.' He turned back to Joe. 'I thought that the place was being watched last night.'

Joe sighed. 'It was supposed to be, but several decided that the Irish wouldn't work on Sunday, so they went home to their beds. The quarry was left vulnerable and at about four o'clock this morning they raided.'

'Jesus, what'll happen now?' Horas said, bleakly.

Behind him, a child shrieked.

'For God's sake, be quiet,' Horas shouted. 'The next one that yells will feel the back of my hand, and then they'll have summat to yell about.' Instantly the room fell silent but for whispered words.

The flash of anger brought deeper lines to his face and Joe saw that Horas looked a great deal older than his thirty-five-years. The man had been thin for as long as he'd known him, but now he was rake thin. Joe guessed that he was going without food to give his share to the children. He was wondering what he and Emily might spare from their store cupboard, when Horas broke into his thoughts.

'How many came, do you know?'

His last hope of staying out of the workhouse was fading fast. On entering, he would be separated from his wife and children. He had no idea how they, or he, would survive the harsh regime. Their only hope of remaining in their home, was if the parish gave them a handout, but the custodians could refuse, as he wasn't a native of this parish. The stark reality was that the family were in dire straits and would need to apply for the workhouse or relief to survive. For more than a week his pride had been in his boots; the news, that the Irish had taken Garddryn jobs, buried it entirely.

Joe was recalling last night's scene, the men crossing the fields to the quarry boundaries, and his temper started to get the better of him. 'There were more than a hundred of the buggers,' he said angrily.

Horas's voice broke. 'With that number, it's hardly likely that we'll be able to throw them off, then.'

Although he was sympathetic, the man was in a terrible mess, Joe didn't think the defeatist attitude was going to help anyone and he answered somewhat more brusquely than he intended. 'Who knows, what we might manage, with a bit of organisation. If we band together, we have a better chance of succeeding.'

The breeze ruffled Joe's pepper-and-salt grey hair and he flattened it back down with his palm.

Moving off the doorstep, he said 'I'm going home to get our Frank. The pair of us will rouse as many quarrymen as we can. When we've got a decent crowd together, we'll meet on the common in an hour. Jointly, perhaps we can sort summat out.'

'I'll be there, Joe. But I don't hold out much hope.'

Joe hid a sigh. Who knew how he might react if he were in Horas's predicament?

He tried to encourage the man. 'We have to hang onto hope, Horas. If we quarriers stick together, there's a chance we could beat this and get back to work.'

'Aye, happen.' Horas said, despondently. His sallow face creased with worry, he turned to go into the house.

Going down the path to the rickety gate, Joe tried to throw off the melancholy that had rubbed off on him. He couldn't afford to be dragged down by Horas's despondency. His optimism was too fragile, born of little more than a refusal to accept defeat.

Turning into his own gateway, he went into Corn Cottage.

Frank was ready to leave, his coat lying across the back of a chair. Emily came in from the scullery in time to see them both off. Over a mug of tea, Frank had told her of the arrival of the Irish tinkers. Her face was anxious, as she kissed them both goodbye.

Frank, his hands shoved into his coat pockets, kept pace with Joe as they walked through the village. There were several homes to visit; at each one, Joe sent the men to notify others that they were needed at the common. In this way, all the houses in the village were informed of the meeting. Men poured out of the cottages to spread the word.

As quarriers drew near to the common, the sheep and roaming goats ambled across the greensward to the far hedge. The few cattle stampeding to the furthest trees, looking on the milling throng with calm bovine interest.

Considering it was early Sunday morning, there was hardly a hangover between the men. Dishevelled, they looked as though they had left home in a hurry with only time to spare for a quick trip to the privy. They stood in groups discussing and cursing the Irish. Some of the quarry boys were young enough to start antics, and were acting the fool on the fringes of the crowd.

When Joe and Frank approached the common, there were more than two hundred there. Others, those from the outlying houses, were walking down the roadway. Glancing to the fields, Joe saw dozens advancing. Although they would have a good number, it was obvious that it would be far from the entire workforce. Quarrymen living on Anglesey were with their families and not expected to return until the following day. Many homes were scattered across the mountainous area, which made it impossible to alert the quarrymen in time.

They waited for the last stragglers before the meeting started. It was Twm Tomos, caban eisteddfod president, who stood before the now hushed crowd. Everyone was familiar with Twm's moderate and lyrical voice and were surprised when he addressed them loudly and with such force.

Impassioned, he yelled 'The Irish have invaded the Garddryn and taken our jobs. They have stolen the bread from our hungry children's mouths.'

The men roared angrily.

With his arms held high, he shouted over the noise, 'As God is our judge, these usurpers will not remain in our quarry, or our village.'

A loud collective cheer rose on the air.

When he could speak over the clamour, he yelled 'We are going to take back our jobs. Together, we will end this infamous lock-out.'

'Let's break their scurvy heads,' someone shouted venomously from the centre of the crowd.

'Violence will get us nowhere.' Twm roared. 'Three have died already. We do not need to add more to this tragedy. Today we will descend on the Garddryn track and as the usurpers come from work we will show the bastards the faces of the men they have thieved from. Tomorrow, I will go back to the management and seek a solution to this problem.'

A voice hollered, 'Oakley and Roberts have not listened to us so far. What makes you think they'll take notice tomorrow?'

A strong voice yelled, 'What makes you think Tommy Standish will let us back in?'

'The bastard will watch us starve first.'

Using his bulk, Ian Griffith, a rubbler, elbowed his way to the front. 'Why should we lie down and let the bloody Irish steal our livelihood? Let's go up the track and beat the tinkers to a pulp. We don't want to just show them our faces, we want to show the buggers our fists.'

The men yelled in agreement.

A loud voice bawled from the rear of the crowd, 'If we don't get back soon, me family will be for Merthyr or Dowlais. We can't stay here and starve to death.'

Twm Tomos raised his arms, calling for quiet.

Joe was fearful that a bloody battle was about to erupt. Twm had raised the men's hopes, promising that they would go down the track to confront the Irish. Then dashed them with the promise of a meeting with the management. It was a surprising about-turn for a man normally so judicious. He had fired their anger, heaped smouldering coals on dry tinder, then promptly doused it with cold water.

'What's the man thinking of?' Joe was unaware that he had spoken aloud.

Frank had to shout to answer. 'I reckon he's just as worried as everyone else. He's afraid for his job, Da.'

Joe recalled that the man did have a large brood of children, most still at home. The thought tempered his criticism. Just because the man was educated, didn't mean that he wasn't poor.

A bullnecked man raised his fist. 'Break their bloody legs. The bastards can't work with smashed bones.'

Joe's temper flared and he roared, 'What? And have the military or the constables down on us like a ton of bricks? Think man, for God sake.'

'What would you suggest, Mr bloody Standish? A trot to the bloody mansion, followed by a civilised chat with your son?'

Joe was curt, 'It's a union we need, not a blood bath.'

Twm Tomos intervened, 'Joe's right, we do need a union, but the lack of one can't be solved in a day.' He was earnest, shouting, 'Let me talk to the management tomorrow; there's no point going off half-cocked.'

Ignoring him, twenty men, mainly those on the quarry blacklist, broke away from the crowd and ran towards the fields that led to the quarry boundaries, eager to fight it out with the Irish and management on Garddryn land.

There wasn't a man there that didn't sympathise with the men on the infamous blacklist; its malevolent tentacles stretched into Penrhyn, Dinorwic, Blaenau, Llechwedd and beyond. There was no hope of them finding work. If they survived today's skirmish with the Irish, it was Dowlais or Merthyr they would head for, where their misdemeanours such as talking out of turn, complaining to management, standing up for a comrade, or speaking out at an inquest, would be unknown.

The crowd watched them go, the younger element and the hotheads cheering them on. When they were no longer in sight, the other men drifted away.

Twm Tomos called to the remaining men to stay within the law, not to stir up a rebellion that would cost them all dear. Promising again to meet with management at the first opportunity ...

Although his words were lost on a babble of protest, Twm kept up his opposition to violence but the men made arrangements to meet at the quarry track at the end of the working day.

Quiet, deep in thought, Joe and Frank ambled home to spend the day tending the vegetable patch at Corn Cottage. There was nothing to be achieved at the quarry until Twm Tomos had spoken again with management. By late afternoon, Joe had dug the potato patch thoroughly and viciously. It was decided that he and Frank would go to the track, to lend their support to their comrades determined to confront the Irish blacklegs.

As dusk fell and the time for shift's-end drew close, the men fell silent. The tension was tangible, a physical force. Bloodshed was imminent and inevitable. Furtive glances passed between mates. Several clinked coins in their pockets and the restive moved their feet as though itching to get things started.

From far off a siren blared, the strident sound swept over the mountain and down the valleys. Holding their collective breath, they waited for the jangle of men on the move, the tramp of boots, the low hum of voices as the itinerants moved towards them.

Quarriers flashed sly smiles to their comrades, clutching weapons concealed in their work-coat pockets.

More than a hundred Irish flooded through the quarry gates. Shoulder to shoulder, they advanced on the curve in the track, oblivious of the reception party waiting beyond the quarry waste dumps.

Coming around the man-made slate mountains, the Irish came face to face with Garddryn men and they came to a sharp halt. Darting eyes roved over the men and seeing they outnumbered the quarriers, they ran towards them, spoiling for the fight.

Their leader, O'Leary, smiled grotesquely. Thrusting out his neck, using his leonine head as a weapon, the mop of unruly red hair a flying pennant, he charged, bellowing.

Paul Jones, a smithy, took the full force of the strike in his midriff. The fierce blow threw him back several yards; landing, he lay in the muck.

Using a similar tactic, O'Leary charged Henry Williams, a rubbler, sending the man flying onto the high grass verge.

Arfon Craven, standing nearby, pulled a homemade cudgel out of the inside pocket of his coat and whacked O'Leary across the back of his head.

Momentarily dazed, O'Leary stopped in his tracks. Touching the wound, bringing away a smear of blood, he roared angrily. His ham-fist snaked out, grabbing Arfon around the neck, he tried to throttle the tubby young man.

Frank grappled at O'Leary's coat, trying unsuccessfully to pull the Irishman off Arfon.

Joe, seeing his son struggling with the giant, clouted O'Leary viciously on the side of his head and the Irishman crumbled to the ground.

Arfon was floundering in the muck, gasping for air, his face ruby red. Afraid that the lad would be trampled, Joe hauled him to his feet. He swayed for a moment before casting in the muck for the cudgel. Re-armed, he set about the shabby Irishmen.

A gunshot blasted.

The fighting stopped and many winded and breathless men, supported by their adversaries, looked around in shock.

Those that could, scattered across the deep verge and scrambled over the hedgerows that had been downed the previous week in the catastrophe.

Twelve hired henchmen stood with Oakley. It was Oakley who had fired the weapon. With the muzzle directed at a group of quarrymen, Oakley bawled, 'Get off this property, you are trespassing. If you do not move immediately, you'll be arrested!'

In shock and confusion the men looked from one to another.

Walking out of the crowd, Joe faced Oakley. 'Is that son of mine so much of a coward that he has to send his manager to do his dirty work?'

Affronted by the outrageous act, Joe snarled, 'Oakley, you'll find that firing on unarmed workers is frowned upon by the specials. And I propose to see that they hear about this.'

Oakley sneered. 'You are on private property, get off and take the rabble with you.'

Woody Pritchard couldn't resist bawling, 'We know our rights and we will use them.'

Oakley laughed. 'Rights? Workers and rabble rousers don't have rights.' He laughed again. 'You don't even have a vote.'

Joe's words were almost obliterated by angry voices and he needed to holler to be heard. 'You're wrong there, Oakley. As a ten-pound householder, I do have a vote, and I'll use it, so that one day, men of your ilk are torn from our society.'

The Garddryn men gave Joe a resounding cheer.

With as much dignity as they could muster, the quarrymen strode away with Joe leading, stoically ignoring the jeers and jibes of the Irishmen.

As Oakley had the weapon trained on them it was prudent to leave; an accident could so easily happen and Oakley would have the upper hand when it came to an explanation. The dozen henchmen would be bribed to give a good account and inevitably it would be the quarrymen that endured the brunt of the blame.

Disregarding their cuts and bruises, they walked as a pack towards the Half-Way inn, their fine Welsh voices singing in praise of God, resonating over the mountainside.

A week passed with little change except the circumstances within the family homes. The Jones family in Bryn Tirion were trying to eke out the pitiful remains of the store cupboard, living on what Joe and Emily could contribute above their own needs. A pair of pigeons, half a hare and a scrawny rabbit had been delivered by Frank, the sum token of many hours of hunting.

CHAPTER EIGHT

Tommy was sitting alone at the breakfast table. Whilst eating he would occasionally glance through the long arched window to the flagged terrace and the manicured lawn beyond. The early roses were beginning to bloom, magenta red against the fresh spring green of the grass. The view was perfect but for an under-gardener stooping to pick stray petals and leaves off the immaculate lawn, carefully placing each find in a small sack he carried. The morning was windless, sparkling, pale golden sunlight shimmering through the leaves of the tall elms. The sapphire sky held the promise of the first decent day for months.

Finishing the meal of lamb cutlet, kidneys, roast ham, eggs and fried potato, he relaxed back in the upholstered chair, with a sigh of contentment.

On soft soled shoes, a footman crossed silently to the table, removing the plate and cutlery without intruding on his master's privacy. With a small bend in his back, the servant took three backward strides and then returned to the carved sideboard.

Instantly and just as unobtrusively, holding a steaming silver teapot in his white gloved hand, the second footman appeared at Tommy's side. Afraid to make the slightest splash on the crisp white tablecloth, the servant poured tea into a bone china cup. With neither word nor sound, the first footman replaced a full toast rack with another holding hot toast.

Shoulder to shoulder, bending subserviently from the

waist, the two men backed away from the table, returning to the sideboard, ready to obey the master's orders on the instant.

Tommy's eyes alighted on the dish of peach preserve. Although he had eaten more than his fill, he took a slice of hot toast and buttered it thickly, topping it with a generous amount of his favourite fruit jam.

It was at his instigation that peaches were cultivated in the orangery. The position of the hothouse was perfect; south facing it virtually guaranteed a plentiful yearly crop.

Sipping tea, his thoughts went to the morning ahead; he was expected at the Garddryn Quarry office. Oakley, the manager, had called a meeting to discuss the closure of the dressing sheds. Although the Irish itinerants had taken over the rough work at the quarry, there wasn't a man amongst the tinkers that possessed the skill to split slate accurately. Several had made attempts at it, but the finished products were useless, only good for throwing into the wagons heading for the waste dumps.

Oakley was positively shackled to the idea of getting the Garddryn men back as quickly as possible and the quarry routine established. But it was up to him, as master, to decide when, and if the buggers went back, and he did not intend to reopen the quarry until the men had learned their lesson. The sods would work all day Saturday, or they wouldn't work at all. The quarrymen had been locked-out for two weeks and they'd stay out until he said differently. It was his prerogative to exercise his authority and by God, he would do just that. It would be at his whim, not theirs, that would see them back in work and even then, not all would be reinstated. He'd make it his business to segregate the trouble makers from his work force. Once their names were added to the blacklist, there wasn't a quarry in the district that would take the rabble rousers on.

Replacing the almost empty cup on the saucer, Tommy

flicked his eyes to the footman, who moved quickly to refill it.

Watching the hot liquid being poured, Tommy enjoyed a self-congratulatory moment. How fortunate it was that he had the good sense to pay a quarryman to bring him word about the goings on in the village, who visited who, which men had found employment elsewhere, what families had left the district to seek work. The majority had remained and he wondered how those men and their families fared. The less provident amongst them would be hungry by now.

Tommy waved the servant away. Spreading butter and peach preserve on toast, he licked a smear of delicious jelly off his finger. The flavour was so superior to the jams his mother concocted; blackberry, crab apple and sometimes quince were the usual choice and even then, the inferior jelly was rationed.

Thinking of his father, Tommy wondered if tightening his belt had loosened his resolve. The men's *rights* were probably less important now, than they had been when all this nonsense began. What was going on in the kitchen at Corn Cottage? No doubt conversation was limited to the lock-out, the old man spouting on about a *union* to the detriment of all other topics. All manner of suspect ingredients simmering in his mother's cooking pot.

Turning his thoughts away from his mother's kitchen, Tommy wiped his fingers on the white napkin draped across his lap.

A silver tray with a small pile of unopened letters was beside his plate. The uppermost envelope was pale cream, the elaborate script written in green ink, the flourishes decidedly feminine. Although the stamp was an ordinary penny-red-plate, Tommy's interest was pricked.

A footman, hurrying from his station, handed him a gilt letter-opener. Without lifting his eyes to the man, Tommy inserted the tip of the blade and slit open the envelope and withdrew a single sheet of expensive paper.

The first line amused him. Under his breath, he said 'So, Lady Isabelle is back in London.'

Reading on, discovering that his presence would be welcome if he should happen to be in town in the near future. Her husband was in Germany, hunting wild boar, so she would be so lonely. A little *diversion* would be most welcome. Picturing exactly what manner of diversion Lady Isabelle had in mind, Tommy was instantly sexually aroused. The lady certainly liked rough handling, too rough sometimes. It was a wonder that she wasn't permanently marked during her forays into the darker side of sado-masochism. Whatever the lady's penchant, the invitation couldn't have come at a better time. A few days in London would take his mind off the troubles at the Garddryn.

Folding the letter, he slipped it back into the envelope and put it into the breast pocket of his coat.

Rising from the table, ignoring the two footmen bowing subserviently, he made for the door. One of the footmen hurried to open it. Tommy was completely oblivious to the man. His thoughts were with Lady Isabelle; he was picturing her lying naked, face down, her perfect and un-blemished buttocks inviting the sting of a riding crop.

There was a ghost of a smile on his face and he mur-mured beneath his breath, 'Lady Issy could get a great deal more than she expected on this occasion.'

Hurrying, trailing his employer, the first footman carried the tray with the unopened letters. His object was to reach the library door before the master. On this occasion the footman failed and he entered the room as Tommy dropped down into the comfortable hide chair behind his desk. The servant felt the master's steely glance fall upon him as he placed the tray on the corner of the desk.

Tommy was brusque. 'Roberts, I want the best carriage brought to the main door.'

Roberts stepped away from the desk. 'I'll arrange it immediately, master.'

'And send Wright to me.'

The footman dipped his head. 'Yes, sir.'

As the door clicked closed behind the servant, Tommy took up another envelope and slit it open. Finding a statement from his tailor, the bill for the new coat ruined in the debacle with his father, he put it aside.

John Wright, the valet, knocked before entering the library.

Tommy looked up. 'Ah, Wright, I'm catching the afternoon train to London. I will be staying at Claridge's Hotel for a few days but dining at the Reform. Arrange that town clothes and accessories are packed in a portmanteau.'

Wright, a servant of long standing, managed subservience with dignity, never compromising his self-esteem. Giving an almost imperceptible bow, he said 'Is there anything particular that should be enclosed, sir?'

'No. The usual will do.' Then as an afterthought, Tommy added, 'I'd like the lapis lazuli cuff buttons and the emerald pair.'

With a slight nod, Wright turned to leave the room.

'I will need your services whilst I'm away, so pack a bag for yourself, Wright.'

Wright's expression didn't alter. Bobbing slightly, he left the library making his way upstairs.

Minutes later a large portmanteau lay open on the chaise-longue in Tommy's dressing room. The maids were gathering the master's toiletries, shoes, gloves, shirts and under garments together. Wright was placing everything carefully into the large hide-bag. The articles were stowed in record time. The maids, hot and flushed from the hurried activity, were sent to the kitchen for a cup of tea. Wright packed a few essentials for himself into a small valise. After dispatching a boy to the stables to order the everyday trap, Wright took a moment to check that nothing had been forgotten.

The trap, drawn by a dapple-grey mare, pulled up at the

tradesman's entrance. The portmanteau and valise were put aboard. With a stable hand driving, Wright left for the railway station to catch the early London train. When Tommy arrived at Claridges, the valet would be installed and the master's personal belongings arranged to his liking.

Yanking the bell-pull beside the chimney-piece, Tommy summoned the butler. When Miles appeared, Tommy was hunting in the desk drawer for a particular pen.

Looking up, he said, 'I will be leaving for the quarry office in a few moments. My plans are to travel to London on the afternoon train. After my departure from the house, inform your mistress that I will be away for several days.'

Finding the gold and mother-of-pearl pen, he slipped it into the inner breast pocket of his coat. Closing the drawer, he stood. 'Should an emergency occur, you will find me at the Reform or Claridge's Hotel.'

The butler's face remained impassive. 'I will see that madam learns of your arrangements at the appropriate time, sir.'

'Good.' Tommy gave a self-conscious smile, slightly embarrassed that the butler was now aware that he was avoiding Henrietta.

'Is there anything else that I could do for you, sir?'

Tommy answered snappily, 'No. There's nothing at the moment.'

A swish of petticoats and taffeta came to them through the barely open door. Expecting Henrietta to appear at any moment, Tommy cursed that he hadn't hurried his departure.

Opening the door a little more, Miles looked out. An upstairs maid was passing, wearing a cast-off dress donated by the mistress from the wardrobe of the late Louise Bellamy.

Miles nose twitched, detecting a hint of perfume. 'It's Becket on her way to the kitchen, sir.'

'When did Becket begin to wear silk and trounces?' Tommy frowned.

'I'm afraid that the mistress gave her a gown or two from the late Mrs Bellamy's wardrobe. As today is Becket's day off, no doubt she thought it an opportunity to wear one of the articles.'

Flabbergasted at the cheek of the maid, and the stupidity of Henrietta, Tommy's face flushed with anger. 'You can tell Becket that whilst she serves under this roof, she'll dress accordingly. I will not have the servants getting above themselves. I expect you to deal with this ludicrous situation during my absence. If the servants wear furbelows and fancy fandangles they can expect to be dismissed immediately and without a reference.'

Miles gave a small bow. 'I will deal with the matter immediately upon your departure, sir.'

'Do!' Tommy answered sharply. 'Miles, if you no longer have authority over the servants, perhaps it's time you moved on.'

This was the first time in all his years of service that a master had spoken to him in a derogatory or threatening way. Furious with the maid that had brought this humiliation upon him, Miles made a low bow.

'I apologise for my dereliction of duty, sir. The matter will be put right immediately.'

Tommy's mumbled answer was hardly coherent, as he gathered documents together to put into the safe.

Backing out of the door, the butler made his way quickly to the kitchen. With every stride he felt the hard tiles through the swan-skin soles of his shoes and as there was a small hard growth beneath his right heel, it didn't improve his temper.

If Becket, he thought irately, made one complaint, he would dismiss her immediately. And he'd warn the other staff that he would not allow anyone to accept gifts from the mistress. Those already accepted were to be handed back immediately. If this wasn't possible because the articles were no longer in pristine condition, then they would be confiscated immediately.

Reaching the closed kitchen door, hearing the laughter coming from within and imagining Becket showing off her *fandangles* as the master had put it, he all but charged through the door, rattling it on its ancient hinges. His sudden presence silenced the servants gathered in the large room.

Tommy was glad to see the back of the butler as at any moment he was likely to lose his temper entirely and reveal what he really thought of the servants and more importantly, Henrietta. His blasted wife was an imbecile, becoming more stupid by the day.

Becket was equally stupid for accepting the expensive clothes. That a servant should ape her betters was an outrage. If he ran across her before his departure, he would dismiss the wench immediately.

Grim faced and his jaw tight with exasperation, he knelt to open the heavy safe. Sitting on his heels, he reached into the interior and from behind a stack of paper and legal documents he took a slim black box. Opening it, his eyes fell on the exquisite string of pearls lying on the black satin. Admiring the fine lustre of the perfectly matched pearls, his angst evaporated. The gems were doubly valuable to him as he had taken them from Louise Bellamy's silver jewel case on the day that George Bellamy was interned in Denbigh Asylum. He ran the tip of his finger over the creamy surface; the pearls would still retain traces from Louise Bellamy's skin.

He gave a small mirthless laugh. How fitting that Louise's treasured possession should go to his mistress. It was a pity that the straight laced old biddy wouldn't see him threading the lustrous gems through Isabelle's dark secret hair of her womanhood.

Closing the box, he slipped it carefully into the inside

breast pocket of his coat. His thoughts turned to the other jewellery he had taken that day, the diamond brooch and precious sapphire necklace that mysteriously went missing between the time he put them in the library in Louise's Chester house to when he arrived back at Plas Mawr.

He half suspected Dr Rogers of the theft but he was too much in the man's pocket to risk accusing him.

There was the sound of horses' hoofs on the gravel and the slow turn of wheels as the carriage pulled up at the front steps.

Finishing quickly in the library, the last thing he wanted was to alert Henrietta of his imminent departure, Tommy crossed the wide hall, his shoes clicking on the polished mosaic floor.

Miles was waiting at the open front door; in a last minute exchange the butler informed Tommy that the servants were warned and Becket had relinquished the elaborate dress. Miles didn't mention the tantrum or the tears but assured his master that all was well and everything would run smoothly during his absence.

Climbing aboard, the horses shifted in the shafts at the redistribution of weight.

As the carriage moved forward, Tommy leaned back on the leather upholstery and gave a long sigh. It was good to get away from the constant intrusion of servants and the niggling feeling that Henrietta was *up to something*.

For weeks now, since her late mother's house had been sold, it had been as though she held a secret. It was so typical of his wife to add to his worries, as though he didn't have enough on his plate with the situation at the quarry.

The new heroin cure that had been recommended for her alcohol and opium addiction could have brought about the change but he doubted it. The woman was planning something and it could only be to his detriment. For the moment he wasn't going to worry about it. The trip to

London wasn't going to be ruined by thoughts of the Garddryn or his wife.

The weather remained perfect throughout the ride. The carriage wheels and the clatter of the horses' tread were the only sound filtering into the enclosed privacy. It should have been idyllic, the warm sun filtering through the open window, the fragrance of wild plants on the clean air but he was too impatient to see the dusty streets of London, the pavements thronging with pedestrians and the thoroughfares flowing with carriages, to be content with the rural setting.

A group of men were on the road and it took them a moment to move out of the path of the horses. Tommy didn't recognise them as quarrymen but he supposed that they were; to a man they were dressed in quarrymen's fustian. Down at heel, unhealthy looking, walking, it seemed, to nowhere. For there was no work for them at the Garddryn and the quarry was the only employer in the district. Tommy didn't speculate as to the men's thoughts on seeing him pass in style on his way to the Garddryn. Quarrymen were two-a-penny, easily replaced, so therefore unimportant. A picture of the empty dressing sheds came to his mind, unsettling him for the remainder of the ride.

The carriage pulled up at the office building and alighting Tommy glanced up at the driver. 'Park up and wait.'

The man doffed his cockaded hat and climbed down, wheezing with the effort. Glancing after the master, he wondered for how long he and the two horses might be kept waiting.

Hearing Tommy's voice in the outer office, Oakley sighed. For a moment he considered rising to meet Mr Standish but feeling extremely unwell he remained in his chair. Oakley was convinced that it was the uncertainty of the lock-out that was taking a toll on his health, that and the problems he had with his young son, Sam. The boy was in charge of progress at Ruby Quarry and he was making demands, insisting that a hundred or so men were sent to dig off the top layer of rubbish to get to the good slate.

His plea had become an incessant litany. Months ago, Sam's head had been turned by the men at the Half-Way spouting ideas of a union. As his father, Oakley prayed that this madness had come to an end because, if it hadn't, they could both be looking for other employment. The boy was still of an age when he might be successful but as for himself, professionally he could quite easily be on the ropes.

Tommy shoved his head around Oakley's office door.

Oakley rose to his feet. 'Good morning, Mr Standish.'

'Good morning, Oakley. Come into my office in five minutes.' Without waiting for a reply, Tommy disappeared.

Feeling many years older than his true age, Oakley eased back into his chair and listened to Tommy's voice, muted by the closed door, giving orders to Elias Hubbard, the office underling. When Tommy proceeded to his own office, Oakley didn't resume work but sat with his elbows on the desktop, head in his hands, staring at the orders for slate tiles from the American agent. When he judged that five minutes had elapsed he rose slowly, inched around the desk, then blowing his nose on a used handkerchief he slipped the square of linen back into his pocket and made for the door.

Entering Tommy's office, Oakley saw that Tommy was cheerful, more positive than he had seen him for a while.

Tommy gave a token smile. 'Take a seat, Oakley.'

A sigh sloughed from the older man as he slipped down slowly into the brown hide chair, the leather creaking with his weight. He waited for a brief moment for Tommy to begin the conversation but Tommy wasn't forthcoming.

Oakley gave a light cough. His serious eyes met Tommy's. 'We really must address the problem of the closed dressing sheds. We need to start splitting slate if we are to fulfil the orders from America.'

Tommy was close to losing his temper. Oakley was

202

harping back to a question that was already dealt with. Reminding him of the fact, Tommy, reiterated sharply, 'Another week will make all the difference to the attitude of the men. They must be feeling the pinch by now. Very soon they'll come back grovelling, thinking how lucky they are to be working all day Saturday. We have to wait, hold our nerve. Stop fretting, Oakley. I'll be proved right. Just you wait and see.'

He leaned back in the chair, a smug smile on his mouth. 'A fortnight at the most, that's all.'

Oakley's exasperation was plain. 'Surely we can't wait that long. We'll never make the shipment if ...'

Tommy's smugness evaporated and he answered with familiar arrogance, 'It's the way *I* want it done.'

With the palms of his hands on the arms of the chair, Oakley pushed himself up. He gave a short sigh as he got clumsily to his feet. 'If that's what you want. I'll see that it's done.'

'Good.'

It was against his better judgement but Oakley felt duty bound to raise a question on his son's behalf. 'Sam is getting on well at Ruby but he wants men to dig the rubbish off the slate. Men placed at ...'

Seeing a ploy where there was none, Tommy's eyes narrowed; interrupting he was brusque, 'How many men did he say he needed?'

'A hundred or so should do it.'

This number confirmed Tommy's suspicions. This was Oakley's way of getting the Garddryn men back in a hurry. 'That's a hell of a lot. We haven't any men to spare.'

With difficulty, Oakley contained his irritation. 'If we send a hundred Irish to Ruby, we could reinstate a hundred Garddryn men to take their place here.'

Tommy spoke sharply, 'No! I'll not have it. Sam will just have to wait until things are resolved. And that will not happen until I return from London.'

Surprised, Oakley's voice flew up on the final word. 'London? Are you going soon?'

Gathering papers together, Tommy said briskly, 'Today, as soon as I've finished here.'

Oakley's jaw dropped. 'But what about ...?'

Exasperated with his manager, Tommy rudely interrupted him, 'I can't sort it out today. I have a train to catch.'

Rising out of the chair, Tommy came around the desk. Oakley had no alternative but to follow the master out of the office.

Disheartened, Oakley went back to his office. Slumping in the chair, elbows on the desk top, he held his head in his hands. The short meeting had been a complete waste of time; nothing had been resolved and the list of problems had not diminished one iota. The quarrymen were demanding to be given their jobs back. Families were near to starvation. Ruby Quarry wouldn't get the labour needed to push the project forward. The Irish tinkers were difficult and sometimes positively dangerous with their fighting and drunkenness. The dressing sheds were closed and likely to remain so. To top it all, the deposed quarrymen had organised the chapels in the vicinity to send the brass bands to travel the country and they were now giving concerts to raise money for the hungry families. It was quite possible that Tommy Standish would see his own men giving a musical performance in Hyde Park or the Haymarket Theatre. The outcome of which didn't bear thinking about. If the lock-out became common knowledge in the city, it would ruin confidence. Tommy Standish, normally a very good business man, had dug his heels in and refused to listen to reason.

Oakley murmured aloud, 'What more could possibly go wrong?'

Tommy arrived at Claridges in the late afternoon. Since the Empress Eugenie had made the hotel her winter quarters and the Queen and Prince Albert had visited her, giving the hotel their approval, Tommy made a point of staying only at Claridges when in London. Henrietta had never accompanied him.

After a change of clothes, the locomotive's windows had been open and sooty particles had blown in spoiling his shirt front and necktie, he left his valet to the debris of his toilette.

Coming down the green carpeted stairs to the ground floor, he was in two minds whether to take tea here or at the Reform. But as a party of people came into the entrance hall from the street, at least three were titled aristocrats, he decided to remain. There was always a chance, now the hotel had a reputation for being *an extension to Buckingham Palace,* of meeting royalty.

His afternoon tea was solitary, served to him in delicate porcelain. As he finished the last dregs in his cup, Sir George Allen, an octogenarian with an immensely long grey beard, approached the table. For the next few moments, Tommy and Sir George discussed the Companies Act before the old gentleman went to join his newly arrived granddaughter.

With teatime virtually over, the room began to clear and Tommy prepared to depart. With a last check to make sure the box with the pearls was still safe in his breast pocket, he rose. Taking his hat and cane from the adjacent chair, he went out to the entrance hall.

A uniformed doorman, an elderly man with the bearing of a grenadier on parade, appeared from the cloaks room; advancing, he bowed. 'Do you require a hansom, sir?' he asked confidently.

'Yes,' Tommy replied briskly, unused to being addressed so heartily by a servant. 'To the Reform Club.'

Trotting quickly down the front steps to the pavement, sprightly for his age, the servant lifted his hand, beckoning to a hansom cab waiting on the opposite side of the road.

Climbing in to the chestnut brown cab, Tommy settled into the cracked leather of the corner seat.

Pulling away from the kerbstone, the cab joined the other vehicles travelling on Brook Street. Tommy took little notice of the journey; his thoughts were centred on the visit he would pay later to Lady Isabelle at her residence and what he expected to take place there.

The hansom was turning into Pall Mall, the imposing edifice of the Reform Club in view before Tommy paid attention to his whereabouts and put his face to the open window.

Several gentlemen were climbing the steep steps to the front door as the cab driver pulled up at the Club. Paying the driver, he crossed the pavement following the men's path.

Walking towards the Club gave him a sense of satisfaction, a man had to be successful to be a member. The dues alone were proof of that, the selection committee also demanded rank.

The building, designed by architect Charles Barry, resembled Michelangelo's Palazzo Farnese. Tommy had learned this information recently which had further impressed him. Built of Portland stone, it was not dissimilar to the stonework of Plas Mawr. Perhaps that was one of the reasons he was drawn to the fine architecture.

The original cost, said to be astronomical, was his thought as he trotted up the steps to the open door. Through the doorway there was a second set of steps, taking these easily, he came into the large square atrium which rose impressively to the full height of the building. The whole, covered by an immense dome constructed from a thousand lead crystal lozenges. The atrium was said to be like an Italian courtyard but he had to take his informant's word for that, as he hadn't personally journeyed to the Mediterranean.

Approaching the library he heard the strident voice of

Philip Hardy and having no wish to get into a debate with the man, Tommy beat a hasty retreat to the smoking room. Sitting on a plush leather chair, he ordered a malt whisky from a servant.

Whilst he waited, Tommy got into conversation with a Lord Ash. They had met some time ago at the House, Tommy had been there as a guest of Edward Pennant, of Penrhyn Castle.

Dining alone on sea bream, mutton cutlets and red-currant sauce, apple cheesecake, and a wedge of Cheshire cheese, with a glass or two of claret and a good port imported by the Reform, Tommy was replete.

As the night promised to be *energetic* and he would need stamina to satisfy her ladyship, he decided to walk towards Park Lane to Lady Isabelle's mansion before getting a cab to complete his journey. Checking once more that the jewellery box was safe in his pocket, he left the table.

In the entrance hall his coat, hat and cane were brought to him by a footman. Donning his lightweight coat, held by the footman who also applied a hog bristle brush to the shoulders, Tommy slipped his hands into calf, lavender gloves and fastened the tiny buttons at the cuffs.

With barely a glance at the servant, he crossed the mosaic floor to the entrance.

Watching his approach, his face wreathed in folds, the middle-aged doorman bowed as he pulled open the heavy door.

The staleness of the city air was immediately noticeable to him. The street was dusty; the pavements, buildings and roadway had soaked in the heat of the day and now leached it into the smoky blue mist of the evening.

Trotting down the steps to the pavement, he glanced up to the orange and cobalt sky where a blood red scimitar arced across the heavens. Nightfall, he thought, with a secret smile.

A club manservant stood on the pavement. Reading

Tommy's face he could be forgiven for believing that something had amused the young handsome man, that his smile was of humour, and not the dark thoughts of sadism.

Doffing his hat to Tommy, the servant said, 'Cab, sir?'

'No,' Tommy said, the ghost of the smile on his lips. 'I think that I will walk a little of the way.'

Minutes later, on seeing an idle hansom, he beckoned to it.

Climbing aboard, he snapped sharply 'Hollybeck House, Park Lane.'

The driver touched his hat with the whip.

Settling into the seat, Tommy dipped his head to look through the small window. The cab was passing the offices of his business agent, inherited from the late Bertram Bellamy. The man now managed the Bellamy and Standish business interests in Cuba. When the abolition of slavery came to many American States it was imperative to turn from the sugar plantations to the tobacco fields of the South where the labour, albeit now frowned upon, was still carried out by people willing to work for food alone.

The hansom slowed and Tommy saw that the trees in the park were ethereal in the gathering twilight. Illicit lovers sauntered, wrapped in secret embraces, oblivious to the outside world and everyday cares.

The cab's wheels scraped on the kerbstone as the vehicle came to a standstill.

Opening the door, Tommy climbed down to the pavement.

The driver doffed his hat. 'Goodnight, sir.'

'Night,' Tommy said. Turning towards the house, he walked up the three long steps to the doorway.

The door opened before he had time to knock upon it. A footman, resplendent in liveried uniform, stood in the opening, the light of a magnificent chandelier behind him.

'Good evening, sir,' he said, bending at the waist in an elaborate bow.

'I am here to see her ladyship,' Tommy said smartly.

The door opened wide and Tommy stepped into the immense hall. A wide sweeping staircase, the banisters a filigree metalwork, took centre stage. Above it, a great chandelier lit by more than a hundred candles, the glittering light reflected in long mirrors and multiplied a hundredfold in the facetted borders. The effect was stunning. The walls were decorated with silk, the background colour the iridescent green of mother-of-pearl, exquisitely embroidered with exotic birds of paradise, the tail feathers scarlet and royal blue. The old fashioned portraits of her husband's ancestors had been removed long ago and were now stored in the spacious attic; Lady Isabelle's taste ran to the modern, the up-to-date.

Tommy compared the hall with that at Plas Mawr and, although it was wonderfully fashioned, it didn't truly compare with the traditional to be found in his own home. This modern decorator's creation would soon date and then it would take another king's ransom to do again.

The footman, well used to the moments it took visitors to appreciate the splendour of the hall, stood silently whilst this new guest looked admiringly at the recent refurbishment. Tommy caught the man's eye and he was slightly embarrassed to be found gawping like a greenhorn.

'Mr Standish to see Lady Isabelle,' he snapped. Drawing a personal card out of his pocket, he offered it to the servant. The address would be enough to scupper the notion that he was just another sycophant.

The footman bowed from the waist again. 'Madam is receiving in the music room. Please follow me, sir.'

If Tommy was disappointed to see a room full of people and several musicians, resting for the moment, he didn't let it show as he walked towards the hostess. Lady Isabelle looked splendid in a gown of oyster silk; the deep décolleté bodice beaded with magenta droplets, showed off her unblemished shoulders and long neck to perfection. Her dark and luxurious hair was dressed in a Grecian style, the dark silken curls piled one upon another, drawn away from her high cheek-boned and almost perfect face.

Lifting her hand, Tommy kissed the soft ivory skin. 'Lady Isabelle, you look ravishing.'

Astonished to see him so soon, a smile lit her face. 'Tommy! What a wonderful surprise.'

Giving the gathering a sideways glance, his mouth quirked ironically. 'I hadn't expected you to be so occupied. Your letter came to me only today and I understood that you were in need of a small diversion. Is this the sort of diversion you were referring to?' He smiled, his dark satanic eyebrows lifting questioningly.

Lady Isabelle giggled. 'You know exactly what I meant.'

Amused, he dipped his head to whisper near her small ear. 'I'm sure you'll punish me. If I am naughty.'

She bent towards him, the outline of her breast touching his coat sleeve. 'Oh, most certainly, I will.' she whispered.

Steering him towards a group of people chatting beside the open window, she was the perfect hostess. 'Let me introduce you to one or two guests.'

It was late, the musical soirée had gone on for an interminable time and supper had been delayed for the arrival of a special guest. The ritual of the light repast eventually completed, several male guests gathered for brandies in the absent husband's smoking room. It was almost two o'clock before Tommy could think of retiring.

Lady Isabelle had insisted he stay overnight. Several other guests were visiting, so his presence would not be thought in the least bit unusual, she said, when he queried the arrangement.

The clock was striking two-thirty as he left his bedroom and made his way silently towards Lady Isabelle's suite.

A grey sea mist lapped at the shore as Joe Standish walked along the water's edge, his boots leaving deep imprints in the damp sand. The sea touched the land in gentle, silvered ripples, soothingly rhythmic, the faint lapping and sucking of the wavelets calming the tension of his restless night. The early morning air was damp and chill, smelling of ozone and the tang of salt. Breathing through his mouth, he tasted the sea and air, seaweed and long dead shells. The murmur of the distant swell was vaguely sinister, heavy, rolling slowly, licking the black rocks that broke the water, drifting the long manes of blistery seaweed below the tide line.

He remembered the last time he'd come down to the shore; it had been too long ago.

On that occasion the dark green translucent waves had been churning, violent, and he'd revelled in the murderous, lonely sea, the stimulating fear of the storm. Today couldn't be more different, the stillness of the blanketed air, smooth sea, and the cries of seabirds on the wing.

Towards the mountains the light mist was gradually clearing, the greys and dark greens of the slopes emerging. It could be a decent day.

He moved on until he was walking on drenched sand, the wavelets receding as the tide turned and he wondered if he imagined that the mist was being drawn out with the seawater. A rock that had been a vague shadow only moments ago was now quite distinct, clear enough to see the ochre lichen growing on the surface. As he made for it he pulled his pipe and tobacco pouch out of his coat pocket and sitting on the rounded rock he filled the bowl. Enclosing the flame of a Lucifer with the palm of his hand he lit the tobacco, sucking in the sweet fragrant smoke. Tranquil for the first time in weeks, he sat listening to the cries of the seabirds and watched a sandpiper turn over the shells left by the falling tide. He was pleased that he had come down to the water's edge; the sea had the power to calm him.

The hours of the long night had been beset with demons; he had woken suddenly during a dreadful nightmare, reliving the calamity that had crushed three men at the Garddryn quarry gates. When his heart had ceased to race sickeningly and he had cooled down, his body had been sweaty with fear; he tried to redirect his mind away from that dreadful day and the terrified cries of the men. But he had exchanged one torment for another and Tommy and his nefarious conduct had circled in his mind until his head positively ached. Banishing Tommy senior, little Tommy, angelic at three-years-old had flitted through his thoughts. Frank, his mate from the Galloway Pit, had eventually surfaced and for a short time he'd held a mental conversation with him.

Then, just when he thought he was going to drop into a doze, the Garddryn families that were so near to starvation, loomed before him. Trying to work out how to raise money to keep the needy out of the workhouse had killed any hope of sleep.

The room was still ink-black and he'd looked towards the window and saw his darling Chloe standing before the flimsy curtain. For long moments he stared, afraid to move, afraid that if he did she would disappear. Tears filmed his eyes and he watched her through a veil of water until she was there no longer; all that remained was the darkness and the empty space. In a panicky urgency he tried to penetrate the shadows but there was no little girl wearing her third-birthday dress.

When he awoke he wasn't sure if he had dreamed of Chloe or if the image had been real. There was no small girl there now, just the small clock on the mantel ticking quietly. An image of the tiny grave on the mountainside came to him and an agonising desolation swept over him. When the worst of this passed, he lay unmoving looking into the blackness, trying to recreate the image, trying to ignore the hands of the clock moving towards the hour of dawn, for then, any hope that Chloe was close would flee with the darkness.

As the first rays of the grey dawn edged the curtains, he rose stiffly and dressed slowly like a sick man. Then lifting

212

the latch on the door he glanced once more around the room, before making his way to the kitchen.

The image of Chloe stayed with him and it was by habit that he threw dry wood to the ash-grey embers in the grate and put the kettle to the new fire to make a brew. Drinking his tea, watching the flames take hold and the log at the heart of the fire turn molten, he listened to her voice and laughter in his mind.

Leaving the cottage before Emily or Frank rose and the noise of a new day banished the precious image, he took the road to the shore, away from the mountainside grave.

His eyes were on the sea whilst he smoked his pipe but he was blind to the movement of the water. It was the sun flickering on the waves, dazzling his eyes, that ended his long reverie and he was surprised to see the mist had lifted and the ocean flecked with white was rolling away from the land. Wondering at the time, he glanced towards the sun and saw that it had moved around to the south.

Deciding he should move and make his way back, he tapped the cold pipe gently against the rock before he put it into his coat pocket.

Standing, finding his knees stiff from sitting motionless, he shook one baggy trouser leg and heavy boot then the other.

His movement disturbed a small flock of sandpipers picking at the tide-line and he was rewarded with the low beat and grey black flash of wings as they took flight. Landing near a rock pool, they began to pick their way elegantly through the wet stones ferreting for shellfish and hidden worms. Taking his eyes from them, he glanced to the horizon to the blue line where sea meets the sky. Then starting back the way he had come he collected driftwood for the evening fire.

Emily was in the back yard hanging wet washing on the line as Joe came through the front door and into the kitchen-cum-living room. Taking the peg from between her lips, she shouted, 'That you, Joe?'

Walking through to the scullery, he came to the back yard.

Dumping the drift wood onto a stack of cut logs, he grinned. 'I'd like to know who you thought it might be, you young vixen.'

Emily smiled, pleased to see that he was in a more relaxed mood. She'd worried finding him gone when she awoke and his side of the bed stone cold. If he had gone to Chloe's grave, the place he still turned to when his mind was troubled, he'd been gone a good while.

Her cheeks dimpled. 'Young vixen indeed, I wish that were still true.'

With mock anger, he said 'Oh, so you'd still like to have the foxes chasing after you, would you?'

She was trying to catch the corner of the flapping sheet. 'Don't be daft, our Joe. Take a hold of this darn thing. Make yourself useful.'

Taking the peg from her he secured the bed-sheet. 'Have you been to the hens?'

'No, not yet. Our Frank let the little perishers out and gave them the scrapings, same with the pigs.'

She didn't like to think of the two pigs. After their next litter, if no wages were coming in, the pair would be off to market, or worse, end up on the table. She couldn't bring herself to think how she might cope if she were expected to roast or simmer Jake and his Missus.

Stooping, Joe picked a stranded peg off the ground and clipped it onto the line. 'I'll go and see if there are any eggs. I could boil one for you.'

'A bit of bread will do Joe. I promised Maisy at the shop that I'd take some eggs down later.'

Joe's eyebrows twitched in a frown. 'I hope she's giving you a fair price. Maisy can be a real skinflint.'

Picking up the washing basket, carrying it on her hip,

Emily made for the open scullery door. 'I know she can. But she's getting to be a real old girl.'

'It's no excuse for robbing folk when times are bad.'

Emily was sympathetic. 'I think that it's a habit with her. She's been doing it so long she just doesn't notice anymore.'

Joe clicked his tongue. 'I'll take the eggs down to the shop and make sure the old bugger doesn't rob us. You're too soft with her.'

'I know. But I like Maisy and I find it hard to say no to her.'

Raising his eyebrows, he sighed. 'I'll do all the money negotiations from now on. Soft isn't the word for you, Emily Standish. You know what you are ...?'

She giggled. 'Get away to the hen house and collect what eggs there are. I'll put the kettle to the fire.'

Joe had four eggs to sell from today's crop and six from the previous day. After rinsing them in cold water he put them into a screw of paper. He wouldn't be seen dead carrying Emily's fancy basket and he told her so as soon as she suggested it. Two eggs he placed carefully into a basin to give to Maud Jones for her two smallest children.

His return from the shop was triumphant; Maisy had argued very briefly before handing him a small block of sugar for the eight eggs. Coming into Corn Cottage he found Horas Jones and Emily at the table sipping mugs of hot tea.

Putting his hat down on the dresser and placing the wrapped sugar on the table, Joe was jovial. 'Horas, how are you?'

It seemed nonsense to ask; the man looked half-starved, his eyes sunk in his yellow face.

'Could be better, but we're getting by.' Horas's red-rimmed eyes filmed with tears.

As she had no wish to embarrass the man, Emily found a job in the scullery that needed her urgent attention.

Joe pulled a chair close. 'Look, Horas, you don't have to

pretend here; if things are getting worse say so. We are all in this together.'

Wiping the end of his long nose on the back of his hand, Horas sniffed. 'You've been good to us, Joe. I don't know what we would have done without the rabbits, pigeons and those fish.' He made an attempt at a smile. 'Well, actually I do know. We would have starved.'

It was a weak joke and Joe's heart went out to the man. With his eye to the scullery door, Joe kept his voice low, whispering, 'Me and our Frank are going out later to get something for the table. With luck we should have a plump rabbit for yours an all.'

'Thanks, Joe. Do you want me to come with you?'

Something clattered to the floor in the scullery and Joe's glance went back to the door. 'No, the fewer the better, we can't afford to make too much noise.'

Horas nodded. 'Joe, you've been good to us, you've looked out for my lot since the beginning of the trouble and it makes what I have to tell you all the harder to say.'

He paused, then said in a rush, 'I can't stay away from work any longer, me little ones cried all night ...'

Tears ran in twin rivulets down his hollow cheeks. 'The little beggars are so hungry, Joe. It would break your heart to hear them.' He sniffed. 'Maud is beside herself, the poor woman has already lost two little ones. I can't stand by and watch her torturing herself about the fate of the others.'

Joe touched the man's sleeve. 'I know that it's hard, Horas. But if we go back we've lost the battle and management will walk all over us. We would be accepting lower wages and longer working hours.'

Joe stood. His hands trembling slightly he took his pipe off the mantel. He couldn't bear to mention his son's name, as he said, 'The bugger would have us by the balls.'

Horas wiped tears off his cheeks. 'Am I to stand by and watch my babies die? God in heaven, what sort of man would I be if I did that? Heartless, a fiend, not fit to live.'

Thinking of the children, Joe felt like weeping. 'Of course, you can't stand back and watch that.'

He imagined the kitchen in his neighbour's house, the children sitting at an empty table. 'I'll do my best to bring something for them tonight,' he said earnestly.

Horas's face contorted with anguish. 'Joe, it's good of you to try, but tiny bairns can't eat rabbits. The little ones are crying for milk. And it's me wages that'll buy that for them.'

For a moment Joe was at a loss for words. Standing he grasped the mantel. 'Jesus. It's that bad?'

Silent tears flowed down Horas's face. 'It's been that bad since the day we were locked out of the Garddryn.'

Joe's eyes filled. 'I'll murder that bugger of a son of mine. One day I'll swing for the bastard. So help me God, I'll swing for him.'

Hearing the vicious tone of Joe's voice, Emily opened the door. 'Joe, don't say that, he's our son.'

'Aye, I know. But there are times when I wish that he weren't.'

Emily's face screwed with anguish. 'Joe!'

Rising from the chair, Horas looked from one to the other. 'I'm causing trouble here. I'm sorry. I'll go.'

Joe gave him a gentle push back into the seat. 'No, don't go. Sit and let's talk this through.'

Glancing quickly at Emily and receiving a small embarrassed smile, Horas sat on the edge of the seat.

That little ones were crying for the want of milk was like a hot poker searing Joe's heart. Only a matter of minutes ago he'd got back from the shop, pleased as punch that he'd got a good price for the eggs. The block of sugar, how unimportant that luxury seemed now! His pleasure so vacuous when measured against the suffering in his neighbour's house.

Emily was vaguely cross that Maud had not mentioned the complete lack of pennies to buy milk. She and Maud had a close friendship, and although she knew it to be ridiculous, she felt somehow slighted that Maud had not confided in her. Because she knew that she was being foolish, Emily went to the scullery to fill the kettle from the bucket. The small chore would suffice *as something to do* until she had time to think about Maud's reasons for keeping quiet. Bringing the kettle back, the scorched bottom dripping on the slate floor she put it to the fire.

Turning, she faced Horas. The man was a shadow, a half-starved shadow. Moved by his vulnerability, in her heart knowing that Maud was in no better state, Emily laid her hand on his shoulder.

'Horas, you must do what *you* think is best.'

The gentleness and wisdom of her words reached through the fog that had clouded his judgment for so many weeks. Of course, he should do what *he* thought was best for his family and stop worrying himself sick about what everyone else would think. There would be harsh penalties to pay but he could accept that to feed his little ones.

The kettle started to simmer and, absentmindedly, her thoughts centred entirely on Tommy; Emily began to make a brew.

Clattering the pots, her head reeling with conflicting emotions, she stirred the teapot viciously. Joe had every right to be angry and perhaps if she were a man she would feel just as Joe did. But she was a mother first and foremost and whatever Tommy did, it didn't stop her loving him. She might wish to God that things were different, but they weren't. Circumstances had to be endured. But that wouldn't stop her taking a broom handle to the bugger the moment he returned from his shenanigans in London. She'd whip his backside if it was the last thing she did.

Horas took a deep breath. Trying to explain, he said 'It's been almost four weeks since we were locked-out and in that time not once has the management at the Garddryn said anything about letting us back in. Face it Joe, whilst they've got the Irish digging slate, they don't need the old workforce. They can afford to keep us out. There's no reason to hurry to reinstate us. You can bet that the Irish are working for a pittance. There'll be no *bargains*. It'll be a set wage and a meagre one that the tinkers are picking up every Saturday.'

The line of reasoning wasn't new to Joe; he'd heard it more than a dozen times from the men that gathered at his home under the cover of darkness.

Reaching for his pipe on the mantelshelf, he gave Horas the same answer he gave the others. 'I don't know what wages the Irish are being paid. But what I do know is that there isn't a man amongst the tinkers that can split slate, so the dressing sheds are closed. Oakley can't keep them closed indefinitely. The Garddryn will go bust if he does. Tommy needs men to dig at Ruby. He'll soon be forced into accepting the men back at the Garddryn on their terms, to free up the Irish for the work at the other place.

It's important, Horas, that the men get back on *their* terms and not Oakley's or bloody Tommy's. If we stick it out just a little bit longer…'

Dragging his hand through his already dishevelled hair, Horas turned a pale strained face to Joe. 'Maybe you're right. But have you considered that with your Tommy starting up his new quarry, perhaps he doesn't need the Garddryn any longer?'

'Don't talk daft, man. The Garddryn is profitable. Even our Tommy is not so stupid as to let that business go to rack and ruin.'

Horas sighed. 'Time will tell, but me and my family might not be here to see the day the Garddryn gates open. If things don't change in the next day or two I'll have to send my wife and bairns to the workhouse while I get down to Merthyr.' He sighed. 'I just hope that I can get work and get them out of there.'

Joe had no truck with the working practises at Merthyr; if anything they were worse than the men at the Garddryn endured. Although the Anglesey copper workings had a regrettable reputation, it offered an instant solution. 'Why not try Parys Mountain? Anglesey is a lot closer than Merthyr.'

Horas snorted. 'Aye, some of the men chucked off the Garddryn are working the copper. The half starved Irish are over it like flies. Only yesterday a dozen Garddryn men came back from there empty handed.'

Standing, Horas turned his hat in his hands. 'Look, Joe, it's no good me going over all my woes, you have enough of your own. I'd best get back.'

'Take these, it's not much but they'll be good for the little ones.' Joe handed him the two eggs from the basin.

'Thanks Joe, it is appreciated .You know I wouldn't accept anything from you if I wasn't desperate for the bairns.'

'Say nowt. If it wasn't for our Tommy...' Joe left the sentence unfinished.

After Horas's departure, Emily and Joe were both quiet, wrapped in their own thoughts.

That night Frank and Joe left Corn Cottage as the mantel clock struck ten.

Emily found it impossible to sit beside the fire looking into the sparse flames waiting for their return. Worrying that one or both would get caught, hurt, or sent to jail.

To distract her mind she tried to read Joe's Friday newspaper. The sense of the paragraphs left her baffled; some solitary words she could understand but she lost the gist of a long sentence before she'd mastered the one that followed it.

Feeling somewhat stupid, how she wished she'd learned to read properly whilst she'd still been young but schooling hadn't been a priority in her farming stock family.

Folding the newspaper she abandoned it on the table and made her way to bed.

Tired, washday was the hardest day of the week, she dozed. The front door opening brought her instantly awake.

Hearing two voices she breathed a sigh of relief, they were both home safe.

Joe's footfall crossed the room to the scullery and she knew that their hunt had been successful and he would be putting what he had in the sack into the stone sink to deal with in the morning. A kill was good for them and for the Jones family next door but bad for whatever creature had been slaughtered that night. There wasn't a time when she didn't feel real compassion, a sadness in her gut for the poor unfortunate animal; were we not all God's creatures when it came down to it?

Joe came into the bedroom quietly, afraid to wake her if she slept. She turned to face him as he climbed into bed, but feigned sleep; tomorrow would be time enough to know what creature had met its maker tonight.

Rising early to skin the two rabbits, it saved heartache if he got the task complete before Emily came to the scullery; she was still as soft as a girl. When the job was complete Joe put one jointed rabbit into the stewing pot and wrapped the other little corpse into a newspaper. He cleaned up the inevitable mess, then scrubbed his hands. Satisfied that all the evidence that would upset Emily was cleared away, he went out the front door to see the Jones's at Bryn Tirion.

Maud, a sleeping child in her arms, opened the door to his first knock. Her appearance came as something of a shock to him. She looked ghastly as though she hadn't slept for nights. Her face was almost as grey as her dress.

She glanced at the parcel in his hand. 'Hello, Joe. I'm afraid Horas isn't here.'

Offering the parcel, he said 'Oh, never mind. I just called to give you this rabbit for the pot.'

Hitching the child on her hip, she took the wet package from him. 'Can you spare it?'

He smiled, delivering a white lie. 'Oh aye, me and Frank had a good night last night, we found plenty.'

Her dark tawny glance dropped to the ground between

them. 'Perhaps you wouldn't want to give it to us if you knew the truth.'

Bewildered, his brow puckered. 'What truth?'

Standing back from the door, she shifted her eyes to him. 'Perhaps you had better come in. I'll explain what's happened.'

In his old kitchen, smart and clean when Emily was the housewife, Joe tried not to glance at the clutter.

'Sit down, Joe. Take that pile of clothes off the chair and put them onto the floor.'

Tidy by nature, Joe couldn't bring himself to do as she suggested and he looked to the littered table and to another chair for a space; as there wasn't a place to put the clothes down, he kept hold of the bundle.

The child in Maud's arms stirred. Stooping to the open drawer at the bottom of the dresser she laid the baby into it and tucked a small sheet around the youngster.

Straightening, she took the clothes from Joe's arms and placed them on a stack of old newspapers on the dresser top.

There wasn't the usual bedlam, noisy children running in every direction.

Glancing at the closed staircase door, Maud explained, 'They are all asleep, we had a very disturbed night last night.' She didn't admit that the children had gone without a proper meal yesterday and hunger had kept them awake.

Sighing, she squatted on the three legged stool before the empty hearth. Her thin arms were bare to the elbows, folding them against her midriff, she sat quite still. Her skirt a circle of grey around her, she looked vulnerable and tired.

She glanced into the empty grate then turned her eyes to him.

'Joe, I don't know where to begin. Horas told you how hard things are for us. He wanted to go to Merthyr to see if he could get work there but the little ones are too young to make such a long journey. We'd have to sleep outdoors.'

222

Tears filled her eyes. 'My children are not well enough for that. So Horas said we must go to the workhouse, but I refused.'

Joe had already guessed what was coming next and he held his breath praying that he was wrong.

Her eyes slid away from him. 'He's gone to get his job back at the Garddryn.'

Joe was slightly contemptuous. 'He's gone back?'

'Yes, Joe, he's gone back,' she said quietly.

Although he tried hard to hide his anger, it broke through and he almost shouted, 'Does he know what this will do to us all?'

Her dark eyes flashed fire. 'Yes, he knows. But the alternative was to watch his children starve and he couldn't do that; he's too good a father. No man should expect a father to kill his children.'

Her words silenced his outrage.

Leaning forward, she clutched his shirt sleeve. 'Think, Joe, what would you have done if things were reversed and it was your little ones crying with hunger?' Her voice rose on the last word, 'would you let them suffer?'

He thought of Chloe, who he would have walked over hot coals for and murdered any man that harmed her. 'No. I couldn't stand by and do nothing. I might have done the self same thing.'

He wondered if she truly appreciated what Horas's return would mean. His eyes sought hers. 'The repercussions will be terrible for the quarrymen who are fighting for their rights, and for Horas. He'll be branded a strike-breaker, a traitor to the cause.'

She bent her head, staring at the grey folds of her skirt. 'I know, as does he. Life will be difficult. He's prepared for violence. He says whatever pain he suffers he'll know that it's in a good cause, his children's bellies will be filled.'

Struggling up from the stool, there wasn't an ounce of

energy left in her; she took the parcel off the table. 'Here, you had better take this back.'

Brushing her words aside, he stood. 'Don't be daft, lass. You still have to eat between now and his first pay. I will not see you and yours starve. When Frank and me go out tonight, there'll be something for your pot if there's summat in ours.'

Unshed tears filmed her dark eyes. 'Thanks, Joe. It means a lot. Not many men would look out for us, especially now.'

Emily was at the table shaking flour into a basin to make a small loaf when Joe came back. Putting aside the crock container, almost dropping it as it slipped through her floury fingers, she looked up. 'Have you been to Bryn Tirion?'

'Aye, I have.'

'Is Maud all right? Is she coping?' Emily poured the risen yeast and water into the flour, stirring it with her hand.

Joe went to the mantel for his pipe.

Glancing at him, she raised an eyebrow. 'It's a bit early for you to take up your pipe.'

'Horas has gone back,' he said with no life in his voice.

She stopped mixing. 'What, to the Garddryn? He never has?'

He gave a long sigh of regret. 'Aye, he has. I took a rabbit round there. She asked me in and explained everything.' He stuffed the bowl of the pipe from the small amount of tobacco in his pouch.

Taking a spill off the mantel, he put the tip to the fire in the grate; when it flared he lit the tobacco. 'The children are going hungry and it looks as though the lass herself hasn't had either a meal or a decent sleep in weeks. It's a bloody mess.'

Forgetting the mixing, Emily pulled a chair from beneath the table and slumped into it. Wiping her floury hands on her white apron, she spoke softly 'What can we do?'

'Not much more than we are doing already. I've done me

best to keep a bit of meat on their table. Poor Horas isn't the best of providers. I know he works his fingers to the bone in the dressing shed to bring home a wage but when it come to foraging and trapping wild creatures, he's not much use.'

In Horas's defence, she said 'He was brought up in a town; there's not much call for those skills.'

Joe sucked his pipe. 'Aye, happen.'

Smoking silently, his thoughts with Horas he wondered what the man was doing at this moment. Was he sitting in an empty dressing shed working alone, splitting the slate blocks that were put there on the day of the lock-out? One thing was for certain Horas Jones would not have been refused work; management would have jumped at the chance of having the first man back and on their terms. If Horas had mastered a few survival skills, this calamity might have been averted.

In his mind, Joe scanned the faces of the dozens upon dozens of quarrymen he knew personally and wondered how many of those were in the same straits as Horas and his family. If one quarryman had gone crawling back to the Garddryn, it would only be a matter of days before others followed him.

'Joe, the men will roast him for going back.'

'Aye, I know. I don't think there is anything we can do to stop it. The worst of it is, that now he's gone back, others will follow. We've lost any hold we might have had over Tommy.' He sighed. 'We can expect to work longer hours for less money. The bugger will keep those that have said a word against him out. They'll find no work in the Garddryn or any other quarry in Wales. It'll mean a great exodus of folk from these parts and Anglesey.'

Emily looked to the yeast and flour congealing in the mixing bowl. Sighing, she stood and began to mix the two together. 'Whatever will happen next?'

Although her question had been rhetorical, he answered, 'The poor sods that are in the same position as Horas will go back and they'll be crucified for doing so. When in reality, all that the men are trying to do is feed and keep a roof over those they love.

There'll be mayhem before the day is out.'

Knocking out his pipe on the side of the grate, Joe gave a long drawn out sigh. 'And our Tommy will have the last laugh as his bloody dressing sheds will open again.'

Emily slapped the dough down viciously on the floured tabletop. 'The scoundrel will not be laughing when I see him. I am more determined than ever to whack the bugger with me broom handle and if the lads happen to be watching, so much the better.'

Joe laughed. 'You tell me when you plan on this little circus taking place. I wouldn't miss it for the world.'

The dough came down heavily again. 'I'll be selling bloody tickets for it, our Joe.'

After a long day in the dressing shed, alone but for a young Irish lad that watched him split slate into duchesses and countesses, Horas Jones, nervous of leaving the safety of the Garddryn, chose not to go through the main gates of the quarry but instead walked to where the boundary fence butted onto an open field. Skirting the village, keeping to the alleys, away from prying eyes, he came to the waste ground at the back of the village shop. Watching from behind the small stone building that housed the privy he watched the flow of customers and when the shop was empty he darted in.

The bell above the front door pealed out; Maisy looked up from the block of suet she was cutting into. Earlier she had heard a rumour that Horas Jones had returned to work, but as it was only a rumour at this stage she decided to serve him. If things changed and the whispering became fact, she proposed to banish him and his family from the shop. She'd not serve traitors. The Jones family would starve if they relied on her to supply their sustenance.

Nervous he stood with his back to the door. 'Maisy, I need milk, flour, lard and potatoes.'

Maisy wiped her hands on her apron. 'Come into money have we, Mr Jones?'

'No. But if you'd be kind enough to put it on the book, I'll see you are paid next week.'

'I don't mind doing that for you as long as you're not thinking of paying with traitor's wages. I'll not serve anyone that's in the pay of the Garddryn.'

Horas's thoughts flew to the kitchen at home, to the faces of his children with no supper to look forward to. He tried to smile but he was too nervous and he was conscious that his eyes were darting this way and that. The lie, when he said it, sounded false and stupid. His heart pounding in his chest he waited for the woman to denounce him as a scoundrel.

'Whatever gives you that idea, Maisy? I've some work in Caernarvon, on the boats. I'll receive my pay come Saturday and I'll be in the shop to buy the week's groceries.'

She didn't look convinced and he was about to add more colour to the untruth when Maisy moved to the end of the counter.

'How much flour did you say you wanted, Mr Jones?

He almost wept with relief and he asked for a large quantity, saying that Mrs Jones found it difficult to carry such a burden, her being under-the-weather at the moment.

He came out of the shop laden and carried his prize home, trying his hardest not to let the threat of reprisals ruin his momentary joy.

Maud had been watching for him, terrified that he might not make it back in one piece. During the course of the day she had imagined every conceivable atrocity befalling him. Near tears on several occasions she thought how unfair it was that a man that was a good and loving father and husband should risk life and limb to do a day's work that he loathed, and all for a loaf of bread and milk for the babies.

Joe was putting the hens away when he heard the

children's cries of delight coming from Bryn Tirion. Horas's voice rang out louder than the rest, then the door closed and the old house fell back into the silence that had become habitual of late. He hadn't the heart to go and confront Horas just now, although he might do so when the children were in bed.

Sighing, his heart heavy, Joe picked up the bucket that had held the scrapings for the hens and walked back across the half-acre field to his own kitchen.

Frank arrived home as darkness fell. He was tired after spending the day rolling great stones off a field in Penygroes, clearing the land so that foundations could be dug for the bonesetter's new house.

He had met the man by chance, when a friend of his was in need of the bonesetter's expertise. Whilst splinting the arm of the young pugilist, the bonesetter told Frank of the proposed house and the problems with the rocky land. Frank had volunteered his services immediately. After delivering his mate back home, where he could bemoan his ill-luck to his heart's content, Frank had gone to the field at once.

Although tired and in need of his supper, Frank explained to Joe and Emily that the job could last till Saturday.

Joe was glad to hear it, thankful that Frank would be away from the vicinity should tempers boil over in Garddryn village.

He was trying to find the words to tell his son of the turn of events at the quarry, never easy to get a word in edgeways when Frank was full of news, when Frank surprised him by pulling out a bag of tobacco.

'Present for you, Da.' Frank grinned, seeing the surprised and grateful look on his father's face.

'Old Bony paid me for today. I knew that your tobacco was a bit low so thought I'd treat you.'

'What a marvel you are lad. That was really thoughtful.'

Opening the bag, Joe sniffed the aroma of the sweet Virginia.

'Pity our Tommy isn't more like you,' Emily said, looking up from darning a great hole in the heel of one of Joe's brown socks.

Frank dived into the inside pocket of his old coat. 'I got this bit of cheese from the woman that keeps the small farm just outside Llanllfyni. It seems like ages since we had cheese. I didn't know I liked it as much as I do.' The lad grinned again.

'Is this Christmas, Frank?' Joe laughed.

Emily put aside the darning. 'I'll get the old cheese dish for it.'

'I don't think it'll need the dish for too long. A bit of today's bread with that will make a real nice late supper. Look, me mouth's watering already.' Joe chuckled.

Delighted to bring a bit of happiness, Frank tucked into the rabbit stew that Emily had kept warm over a pan of steaming water.

It wasn't until Frank had wiped the plate clean that Joe mentioned Horas and his return to work.

Frank was as indignant as Joe expected him to be.

Righteous indignation wasn't the sole prerogative of youth, Joe thought meditatively.

He was pretty narked himself. It was just the older you got the more likely you were to see that problems were many facetted.

The following day, the quarrymen, discovering that Horas Jones had returned to the quarry, were waiting up the lane as he came towards his home that evening. As Horas neared his gate a few dozen men walked towards him.

Terrified, Horas froze.

In a pack, the men surrounded him, goading and jostling, until he almost lost his footing.

'Trip the bastard,' someone shouted.

Grabbed by the back of the neck, Horas's head was

pushed down. He was looking at the ground and the dirty boots stamping the dry dust. In the confusion he heard Joe Standish, shouting angrily.

'Leave the poor bugger alone, you bloody bullies. Typical of you lot, can't fight a man single handed, you have to brawl in an effing mob.'

Joe elbowed his way through the men. Clouting the ear of the lout that held Horas's head in a fierce grasp, he roared, 'I said, leave him! This is no way to settle the matter.'

The blow was fierce. The youth's ear smarted and in anger he hung onto Horas brutally.

Joe clouted the youth hard and the bully suddenly let go.

Red in the face, cupping his split ear, the lad shouted angrily, 'Standish, you'll pay for this.'

'Aye, I probably will. But it won't be by your hand, you bloody pipsqueak. Now stand back and let the air to the man, before I do the other bloody ear for you.'

The young man's eyes filled with tears of pain.

The rabble around him laughed. Nudging him painfully in the ribs, they ignored the blood seeping from beneath his hand.

The front door of Bryn Tirion opened and the Jones family spilled out. Maud was in the centre of her brood of children and she gathered the youngest to her as the others ran to their father. The children penetrated the crowd, little elbows and fists fighting the way through the trousered legs.

The childish squeals split the mob's ranks and the men fell back. The young Jones's surrounded their father; hanging onto his arms and legs they tried valiantly to drag him towards the garden gate. Their dirty tearstained faces turned towards his aggressors.

No one tried to stop the family retreating into the cottage and all were watching as the door slammed shut.

Joe spoke out angrily, 'Tomorrow morning at eight o'clock, there'll be a meeting on the common. We'll talk this through and decide a course of action that doesn't involve the murder of a solitary man or bring harm to little children. We are not in a fight for justice to create a bigger injustice. We are men, not animals.'

His words embarrassed some of the men, whilst others felt their actions were perfectly justified.

In groups they began to disperse. There was no point in hanging around; there was nothing more to see. The cause of all the trouble was safe in his cottage surrounded by a veritable army of pint-sized warriors. Reaching the centre of the village some went to the Half-Way. The men without funds gathered on the low walls outside the inn to discuss the situation.

The following morning, Joe was the first to arrive on the common. As the quarrymen began to arrive they brought unwelcome news, several reporting that neighbours had followed Horas's move and had returned to the Garddryn. The mood amongst the crowd was sombre. The sacrifice they and their families had made had been for naught. They had tightened their belts, gone without the luxury of a few ales at the Half-Way. There had been many hungry days, when there was no credit to be had, and a man could only feed his family if he lived off his wits. The less fortunate, caught in the act of poaching, were awaiting the court's pleasure. Three men were in jail for theft. One man, his family threatened with the workhouse, had killed himself.

Looking at the gathering crowd, Joe saw that the men that had started the battle for justice were now harrowed, lean and sickly. For the moment they were beaten. He kept the call for a union to himself, for men seeking a Society of Welsh Quarrymen would need to be a great deal stealthier if they were to win their goal.

CHAPTER NINE

Although Henrietta half-expected Tommy to return imminently, she was disappointed to hear a vehicle bowling down the avenue. She had hoped, though it was a rather vain hope, that Tommy would stay in London just a day or two longer.

Whilst he had been away she had calmed down, relying less on the heroin cure that Griffith the surgeon had recommended to counteract the dependence she had to the laudanum medicine.

With the return of her energy and appetite, she had felt well enough to take delightful walks with young Edward and his nanny. Many amusing hours had been spent in the nursery playing with her son. Several times she had stayed for afternoon tea and sitting at the small table in the window they had shared the tiny pastries so loved by little Edward. Tommy would disapprove wholeheartedly if he were to learn of the enchanting episodes.

Clinging to the small hope that it may not be Tommy, she went to the window, her mauve silk skirt brushing the Turkey carpet. Drawing aside the lace curtain, she looked out to the carriage-turning circle.

The carriage had come to a standstill. Tommy was alighting. So there was no mistake. He had returned. She had so hoped that the vehicle had brought a visitor. But guests hadn't called for some while now, not since the demise of her mother. Casual visitors did not make their way to Plas Mawr as they had in the days of her parents' residence.

Watching her husband, tailored impeccably, she wondered how he managed to travel and remain so neat. Other mortals looked dishevelled and drab well before they had reached their destination.

Tommy went up the steps to the front door, his cane tapping once on each tread. Two footmen had come hurrying at the sound of an arrival and they stood aside, bowing from the waist as the master passed into the house.

His strident voice echoed in the large hallway and she physically braced herself for his appearance.

With her arms folded across the bodice of her lilac blouse, she stayed at the open window, the light breeze drifting across her face. She thought back to the time when waiting for him had been torture, every moment apart an agony. Now she dreaded the moment he would appear. Praying that he would be absent for days rather than minutes.

Her eyes passed over the gardens and then her attention was caught by the everyday trap drawn by a dapple-grey mare coming down the avenue at a spanking pace. It came to a standstill, the trap aligned to the front door.

On cue a footman trotted down the steps, the large silver buckles on his shoes glinting in the sunlight.

Alighting, Tommy's valet immediately began issuing orders, gesticulating towards the stacked baggage.

Wordlessly, the footman lifted down a large and obviously heavy portmanteau and lowered it carefully to the ground. Another servant appeared and began retrieving large packages from the seat. A second footman came on the scene and he began to cart the luggage into the house.

The valet trailed the two servants into the house. His own bag tucked under his arm.

The butler came down the steps and spoke to the driver. The man shouted, waving his arms angrily, and then the trap moved on.

A maid wearing a white mop-cap over her dark curls peeped around the open door and then bobbed back quickly.

Henrietta sighed. 'What a circus!'

Watching her husband's return brought the familiar blanket of ennui down on her. She wondered if she could escape seeing him until she had visited her room and taken a dose of her medicine. If she cut short her visit to the nursery, or better still didn't go there, she would have time to lie on the chaise-longue in her dressing room and give the medicine time to sweep away the gnawing sense of futility.

Climbing the stairs, Tommy turned to look at his butler as the man came through the front door. 'Miles, I want that small black bag put into the library.'

Henrietta pictured Tommy on the stairs. To avoid him on the landing or in the long corridor, she decided to wait a few moments before leaving the sanctuary of the drawing room.

Turning from the window, her eyes caught the display of magenta peonies set on the small inlaid table. In full bloom the heads were nearly overblown. Putting her nose near them she inhaled the sweet fragrance and clean sharp astringent perfume of the dark glossy leaves.

Striding into the room, wasting no time on preliminaries or a greeting, Tommy threw papers onto a small table. 'I want a music master and a Christian cleric to start on Edward's education immediately.'

Startled, Henrietta turned sharply, almost knocking the flower arrangement over. Putting a hand out to steady the Chinese vase she touched a showy bloom and the petals disintegrated. Her eyes darted from the fragmented flower on the table top, to Tommy.

'Edward's still so young.'

He didn't reply instantly but crossing to the console table he lifted a decanter from a silver tray and poured a measure of port into a glass. 'Education cannot begin too soon,' he said, replacing the glass stopper.

Watching him, wondering if he had always been so

arrogant, and if so, why she had not noticed it in the early days, her glance and tone were dismissive. 'I'll begin to make enquiries.'

Her haughtiness was not lost to him and his eyes narrowed. 'I can see to the matter perfectly well without your interference.' He took a draft of the deep red port. 'The education of my son is of supreme importance.'

'Edward is *our* son,' she corrected him.

He gave a long drawn out sigh. 'Why are you always determined to be so difficult, Henrietta?'

It was a struggle not to retaliate. Feigning calmness, she said 'I wasn't aware that I was being difficult.'

He brushed off her remark. 'I will deal with the matter tomorrow. You can sort out rooms for the two men.'

It was impossible to hide her surprise and her voice darted up. 'Oh! You want them to live here? Surely in the very early years a man or a female music teacher could be found locally ...'

Rudely interrupting, he sneered. 'Of course I want them to live here. Surely you don't think that men of distinction and letters will be found amongst the rabble that resides in Garddryn village?'

He laughed. 'Even you, Henrietta, must think more clearly than that.'

She would have loved to possess the courage to remind him that he had been educated locally. Until her father had taken him in as a protégé and drawn him under the wing of Plas Mawr, his teachers had been drawn from the Garddryn community.

To annoy him she mentioned only George's tutors, omitting that they had been his also. 'The rooms that George's teachers occupied could be put to use again with very little trouble. No doubt they have been kept in a good state of repair and if some decoration is needed it can probably be accomplished with minimum bother.'

The sound of an approaching horse and vehicle came

through the open window. Putting aside his glass, Tommy went to look out. 'It's Oakley.' His brow furrowed. 'Now what the deuce does he want?'

Without a backward glance, he left the room.

Henrietta waited until he and the quarry manager had settled in the library before making for the staircase and her room, her fingers itching to hold the bottle containing her medicine.

In the library, sitting at his desk, the manager seated opposite, Tommy was smiling. 'So the bloody rabble has begun to return to work. You couldn't have brought better news, Oakley.' Laughing loudly, he slapped the palm of his hand down on the desktop. 'Didn't I tell you, all we needed was patience? With the Irish tinkers taking their jobs, the men were sure to come to their senses. If we'd done it your way and pandered to the bastards, they would be no nearer going back to work than, than ...' he was lost for words.

Gritting his teeth, a slight sheen of perspiration on his deeply lined forehead, Oakley listened to the master congratulating himself, when in reality Tommy Standish had disappeared to London at a crucial time. It had been his own management skills that had got more than three dozen men back labouring at the rock-face and another sixteen splitting slate in the dressing sheds. Thankfully the summer evenings were long and light making it possible for them to work until after eight o'clock to make up the lost time. With the Irish working at the slate-face alongside the returned men, the quarry would be back in full working order within weeks.

Jovial, grinning, Tommy slapped his hand on the desk again. 'It's absolutely capital news.' Rising from the comfortable hide chair, ignoring the bell-cord beside the fireside that would summon a servant, he strode to the library door and pulling it open he yelled for a servant.

A flustered footman was the first to appear. Straightening his jacket, fastening the last button over his developing paunch, the man gave a quick bow. 'You called, sir?'

Tommy's eyes were on the servant's gaping coat. Frowning, he bawled, 'Tell Miles to bring a bottle of the best champagne and make it quick.'

As he was about to close the door on the retreating man, Tommy had a compulsive desire to call him back to sack him for slovenliness. It would be a lesson to any servant who thought to appear in an untidy fashion. The man was spared for the moment as there were other issues to think about. The labourers were starting to get back to the quarry; that's all that was important today.

Rubbing his hands together, giving Oakley the benefit of another grin, Tommy crossed to his desk. Sinking back into the chair, the soft leather creaking, he sighed with satisfaction.

'The day couldn't have turned out better, Oakley. A glass or two of the finest champagne to celebrate our victory is what's called for.'

Oakley would have preferred to get back to the Garddryn. There was still a great deal to accomplish at the quarry. Only a few men had returned to work. There were hundreds still to be reinstated before the quarry could get back to operating fully.

Tommy was talking over Oakley's thoughts. 'What I want are the names of the dissenters. I'll not let the rabble rousers work again at the Garddryn or any other quarry in the district. If they want work, they'll have to go far-a-field to find it.'

Hiding a sigh, Oakley reached into the breast pocket of his jacket to retrieve the list he'd compiled of the men that had organised or held meetings during the lock-out. He was about to hand it across the desk when there was a light knock at the door.

The butler entered carrying a tray with two glasses and an open bottle of Veuve Cliquot, chilled from the cellar.

Carefully, afraid to over stimulate the wine, he placed the tray onto the corner of the desk.

Before the butler lifted the bottle, Tommy said roughly, 'Get on with it.'

Miles was well-used to Tommy's abruptness. Leaving the room, closing the library door quietly, he made his way back to the wine cellar. There was a bottle of port coming to perfection in bin 58. It wouldn't be missed from the inventory, and if it was, the blame would fall on Henrietta Standish. Remembering the last occasion he had been asked to account for an expensive bottle of wine, he smiled. The explanation had run off his tongue like honey. 'Madam asked for that particular bottle to be served sometime ago, sir,' he had told the master.

Wheezing slightly, he came to the heavy oak door to the cellar, pulling it open he went through. Just inside the door was a stone lintel where he kept a candle in an old holder. As he put a flaring Lucifer to the wick, grotesque shadows appeared on the bellying stone walls. Holding the candle cautiously, he went down the old worn steps to the cool realm of wine. Theft, he had discovered, compensated for his master's rudeness.

As the library door clicked closed on the butler, Tommy stood. 'To Ruby Quarry,' he said, raising a brimming glass.

Oakley raised his glass. 'To Ruby and the thousands she'll make for...all at Plas Mawr.' He had almost said 'Standish family' but stopped in time.

Tommy took another mouthful of wine, the bubbles tiny explosions on the roof of his mouth and tongue.

With a wave of his hand, he said, 'Hand over that sheet of paper you're clutching so tightly, Oakley. Let's take a look at the names of the reprobates you've managed to catalogue.'

Grunting as pains of rheumatism shot through his bones as he leaned forward, Oakley passed it to Tommy.

Tommy laughed as his eye fell on the name heading the list. 'So the old bugger's still at it. Well, it's no surprise.'

Earlier, whilst in the office, Oakley had prepared a letter for Joe Standish informing him that his labour was no longer required. Tommy's response came as a surprise; he expected an angry outburst.

'Shall I get rid of him?' Oakley asked, one of his grey eyebrows rising quizzically.

Answering without looking up, Tommy said, 'No! No! If he's working at the Garddryn, we have a better chance of keeping an eye on him. But we'll watch every move the bugger makes.' He grinned. 'The same applies to his son, Frank Standish.'

If Oakley was surprised to hear Tommy refer to his younger brother so, he made no reference to it. Taking another mouthful of champagne, he kept his thoughts veiled.

Running through the rest of the names, Tommy was thoughtful. Placing the paper on the desktop, he looked Oakley in the eye. 'Get rid of the rest of them. Send a letter to every quarry manager in the district explaining that these men are on a blacklist because they are work-shy troublemakers, dissenters, scum.'

Reaching across to the bottle of wine, Tommy replenished both glasses.

Eager to be away, Oakley drank the contents in one swallow. 'I will see to it immediately, sir. Are there any other instructions?'

Tommy thought for a moment, then with a small smile touching his mouth, said 'Who was the first man to return to work?'

'It was Horas Jones. He works in the dressing sheds. He's a good worker and first rate at his job.'

Tommy leaned forward in his chair. 'Promote him to position of steward.'

Askance, Oakley said 'If we did that, we would lose a good slate dresser.'

'That's true.' Tommy thought for a moment and then said

positively, 'Promote him to something else. There must be an overseer's job vacant in the dressing sheds and if there isn't, fabricate one.'

Oakley's words sighed from him. 'Leave it to me, sir.'

Rising out of the chair awkwardly, his rheumatism plaguing him more than usual today, Oakley picked the paper up off the desk. His eyes ran quickly down the names. 'I'll send out the letter to the other quarries today.'

'Do that. The sooner the other men hear that we are not reinstating everyone, they'll know that they are lucky to have a job themselves.'

Oakley hid a groan.

Left alone, almost half a bottle of the wine remaining, Tommy relaxed back in the comfortable chair. His feet on the corner of the desk, he sipped from the glass. Today had been good. There had been only the briefest encounter with Henrietta and he had kept the upper hand in that. The brat, young Edward, had not been seen or heard; his childish shrieks had not infiltrated the house from the garden. Was there anything more likely to set teeth on edge than the racket a child made? What had happened to the notion that children should be seen and not heard? Recognising that this train of thought would ruin his equilibrium, he changed tack. The lock-out was virtually over. And what better news could there be, but that? Within days he would be in a position to send a hundred of the Irish papists to Ruby to get the project well and truly underway. The sooner they were digging slate, the sooner his profits would multiply and the reward would be his alone.

Lifting the glass to his mouth, he savoured the tingle of the wine as it trickled over his tongue. He tried to equate the tang of the champagne with the subtle fragrance of Lady Isabelle's perfume on her warm skin. But it was too different; both were heady, intoxicating, but distinctly individual.

The recent nights he had spent with Lady Isabelle had

been wonderful, so much so that this morning he had been reluctant to leave her company. At first light she had brushed his lovemaking away with a wave of her lovely pale hand, mentioning the return of her husband from his sojourn, killing wild pigs in Germany. But he knew that her dismissal had been faked, that she craved another meeting with him as much as he did with her. The Lady protests a little too often and so charmingly how could it be anything but an act of play? Love foreplay?

If he were a betting man, he'd gamble a hundred guineas that he would be back in her London house before the end of the following week. If her husband's return prevented that, then they could meet at a hotel. In the longer term, should Isabelle's husband decide to spend more time at his home, Hollybeck House, then he would purchase a convenient townhouse where they could be together without prying eyes being any the wiser.

At this delicious thought, Tommy laughed out loud. Still smiling, he raised the glass to his mouth again. Not even Henrietta would need to know that he had set himself up with a comfortable *nest* in the city.

* * *

Amos Ridley, the ancient book peddler, had arrived at Corn Cottage a short time after supper bringing Joe Thackeray's *The Adventures of Philip.*

Sitting before the meagre fire in his old but clean work clothes, Joe held the book in his hand, resisting the temptation to open it and read the first paragraph or two. It wasn't the first time that Amos had brought him a Thackeray novel. He'd read and reread *Vanity Fair* and *The History of Pendennis.* This newest book had come at a bad time financially, which was a pity.

Amos could see how appealing Joe found the book by the way he was fingering the brown cloth cover.

Joe handed the volume back to Amos. 'It looks

interesting. Perhaps when everything's settled at the Garddryn ...'

Amos pushed the book back into Joe's hand. 'Take it now and pay me when you can.'

Frowning, Joe said 'I couldn't do that, Amos. I'm not a man to get into debt.' He gave a weak smile. 'Not even for Mr Thackeray's newest book.'

A light knock on the back door ended the discussion.

Emily, leafing through a booklet that Amos had given her, jumped in surprise. 'Who on earth can that be coming to the back of the house?'

Joe was out of his chair, striding towards the kitchen door, before she had finished the question.

Good manners forbade Amos to remain present if visitors called. But he was disappointed not to have the opportunity to spend an hour or so with Joe. His company was a rare treat. Wheezing, the old man bent to the small stack of books he'd piled at his feet and he started to pack the volumes into his old leather bag.

Mindful of the rheumatics in his joints, he pushed himself up off the seat. Early rickets had bowed his legs and his old moleskin breeches failed to hide the curvature of the old bones as he stood. Giving a short grunt, he pulled his old cape-coat off the back of the chair.

Joe came back into the room with Woody Pritchard in tow.

Woody, looking slightly abashed, tipped his hat towards Emily. 'Sorry if I startled you, Mrs Standish.'

Amos shrugged into his coat. 'I'll leave you in peace.'

Joe put a hand on the old man's coat sleeve. 'Don't go, Amos. Your counsel will be useful.'

Joe's eyes flicked to Emily. 'Woody says there are several men coming here to talk about what's to be done, now so many men have returned to the Garddryn.'

Amos pulled off his coat. 'If you're sure that I can be of help, I'll stay.'

Taking the garment, Joe draped it over the back of a chair.

Amos sighed as he sat down. At least he would be comfortable for a while longer. His bones needed more than half-an-hour to recover from the walk to Corn Cottage from his own neck of the woods.

Joe moving a newspaper off a chair, said 'Park yourself, Woody, you make the place look untidy.'

Unaccustomed to visiting, Woody was sorry that he had arrived before the others.

Joe looked about for somewhere to dump the bag and paper and then placed both articles on the corner of the dresser.

'Emily,' he said disturbing her from a rare moment of relaxation, 'would you put the kettle to the fire. The men are sure to want a brew.'

'It'll have to be without milk,' she said, rising out of the chair. Abandoning the booklet on the table, she left it open at a picture of the Queen at her Scottish residence.

Going to the fireplace she lifted the kettle from the ashy hearth. As she passed the table the movement of air flipped the page over, revealing a picture of Victoria feeding several dogs with morsels of cake. Victoria was laughing like a young girl.

Joe touched Emily's arm. 'Don't worry about the milk, lass. The chaps will be used to tea without it by now.'

She dragged her eyes off the picture. 'There's no milk shortage for some folk to worry about.'

Never before had she thought of the monarch with anything other than affection and loyalty. Discontented, she went to the cold scullery. The lean-to was in darkness but for blue starlight coming through the small window. An old fashioned candlestick was kept at the side of the shallow sink; after lighting the stub, she dipped the end of the hot Lucifer in water before discarding it.

'Who in their right mind would feed cake to dogs?' she

muttered. 'A wanton waste, whilst Garddryn children are going hungry.'

Disgruntled, she lifted the bucket and poured icy cold water into the kettle.

An image of Tommy came to her and she sighed sadly. There was only one person to blame for the children going hungry and that was her own son.

Cheerless, she put the lid on the kettle and went back into the living room. At the table she glanced at the booklet but she had little interest in it now.

Boots grated on the slate paving in the backyard. Joe went out to the scullery to open the door. Dick Lord and Fergus Holmes were there and Joe brought them into the kitchen-cum-parlour. The door was left ajar for the others.

The room was soon hazed with pipe smoke.

Emily had made tea in two batches, the teapot only held four cups. Several times she made her apologies for the lack of milk.

Taking a mug from her, Fergus smiled. 'I'm beginning to enjoy tea better without, which is good, seeing as we haven't had a drop for the past month.'

Woody Pritchard, feeling less nervous, started a tirade against Horas Jones. 'He's a bloody traitor, sneaking back to work like that,' he said, full of righteous indignation. 'None of his family will set foot in our house after this. It's a disgrace. They should be ostracised by everyone in the village. If any of my family so much as speaks to Horas and his ilk, they'll get tanned arses. If the traitors have the brass neck to come to chapel on Sunday, they'll get short shift from everyone there, the minister included.

I just hope to God that I meet the bugger out after dark. He'll know about it then. I'd like to break his bloody traitorous neck.'

Dick Lord nodded in agreement throughout Woody's rant.

Frowning, working himself up, Dick said 'You're not the

only one. I'd like to snap his blasted legs first and leave his neck till later.'

Woody nudged Dick in the ribs. 'We could do him over tonight. Wait for the bastard to come out of the Garddryn gates and then let him pay for what he's done.'

Joe understood Horas's reasons for going back; what sane man could ignore his children's cries of hunger? But he had sympathy for these men also. They had been locked out of their workplace. Three of their comrades had been killed at the quarry gates. When they were allowed to work they endured appalling conditions, for long hours, and all for a pittance. A fair day's pay for a fair day's work, that's all they wanted. But because of Horas and a few like him, they had lost the chance of achieving that on this occasion.

Joe shouted above the racket. 'It's only natural to feel angry, especially after everything we have been through. But this idea of retribution will only bring calamity down on the lot of us. Stop looking back and start going forward. What we have to decide is what's to be done *now*?'

Woody glared. 'It's all right you saying that, but the traitors will have to be dealt with at some point.'

Joe brushed this comment aside. 'That's for a later dis- cussion. We must remember that whatever happens, even if we go back tomorrow, all is not lost. We still have the opportunity to create a union. When the men are tied to a union they will not be allowed to break strikes. Lock-outs will be a thing of the past.'

Joe glanced at the disillusioned faces. 'Blacklists and victimisation, that's our next battle to fight at the Garddryn. Oakley and his mob will have the name of every man that went to a meeting, organised funds or played in a brass band to raise money. He'll have thought of a way to keep those men out of the Garddryn and every other quarry in the district.'

Joe looked to Tom Hughes who had organised music and

245

poetry sessions in the makeshift caban in the village to collect funds.

Lowering his voice, his eyes going from one man to another, he said 'Our strength as working men lies in a union, a united society for quarrymen. When we accomplish that, the most strenuous efforts put up by management to oust, torture, victimise and kill us will be in vain. With the strength of a union we'll be nigh on invincible.'

Fergus Holmes was smoking his pipe, his back against the kitchen wall, his feet planted firmly on the slate floor. 'We are with you on that, Joe. But we can't forget about the buggers that went back before anything was decided between us all. Woody's right; those men are traitors and should get their comeuppance.'

Joe wondered if he could really hope to protect Horas. Patiently and calmly, he said 'Fergus, for now let's concentrate on what we can do to strengthen our position. Firstly, does anyone know how many men are now at work?'

Tom Hughes, a team leader, twice widowed, was thinner now than when the lock-out began. His coat hung from his shoulders as though it had been made for a larger man. In two months he'd aged by ten years. Tom had earned the respect of the men at the quarry, unflappable, precise, a hard worker.

Matter-of-factly, he said 'There's about fifty or so, including Tommy Standish who returned to his home today.'

Emily's head snapped up. 'Tommy's back?'

Tom glanced towards Emily and he wondered how she felt about her son. The other womenfolk in the village were probably treating her badly because of the family tie. He suspected that she got a hard time from most of them. Whatever everyone said about Tommy and his rotten character, he was still her son.

Out of respect for her motherhood, Tom answered kindly, 'He came back this very morning. He hasn't been seen at the quarry. Oakley went up to the big house for a while and then he went back to the office.'

Joe knocked cold ash out of the bowl of his pipe into the hearth. 'Your intelligence is pretty good, Tom.'

Tom smiled. 'The news comes from Sam Oakley. He was at the Half-Way earlier. A few days ago Sam came to the Garddryn office to beg his Pa to send a hundred men to Ruby to start digging. Oakley promised to talk to Tommy Standish about it when he called at Plas Mawr. Sam is spending tonight at home with his family and riding back to Ruby tomorrow. I'm meeting him up on the high road tomorrow morning to get an account of what's going on.'

Thoughtful, Joe filled his pipe. 'So Sam's still loyal to the cause even though he's promoted to managing Ruby.'

'Yes, but he's not so daft as to think that he'll be kept on as soon as things start to happen there. Sam's no fool. He knows he hasn't got the brains to make a manager. He can't really understand why the master wanted him at Ruby in the first place.'

Joe clicked his tongue. 'Whatever the reason, it'll be for the benefit of Tommy, not Sam, that's for sure.'

Woody frowned. 'It'll be for the benefit of Oakley more than likely.'

Ignoring the remark, Joe glanced at Tom. 'What time you meeting Sam?'

'About eight o'clock.'

'Good. So tomorrow morning at ten o'clock we'll have a meeting on the green. With luck, we'll have information for the men. We can then decide what's to be done.'

Standing at the back of the room, Arfon Craven was sceptical. 'It's not possible to get all of the men there. Too many of them live so far away.'

Joe wasn't surprised by Arfon. He was a nice chap but not the brightest. Joe's explanation was simple. 'We have had this problem before and we managed to get a good crowd together. It's just a case of you men going about the village

247

and telling as many people as possible. Those men go further afield to tell more, and so on. We can cover a lot of ground working as a team.'

There was little to discuss after that and the men started to melt away into the night. Amos trundled off in the company of Dick Lord and Fergus Holmes. Although Amos hadn't contributed anything to the meeting, Joe was aware that the hour or two that he had sat had given the ancient bookseller time to gather his strength for his walk back to his village. No doubt he'd stop at the Half-Way for a refresher before ambling home.

Tom Hughes was the last to leave. For no reason other than the night was warm and dark, Joe stood in the small garden enjoying the coolness and the fragrance of night-scented stocks on the still air. Tom's footsteps were evident for some time but when he was far enough away from the cottage that his steps were hardly perceptible, Joe heard another set of footfalls, clandestinely keeping to the soft verge.

Leaving the garden quietly, Joe trailed the dark shadow walking ahead. Dismissing the idea that a footpad followed Tom, he came to the conclusion that it was Corn Cottage that was being watched. The only people interested in the comings and goings of Corn Cottage would be the quarry steward, Oakley or Tommy Standish.

Long minutes later, Joe came near to the house where Tom rented a room. Tom entered the low-roofed stone cottage. Joe saw a light as the door opened. As it closed the cottage melted into the darkness again. Although the light was brief, Joe got a glimpse of a man stepping into the shadows to watch the building. Shielded by an open porch, Joe patiently watched the watcher.

The lane was quiet, no living thing passed but a cat, the animal paused to spray a doorway before moving stealthily on. The stink caught at the back of Joe's nostrils and he tasted the tang of tomcat urine.

Ahead, a footstep crunched on grit. Joe sensitive to the night sounds tensed. In the near distance a nightjar called. Looking to the tall trees behind the cottages, he saw the bird, silhouetted against the ink black sky. A light breeze fluttered the dry leaves of the rambling rose growing over the porch and the stems of the nearby hollyhocks quivered. The fragrance of the blooms was lost to the overpowering stink of cat.

Footfalls, hard leather soles on sun baked earth, came close.

Joe stood in the shade, as a darker shadow fell across his path, his arm snaked out and he grabbed the interloper. Held firmly, the man wheezed for air. Roughly, Joe hauled him to the next cottage, to a curtain-less window, lit with the flame of a single candle. In the meagre light he recognised the stalker at once.

'Rees Roberts,' he hissed. 'What the devil do you think you're doing?' He shook the steward violently.

Caught off balance, Roberts staggered. Spluttering, he shouted 'Let go.'

Joe tightened his grip. 'I'll let go when you tell me what the bloody hell you think you're playing at.' Joe shook him again.

With hardly enough air to breath, Roberts gasped, 'Ask your son, if you really want to know.'

'Our Tommy, what's that bugger got to do with it?' Joe snarled.

Roberts gave a choking cough. 'He wants an account of all unlawful assembly.'

Doors nearby began to open. Occupants dressed for their beds, held candlesticks aloft.

Someone called out, 'What's the racket?'

From an open window an old lady shouted contemptuously, 'It is only two drunks fighting.'

'Let them leather each other. I'm away back to me bed.' A door closed.

A small dormer window set in the roof was thrown open and a baby's cries shrieked into the night. An angry woman called down, 'Now look what you've done, woken our Mary. It'll take half the night to settle her.'

Joe glanced up but made no comment. Giving Roberts a shove with his boot, he grunted.

Caught off balance, the steward fell with a dull thud into a flowerbed.

Hauling him away from the hollyhocks, Joe hissed near the steward's ear. 'I'll find you tomorrow and you'll tell me everything if it's the last thing you bloody do.'

Scowling, Rees Roberts retreated. Walking at a fast pace he trotted through the village.

Seething, Joe made his way back to Corn Cottage.

The following morning Joe rose early and donned grey trousers and old white shirt, frayed at the neck and cuffs over his combinations. Grey hand-knitted socks were the first to hand and although too warm for the weather, he pulled them on. Aware that Emily would say something about it later.

His boots were beside the fender where he had left them on coming in last night. Dark mud and short blades of cut grass were caked where the uppers met the soles. Sitting in the fireside chair, he slipped his feet into them and tied the worn laces.

After resurrecting the fire, he put the kettle to it.

In the scullery he doused his face with cold water and then went out to the privy.

Opening the back door onto the yard he was met with the gentle ripple of the mountain stream, a dry weather sound. On wet days it was a torrent, hurtling over the hidden and half submerged rocks. The privy was shaded by the tall trees growing on the opposite bank. Going towards the small wooden building, he left the warm bright sunshine for the green, dappled light.

On his return to the kitchen he made a quick brew and

drank half a mug of the hot tea. Too restless to settle, the encounter with Rees Roberts not far from his thoughts, he collected the swill bucket kept at the back door and went to release the two pigs.

Jake and his mate came out of the sty at their usual break neck speed, throwing the door wide. Joe had scattered the contents of the bucket, last night's vegetable parings and a few old apples, before freeing the pair. Fortunately, neither pig took a blind bit of notice of him; going straight to the food they buried their snouts. Whilst he made it safely back to the gate.

The pigs were entertaining, and standing with his elbows on the ancient stone wall he watched them for a few moments, amused by Jake's atrocious manners towards his only slightly daintier mate. The sow presented her stern and a swift glance told him that there would be piglets after all. It had looked like a barren year. Cheered by this, he watched the sow chew an apple.

The morning sun was warm on the top of his head. Rolling up his shirt sleeves, he felt the sun's rays penetrating the thick hairs on his lower arms. Chuckling, he watched Jake try to pinch an apple off his mate and get a nip on his slobbery jowl. Ructions looked to follow and picking up the bucket, he left them to it.

The hens were penned closer to the cottage and had been for the last month. The risk of losing them to someone's pot had been too great. The village harboured many hungry families.

Walking through the lush grass, speckled with dandelions and daisies, his thoughts were with the meeting that would take place later on the village green. After being out of work for weeks, he wondered what chance there was of going back today or tomorrow.

This thought brought him to the fierce encounter he'd had last night. That Corn Cottage was watched was disturbing. It could only be for one reason and that was a *blacklist.* If Tommy was keeping one, and it looked very much as though he was doing so, he reckoned that he would be on it. Unlawful assembly had been quoted to him last night. It had got his ire up so much he came close to thumping the living daylights out of Rees Roberts.

Near to the henhouse, he took a bag of sunflower seeds from his old coat pocket. Opening the wooden framed chicken-wire gate of their small run, he heard the shuffling in the henhouse as the birds anticipated the lifting of the wooden trap door. One by one they jumped through the aperture, squawking and ruffling their feathers, strutting like vicars' irritated wives.

When the last of the birds were out, clucking over invisible morsels in the dry dirt, he opened the bag and threw seeds to them. With his arms resting on the fence, he waited until the brown feathered hens had taken most; the wild birds would be down in seconds to steal from the dozy creatures.

Watching the hens pecking the dirt with their gaudy beaks, he weighed the problem of the *blacklist.* If it existed, and he was on it, there would be no work at the Garddryn for him. It made him hot under the collar, clammy beneath his shirt, to think of it. What would he do? And if he was on a list, did that mean that Frank was also? Two men of the family out of work would be a catastrophe. No other quarry would take them. They could be forced to go to Anglesey to the copper works, the abscess on Wales to rival Hades.

His mind flashed to the other Frank, his old mate in the Galloway, still a young man in memory.

'What would Frank think of all this? Would he think me a fool for supporting the idea of a *union*?' he asked the hens, scratching in the dry mud.

Sighing, he pulled himself away from the fence. The day and the inevitable outcome had to be faced. Thoughtful, he went to open the henhouse to collect the night's harvest of eggs. Three perfect eggs lay in the wheat straw; picking them up, one still warm, he decided to boil it for Emily's breakfast. He'd cook it, before she had a chance to say she'd save it to take to Maisy's to sell. It had been weeks since she'd enjoyed a fresh egg; it would be a treat.

Locking the henhouse, the eggs safe in his pocket, he collected the pig bucket from the top of the wall where he'd left it balanced between two upright coping stones. Accompanied by the rattle of the handle, he strode through the long grass making his way back to the cottage, rehearsing a conversation he meant to have with Emily.

She'd be furious to discover that their home was watched; when she learned that it was on Tommy's orders, she would be murderous.

Coming into the house, he shed his dirty boots and carried them to the back door, dropping them on the slate step, leaving the bucket beside them. Taking the eggs from his pocket, he washed them in the scullery sink before placing them in a bowl on the table.

Emily was moving about in their bedroom. A moment later she appeared in the kitchen, her face soft from sleep.

Tying a white apron over her moss-green skirt, she yawned. 'Joe, you were out of the house early.'

He glanced at the clock on the mantel. 'I couldn't sleep.'

Seeing the eggs, she smiled. 'The hens are doing well. I thought this heat might put them off laying.'

'It won't last.'

She smiled. 'What the heat or the eggs?'

'The heat, it looks like rain is brewing out to sea.'

Emily sighed. 'Well, we've had a week of sunshine. The weather was beginning to feel a bit foreign.' She glanced through the small window to the yard. 'It would have been nice to get a bit more washing done before the weather broke. I was thinking of washing the blankets.'

He kissed her cheek. 'There are more important things to face today.'

'Aye, I know. I was just putting off thinking of our Tommy.

253

I should go to his house and see him today, even if it's only to give him a piece of my mind.'

'Emily, you can decide what to do when I've told you summat else.'

'Oh Joe, don't tell me he's been up to more mischief.'

A sigh escaped Joe. 'I'm afraid so.'

'What is it this time?'

Emily listened to Joe's explanation and as he came to the end of the tale of Rees Roberts and his late night excursion, her face was stern with anger.

An hour, later a hundred men gathered on the green. At the forefront stood Rees Roberts, the steward. Beside him was the minister from Bethesda chapel. Twm Tomos, president of the caban, stood a pace behind them.

Rees Roberts was enjoying a moment of self-glory, standing with his legs apart and his great spade like hands drawn into fists at his side, he looked ready to take any one of the men in the crowd on. It was obvious by the size of his belly bulging over his wide belt that the famine that visited almost every house in Garddryn village had failed to find the Roberts household.

For no other reason than Roberts stepped forward first, he got the proceedings off to a start. It took less than a minute for it to become clear to the men that Roberts proposed to use the meeting to deliver a rant about men and their responsibilities.

Listening to the diatribe the men grew restless and from the centre of the crowd a voice split the air. 'Let Twm Tomos speak for us.'

'Come on, Twm, knock the bugger Roberts off his pedestal; he's only talking rubbish.'

Twm had lost weight, beyond thin, he was emaciated. The flesh on his face had a yellow tinge and had thinned; it no longer fitted the bone structure. His old work coat and trousers drooped from his slight frame. Looking absent-minded, he stood for a moment as though wondering where to begin. He started blandly, his usual gift for oratory deserting him as he faced the crowd. 'Garddryn quarrymen, I'm sure you can find a better man than I to help you in your search for an answer.'

Many quarriers looked from one to another in bewilderment, whilst others waited for the president of their caban to warm to his task and set the morning air ringing with his lyrical speech, wisdom and wit.

Twm's voice was weak. As he tried to raise it for all to hear, it cracked. 'I'm at a loss to advise you on such an important matter. I am probably as confused as any one of you ...'

Twm staggered, two men standing near caught him before he collapsed to the ground. Laying him down carefully, one of the men loosened his shirt collar and belt.

Flustered, the chapel minister waved a blue handkerchief over the fallen man's face. 'Let him have some air.'

Twm coughed, choking.

The minister looked to the crowd, shouting, 'We need a doctor to see to the poor man. Could someone fetch the surgeon?'

Twm caught hold of the minister's coat sleeve. His voice barely a whisper, he said, 'No doctor. I'll recover in a moment.'

Speculation in the crowd was rife and most believed that Twm was near starvation. Someone said that he had been poorly of late but there wasn't a shilling in the house to pay the doctor.

Twm took several minutes to recover. When he was able to sit up, he asked those close by to fetch Joe Standish to him.

Joe was shocked by Twm's colour; he was as pale and as yellow as a mending bruise.

Hunkering down, Joe said 'What can I do for you, Twm?'

The sick man's voice was weak. 'Speak to the men, Joe. You understand the matter better than most. Advise them.

Tell them what to do.' Coughing again, he held his midriff, wincing with pain.

'I don't think they'll listen to me, Twm. I'm Tommy's father. It would be better if I'd fathered King Herod, than the bugger I foisted on the world.'

What passed as a smile came to Twm's dry lips. 'You'll see Joe. They'll listen. You have the men's respect. Take the burden from me, Joe. I'll rest easier knowing that it's in your hands.'

Joe had a premonition that this would be the last time he'd have the privilege of being with Twm Tomos. That the man was dying was obvious. A great sadness swept through him. What a terrible loss Twm's intelligence, wit and laughter would be.

He touched the sick man's hand. 'If it helps, of course, I'll talk to the buggers.'

A stretcher was brought from the doctor's house and three men lifted Twm onto it and carried him to his home.

The minister who had heard Twm's request came alongside Joe. 'Mr Standish, before you speak to the men would you allow me to have a few words. Everyone will be concerned for Twm?'

'Good idea.'

Facing the crowd the minister raised his voice. 'Twm Tomos has been taken home. The man is obviously not well. I will call on him when I leave here and leave a report at the Half-Way of his state of health. Before he went home, Twm asked Mr Standish to speak to you. Twm holds Joe Standish in the highest regard and trusts him to help you to come to a decision with regard to the quarry.'

Turning to Joe, the minister smiled.

Joe's naturally powerful voice reached all in the crowd. 'We have a decision to make. We started this battle because management expected us to work a full day on Saturday, when traditionally Saturday has been a half-day. There are many other bones of contention between management and the workers, not least the dangerous working conditions at the Garddryn. I could go on all day spouting about *piss poor pay*, the lack of a hospital, etcetera. But these are issues we must come back to at another time.' His voice rose, 'These problems cannot be ignored and will not be ignored.'

The men cheered.

Someone shouted, 'You tell 'em, Joe. Stop the buggers exploiting us quarrymen.'

Joe shouted over the noise, 'The Garddryn quarrymen need the protection of a society, a quarryman's union. And they need it now more than ever. We have bad management, bad work practises and poor pay. Help for the injured is virtually non-existent at the Garddryn.'

His anger bubbled for those comrades lost. He bawled, 'No more lies penned on death certificates. If a man falls, let the doctor state that he fell, and not that he died from pneumonia in his bed a week later.'

Rees Roberts face was red with anger. A thick vein, like a worm under his skin, throbbed to the fast beat of his heart.

The steward's anger was obvious. As Joe's words were the cause of it, the men cheered him. It took courage to shout about the disgrace of the certificates.

Joe raised his arms for silence. The tone of his voice changed from angry to practical.

'These are discussion for the near future. Today we have a different agenda. We all know the score, three dozen men have returned to work...'

His words were drowned by angry shouts. 'Traitorous bastards, they've sold our bloody souls.'

Several more voices joined the racket and Joe paused until they quietened.

'Many of those men had children starving at home.' Joe's voice reached to the back of the crowd and beyond. 'If you want to blame somebody, blame Tommy Standish.'

With the name of his son surfacing and the culpability put squarely where it belonged, Joe saw his chance of ever getting back into the quarry, as finally lost. Now he had nothing to lose, he put his soul into uniting the men.

'Three dozen have returned; everyday the trickle of men showing up for work increases. Like it or not, because these men have returned they have accepted the Saturday extra hours, accepted the conditions and the poor rate of pay. They have accepted this on your behalf. With men going back, how long can the rest of you stay out? What voice do you have on the outside, when work goes on inside? A hundred men have been dragged into your jobs. A hundred men are needed at Ruby and I have it on good authority that the Irish tinkers are leaving next week for Ruby. That could mean that another hundred are coming across the water at this very moment to fill Garddryn vacancies.'

This was news to them and they looked from one to another for confirmation.

Joe dragged their attention back. 'Forty days with no work. Forty nights lying in bed worrying about it. Make this day the last. Go back and reclaim your livelihoods. When we are strong again, we will fight for the justice we deserve. Together, we'll fight from a strong base, with a quarryman's society behind us.'

The air drummed with their cheers.

Joe shouted, 'Who says aye for a union?'

Their roar reverberated on the mountainside, echoing in the labyrinths of galleries in the Garddryn.

Joe didn't need to glance at Rees Roberts to see that he was fuming, hatred oozing from the man.

The following day, Joe rose at five o'clock. Dressing in his clean work clothes, he wondered why he was bothering, he didn't really expect to be allowed past the Garddryn gates. When he was ready, he roused Frank. After a quick breakfast of porridge, they left the cottage.

There was an air of a holiday, a celebration amongst the men they met en route to the quarry. They were carrying newly oiled tools and their hobnailed boots were shiny with boot black.

Oakley and Rees Roberts were waiting at the gates. Roberts had a sheet of dirty paper in his hand and before each man drew near, he scrutinised his face, checking his list before letting him in.

Twenty four were turned back.

When it came to Joe's turn, there was a sour sick feeling deep in his gut. Reaching the metal gates he refused to let his eyes be drawn to Oakley or the steward. As he passed under the decorative arch, he expected to be hauled out, clouted and banished from the property.

Rees Roberts had his orders to let Frank and Joe through. It went against the grain to accept the order but, as it came from Tommy Standish, he was forced to obey.

Astonished, he never believed that they would be let through, Frank left his father and made his way to the dressing sheds.

With a tamping rod in the crook of his arm, Joe went to find his team beginning work on Jericho. In his pockets were a bag of Bickford fuses, a small sack of explosive, and a box of Lucifers. More than anything he was looking forward to getting a loud bang out of the rock today. He'd set the Garddryn Quarry office windows quivering, if it was the last thing he did.

Reaching Jericho, he saw his team gathered on the floor of the gallery inspecting a good size *bargain*. They looked up at the sound of his voice and smiled a welcome.

Tudor Williams pointed skyward and Joe looked up to the dark grey clouds threatening rain.

Joe smiled at the irony of it. The weeks that they had been forced out of work the weather had been magnificent, best in living memory, on the day the quarriers returned to the Garddryn, the skies cried.

Looking down to the team, Joe shouted, 'Everything's back to normal then. We've got the rotten rain. Oakley's on the warpath. Rees Roberts is slithering around like the snake that he is.' He grinned. 'Welcome back.'

The day was like any other. Hardly any reference was made about the lock-out. Four Irish tinkers were sporting black eyes and sore jaws before dusk.

It was late in the day, on the last trip to the cabanod, high up on the mountain, that Joe heard the news of Twm Tomos. The poor man had failed to awaken this morning.

On hearing it, Joe came close to tears. Walking out of the cabanod without his tea, he took himself off to smoke his pipe. Climbing to the summit, he sat quietly, listening to the lilting lyrical voice of Twm in his head.

Emily spent the day anxiously. There was a certain relief in having Frank and Joe out from under her feet, but she half expected to see the pair at any moment. As the day drew on, she guessed that their names were spared the blacklist which was a small miracle.

When there was neither sight nor sound of the pair, she scrubbed the slate floor until there was no trace of a man's boots passing over it. Then she turned her attention to the small windows, polishing until the haze from pipe smoke was obliterated.

Late afternoon she prepared a stew of beans and salt pork; the meat was the last of the supply. When this was simmering gently over the fire, she sat beside the window to darn. Would there ever be a time when Joe would not have a hole in the heel of one of his socks, she wondered.

At six, she began to look out from the garden gate; at half-past she knew that Joe and Frank would be having a sup of ale in the Half-Way. The landlord would see his profits appearing again, now the men were back at work.

Returning to the kitchen, she put the kettle to the fire to make a brew.

CHAPTER TEN

A hundred Irish workers had been digging at Ruby Quarry for three months and to Tommy's chagrin had found no evidence that a large deposit of slate was buried beneath the deep, springy loam.

To add to his ill temper, although he had purchased a townhouse in Mayfair, Lady Isabelle had yet to visit there. She claimed that her husband, who was still residing at Hollybeck House, had become suspicious and was keeping a watchful eye upon her. She went as far as to say that she thought a firm of private detectives was following her.

Furious, the expenditure on house and furniture had been enormous, he had insisted that she call on him during his last visit but at the last minute she had made her excuses and refused to call.

Returning to Plas Mawr, leaving the Mayfair house in the capable hands of the new housekeeper and her recently employed staff, he had taken his frustration out on Henrietta and they argued bitterly.

The row centred on the amount of time Tommy absented himself from Plas Mawr, but it soon turned to Edward's new music teacher and the retired church deacon now living in the mansion. Henrietta, with tears of anger shining in her eyes, had complained that the two men were creating extra demands on the servants and monopolising young Edward's time.

Rudely, Tommy laughed and asked what she expected teachers to do, if it wasn't to monopolise a young student's hours. Henrietta, losing control, threw an expensive vase in his direction before she ran from the library to the sanctuary of her private sitting room. The incident creating more merriment for Tommy.

Left alone in the library, Tommy soon dismissed Henrietta from his thoughts. He had bigger problems than his wife's jealousy, concerning teachers, to deal with. Ruby Quarry was the priority. It was becoming evident that an outright failure of the quarry was imminent. The only option was to try and sell the worthless land, and the best way to do that, was to form a company. *The Quarry Lands Consortium* sprang to mind as a possible title for the organisation. It was imperative that he re-coup his losses and save face. In the future, he would put his entire energy into drawing money from the profits of the Garddryn. He would instruct Madoc, the solicitor, to create a company. Ruby could be sold as a going concern, as a neighbouring quarry to the massive Penrhyn Quarry. Advertising the property in the London papers should certainly create an interest amongst speculators. With luck, he could make a handsome profit and not a substantial loss, as looked likely at the moment. The sooner Ruby was sold the better. The last thing he needed was anyone to get wind that the land was barren of slate.

If the problem of Lady Isabelle was half as easy to solve, he'd consider himself a fortunate man, but Issy was a different dilemma entirely. For weeks now, he had listened to her aggravating excuses of why she couldn't visit him at his new town house in Mayfair. Jesus! Hadn't he gone to enough expense to create a *nest* for their brief encounters? The house had cost a king's ransom. The furnishings were the best that money could buy. Staffing the three storey house and finding servants that would exercise complete discretion, had been a nightmare.

Isabelle said that the problem lay with her husband; he had become suspicious of her excursions and she was now followed by a private detective. If this were so, should he invite her for a very private sojourn in Paris? Would such an exciting adventure arouse her interest? Or was Lady Isabelle using her husband as an excuse? There was only one way to find out.

Rising from the chair, he rang for his valet.

When the man appeared, Tommy gave him hurried instructions. 'Pack a portmanteau. I'm going back to London on the late train. Make arrangements for the brougham to be brought round to the front door. I have a call in Caernarvon to make before my departure. Oh! and put out the new black frockcoat and trousers, with a light grey shirt. I'll change before I depart.'

With a slight bow, John Wright stepped backwards out of the door, closing it quietly. The master had made no mention of needing him during his stay in London and it was with disappointment that the man climbed the stairs to Tommy's dressing room.

With the problem of his clothes and the brougham dealt with, Tommy opened the top drawer in his desk and pulled out the relevant papers for Madoc. Placing the legal documents into a leather bag, he closed the fastening, locking it with a tiny brass key.

If it was necessary he'd take the solicitor to London with him. Or, get him to join him there tomorrow. There'd be enough money in this venture to appease the solicitor for any inconvenience.

It was at the very last moment that Tommy boarded the Euston train. As he didn't have time to check the carriages for occupancy, he shared a carriage with two elderly gentlemen. Fortunately the corner seat next to the window was unoccupied and wedging his portmanteau beneath the seat, he settled down for the journey.

A whistle blew and a moment later the locomotive moved forward. Coming from under the canopy of the station, the train picked up speed, the metal wheels clacking on the rails. As it crossed the first set of points Tommy relaxed back in the seat. There was nothing now that he could do until the journey ended. In a strange way, it was liberating to cede control for the next few hours.

Daydreaming, he imagined the scene up ahead in the noisy locomotive, the stoker shovelling coal into the red-hot furnace, the driver looking out into the darkness, the cold air blowing on his face until his nose ran. Along the track, the signal men would be waiting in their solitary boxes for their puffing charge to make safe passage out of their domain.

Travel had changed with the coming of the railway. It was not so long ago that journeys were a nightmare that lasted for long periods of time. Now, at a whim, a person could travel a hundred, two hundred miles in a day. Immense progress had been made in his lifetime.

The train crossed points. The lights of a signal box rushed by the window and then there was impenetrable blackness. On the glass his reflection looked back at him.

Turning his eyes away, he looked to the empty seat opposite. The sway of the train was pleasantly soporific.

Dozing, he imagined the scenario of tomorrow's interview with Lady Isabelle's husband. Ignorant of the adulterous affair, Lord Harvey would talk proudly of his wife and her social commitments. The image that followed this domestic idyll was of Lady Isabelle sweeping into the room and hiding her surprise at seeing Tommy Standish there. Her expression changing suddenly, when it occurred to her that he had come to denounce her. The unfolding fantasy was interrupted by the train slowing for a signal.

The train built up speed again and they were passing through a residential area, the windows of the houses, flashes of light. Then there was nothing to see but his own reflection in the glass and the blackness beyond as the train journeyed through the rural miles between Crewe and Birmingham.

Tommy slept for the last part of the journey and woke with a start as the train came to a standstill at Euston Station. Half-asleep he fumbled for the portmanteau. Dragging it from beneath the carriage seat, he followed the two elderly gentlemen whom he had travelled with; neither had spoken a word to him or each other.

Alighting, Tommy walked with other passengers to Euston Arch fronting the station.

There were several hansoms waiting and choosing the nearest, he spoke briskly to the driver. 'Mayfair,' he said, following the direction with the address of his townhouse.

It was almost three o'clock on the following afternoon when Tommy walked along the pavement towards Hollybeck House, Lady Isabelle and Lord Harvey's Mansion. The grand house fronted onto Hyde Park.

At this time of the year the park was magnificent, the trees draped in shades of early autumn. The grass, still lush, was littered with brittle brown leaves. The trees overhanging the park fence had spilled leaves onto the street and small flurries of crackling flotsam scurried across the pavement in the light breeze, crunching under the soles of his shoes.

His mood was excellent. His temper in London was generally better when there was a distance between him and Henrietta. There were times at Plas Mawr when he would own to being somewhat fractious. The close proximity of family, ungrateful quarrymen and the thousand responsibilities of running a large estate and two quarries, plus his interests abroad, were likely to ruin anyone's equilibrium in his opinion. But today these worries were nearly two hundred miles distant and that was far enough away to put them from his mind. The chance that he may see Lady Isabelle was another reason for his light-heartedness.

Swinging his new Malacca cane, a jaunty spring to his step, Tommy trotted up the wide stone steps to the impressive front door of Hollybeck House. The paintwork of the dark green door was faultless, the brass adornments unmarred by a single finger mark.

Pressing his finger to the bell button, he listened for footsteps, but beyond the door was silence. It crossed his mind that Lord and Lady Harvey were abroad, leaving a skeleton staff in residence.

Anxious, he put his head closer to the paintwork and heard footsteps. To appear nonchalant, he turned his back to the door and looked out over the park. Touching his lavender necktie, he checked the diamond pin was still in place, an expensive frippery that he had purchased recently for himself. With one hand resting on the silver top of his cane, he pulled the hem of his skirted jacket straight.

As the door opened, he turned slowly to the footman. The man was clean shaven and his dark hair was tied back in a periwig style. Wearing a long skirted green coat with golden braids on the shoulders, and white knee breeches which accentuated his rather shapely calves, the man looked as though he had stepped from the previous century. Tommy was rather startled by the apparition. On his last visit, the servants' uniforms had been modern and nondescript.

The overlarge buckles on the man's shoes twinkled and Tommy's eyes dropped to the decorations. Hardly raising his glance, he said 'I have called to see Lord Harvey.'

The servant gave a deep bow from the waist. 'I'll see if he's receiving visitors, sir. Would you care to wait in the guestroom?'

Opening the door wide, he stood aside to permit Tommy to enter.

From a previous visit Tommy remembered the details of the grand hall and on this occasion he didn't stare at the modern and unusual décor but his eyes did stray to the beautiful silk wall covering. He was tempted to redecorate Plas Mawr with similar. The iridescent green of mother-of-pearl with embroidered exotic birds of paradise, the tail feathers scarlet and royal blue, was a masterstroke of the decorator's skill.

Before retreating to find his master, the footman led the guest to a side room.

Tommy was somewhat disappointed with the rather drab furnishing; the predominant colour was beige, the furniture was heavy and there was too much of it cluttering the available space. Was it meant as a startling contrast, he wondered? Rather like the cloister appearance of the entrance at Penrhyn Castle which opened onto the truly magnificent grand hall. But at Penrhyn the entrance was designed to accentuate the grandness and the immensity of the hall. Here, the hall had already been viewed.

Another idea came to him and it raised a smile. Perhaps after decorating and furnishing so elaborately there was no money left to attend to this room. His mother had a country motto for such circumstances, *kippers and curtains,* which he took to mean, that to pay for the new curtains it was necessary to dine on kippers yet again.

The sound of footsteps on the Italian marble came to him and Tommy ceased to study the drab wallpaper.

Entering the room, the footman bowed deeply. 'Lord Harvey would be pleased to see you, sir. He's in the orangery.'

Lord Harvey, a large man bordering on obese, was standing beside a spindly lemon tree, inspecting the rather puny single fruit. An overbearing man, a keen hunter and innate gambler, he rarely missed an important race meeting and would travel as far as France for equestrian sport.

From Lady Isabelle, Tommy had learned that her spouse was inclined to over-indulge in fine wines and insisted that only the best and most expensive food be presented at table. Aware of the man's reputation for enjoying an afternoon drink, Tommy wasn't surprised to see a glass in Lord Harvey's hand.

Turning from the lemon tree on seeing Tommy enter,

Lord Harvey raised the glass in a salute. 'Madeira, Standish?'

'Excellent,' he answered, matching the jovial tone of his host.

The footman hovered.

Turning, seeing the servant standing between the door and the table, Lord Harvey spoke stiffly, 'Squires, get the Madeira for Mr Standish and a refill for me whilst you're at it.'

Tommy was pleased to note that Lord Harvey's speech was slightly slurred, which suited his purposes exactly. Inebriated, his lordship's guard would be down and he would be more likely to discuss the curtailing of Lady Isabelle's social life.

The servant moved across to a cabinet and in virtual silence he filled two glasses from a decanter. Placing these onto a silver tray he crossed the room to Tommy.

Without acknowledging the man, Tommy took a glass and sipped the Madeira. It was excellent.

Downing what remained in his glass, Lord Harvey took the other from the tray.

His lordship's voice was overloud as he said, 'Fetch the decanter, Squires. Leave it on the table. We'll help ourselves. Get the butler to look out another bottle from the cellar; we are sure to need one.'

Lord Harvey winked at Tommy. 'What do you say, Standish? We'll need another, won't we?'

'Good idea, Lord Harvey. Another bottle seems an excellent idea.'

Tommy resolved to remain sober. When he had extracted the information he wanted, he would retreat to his club for a good dinner.

Lord Harvey pointed to the lemon tree. 'You know anything about foreign fruit trees?

Tommy said that he didn't, although the head gardener

at Plas Mawr had great success with peaches and apricots in the orangery there.

Lord Harvey sniffed. 'I'll have to sack my fellow if he can't do better than this.'

A thought came to him and his lordship smiled. 'Of course I could always send my man to your place in Wales. He might learn how to grow the exotics properly.'

Tommy took a sip from his glass. 'Good idea. You could come along too and bring your lovely wife with you. Henrietta would be delighted to entertain Lady Isabelle for a month. The air in North Wales is bracing, extremely healthy.'

Lord Harvey sat heavily on a pale blue brocade sofa, the delicate gilded legs looked dangerously inappropriate for his weight.

Tommy held his breath, expecting the whole frippery to collapse under the strain.

Settling himself, sitting with his legs apart, his belly protruding above and between, Lord Harvey burped loudly. Ignoring the indiscretion, he enquired, 'What's the hunting like?'

Never having mixed with the hunting fraternity, Tommy had no knowledge of the meets or the extent of the game. Lying convincingly, he said 'The hunting in the area is superb and there are plenty of meets. A week doesn't go by when the hounds are not out getting good exercise.'

A matching sofa was positioned opposite to the one that his lordship occupied. Lifting the skirt of his coat, Tommy sat upon it rather gingerly, suspecting that the furniture had been designed for the ladies' crinoline dresses.

Slightly cross eyed, Lord Harvey swallowed the contents of his glass before topping it up from the decanter. 'I've never visited Wales. Paris, Rome, Switzerland, those are my usual ports of call. I was recently in Germany, shooting pigs.'

Although Tommy was aware that Lady Isabelle had not shared his lordship's trip, she had slept with Tommy on

269

several occasions whilst Lord Harvey was away, he couldn't resist making a little mischief. 'Sounds like quite an adventure. Did you take your wife with you?'

Lord Harvey laughed. 'No! It'd be far too boring for her ladyship. Isabelle prefers being in London to anywhere.'

Inching his bulk to the edge of the sofa, Lord Harvey spoke in a conspiratorial fashion. 'I have no control over her. Isabelle does as she likes and dashes from one social engagement to another. She's forever wining and dining. Twice a week she's at the theatre, and if it's not the theatre, it's concerts and art galleries. I don't know how she finds the energy. She's never at home. Always busy, flitting from one place to another. This afternoon she's at a matinee of something or another. The little vixen is out every night of the week.'

As Lord Harvey prattled on, Tommy's ire rose. The traitorous hussy had told him a pack of lies. She had said she was never out and hardly allowed from her husband's sight. She went as far as to say that she was followed by a private detective. What poppycock! What brazen balderdash! The traitorous bitch!

Tapping the side of his thread-veined nose twice, Lord Harvey giggled drunkenly. 'I have my reasons for not minding that Isabelle gets out and about.'

Tommy's interest flamed.

Taking a slurp from the glass, his lordship burped. 'I have a little filly who I like to visit. A sweet little thing and only seventeen, with skin so perfect you could eat it. I love my little filly.' He hiccupped. 'Has a perfect little bottom, round and unblemished.'

Tommy's mind went to Lady Isabelle's derrière, also round and also perfect. Caned, the flesh took on a pink glow. The sexual interlude with her had been perfect, exciting and demanding. That she had lied to him, ended any feeling he had for her.

Lord Harvey was helping himself from the decanter. 'My

perfect filly is housed close by, so at a moment's notice I can pop around there for a little visit.' He touched the side of his nose again. 'Bet you'd like to take a look at my poppet?'

Malicious and wishing to wound Isabelle in any way that he could, Tommy said 'I would be honoured to meet your special friend. And of course, I would be extremely discreet.'

Tommy's glance went to his lordship. If the old sod believed that, he'd believe anything, the drunken sop. What a cracking bit of news this would be to fling into Lady Isabelle's face. How would she react when he told her that he had visited her husband's paramour and made love to the woman?

Hurriedly, Tommy rose from his seat. 'How far is it?'

Lord Harvey was slightly taken aback, as he had not truly meant to invite Standish. He eyed the young handsome man with drunken suspicion.

Obviously his lordship was trying to back-out and Tommy laughed. 'Oh, I understand, it was just a joke, there's no pretty filly.' Sitting again, he chuckled as though he found the whole thing highly amusing.

Offended, Lord Harvey rose from the low sofa with some difficulty. 'It's not a joke.

Come, I will take you. We can walk.'

Outdoors, the fresh air hit Lord Harvey and he staggered. Tommy took his arm to steady him.

Several minutes later, they were standing on the steps of an unimposing double storey house in a street bare of trees. At the first ring, the door was answered by a youth. The boy looked surprised to see visitors.

Tommy's first thought was that it was the boy's sister they had come to visit.

The youth stepped into the house and the door was closed. The boy's eyes darted between the two men.

Exhaling alcohol fumes into Tommy's face, Lord Harvey laughed. 'Didn't I tell you my filly had perfect skin? Turn around boy and show the master of the Garddryn Quarry your pert little arse.'

Tommy was thunderstruck. The revelation was the very last thing he expected. Neither in demeanour or character had Lord Harvey ever given a clue to his proclivity.

The boy's face flamed pink. 'Harvey, I wasn't expecting you.'

It was dusk when Tommy escorted Lord Harvey back to Hollybeck house.

Staggering drunk after a glass of port, Lord Harvey had disappeared with the boy and had been missing for awhile.

Left to his own devices in the drab sitting room, Tommy plotted.

The following day at around three o'clock, Tommy dressed fashionably in a knee length black coat and trousers, ivory shirt and grey silk necktie, walked towards Hollybeck House. He hadn't thought it worthwhile to call at Hollybeck earlier, as he expected that Lord Harvey would be sleeping off his debaucheries of the previous day.

A green-clad footman answered the door. On this occasion Tommy wasn't surprised by the man's eighteenth century attire or by the fleeting sight of a maidservant hurrying across the hall dressed in an outfit from the same century.

As he entered the house, Tommy waved away the footman's enquiries, saying stiffly and with authority, 'Take me to Lord Harvey.'

It was against the footman's better judgement to let a visitor pass without the rigmarole of announcement but as this particular caller appeared determined and authoritative, he lead Tommy at once to the library

His Lordship was alone. Dyspeptic, he was slouched in a brown leather chair beside a small fire. Sitting idly, his gaze, although directed at the large window overlooking the park, was unseeing. His appearance was dishevelled as though he had taken little trouble with his morning toilette, his dark grey coat and trousers were creased and wrinkled from sitting over long.

Tommy's unannounced arrival startled him and his naturally ruddy cheeks flushed with embarrassment. 'Tommy!'

Lord Harvey began to rise from his seat.

'Don't disturb yourself on my account, Lord Harvey,' he said gently.

Gratefully, the heavy man slumped back down. In a lacklustre voice, he asked, 'Would you like some refreshment?'

His eyes went to the small table close at hand to the jug of water and glass. 'I'm only drinking water today as I made a bit of a fool of myself yesterday.'

Taking a nearby seat, Tommy crossed one leg over the other. 'I would enjoy a small port.'

The footman gave a small bow before retreating.

As the door closed, Lord Harvey turned his morose face to Tommy. 'Why did you come? Not to commiserate on my thundering headache, I assume.'

Tommy looked slightly taken aback. 'I came to see how you are.'

Lord Harvey shook his head, his untidy hair flopping over his brow. 'I feel like death and I might just as well as die.' Tears misted his liverish eyes. 'If this scandal should get out, I would be ruined.'

Tommy's face was devoid of expression. 'You could be imprisoned.'

Unable to sleep beyond the early hours of the morning, thoughts of his ruin spinning round and round in his mind, Lord Harvey's nerves were near to breaking point. He snapped waspishly, 'Do you think that I don't know that?'

Tommy looked genuinely contrite and concerned. 'I'm sorry. I didn't mean to upset you further.'

The butler knocked softly on the door and entered

quietly. Carrying a small tray, he came alongside Tommy's chair and gave a slight bow. 'Your port, sir.'

Ignoring the servant, Tommy lifted the glass off the tray. He took a sip, then said appreciatively, 'I congratulate you on the quality of your port Lord Harvey; this is superb.'

Looking slightly nauseous, his lordship turned his eyes away from the glass.

The butler bowed to his master. 'Can I get something for you, sir?'

Lord Harvey's stomach turned and bile rose to his throat. 'No, you blasted well can't! Get out of here!' he snapped rudely.

Familiar with his lordship's temper, the butler retreated at once.

When the door had closed, Lord Harvey fixed Tommy with an ill tempered stare. 'What do you want? What brought you here today?'

Tommy looked astonished. 'Why, absolutely nothing but friendship.'

'Friendship? How can we be friends now that you know everything?' Leaning forward, head in his hands, Lord Harvey began to cry quietly.

Tommy remained silent until the man had recovered himself. He spoke gently, 'Why think of ruin? Please stop torturing yourself like this.'

Lord Harvey sniffed. 'I have put myself in a very precarious position. Our acquaintance is new; how am I to know that you will keep this unfortunate business to yourself?'

Tommy gave the man an appealing smile. 'Our friendship may be new but that does not mean to say that it is not true. I offer you my loyalty; what more can one man give to another?'

A weak smile passed over Lord Harvey's face and he sniffed again. 'I thank you for those kind words. I feel a little relieved by them. But all the same, in a day or two I will call on my friend and tell him our companionship cannot go on. It's the only thing that I can do.'

Tommy looked askance. 'Don't do that on my account. I beg of you, reconsider this hasty decision. I understand these things and take them with a pinch of salt. What another man does is no concern of mine. Gill's a good friend to you, why finish with him now?'

Tears filled Lord Harvey's eyes, spilling onto his thread-veined cheeks. 'Oh, it's impossible.'

Sounding sympathetic, Tommy said, 'Why shouldn't you have a particular friend? Two men sharing an alliance, what's so unusual about that? If Lady Isabelle remains none the wiser, what harm is done?'

'Lady Isabelle would not care who I spend time with. I hardly ever see my wife. She came home around two o'clock this morning and she was gone again by noon today.' Pulling a linen handkerchief out of his pocket, Lord Harvey blew his nose noisily.

Tommy found it hard to keep his face impassive with the knowledge that Lady Isabelle was out of the house until all hours. Obviously, the traitorous bitch had a new lover and was giving the man a great deal of her time, much more that she had bestowed on himself when his star was in the ascendancy.

Hiding his true feeling and sounding positively cheerful, Tommy rose. 'Now that I have seen for myself that you will make a complete recovery, I will leave you in peace.

Perhaps you will permit me to call in a day or two? We could dine together at the Reform or at any other place you would like to name.'

Lord Harvey eased his heavy bulk out of the chair and taking Tommy's hand, he clasped it tightly. 'You are a good friend, Tommy. Your visit has relieved me greatly. I feel so much better having had this conversation. Dining together is an excellent idea.' He laughed. 'In a day or two I will no doubt be back on the port, but perhaps I'll leave off the Madeira wine for a while.'

Tommy held onto the man's hand. 'Come Friday you'll be imbibing your favourite tipple again. You mark my words.'

Departing Hollybeck House, his Malacca cane tucked under his arm, Tommy crossed the street to Hyde Park. It was only necessary to walk a few yards along a narrow path bordered with gaudy dahlias before he came to a wooden bench that overlooked Lord Harvey's and Lady Isabelle's mansion. The seat was unoccupied, the park virtually devoid of pedestrians.

Sitting, crossing one leg over the other, the cane propped against his knee, an arm stretched across the back of the bench, he turned his head a little to view the dark green door.

The branches of a copper beech splayed above the bench, the autumn leaves rustling in the light breeze.

From the roadway came the sound of horses' hoofs and vehicles, the murmur of voices of the people walking on the pavement and from an open window the dreamy notes of a piano floated out.

Few people walked along the path and those that did ignored the solitary man who sat engrossed with his own thoughts. Only one small child took momentary interest in him, hanging back from a uniformed nanny to stop and stare. Then the child ran on. Her small red jacket and blue skirt, a rich flash of colour as she darted between the bright flowers.

For more than an hour he gazed fixedly at the door and windows of the house, for no other reason than it helped him to think and to plot revenge on Lady Isabelle. Dark thoughts circled in his mind and he made an effort to harness them, to consider his retribution coherently, the punishment to fit the crime. He would show her no mercy and teach her a lesson she would long remember. The fool of a husband would be the instrument he would wield to orchestrate her ladyship's fall from grace and financial ruin. Plotting his moves, pleased with the ideas that came to him, Tommy found it almost impossible not to act immediately but it was imperative that he remain impassive for at least two more days.

After Tommy's departure from the mansion, Lord Harvey, feeling immensely relieved, retreated to the quiet of his bedroom to sleep off the debilitating effect of the previous day.

Later he would visit Gill to explain the position. Although he dreaded the interview, it had to be faced. The boy wouldn't like giving up the house and the light attic rooms there. Gill was an aspiring artist of life figures. Lord Harvey had promised to pay for his first exhibition and the boy was working towards this goal by painting at every available moment. If he were to end the friendship, it would be necessary to see that the boy, who was very special to him, was financially secure for a while.

Within minutes of climbing between the crisp clean sheets of his bed, Lord Harvey fell into a deep sleep. His dreams were of Gill. The boy was painting at his easel, his long slender hands daubed with pale-blue oil paint ...

A few hours later when he awoke, his lordship was resolved to stay with Gill. Tommy Standish was the only person that knew of the relationship and he had promised faithfully not to divulge the secret. Climbing from his bed, feeling very much better than he had earlier, Lord Harvey rang for his valet. As soon as he was dressed, he would visit Gill.

Tommy shivered. The breeze had picked up and there was an edge to it now. There was a definite autumnal feel to the late afternoon. The smell of smoke from household fires was on the air. Now the light was failing, the leaves of the copper beech over the bench were darker, less attractive than when caught in the afternoon sunlight.

Rising, slightly stiff from sitting in the same position for too long, he took his cane and walked along the path to a gate which came out some way from the mansion. As he didn't wish to be discovered loitering near Hollybeck House if Isabelle made an appearance now.

From the pavement, he raised his cane to hail a passing hansom. Turning, the vehicle came alongside.

Tommy glanced at the driver as he boarded. 'Take me to the Reform on Pall Mall.'

Settling into the small interior, gloomy with the loss of daylight, he banished thoughts of Isabelle to concentrate fully on the evening ahead. He was meeting Madoc at the club for an early dinner. The solicitor had been occupied for the past two days making arrangements for the formation of the new company that would ultimately dispose of shares in Ruby Quarry. He almost laughed aloud as he thought of the interesting tale of drunken debauchery he had to tell the solicitor over the entrée.

Pall Mall was busy. It never failed to amaze him how many hansoms and other equipages besides pedestrians thronged the streets of London at this particular hour. His hansom was forced to make two changes of direction to avoid clogged junctions and Tommy arrived at the club slightly frustrated.

The solicitor was waiting for him in the library. Seeing him there sitting in a dark green leather chair, Tommy knew at once that Madoc had succeeded.

Rising, Madoc watched Tommy's approach.

'How was the journey?' Tommy asked as he shook the solicitor's hand.

'There were no problems.' Madoc picked up several papers lying on the low table. 'I came down on the first train of the day. The early start enabled me to formalise the arrangements for the new consortium this afternoon.'

Tommy smiled. 'Good. So everything is in order?'

'Absolutely, no problems whatsoever ...'

Tommy laid a hand on the solicitor's coat sleeve. 'Tell me everything over a drink. What'll you have?'

'A brandy, please.'

Tommy beckoned to a passing waiter. 'Bring us two large brandies.'

The manservant gave a swift bow. 'Yes, of course, Mr Standish, at once, sir.'

The two men sat in adjacent chairs, sinking into the soft leather.

Madoc handed the papers in his hand over to Tommy. 'I did everything as you instructed. The Quarry Lands Consortium, your new company, is now operational.'

The manservant brought the two brandies and the men fell silent as he placed them on the table.

As the waiter retreated, Madoc went on, 'Ruby Quarry is now ready to be sold to shareholders. You will keep ownership of the land, leasing it to the shareholders for a nominal price. The shareholders will have the rights to quarry the land. This paper,' he leaned forward and tapped the topmost sheet Tommy was holding, 'is your shareholding in Ruby Quarry. The share is the smallest, which will preclude you from contributing to any expenditure should the other shareholders decide to put in rail track and rolling stock or any other innovation. Your contribution would be nominal as the smallest shareholder.'

Tommy was impressed with progress. 'You've done remarkably well in the short time available. Well done, Madoc.'

The solicitor gave a self-effacing smile. 'We do our best to please.'

A manservant approached with two menus. 'Would you like to order dinner, sir?'

'Yes,' Tommy answered abruptly, 'we'll have the table d'hote and a bottle of the best claret.'

With the slightest nod of his head the man moved away.

Picking up his glass, Tommy sipped the mellow brandy.

Then smiling wickedly he said 'I already have the first shareholder.' His smile deepened. 'And he'll be the biggest of them too.'

'Oh, do I know the gentleman?'

'I don't think that you do, Madoc. But you soon will.'

'You make it sound like a mystery.'

'There's nothing at all mysterious about this particular man. In fact you could say I know everything about him.' Tommy smiled again.

The solicitor's eyebrows rose quizzically. 'I'm intrigued.'

Tommy rose. 'I'll tell you everything over dinner. Roast beef at the Reform is always excellent.'

Although Madoc laughed uproariously over Tommy's tale of Lord Harvey's drunken spree and the visit to the drab house on Pendon Street, he made a mental note to never allow Tommy Standish to discover a single thing about his own private life. The man was positively dangerous.

Dinner was a success and later the two men retired to Tommy's Mayfair house where over a post-dinner brandy, Tommy explained his disappointment that Ruby wasn't the viable quarry he had so wanted it to be. His disappointment was tempered with pleasure that he would make a great deal of money by selling shares. What he didn't explain to Madoc was his scheme to bring about the downfall of Lady Isabelle. As it involved shares in Ruby, Madoc might disapprove of him allowing his personal life to spill into his professional.

Tommy's next visit to Hollybeck House took place at the end of the week. As he crossed from the park to the mansion, on the first crisp clear autumnal day of the season, he saw Lady Isabelle alighting from a smart carriage. Hurrying across the road, Tommy was ready to take her hand as she stepped onto the pavement.

For a moment she didn't see him, her eyes were shaded by a wide hat the colour of ripe lemons. As her shoes touched the paving stones she looked from under the green feathers adorning the brim.

Her eyes darkened instantly. 'Tommy!'

There was searing malevolence in his voice. 'Lady Isabelle, I didn't expect to see you today. I hear you spend little of your time at home. I count myself fortunate to find you here. Your husband tells me that you roam at will and until all hours.' His eyes narrowed spitefully. 'It's a different tale than the one I heard from your own lips. I was led to believe that a private detective watches your every move and that is the reason you are so afraid to call at my new Mayfair home.'

She was afraid that he had come to denounce her to Lord Harvey. Her face paled as her heart began to race sickeningly. As much as she would have liked to drag her eyes from his face, she was compelled to stare into the dark pools of his pupils.

He smiled facetiously. 'Lord Harvey and I have become such friends during your absences. His lordship and I are dining at the Athenaeum tonight. There's no doubt that we'll find a great deal to talk about. The evening promises to be most interesting.' His smile deepened. 'There's a certain satisfaction in trading confidences with new friends. Discovering mutual interests and comparing notes is so entertaining. Yes, Lord Harvey and I have so very much to talk about. Wouldn't you say so, Lady Isabelle?'

Tommy's eyes were alive with mischief. 'Please let me escort you inside the house.'

Shocked by his revengeful manner, fearful what the next few moments might bring, Lady Isabelle scooped up the hem of her dark-yellow dress with trembling hands and walked as steadily as she could up the steps to her front door. Tommy had her elbow in the palm of his hand leading her forward possessively. His grip was a little harder than necessary. Lady Isabelle wished desperately to shake him off but was quite unable to do so.

At one time the gesture would have pleased her but Tommy's possessiveness and demanding invitations of recent weeks had irked her. The passion she had felt vanished under the constant claims for her attention.

With her heart beating fast, drumming loud in her ears, she wished more than ever that she had turned away from him on the night they had been introduced at Penrhyn Castle. Instead she had given herself to him at the first opportunity.

Glancing down at her, Tommy rang the bell. She couldn't fail to see the hatred in his eyes and her stomach churned in dread.

The footman opened the door and as Lady Isabelle stepped into the hall, Tommy relinquished his hold. Lady Isabelle was grateful. His touch had made her flesh quiver.

Her hands were still trembling as she took the green feather boa from around her jacket and handed it to the footman. Removing the yellow hat she caught sight of her face in the mirror and saw the drawn look. It seemed only a moment since she had adjusted the hat in another mirror. Her new lover playfully urging her to stay a little longer, pouting at her insistence that she really must leave for home. She had laughed at his boyish antics. Now she wondered if she would ever laugh again.

The footman took the hat from her trembling fingers and handed it to a maid.

'His Lordship is in the library, your Ladyship. He asked that you go to him upon your return home.' The servant dipped his head in a shallow bow.

Isabelle would have dearly loved to go to her private rooms and hide from the evil that had descended upon her. She glanced at Tommy and saw that he would not be swayed from his chosen path. His eyes spoke of retribution, not mercy.

She wondered if she dare leave him with her husband for just a few moments, whilst she changed from the new crinoline into something lighter. Although the support for the skirt was made of the lightest watch-spring metal it had become uncomfortably restrictive.

Tommy's glance convinced her that the threat he posed was far too serious to worry about the mere discomfort of a skirt and corset.

Isabelle's voice faltered as she spoke to the footman. 'I will take Mr Standish to the library, Squires. There is no need for you to trouble yourself.'

'Thank you, your Ladyship.' With a small bow the footman turned away to take his place again in the hall.

When the servant was out of earshot, Lady Isabelle pleaded, 'What is it that you want, Tommy?'

Tommy laughed. 'You know what I wanted.'

Lady Isabelle glanced sideways, betraying her nervousness in her dark eyes. 'That is hardly the point is it? I asked what you wanted now.'

Tommy sneered. 'I hardly know what I want myself. But I'm sure to think of something, your Ladyship.'

They were standing outside the library door, talking in heated whispers.

Lady Isabelle said, 'What have you to gain by ruining me?'

Tommy's hand was on the brass doorknob. 'Satisfaction,' he snapped.

'And what will that gain you?' She felt like adding, *you bastard*. But antagonising Tommy Standish would only make matters worse.

Feeling light-headed, Isabelle entered the library with Tommy following behind her.

His lordship was sitting in a leather chair, his bulk splayed across the width of the seat. He began to rise clumsily. Isabelle gestured for him to remain where he was.

Crossing to her husband, she kissed his brow. 'How are you?'

She turned briefly to Tommy and he saw the fake smile

on her lips. Then bending to her husband, she touched his lordship's arm. 'Look who I found on the doorstep. Tommy tells me that you and he are going to the Athenaeum to dine.'

Pleased to see his wife, Lord Harvey was jovial. 'Tommy, we'll have a drink here with Issy before we leave. We can get a hansom to the club. It's not worth getting the carriage out again for the short trip to Pall Mall.'

He turned to his wife. 'Ring for Kendal. Get him to bring up a bottle of champers.'

Lady Isabelle crossed to the bell-pull beside the stone fireplace.

Both men watching her.

Lord Harvey admiring the new addition to her wardrobe thought how lovely she looked in the dark yellow gown, which was exquisitely embroidered with green. Her jacket was of the same colour, but lightly padded and trimmed with shoulder epaulettes. It was cut short at the front to show off her trim waist, and at the back it came to a peak to accentuate the line of the crinoline.

The extravagant cost of such an outfit passed through his mind; the dressmaker must have charged a pretty penny for such a creation. No doubt there was a hat and shoes to match. A short sigh escaped him.

Catching the sound, Isabelle turned too him. 'Is everything all right?'

Lord Harvey gestured to the dress. 'I was just admiring the new frock, my love.'

For a moment Isabelle forgot the threat that Tommy posed, as she considered the trouble there would be when the dressmaker's extravagant fees came to her husband's notice. This yellow dress was not the only one she had ordered recently. There was a red and mauve in similar design.

The butler appeared and Lord Harvey gave the servant instructions. The man disappeared quickly.

It hadn't passed Tommy's notice that Isabelle was elegantly and expensively dressed. If he had read the signs correctly the financial situation in the household was already under strain. The lady did have very expensive tastes in décor and apparel. But his lordship wasn't averse to a flutter on the horses and there was talk that a pretty penny had been lost recently.

The champagne chilled from the cellar arrived and was served by Kendal the butler.

Isabelle took a seat next to her husband. Glancing at Tommy she felt rather like a terrified mouse in the sights of a playful cat.

Tommy was charming, entertaining Lord Harvey with the tale of a recent official opening of a smart art gallery in Piccadilly. During the opening speeches, a couple from Burnley had walked into the gallery, and when a member of staff discreetly offered them a glass of champagne the pair had accepted gratefully. Drinking the wine in a swallow, they had turned to the guest of honour and asked if they might see the parrot feathers. They had mistaken the establishment for a feather and skin importer's shop.

It was difficult for Lady Isabelle to find the story amusing but at the appropriate moment she forced a laugh.

Lord Harvey was pleased with his new friend. Tommy Standish was a good raconteur, and without doubt his character was an open book. He had absolutely no misgiving regarding his friendship with Gill. There was no possibility of a scandal coming to light when only Tommy Standish knew the facts. Without a doubt he was a man of honour and could be trusted to keep his word.

Tommy's story had been delightful. In an excellent mood, Lord Harvey looked forward to an entertaining evening in his company.

It was early dusk when the two men left the mansion. Isabelle fled the library on their departure making for the sanctuary of her private rooms. Summoning her personal maid, she climbed out of the crinoline and tight jacket.

The maid noticed the tremor in Lady Isabelle's hands and went to the butler to request a brandy for her mistress.

Changed into a lighter dress, Isabelle paced back and forth wringing her hands. At every sound she imagined her wrathful husband returning and crossed to the window to look out, only to return to pacing until the next vehicle approached. Unable to keep an appointment she had made earlier, she despatched her personal maid with a sealed note to an address in Sloane Square.

Isabelle waited fearfully through the long hours, imagining that at any moment her husband would return to denounce her and banish her from his home. The waiting a torment, she watched the hands on the little Faberge clock move with sickening slowness around the pink and green enamelled dial.

Tommy was in ebullient mood as he and Lord Harvey entered the Athenaeum Club.

It was Tommy's first visit. The membership of the club was made up of artists, writers and scientists. It was very different from the Reform, which had political leanings.

Lord Harvey led the way to the billiard room. It had been decided between them in the hansom that they would have a game before dinner. Later they would spend an hour or two in the gaming room. It was a favourite haunt of his lordship's though recently he had lost a considerable amount of money there. His banker had sorted out the matter only this morning so he felt able to call in and place a bet without embarrassment.

Tommy lost at billiards. But on the promise of a return bout, the two men went into the dining room.

Lord Harvey had consumed several brandies beside the two glasses of champagne served earlier in his library and his mood was expansive. Ordering lobsters from a waiter he asked for a bottle of champagne to be served with the dish and two bottles of claret for the saddle of lamb that was to follow.

Resolving to remain sober, Tommy thought of the business deal he planned to negotiate. Not that he expected much trouble from the drunken sop sitting on the other side of the table. If it became necessary to mention Gill's name, he would do so without a second thought. Lord Harvey would agree to anything to keep his name out of the newspapers and courts. What a field day the press would have if it should leak out that Lord Harvey had a pretty boy for a bedfellow!

Tommy's ruminations were interrupted by the delivery of a large bowl of split and grilled lobster.

Tucking his napkin into his shirt collar, Lord Harvey took two open shells from the dish and attacked them quickly with a fork.

Pulling pieces of succulent flesh from the shell, Tommy's thoughts went to Corn Cottage and he speculated on the fare placed on his parents' table. He glanced at the long case clock and saw that it was after his father and mother's bedtime. Satisfied with his own lifestyle, thankful it wasn't the meagre drudge that was their lot, he chewed the morsel he had popped into his mouth.

Later, he made a small amount of money at the baccarat table. Lord Harvey lost a little but was well satisfied. In the recent past he had lost a great deal, some would say a fortune at baccarat. Tommy was no gambler. The fate of George Bellamy had taught him long ago that it was a game for idiots that could bring eventual ruin.

Lord Harvey's suggestion that they should retire to Hollybeck House for a nightcap came as a welcome end to the evening for Tommy.

Climbing aboard the hansom, a manservant had been sent out of the Athenaeum to hail a passing cab, Tommy's blood buzzed with excitement.

For several days he had looked forward to the oppor-

287

tunity to offload shares in the defunct Ruby Quarry to the husband of Lady Isabelle. The acquisition could bring ruin to the Harvey's. As the former owner of Ruby Quarry and now leaseholder of the land he could manipulate the outcome of the debacle. What a pleasure it would be to watch the charmed existence that was Lady Isabelle's, crumble to nothing. Vengeance would be his. Whoever said that *revenge was a dish best served cold* was wrong, it was better delivered *whilst the blood was still hot, boiling with righteous anger.*

It was becoming increasingly obvious to Tommy that the Harveys were hopelessly overstretched financially. His lordship made no bones about his losses at the gambling houses. Lady Isabelle spent money like water. The Harveys' business interests, like so many of the aristocracy, had been tied up with plantations, where black labour had come virtually free. With the abolition of slavery the Harveys' plantations had disintegrated. Tommy was no stranger to the problem, but looking ahead he had moved his interests to Cuba where he still enjoyed the advantage of *cheap labour*, a quaint but necessary euphemism for slavery.

All this information was rattling around Tommy's head as the hansom pulled up outside Hollybeck house. Looking out on the dark street, he was delighted to see that most of the upstairs lamps were still burning. Fervently hoping that Lady Isabelle watched and waited, dreading the return of her husband and his guest. For surely after a night out together, exchanging confidences, what could they bring but her ultimate disgrace?

As the hansom drew up, Lady Isabelle rose quickly. During the hours she had waited her face had grown pale and she had come close to sickness on several occasions.

The hours had drawn by slowly and she'd had time to consider her future. If she were to come through this episode unscathed, although her husband was virtually impotent, never again would she look elsewhere for affection and sexual gratification. Her new lover would be deposed immediately. She didn't dare think what Tommy would want in exchange for his silence; whatever it was, she was forced to accept his terms.

Hearing the front door open, she crossed the room nervously to listen at the bedroom door. Her husband's jovial, though inebriated voice, drifted up the wide stairs. Closing her eyes she thanked God for small mercies. Then Tommy's laughter rang out. Her heart sank as his purpose became clear. It was obvious that he planned to denounce her to her husband as they shared a late drink together. Her ruin was guaranteed.

Biting her fingernails, she crossed the room and sat on the edge of the chaise-longue debating whether to join the two men or sit the agony out here in her room. Indecision kept her rooted to the seat, her heart aching with uncertainty and fear.

Tommy accepted the brandy from Lord Harvey. The butler had thoughtfully left the decanter and glasses to hand in the library. Sinking into a large leather chair, Tommy waited for his host to take a seat.

Immediately they were settled, his lordship splayed over the seat, Tommy came to the point.

'Did I mention that I have another quarry besides Garddryn?'

Looking over the rim of his glass, Lord Harvey frowned. 'I didn't know that. Where is it?'

Tommy chose his words carefully. 'It's very close to the massive Penrhyn Quarry. You know the owner, Colonel Edward Douglas Pennant, Member of Parliament for Caernarvonshire. Edward owns the immense Penrhyn Castle near Bangor.'

Lord Harvey smiled. 'Yes, I know him. He's a fabulously wealthy man. I meet him occasionally in the House.'

Tommy the perfect salesman changed tack; becoming conspiratorial, he said 'Edward's a good friend of mine and

289

he wouldn't mind me telling you that his wealth comes from the quarry. The yearly profit at Penrhyn is in excess of one hundred thousand pounds and he employs two thousand five hundred men in Penrhyn.' Tommy didn't feel it necessary to say that the bulk of Edward's wealth came from his land holdings.

Lord Harvey looked shocked. 'That's a hell of a lot of money by anyone's standards.' He chortled. 'I wouldn't mind a slice of profits like that. It would keep Lady Issy in trinkets and me in spirits for very long time.'

Paying attention to his glass, Lord Harvey gave a little burp after swallowing most of the contents.

Tommy sensed that he was close to a deal. 'I'm surprised that you haven't gone in for minerals. Mining and excavations are very profitable.'

Draining his glass, Lord Harvey reached for the decanter. 'It isn't something that I know anything about,' he said, upending the decanter to fill his glass. 'It might have been a good idea when the business in Jamaica became too expensive to run. It's probably too late now to get into something new.'

His lordship was thoughtful for a moment turning an idea over in his mind. 'I don't suppose you could advise me, Tommy? I might find the capital to invest. It wouldn't be a great sum but it'd be something.'

Although Tommy felt as tight as a drum with excitement, now that he had the old sot on the hook, he looked relaxed and nonchalant. 'You need to invest a lot if you're going to earn vast profits.'

Lord Harvey didn't say that Tommy was stating the obvious, but asked politely, 'How much?'

Tommy thought for a moment, assessing how much his lordship could lay his hands on. There was no point to this exercise if the silly old fool didn't overreach himself. Coming to a figure, Tommy said confidently, 'I reckon twenty thousand should be enough.'

Lord Harvey came up in his chair. 'Phew! That's too rich for me.'

His reaction didn't surprise Tommy. 'Surely you could borrow? A short term mortgage on the house should do it.'

'Lady Issy wouldn't like that. She's afraid to mortgage the property in case anything should go badly wrong and she should lose it. Lady Isabelle does love this house so.'

Tommy's eyebrow rose. 'Does she need to be aware of all your business dealings?'

Chewing his bottom lip, Lord Harvey was thoughtful. 'I suppose I could get away with it.' Chuckling, he said, 'Listen to me going on about raising the money when I haven't a quarry company to invest in.'

Tommy's eyes fixed on his target. He smiled. 'Oh but you do, Lord Harvey. And a safer bet you couldn't make. I'm selling a few shares in my new quarry, Ruby. Situated where it is, the land has massive potential. I already have over a hundred men working there. My manager is employing five hundred more. Of course as we get into full production that figure will rise dramatically.' He smiled confidently. 'I expect to reap as big a profit as Penrhyn in the next two years.'

Thoughtful, Lord Harvey was silent for a moment. Then he said quietly, 'It seems like an offer I can't refuse.'

'It would be foolish to do so,' Tommy said softly.

A sigh escaped Lord Harvey. 'I'm certainly tempted. It's been a while since I've made any amount of money. Of course there's the family trust fund, but that's meagre when compared to the expenditure of running a house like Hollybeck and all that goes with it.'

Tommy was sympathetic. 'Things have changed; what was a great deal of money some years ago is no longer so. That's why it's become so important to diversify to keep these great houses standing. And our ladies in the manner to which they have become accustomed.'

Lord Harvey grinned. 'You can say that again. Lady

Isabelle is a terror when it comes to dressmakers, shoe-makers, hat makers, any maker at all come to that.'

Tommy gave a short laugh. 'You're not alone there Lord Harvey. Tell me what wife is circumspect when it comes to a pretty gown or hat.'

'To cover her ladyship's expenditure is probably a good enough reason to think seriously about investing in one of the mineral companies.'

Eager, Tommy pushed his point. 'You couldn't do better than come in with me. I know the business inside out. The land is perfect. It has great scope. It'll be as big as or even bigger than Penrhyn within twenty four months.'

Lord Harvey sat thoughtfully for a moment, problems and solutions tripping through his mind. How could he refuse such a lucrative offer with his finances in such disarray? His wife was hardly likely to curtail her spending. He needed more money desperately to meet his obligations in the very near future. But how was he to raise a second mortgage? Lady Isabelle was already ignorant of the first. There was the Birkbeck Bank on Chancery Lane; he hadn't yet tried to borrow money from them. Perhaps they could be persuaded to part with some. Taking a sip from the glass he decided to approach a director there first thing in the morning. Surely his title and mansion would be enough to impress the man.

Pleased that he had thought of the Birkbeck, Lord Harvey smiled confidently. 'It sounds like a good idea to invest early.'

'The real money is always made by the early investors,' Tommy agreed.

Lord Harvey chuckled. 'You had better count me in then.'

Tommy smiled. 'Welcome to the board of Ruby Quarry, Lord Harvey.'

Beaming, Lord Harvey raised his glass. 'To Ruby.'

The following day Lord Harvey called at Birkbeck Bank on Chancery Lane. The managing director accepted his lies without question and Hollybeck House was re-mortgaged for twenty thousand pounds. This success made Lord Harvey expansive and he promised the director that he would introduce Tommy Standish of the Garddryn and Ruby Quarries to the bank.

On departing from the director's office, standing beneath the spectacular fan dome in the main hall to don his gloves, Lord Harvey congratulated himself on his business acumen. Hiding the fact that Hollybeck House already carried a mortgage was a masterstroke. It had necessitated a little jiggery pokery but thankfully he had got away with it. Pleased, he sighed contentedly. Swinging his ebony cane he came from under the grand portals of the bank and onto Chancery Lane.

Hailing a passing hansom he travelled to Mayfair to call on Tommy. Boarding he settled into the grubby cracked leather seat, his knees spread, tight trousers stretched across his paunch.

Pleased with himself, he imagined the pile that twenty thousands pounds would make. It was large but nothing like the heap that his share of one hundred thousands pounds would be.

Anxious to get to Tommy's house, the sooner he signed the paper and became a shareholder the better, he glanced out several times checking on the progress of the vehicle. He couldn't wait to tell Tommy the good news. What a stroke of luck that he'd made such a good friend of the quarry master.

Tommy was in the small study when Lord Harvey was shown into the room by the housekeeper. Seeing his Lordship's ebullient face, Tommy knew that he had secured his loan. Coming from behind his desk, he took the older man's hand.

'I guess you got what you wanted,' Tommy said, his face wreathed in a smile.

Grinning, Lord Harvey was slightly breathless. 'I got it

without question. Which was a good thing; too many questions would have upset the apple cart.' He chortled.

To hear that his lordship was in deeper trouble than he had let on last night, was a gift from heaven.

Crossing to the fireplace, Tommy pulled the bell-rope. 'This calls for a celebration. A bottle of champagne at the very least and we'll dine out.'

On the appearance of a manservant, Tommy ordered that a bottle of Veuve Clicquot be served at once. 'Bring three glasses, I am expecting another caller,' Tommy instructed.

Looking slightly embarrassed, Lord Harvey began to apologise. 'Oh I hope I'm not interrupting. If you are expecting a guest, perhaps I should leave.'

Tommy laid a restraining hand on the man's sleeve. 'I wouldn't hear of it. You must stay. It's fortuitous really as the guest is Madoc, my solicitor. He promised to call in before he sets off back to Wales.'

In reality, Tommy had sent a note via a servant to summon the solicitor at his hotel. The servant had been ordered to go immediately should Lord Harvey arrive on the doorstep. Madoc was expected at any moment and naturally the solicitor would bring the necessary papers for Lord Harvey to sign. With the signature on the deed there would be no going back for his lordship.

Gleeful, Tommy opened the door on the servant as he came with the Veuve Cliquot. Everything went according to plan and within minutes of Tommy handing a glass to his lordship, there was a ring of the bell.

Madoc, wearing a sombre dark suit, entered the room. A leather case tucked beneath his arm.

Tommy made the necessary introductions and Madoc was handed a glass.

As it was impossible to hide his grin, Tommy kept his back to Lord Harvey, as he said 'You couldn't have come at a better time, Madoc. Lord Harvey and I were just beginning to celebrate the fact that his lordship has decided to come on board with the Ruby project. His share will be twenty thousand pounds.'

He made a half-turn towards his lordship. 'Isn't that so, Lord Harvey?'

'Absolutely correct and I can't wait to sign up. The Birkbeck Bank will release the money immediately,' Lord Harvey explained to the two men watching him closely.

Madoc gave one of his rare smiles. 'You're in luck, your Lordship. I actually have the papers with me.'

Striding to a chair, Madoc took the leather case that he had downed casually and opened it. Withdrawing a sheaf of papers, he took the uppermost and held it close to his chest.

Tommy's heart drummed in his chest. How likely was it that at this late stage his lordship would have second thoughts and back out of the deal?

Madoc turned to the desk and taking a pen he dipped the nib into an inkpot.

Tommy's breath stilled in his chest.

The scratch of the nib was the only sound in the room.

Writing the number of shares and the monetary value, Madoc handed the pen to Lord Harvey. Standing aside he watched the man sign.

Lord Harvey gave a happy sigh.

CHAPTER ELEVEN

Feeling lost and slightly vulnerable, Henrietta walked down the long wide corridor of Denbigh Asylum, looking for the superintendent's office.

From behind closed doors came the soft murmur of solitary conversations. From some hidden realm, where she supposed the kitchen to be, there was the clatter of metal pans. Trapped in the warm air was the vague odour of countless past meals.

She wondered if she should have come. Would George even recognise her? The last time she had seen him had been at her mother's house in Chester. With his faculties hopelessly damaged, poor George had been confined to his bedroom there. The very last time she had visited him, a nurse had been sitting besides his chair reading aloud from a book. Why had she never asked what had become of the compassionate woman when Tommy exiled George to this place?

Coming to a door with the superintendent's name painted in black on it, she knocked tentatively. Waiting for a reply she glanced along the corridor; the ceiling was lofty, spanned by many arches. The narrow windows were so high that only small patches of egg-blue sky hinted at an outside world. With no furniture, plant, or ornament, the passage-way had an institutional emptiness.

Her eyes came back to the printed name on the closed door. Nervously she straightened the short veil on her blue hat and then fiddled with the waistband on her navy dress.

A masculine voice called sharply from within.

With a sense *that it was now or never,* Henrietta took a deep breath, turned the brass doorknob and entered.

The large man sitting behind the desk rose as she came into the room. He looked imposing in a black suit, a black cravat tied neatly over a stiff high collar. White side whiskers and a thick moustache, yellowing at the fringes, almost hid his lower face, but above, his grey eyes were kindly.

Henrietta's voice was unsteady. Her face flushed slightly and she was aware that colour stained her cheeks. 'I'm so sorry to disturb you, Superintendent. I was told by a gentleman at the main entrance that I would find you here. I hope you don't mind my coming without an appointment.'

The man's untidy eyebrows rose, giving him a perplexed expression. 'Whoever directed you here should have had the courtesy to escort you to my office. I apologise if a member of my staff is at fault.'

Henrietta brushed the apology aside. 'I found my way, so no harm done.'

Sitting again, he gestured to an old library chair on the other side of his desk. 'Please make yourself comfortable and tell me what can I do for you.'

Arranging her skirt, Henrietta sat on the polished wooden seat. Fully expecting the man to think badly of her for abandoning a member of her family, she nervously picked at the fingers of her gloves.

Her eyes met his. 'I would like to see my brother, George Bellamy. He has been with you for some time. My husband sent him here.'

A frown drew the superintendent's white eyebrows together. 'And your name madam?'

'Oh, I'm sorry, how silly of me; it's Henrietta Standish.'

It wasn't the first time that a long absent family member had come looking for a confined relative. He prided himself on knowing the name of every one of the two hundred inmates and he'd recognised Bellamy instantly.

Taking off his glasses he gave them a polish with a pristinely white handkerchief. 'A visit isn't a problem, Mrs Standish. Your brother has his own room. I will show you where he is.'

Picturing George alone in a dreary room, a film of tears came to Henrietta's eyes. She gave the superintendent a smile that wasn't really a smile. 'It's so long since I saw him. Too long ...'

Rising from the chair, he stepped around the desk. 'That can easily be remedied, he said kindly.'

As Henrietta rose she took her parasol from the side of her chair. Clutching her bag against her midriff, she followed him to the door.

Opening it, he stood aside to let her pass through. Making conversation, he said 'This obviously is your first visit to the hospital, Mrs Standish?'

Henrietta watched as he locked the door and pocketed the key. 'Yes, it is the first time.'

She glanced down the corridor. The sun had ceased to shine through the high windows and the passageway was gloomy. They walked side by side towards the door at the far end, their footsteps echoing hollowly.

Neither of them spoke and she felt obliged to fill the void. 'I have found it difficult to come here before today as my husband is not happy about me doing so.'

The superintendent pushed his hands into his coat pocket. 'Oh! Your husband has had a change of heart?'

Henrietta gave him a quick sidelong glance. 'No, never that. He is away in London. I took the opportunity to make the journey.'

The superintendent read a lot into what she said. Although he had no knowledge of Tommy Standish, he jumped to the conclusion that the man was not a considerate person.

George Bellamy was already a patient when he took over the position of managing the affairs of the hospital. For his entire working life he had been involved with broken lives and broken people and he believed that he had a good insight into the human character.

He avoided glancing at her, as he thought, that it didn't take a professional to see that Mrs Henrietta Standish was an unhappy, unfulfilled young woman.

Henrietta judged from his silence that her disclosure had shocked the man and she instinctively tried to make amends by taking an interest in his domain. 'Are all the patients in single room? For some reason I had an idea that they would live in dormitories. Do they share areas for recreation?'

'Most patients do share rooms. George Bellamy has a benefactor. I believe that she was his old nurse from the time that your brother lived at home in Chester.'

Her voice rose slightly in surprise. 'How very strange; I was wondering what had become of her, only a few hours ago. But how on earth has she been able to afford to pay for a private room for such a long period? And why hasn't my husband taken care of the expenses?'

He gave a small smile. 'I'm afraid I don't know the answer to either question, Mrs Standish. But you may be able to ask her yourself. She visits most days. George is calmed by her reading to him.'

Henrietta felt overwhelmingly guilty. George was her brother, yet she had allowed this terrible situation to carry on and without even inquiring into his welfare or how he managed financially. Her mother and father would be ashamed and saddened by her appalling behaviour. She had thought only of herself and her unhappy position with Tommy. When she should have insisted that George come to Plas Mawr or at the very least visited him to see how he fared.

The far door opened and a middle-aged heavily bearded

man wearing a dark shabby uniform came into the corridor. Seeing the superintendent, he touched the brim of his dark hat.

The superintendent beckoned to him. 'Keeper, we have come to see George Bellamy. Can you tell me if he is alone and how his health is today?'

The keeper's eyes went to Henrietta; it wasn't often that a woman of such high breeding visited the hospital. His glance came back to his master and he touched his hat again.

'Bellamy is alone at the moment, sir. A nurse has just seen to his dinner. His usual visitor will come at about three, same as always, I guess.'

'Thank you, Keeper. We will go in to see him. Please open the room. Get a nurse to come and stay with Bellamy until Mrs Standish wishes to leave.'

The keeper had a ring of keys chained to his belt; selecting one he opened the door. Standing back he waited for the superintendent and visitor to pass through. 'I'll fetch someone now, sir.'

Henrietta was shocked seeing George. He looked older than his years and he had lost weight; the old clothes he wore hung from his frame. Sitting besides the window he was looking out. He turned as his sister entered but there was no sign of recognition in his blank eyes.

'George.' She stooped to the ground and took his limp hand in hers. 'Do you remember me, George?'

The lifeless eyes looked into her face and then he glanced up at the superintendent before looking away again and glancing back out of the window.

Henrietta held George's hand tightly, tugging him gently to bring his face back to hers. 'You must remember Plas Mawr, the house where we grew up. We used to play there together and ride across the fields. Do you remember how we used to fly at the five bar gate near the wood, you on Dromineer and me clinging to Shelley's mane?'

George's brow furrowed as though a distant memory stirred.

Henrietta's face lit with hope. 'You do remember! Dromineer was your very favourite steed. He was coal-black and flew like the wind. You loved him dearly, George.'

George's lips moved.

Henrietta was recalling the names of the men at the stables where young George would spend so much time, when a light knock sounded on the door. George's eyes flicked with interest. When a woman entered followed by a nurse, a tentative smile came to his lips.

Seeing a well dressed woman kneeling besides George's chair, the woman glanced from her to the superintendent.

Stepping forward, the superintendent explained. 'Miss O'Donnell, this lady is George's sister, Mrs Henrietta Standish.'

Mary O'Donnell's eyes flashed fire. 'You're Tommy Standish's wife?'

Henrietta stood. 'Yes, I'm Tommy's wife. Do you know my husband?'

'I certainly do, Mrs Standish. I was at your mother's house the day that Tommy Standish and Doctor Rogers came to take George away from home.'

Recalling the theft of Louise Bellamy's jewels, Mary O'Donnell paled. If Henrietta Standish were to tell her husband that she had met George's former nurse, he would hunt her down for that theft and she would find herself in prison.

Oblivious to Mary O'Donnell's torment, Henrietta took the woman's hands in hers. 'I want to know everything,' she said earnestly. 'The superintendent has already told me that you pay for George to have his own room and that you have been a good friend and companion to my brother. How can I ever repay your kindness?'

Friendliness was the last thing Mary expected. She assumed that Henrietta took the same stance as Tommy

Standish and wanted to see George put out of the way. If their views differed, why didn't she visit her brother and send money for the small extras that would make such a difference to his welfare and happiness?

Mary O'Donnell's priority was George and she said, 'I will tell you everything that you want to know, later. For the moment I must see to George or he will grow restless. At this time of the day he likes me to read to him. Mrs Standish, if you would be kind enough to leave us for a little while, we could meet later in the garden. I will tell you everything I can then.'

Henrietta glanced at George clinging to his old nurse's hand. 'Of course I'll go, Mary. I will wait for you. Please don't hurry on my account.'

Henrietta stooped to George. 'I will see you before I go back to Plas Mawr.'

The man's eyes were on Mary and he made no sign that he had heard Henrietta.

Opening the door, the superintendent came out of the room with Henrietta, the hospital nurse following.

Leaving the superintendent in the corridor, Henrietta went out into the garden. Finding a quiet place under an elm tree, she sat listening to the birdsong. Several hospital inmates and nurses strolled in the autumn sunshine and she imagined walking with George on a future visit.

Eventually Mary O'Donnell came out of a side door into the garden. Henrietta watched her as she walked steadily across the short grass. Henrietta had noticed earlier that the woman's pale blue dress was of simple cotton, her shoes and green straw bonnet of a cheap quality. She wondered why such a person, a woman of thirty five or thereabouts, would take such care of her previous charge. The finances must surely be crippling for a woman in modest circumstances.

Mary O'Donnell was agonising about how much she should say to Henrietta Standish. George sensing that something was wrong became agitated and it was difficult to calm him. It was necessary for a nurse to administer a dose of opium. How she hated abandoning him so she could attend to his sister. If it wasn't for the stolen jewels there would not be a problem in talking to Henrietta. George was kept in simple comfort at the asylum with the money gained from the theft of his mother's gems. To explain this to Henrietta Standish would be ludicrous but what was she to say in place of the truth?

Coming alongside Henrietta, Mary sat down.

Anxious, Henrietta began at once. 'I can't thank you enough for taking such care of my brother.' Tears were not far from her eyes. 'I feel terribly guilty for not helping. I abandoned George when he needed me most. I can't expect you to forgive me for that, when I find it impossible to forgive myself.'

Mary touched Henrietta's hand. 'Mrs Standish, I know that you must have had your reasons and they would be strong to keep you from your brother. You mustn't blame yourself.'

'But the expenditure, Mary, how do you cope?'

Mary thanked God that the lie came easily. 'I was left a small legacy. It was unexpected so I was happy to make use of that.' She glanced away as she spoke.

'It's so generous of you,' Henrietta said, touching the woman's arm.

Mary gave a small smile. 'I work as a night nurse to a small disturbed boy. The wages from that take care of my four children and mother-in-law. The old lady keeps house for us, so it works out well enough.'

The admission made Henrietta even more ashamed and she hurried to make amends. 'I will reimburse you in full and from now on I will pay for all George's requirements.'

Mary was at a loss to know how she could accept the generosity when she had stolen for the sole purpose of using the money for George. 'There's absolutely no need for you to do that, Mrs Standish.'

'Please Mary, call me Henrietta. I feel that we are already friends.'

Near tears, Mary sniffed. 'I have enough money to take care of him.'

'But, Mary, he is my responsibility. I must take care of my own flesh and blood. I have to make amends for my appalling behaviour.'

Although Mary had met Tommy Standish on only one occasion, she was sure that the reason Henrietta did not visit her brother lay with the evil man. No doubt he forbade a visit or had not told his wife where he had dumped poor George.

It hadn't been her intention when she entered the garden to relinquish the responsibility of George. But understanding that Henrietta might *need* to help, she came to a rapid decision. The money and how much was left from the sale of jewellery she would deal with later.

'If you could take care of the costs of George's room...'

Relieved, Henrietta took Mary's hands in hers. 'I would so like to do that and if there's anything else that I can do, I most certainly will. I promise.'

Pleased to see a smile on the poor girl's face, she looked as though she needed every bit of happiness that came her way, Mary squeezed her hand. Saying practically, 'Mr Ashton, the superintendent, will give you details of the payments,' she began to rise from the seat. 'I'm sorry I cannot stay to deal with the matter but I really have to leave. If I don't, I will be late getting to my other charge, little Roger Greenwood.'

Henrietta stood, holding the nurse's hands in hers. 'Don't worry, Mary. I'll write to Mr Ashton and settle the matter. You go and see Roger. Do you have to go far? I have a carriage waiting, it could drop you off.'

'That's not necessary, the Greenwoods live close by. I can

be there in a moment. But I really must go, so goodbye, Henrietta. Take care of yourself.'

'Bye, Mary. And thank you for everything that you have done.' Impulsively, Henrietta kissed the woman's cheek.

From beneath the tree, the sunlight dappled by the autumn leaves, Henrietta watched Mary trip across the lawn to the pathway. She was gone in a moment, hidden by overgrown bushes.

Although she had promised that she would see George before she departed from the hospital, Mary had advised against it, explaining that a nurse had given him medicine to settle him down and he would be sleeping.

Feeling that she had accomplished more than she had hoped to, Henrietta picked up her black parasol and small bag and walked to the front entrance where a carriage waited to take her the twelve miles back to Rhyl railway station. It would be a while before she reached home but a cup of tea could be had at the station tearooms.

It was on the spur of the moment, on the following day, that Henrietta called for the brougham to be brought to the front of Plas Mawr.

Hurrying to the nursery, she dressed young Edward in a blue woollen jacket over a cashmere navy dress and short pantaloons. As she buttoned the jacket and placed a hat on his fair curls, she told him that they were going on a secret visit and no one, not even Papa when he returned from London, must know of it. Edward's nurse watched the proceedings with misgivings, guessing correctly where Henrietta was headed.

There was a sense of holiday as mother and son cuddled close together on the leather seat of the small carriage as it travelled down the long drive to the roadway, a chestnut mare in the traces.

Looking over her son's head, to the sloping meadows and to the pale sapphire sea, Henrietta was glad that they had fled the house to enjoy the crisp autumnal day. The brilliant sunshine was a bonus and it was probably the last warm day of the season.

The scene was typical autumn, the trees shedding russet leaves and the hedgerows blazoned with ruby and orange of hips and haws. The blackberries were abundant. Several women were thigh-deep in the long grass gathering the fruit into pudding basins or baskets, their drab shawls draped on the robbed bramble branches. Ink-black sloes peppered the vicious blackthorn. Heavy clusters of glistening elderberries drooped from the elders' dry branches.

Resting back in the seat, Henrietta was content to yield to the velvety emptiness of the day.

Emily was in the garden, pulling carrots from Joe's vegetable plot, when she heard the wheels of a carriage and the sound of hooves trotting down the lane. The vehicle came to a standstill at the gate and her hopes soared at the thought that it may have brought Henrietta and Edward.

Quickly, laying the carrots into the garden basket and abandoning it where it lay, Emily wiped her hands down her soiled apron. Hurrying, stepping over the raised vegetable beds she made it to the gate just in time to see Henrietta lifting Edward down.

Beaming with happiness, Emily opened the gate. Throwing her arms around Henrietta she hugged the young woman close.

Standing beside his mother, smart in his new outfit of navy and pale blue, Edward grinned up at his Nana. Scooping him up, mindful of her slightly soiled hands, Emily hugged the laughing boy.

The groom touched his cap. 'What time shall I return, Madam?'

Henrietta glanced at Emily for direction, aware that her mother-in-law may have plans for the day.

Emily gave the man a dismissive wave. 'Not until after tea, young man. And not a minute before or you'll have me to answer to.'

Henrietta laughed at Emily's easy handling of a snooty servant. Seeing his mother happy, a rare treat, Edward laughed.

Emily bundled the pair towards the cottage door, her skirt skimming over the heads of the remnants of the short stemmed summer flowers.

Indoors there was the sweet fragrance of cooked apples, newly baked pastry, and lavender scented wax polish. Shafts of sunlight fell across the table, shining on a drinking glass filled with full-blown tawny roses.

Visiting Corn Cottage had a sense of coming home for Henrietta. There was love here as there had been in Plas Mawr when her mother and father had lived there.

Emily bustled to the fireplace. 'I'll put the kettle to the fire. We'll have a cup of tea.' She beckoned to the small boy. 'Come to Nana, Edward. Let me take off your coat.'

Edward stood pressed against Emily's knees as she undid the bone buttons on his short jacket and removed his blue hat with the white feathers.

Sitting beside the dresser, Henrietta untied the ribbons on her frilled hat and placed it on the back of the chair.

Emily cuddled Edward to her, whispering, 'Would my little angel like some apple juice?' As she spoke she mentally thanked Joe for suggesting she make the juice with some of the glut of apples; it wouldn't have occurred to her, she was quite happy to lay the fruit in paper and store it over the winter in the loft. The apples might be a little wrinkled come Christmas but it was normal and to be expected. But Joe's idea got her squashing a few pounds into a pulp and straining it through muslin. She had ended up with three pints and decided to take some to the Jones's next door.

The Jones family were ignored by most of the villagers. Horas, the first man to break the lock-out, was named a traitor. His wife and children were finding it hard to bear life in Garddryn village.

Folding Edward's little coat carefully and putting it

aside, Emily looked to Henrietta. 'It's ever so fortunate that you have come today as Joe is helping bring the harvest in at Coots Farm. If we walk over that way we could take some apple pie to him to have with his tea. He'll be so very pleased to see you both. This day will be the topic of conversation for weeks to come.'

Henrietta loved Emily's plain truths; there was no falseness, posturing or affectation in her character. It was just another reasons why she so loved coming here.

If Tommy were to discover that she visited occasionally, there would be a serious row and she feared that more than anything. Recently their arguments had become aggressive and out of control. Following the quarrels she relied on the heroin medicine to get through the days and sometimes she took laudanum, although she knew that it was foolish.

Banishing these dark thoughts, she said 'That's a lovely idea. Little Edward would love to see his grandpa.'

Reaching for her child she held him close. 'Grandpapa is a favourite person. Isn't he Edward?'

Joe finished tying a corn stack and rose from his stiff knees slowly. The work was hard but it paid fairly well. Enough to take a day off from the quarry like a hundred or so other men were doing today to help get the harvest in. Management at the quarries might complain but they couldn't stop the quarriers from doing as they had for decades or longer. The harvest was important and the men felt a certain responsibility in securing the crops that God had been good enough to bestow.

Wiping the sweat off his brow with the back of his dirty hand, spreading dry husks into his wet hairline, Joe glanced to the edge of the field where a colourful trio were coming through the five bar gate. Without a doubt the one in the green dress was Emily; he'd recognise her walk anywhere. The lass in the magenta frock, holding a child by the hand, he guessed at immediately.

Smiling, he trod over the sharp stubble to greet them.

When they were in hailing distance, he shouted, 'What a lovely surprise. Like manna from heaven.'

Moments later he came alongside and lifted Edward off his feet, swinging the laughing child high.

'Mind his clean coat, our Joe,' Emily remonstrated.

Joe laughed, swinging Edward again. 'The child's got an army of folk on hand to clean his little coat.'

Joe put the boy back on his feet and the child clung to the leg of his grandfather's grubby trousers.

Putting his damp cheek to Henrietta's, Joe gave her a light kiss. 'It really is good to see you both. We've missed the pair of you. What a good girl you are for making our day.'

Henrietta flushed faintly pink. Placing her hand on Edward's fine curls, she said, 'Try keeping this little ruffian away from his grandparents.'

The four sat beneath the overhang of an unkempt hedge, eating pie and drinking tepid apple juice. Henrietta hardly mentioned Tommy and both Emily and Joe guessed that all was not well between the couple.

Young Edward scampered around and eventually settled on his grandpa's knee to listen to tales of fishing in the nearby river. Joe said that he would teach Edward to fish and Edward made him make a solemn promise that this would happen very soon. Laughing, Joe vowed that it would be so.

Promising Cecil Coot, the farmer, that he would make up the hours the following evening, Joe finished work early.

The walk back to Corn Cottage was slow, Edward riding on Joe's shoulders. Emily and Henrietta were in deep conversation. What they found to talk about was a mystery to Joe but he supposed it was children. For what else could two women coming from such different stations in life find to talk about so earnestly?

On the last stretch of the lane, the pale blue sea was before them, the dying sun flickering on the water. The last of the dog roses were still blooming in the tangled hedge. The verges were thick with long grass and pink and white flower heads.

If this was the last of the summer days, it had been extra special, Joe thought, as the cottage came into view.

The brougham from Plas Mawr was waiting at Corn Cottage gate. Seeing it there, Henrietta stiffened. Reaching up, Joe lifted Edward down from his shoulders and stood the lad on his own two feet.

As they came alongside the vehicle the driver tipped his hat to Henrietta. 'Madam.'

Slightly flustered, Emily opened the garden gate and going up the short path she unlocked the cottage door. Dashing in, she retrieved Edward's and Henrietta's hats and brought them out to the little group standing at the gate.

There was a great sense of parting. Joe made Henrietta promise faithfully to come again soon.

Tears brimmed in Henrietta's eyes.

Stooping to the boy, mindful that he could make matters worse by showing his own emotion, Joe kissed his chilled cheek and made a joke about fishing. Until he was rewarded with a half-smile he didn't lift the little lad into the brougham.

Before climbing aboard, Henrietta kissed Emily and then on tiptoe reached to kiss Joe's cheek. Holding her close he reminded her of the promise to return soon.

Joe closed the door gently and the vehicle moved away.

Emily and Joe stood together at the gate watching until the carriage disappeared around the bend in the road. They stayed several more moments listening to the wheels turning and the beat of the mare's hooves.

The evening fell flat and after supper they retired to bed early. Frank arrived in. They listened to the locks on the back and front door being turned and then Frank went to his own room and silence fell on the cottage.

Joe blew out the candle and they lay in the dark with their own thoughts.

A light breeze blew in through the small opening at the window, moving the flimsy curtains. The moon was high and bright, casting a silvery light over the small bedroom.

Emily spoke into the darkness, 'Young Edward favours you, our Joe. He has your china blue eyes and your temperament. It makes me happy to thinks he's like you and not like his father.'

Silent for a moment she was thoughtful. 'When Edward comes into his inheritance, the Garddryn will have a good and kind master. The men that work there in the future will have nothing to fear from Edward.'

Joe was touched by her words and for the moment he had nothing to say.

Emily put her arm around his midriff. 'I love you, Joe Standish.'

Smiling, he pulled her close. 'I love you, Mrs Standish. And I'm proud of our grandson, he's a smasher.'

'You ready for sleep, Joe?'

'Aye, the little perisher has worn me out.'

Joe slept and Emily listened to the sound of his breathing. Tommy was on her mind and she hoped that he was kind to the little boy, for she feared that he wasn't to his wife.

Tommy arrived back at Plas Mawr before Henrietta and Edward. Angry to find them away from home he ordered the servants to inform him the moment of their return. Striding bad temperedly towards the library, his good mood at securing Lord Harvey's twenty thousand pounds, plus the other thousands selling shares of Ruby Quarry to four unsuspecting investors, evaporating quickly.

There was no doubt in his mind that Henrietta had taken Edward to Corn Cottage though he had expressly forbidden it. Calling for a footman, a stable-hand and Henrietta's personal maid his suspicions were confirmed.

Dismissing the servants, his temper at boiling point, he poured a generous measure of brandy into a glass.

A short time later he heard the brougham returning and went to the window to look out. Henrietta was lifting Edward down. The child was happy, laughing at something his mother said and she kissed his cheek, laughing with him.

He put the glass down violently, several drops of brandy splashing onto the desktop. Striding to the door he pulled it open.

As Henrietta walked into the house, he shouted 'In the library on the instant.'

The child was in her arms and she felt his small body stiffen at the sound of his father's angry voice.

Calmly, though she was feeling far from composed, she handed the boy over to a servant. 'Please take Edward to his nurse.'

Henrietta kissed the child's face, saying, 'I'll come up to you in a few moments, my darling. Be good for nurse and do as she tells you, sweetheart. I'll read you a story before you go to sleep.'

'Promise me, Mama.' His china blue eyes looked grave.

Henrietta kissed his small hand. 'Of course I promise. I'll see you in a few moments.'

Tommy's voice roared. 'Leave the child alone, you ruin him. Come here at once!'

Reluctantly, Henrietta walked towards the library. Tommy's return had spoiled the day, she and Edward had been so happy. Now there would be another row.

Slightly drunk, Tommy lashed out as she entered. She had barely time to close the door before the back of his hand swiped her face.

Stung, Henrietta covered the red mark with the palm of her hand. 'How dare you.'

His eyes blazed. 'I strictly forbade you to go to my parents' hovel.'

Henrietta's hand remained on her face. 'I have never heard anything so ridiculous. Corn Cottage is warm and clean and there's more love there than can be found here. If anywhere deserves the name Hovel, Plas Mawr does, since your arrival.'

Tommy face was beetroot red. 'You bitch, you'll pay for that!' He hit her again with the flat of his hand.

Henrietta gave a haunted laugh. 'Oh, Tommy Standish, I have paid dearly enough already. My life has been purgatory since the moment you entered it.'

His jaw hardened. 'You were pleased enough to marry me, to give a name to your bastard child,' he sneered.

'Our child, it took two of us to conceive him,' she said bitterly.

He used the weapon that he knew would inflict greater pain than his fists ever could. 'I have decided to send the boy away to a school in Ireland that specialises in educating children as young as Edward.'

A cry wrenched from her. 'If anyone's a bastard it's you, Tommy Standish. How I wish that my son and I bore any name but yours.'

He grabbed her hair, tugging viciously. 'And how I wish another had borne my child.' Out of control, he thrust her aside viciously.

Thrown off her feet, Henrietta hit the sharp edge of the desk, taking the blow in her ribcage. Winded she stayed down for a moment but when she had breath enough to move she staggered up. With as much dignity as her torn dress and escaped hair would allow, she moved painfully to the door.

The noise of her crashing into the desk sobered Tommy. For one moment he thought he had killed her and the old fear of the hangman's noose overshadowed all other thought.

With the help of a footman, Henrietta made it to her bedroom.

Edward's nurse, a kindly young woman with some training from a local doctor, was called to take care of her mistress. Easing Henrietta out of her ruined magenta dress, the nurse was horrified to see the large bruise already beginning to show. Henrietta scalp was reddened where the hair had been wrenched out at the roots. Afraid to injure her mistress further the nurse carefully slipped the hairpins from the fallen tresses.

Her mind in turmoil, Henrietta ran through a dozen scenarios in which she and Edward escaped from Plas Mawr.

Remembering her promise to Edward, she started to rise from the dressing stool. 'I must go to Edward. I said that I would read him a story.'

The nurse put a restraining hand on Henrietta's shoulder. 'Madam, it's not good that the child should see you in this condition. What would he think of his ...' She had been about to say his father but stopped in time. It wouldn't be wise to accuse Tommy Standish of trying to murder his wife.

Henrietta's shoulders slumped. 'You're right.' She laid a hand on the nurse's arm.

'Would you see that he is read a story and tell him I will see him in the morning? Give him a goodnight kiss from me.'

'Of course, I will Madam. Leave it to me.'

Henrietta winced, holding her ribcage as she turned on the stool. 'Would you be so kind as to fetch me the bottle of laudanum from my dressing table, nurse?'

Putting aside the hairpins, the nurse went to the other room and brought an unopened bottle to Henrietta. A few moments later the young woman left the bedroom to go to Edward.

In the library, Tommy poured more brandy and he sat at the blazing fire to drink it. His thoughts went from Henrietta to Lady Isabelle. The woman had treated him very badly and had practically shown him the door when he had called at Hollybeck House before his departure from London.

Lord Harvey had been at his club, still celebrating the acquisition of his shares in Ruby Quarry. The silly fool had absolutely no idea that he and his family were on the road to ruin.

Tommy almost laughed aloud as he thought of the day that Lady Isabelle would realise the situation she was in. Would she think herself so clever then? Dismissing Tommy Standish was not the brightest thing the whore had done to date.

His mind came back to Henrietta. She was another whore who was getting above herself. Calling on his parents when he had expressly forbidden such an excursion was pure defiance.

As soon as he had finished his brandy he would go to her room and tell her again what he thought of her.

The following day the autumn dawn came slowly to the mansion, creeping across from the east; it spread silver-gilt across the manicured lawn and warmed the stone of the house to a shade of honey.

Beneath the great roof, Tommy slept restlessly.

Edward in the far wing lay sucking his thumb, the blankets tossed aside.

Henrietta, wearing a simple underskirt, the ruined magenta dress draped across the end of the bed, lay with her face to the bedside table staring unseeing at the bottle of laudanum. She had been dead for almost five hours and now lay stiffly, her glazed eyes staring at the dregs in the bottom of the bottle.

CHAPTER TWELVE

Joe ran down the quarry track heading for the refuge of home, there was a pain in his side and his breath rasped in his chest, he was crying noisily, tears running down his darkly tanned face. It didn't concern him that others might see him like this; his grief and shock were too great to be aware of the outer world.

At first, on hearing the news, he didn't believe it; how could Henrietta be dead when only yesterday she had sat under the hedge at Coots Farm eating apple pie, laughing at her young son's antics?

Dead, it just wasn't possible. Young Edward without his mother. God in heaven, where was the justice in that?

He found that he had passed the quarry gates and he was on the lane in the centre of the village. To the right was the Half-Way Inn and opposite to this was Maisy's shop. Beyond, there was a slight incline with a terrace of low straggling cottages. The doors and windows open to let in the dry air.

Ahead was Corn Cottage, the last building of the village. The gable-end came into view. The light-grey stone mellow in the sunlight. A moment later he was passing through the open gate and running to the front door that was ajar.

Emily was elbow deep in soapy water, humming a popular tune, when she heard a clatter coming from the living room. Believing a stray cat had got in, she grabbed a towel and came ready to shoo the creature out.

Opening the scullery door, a shout ready on her lips, she

started at seeing Joe bent forwards over the table, out of breath and crying.

The colour was drawn from her face. 'Is it our Frank? Has he had an accident?' She could hardly bear to wait for Joe's reply.

Joe sniffed back tears. 'No. Not that.'

'Thank God!' The sudden relief brought a weakness to her legs and it felt as though her limbs wouldn't support her.

'It's Henrietta. She's dead,' he sobbed.

This was a mistake. Somehow Joe had got it wrong. Emily said with certainty, 'No Joe, that's just not so. Henrietta was here yesterday. She'll be at Plas Mawr with Edward.'

'No, Emily.' Straightening, he wiped his wet face with his hand. 'She's not. She died last night or early this morning. They found her in her bed.'

Emily slumped on the nearest chair, too shocked to stand. 'God in heaven!'

Joe sniffed back tears. 'It's little Edward, how must that little boy be feeling right now? Oh, Emily, I don't think that I can stand this.'

The towel in Emily's hand was held so tightly that her fingertips were tinged blue. 'What of Tommy?'

Joe sneered. 'Tommy didn't even have the decency to send someone to tell us. I had to find out from the men at work and they only knew because one of the chap's daughter's works as a maid at the big house.' His voice cracked, 'Emily, they say that poor Henrietta was still wearing the clothes from yesterday, she never even got into her bed properly.'

'Where is she now?' Emily asked softly.

'I think she's been taken to the doctor's house.' His eyes filled. 'There'll have to be an inquiry I suppose. A young girl in the prime of life doesn't slip away for nothing.'

'She never said she was sick. I thought her thin but not sick, Joe.'

Joe held his breath for a moment, trying to find the words

to speak of the rumour. 'It seems she might have had an accident.'

Tommy's face came into her mind. Emily's head snapped up and her eyes flared.

'What sort of accident?'

The strength went out of Joe and he slumped into a chair, the base of the wooden legs scraping on the slate floor. 'She could have taken too much laudanum. They reckon she'd had a fall and really hurt herself; she must have taken the medicine to ease the pain.'

She glanced sideways, almost too afraid to ask, 'You don't think our Tommy had anything to do with it?'

The possibility had crossed Joe's mind. He said bitterly, 'I hope to God he hasn't, because if it comes out that he has, so help me God I will kill him myself. '

They both heard Frank's hurried footfalls on the garden path and were looking in the direction of the door as he rushed in. He took in the scene at a glance and knew immediately that the rumour spreading through the dressing sheds was true.

Tears came to his eyes. 'Mam, it's so sad.'

Rising, Emily held him close. It was almost impossible to speak coherently, as she said, 'Yes, it's the saddest thing I've heard for a long time.'

Sniffing, Joe wiped the end of his nose with the back of his hand. Automatically he lifted the kettle and as there was water in it he put it to the fire.

The black carriage carrying Henrietta's body to the surgeon's house left the grounds of Plas Mawr and turned into the roadway.

Tommy's thoughts were confused, as he stood at the window watching the vehicle's progress down the avenue. The carriage disappeared through the far off gates and he stood for a moment longer looking towards the entrance but it was too far away to see the servant in the lodge come to close the immense black gates.

His hangover was dreadful, probably the worst he had ever suffered. His drunken slumber had been nothing more than a comatose interlude during the early hours of the morning, which had been noisily broken by the devastating news that Henrietta lay dead in her bed.

His valet had shaken him awake and pain seared through his brain as he came up too quickly from his pillow. His stomach turned so violently, he vomited.

This reaction had more to do with his physical state than shock. But he wasn't such a fool as to think this wouldn't enhance the reputation of the marital union. Those that suspected that his love for his wife ran less than deeply may revise their opinion as word got out of his corporeal response to the dreadful news.

An almost imperceptible knock sounded on the drawing room door. The butler entered carrying a silver tray with a coffee pot and a bone china cup and saucer. There was a decanter of brandy beside the cut-glass sugar bowl. Putting the tray down, the servant poured coffee into the cup.

Turning from the window, Tommy sat at the table. 'Miles, would you see that all the servants are wearing black arm bands, and please deal with anything else that is appropriate for a house in mourning. If the curtains are not already drawn in the other rooms, please see that it is done immediately.'

The butler's eyes went to the curtains at the windows and he made a move towards them.

Tommy, with no intention of sitting in the dark until protocol demanded he pay his respects to the dead, said sharply, 'I will see to these drapes myself.'

With a slight bow and polite commiserations, the servant left Tommy alone.

Tommy poured a large measure of brandy into the cup of coffee; the smell rising from the hot liquid was momentarily sickening and he held his breath until he had swallowed half the contents of the cup. Warming his gut it revived him and he took another mouthful.

Relaxing back in the upholstered chair, feeling slightly better, he began to review the situation. Henrietta was gone. Her passing would make little difference to his life other than he would inherit what money and property she owned. The major and immediate problem to be faced was that Henrietta had been badly bruised. Griffith the surgeon had documented the injuries and would no doubt state this when he was called as a witness at the inquest. There was also the possibility that an examination would reveal that Henrietta was bruised about the face too. How far would the doctor probe for the truth?

Restless, carrying the cup and saucer, he went to the window checking that the avenue was empty. Taking a sip from the cup he continued the thread of his thoughts. Would the police call? If so, he needed to have a story ready. Were the servants aware of the fight? It was hard to believe that they weren't. Should he pay them a bonus as compensation for their upset or should he sack whoever had seen Henrietta after she left the library and anyone else that wasn't prepared to toe the line?

Leaving the window, crossing to the table, he poured a little coffee into the cup topping it up with brandy.

Sitting again, his eyes on the silver coffee pot, he thought back to the hours before the calamity. He had been drunk, very drunk, so drunk in fact that he couldn't remember if he had gone to Henrietta's room.

Hearing the approach of a vehicle, fearing that it was the police, he stood on trembling legs and crossed the Turkey carpet to the window. A black carriage was turning on the circle before the house. The driver jumped down from the box and opened the door. Two uniformed police specials stepped out.

Tommy's heart fluttered and he felt faint and nauseous again. Putting his hand to his brow he brought it away damp with perspiration. Drawing a silk handkerchief from his pocket he wiped his face.

The policemen's voices came to him and the tread of boots on the mosaic floor as they approached the drawing room. Fearing the worst, a queasy feeling came to his guts and his bowels turned to water.

There was a slight knock. The door opened and a footman came in.

Bowing, the servant spoke quietly as though he had entered a sick room. 'Master, there's two specials to see you.'

The uniformed men were only a step away from the footman. They entered before the man had taken Tommy's instructions.

The taller of the two spoke loudly as though compensating for the timidity of the servant. 'Mr Standish, we need to ask you a few questions.'

Tommy felt weak. He was sure that they thought him guilty of murder. Millie Barker's face came to him, blue-grey in death.

His stomach cramped and for a dreadful moment he thought he would need to rush from the room without being sure he would make it to the privy in time. The spasm passed but it drained his face further.

'I'll help all that I can.' Tommy stammered as he picked up the china cup. His hand trembled and the cup clinked in the saucer.

Fighting to regain control of his nerves, to look less guilty before the police standing impassively, he put the cup down. He could read nothing in the eyes of the two men, neither compassion nor doubt, and he wondered if they actually saw anyone as innocent. It passed through his mind that men do beat up their wives and don't go to jail for it. So why was he getting into such a terrible state? He hadn't killed Henrietta!

One of the policemen shifted his boots. 'We would like to see your late wife's bedroom. Also we would like you to answer a few questions, Mr Standish. It's customary when there's been a sudden death.'

Tommy considered summoning a servant to show the police to Henrietta's suite, but the less the police had to do with the servants the better. He led the way up the stairs.

Edward's nurse was crossing the landing as the threesome reached the head of the stairs and she glanced coldly at Tommy. He looked long and hard at the woman, wondering how much she might know of last night's fracas.

The bedroom still held the scent of Henrietta. There was an array of pots and potions and several glass perfume bottles on the dressing table. A silver backed hairbrush had been put down with the bristles uppermost. Several strands of Henrietta's long, dark hair were entwined in the fine bristles.

The almost empty laudanum bottle was still on the bedside table and one of the policemen picked it up and sniffed what was left of the contents. Putting it into his pocket, he began to search the drawers. Three more bottles of the opium-based drug were found in the dressing room and three larger bottles of heroin mixture with the local chemist's label attached were found beside them. A decanter of sherry was on a table in her sitting room, a sticky glass beside it.

Tommy sounding sorrowful explained, 'I'm afraid my wife was of a very nervous disposition. Her mother's death didn't help the situation. Recently I had cause to consult with Doctor Rogers of the Denbigh Asylum about my wife's worsening condition. He advised restraining her at the asylum ...'

He glanced down to the pink and green carpet for affect, as though ashamed of what he had to reveal next. 'Henrietta's brother is confined at the asylum in Denbigh. So the family are familiar with the hospital.'

It was all the police needed to hear. Madness ran in families. Departing from the house without questioning the servants, the police specials climbed back into their waiting vehicle.

It was the police opinion that the case was cut and dried. Henrietta Standish, whilst under the influence of laudanum, had fallen and had taken more laudanum to ease the pain. She had died of an overdose. It was a simple case of a lunatic, neurotic woman, who on this occasion was not fortunate enough to be protected by her husband.

Mr Standish stated that he had arrived home from London to find that his wife and child were out visiting his parents. He had retired to his library to await their return.

Mr Standish had been most forthcoming in explaining that fairly recently he had consulted with a Doctor Rogers in Chester regarding his wife's addiction to opium and it had been decided that she should enter Denbigh Asylum for a cure. Upon the sudden death of her mother, Mr Standish had decided that Henrietta should remain at home as he was reluctant to be parted from her in his grief. Mrs Bellamy and Tommy Standish had enjoyed a close family relationship. Now the poor man blamed himself; had he not selfishly kept his wife close by, this terrible tragedy might not have happened.

Joe heard this version of events from Oakley who summoned him to his office to supposedly commiserate on the loss of his daughter-in-law. Oakley suggested that Joe couldn't expect time off to go to the inquest or the funeral as he had already taken a *harvest* day without sanction. Listening to the man pontificating, Joe realised that the speech had all the hallmarks of Tommy Standish. Joe understood that he was being told not to attend the funeral.

After the one-sided interview, Joe returned to Jericho gallery where he was setting Bickford fuses. Raging inwardly, he packed explosive into the gimlet holes he'd made earlier. When he fired the black powder, the roar was loud enough to shake Oakley's office windows and bring flakes of white distemper off the privy wall.

At the end of a morose day, when each explosion that Joe set brought great quantities of slate tumbling from the rock-face and every occupant in the office building would look to the skyline to check that Garddryn Quarry still existed, Joe left the property. His mood no better than when he had come from Oakley's office.

At Corn Cottage the curtains remained drawn night and day in respect of the young woman the family had taken to their hearts and it was to this gloomy atmosphere that Joe returned from work.

Breaking the habit of a working lifetime, he would generally slip out of his dirty work clothes in the scullery before settling in the kitchen, but this evening he sat in the chair beside the fire and took off his boots. He was staring into the flames in the grate as Emily came in from feeding the hens.

She saw immediately that he was cross. 'What's a matter, Joe?'

'Nowt.'

Slipping off her shawl, she hung it on the peg at the back of the door. 'Doesn't look like nowt to me. You look as though you've found a frog under a stone, when you expected to find a penny.'

Her eyes were on him as she crossed the room. Picking up her white apron from the back of the chair, she tied it around her waist. There was a pan of haricot beans simmering on the hob. She glanced sideways at Joe as she put a spoon into the pot to stir them.

The scowl scoring his face deepened. 'Have you got a black dress?'

Emily's brow puckered. 'Aye, it's an old one, mind.'

'Will it do for the lass's funeral?'

'I've already washed and pressed it for that terrible day. Same as I did with the grey shawl. What's on your mind, Joe?'

His lip curled. 'That lad of ours doesn't want us at Henrietta's funeral.'

Emily was matter-of-fact. 'I didn't expect him to want us there. He hasn't stopped being ashamed of us, Joe. But his attitude will not stop us going to pay our respects to the mother of our grandchild, will it?'

Frowning, Joe rose from his chair. Taking his tobacco pouch off the mantel he filled his pipe, tamping down the tobacco with his pipe scraper. 'It might.'

Emily put the spoon aside. 'How's that then?'

'Because,' he said with indignation, 'Oakley called me into the office and said I cannot have time off for the funeral because I had an unauthorized day to go harvesting.' His voice rose, 'It's our Tommy's doing.'

Emily's mouth pursed in annoyance; bustling to the table she picked up the bread knife and cut viciously into Wednesday's loaf. Cutting again, unevenly, she glanced up flushed and outraged. 'Well, you might not be able to go, but I will.'

Joe's mouth quirked and the folds that ran perpendicularly down his cheeks deepened.

It was the first hint of a smile Emily had seen on his face for long, sad days.

'I knew you would, our Emily.'

Waving the knife to punctuate her words, Emily snapped, 'You had better bloody believe it, Joe Standish. Ashamed indeed, I'll show the bugger who's ashamed!'

Joe chortled. He wouldn't like to be in Tommy's boots not with his mother all riled up. She was a fiery little minx when her goat was up.

With the inquest over, Tommy arranged the funeral for the following Wednesday, two days hence. It would be a simple affair, just a few invited guests. The funeral service would be held in the small chapel in the house, the interment in the family mausoleum in the grounds. Henrietta would be buried next to her mother, who had so recently preceded her daughter.

The day of the funeral dawned grey and chill; a blanket

of soft vapour lay over the house and grounds. The trees along the long avenue were hidden in wet, grey mist. The lawns were beaded with water, imprinted with the soles of the boots of gardeners collecting fallen leaves.

A glass-sided funeral carriage carried Henrietta in her coffin from the funeral directors' establishment to her home. The carriage remained at the front door of the mansion, four sombrely plumed black horses in the traces, wet and disconsolate.

Water dripping from the stonework of the house spotted the maple coffin as it was carried into the grand hall. The crystal droplets lay like tears on the polished wood.

Four solemn men in tall hats, black suits and caped frockcoats, reverently placed the coffin on a catafalque that had been draped with black silk.

Tommy stood in the shadows. As the men stepped aside from the burden he came forward and placed a wreath of white lilies on the closed lid. Bending his head in prayer, he closed his eyes, his lips moving to silent words.

There were few mourners. Since her marriage, Henrietta had been sadly lacking in friends. The invited guests that would attend the service were already in Plas Mawr.

Lord Harvey and Lady Isabelle had arrived yesterday afternoon. Tommy had been quite insistent that Lord Harvey should come to the funeral and had persuaded him to combine the stay with a visit to Ruby Quarry, to see for himself how his investment was progressing.

Tommy had taken immense delight in showing Lady Isabelle around the mansion and grounds, secretly delighting in her lightly disguised awe at the magnificence. It would probably be the last time she would enjoy absolute luxury as her days of extravagance were coming to a close, although she was still unaware of the fact.

Edward, wearing a little black dress and pantaloons, came down the wide stairs holding his nurse's hand; on each step he paused, his black shoes coming together before he stepped onto the next tread.

The funeral guests' eyes were on the little boy and their expressions were sorrowful.

The footmen along with the other servants were standing to the back of the grand hall, almost hidden by the dark marble pillars. The large group stood erect, motionless and silent. They had received a lecture on decorum from the butler; a show of tears was forbidden.

Reaching the final step, Edward was ushered to a far corner where he remained with his nurse.

Tommy was standing at the head of the coffin, in silent prayer. Becoming aware that he was observed he lifted his head and looked to the open front door. His mother stood framed in the doorway, a damp grey shawl covering her head, the hem of her black skirt splattered with wet clay. To his horror she advanced, slowly climbing the stone steps. Her eyes didn't leave his face until she crossed the threshold, then walking to the coffin, she knelt in prayer.

'Nana!' Edward shrieked with delight. Caught fast by his nurse, he squirmed to get away from her arms.

Emily raised a finger to her lips to shush the child and Edward fell still. She remained for a moment longer, then getting up slowly, her knees stiff, she crossed to the shadows.

To cover the moment of embarrassment, the vicar came forward. Whispering to Tommy, he said 'I think it would be appropriate to go to the chapel now and begin the service.'

The four funeral directors, alert to every nuance from the vicar, stepped forward and lifted the coffin off the catafalque. Shouldering their burden they reverently made their way to the open front door.

Matching his pace to theirs, Tommy walked behind the coffin.

His thoughts were entirely with his mother; she was following behind him. How was he to explain the woman's presence? He would die of shame, should anyone ask who the late arrival was. How was he to get rid of her? No doubt she would stay until after the internment. And after that, he dare not think. Would she be so crass as to invite herself for the repast that had been prepared for the funeral guests and the vicar?

After a brief ceremony Henrietta's coffin was laid beside her mother.

As the last words from the vicar died on the wet air, Emily turned away from the mausoleum and took the path to the avenue. Her head covered by a grey shawl, the rain drenching her skirt and leaking through the crack in the sole of her boot, she made for home. She had done what she came to do, to pay her respects to the mother of her grandson.

In the dining room where the small group of people had congregated to enjoy glasses of Madeira, the rumours regarding the uninvited woman were rife. Tommy had disappeared briefly with the funeral director; as he re-entered the dining room conversation ceased, all eyes on him.

The butler came alongside him, and Tommy took a glass of wine from the offered tray.

Lord Harvey guffawed as Lady Isabelle suggested the peasant woman might have been one of Tommy's earlier conquests. After consuming three glasses of Madeira quickly, Lord Harvey couldn't resist saying vulgarly, 'Come on, Standish. Tell us who the damp spectre was.'

Tommy was at a loss of how to answer him.

Lady Isabelle remembered that the child had called the visitor, Nana. Smiling vindictively, she said, 'Nana, an unusual name. Isn't it a title reserved for the poor for a grandmother?'

Slightly red in the face, Tommy made a hasty reply, saying 'Nanareen, I believe. The old woman was an ancient retainer of Henrietta's mother.'

The guests, losing interest, moved to the table to help themselves to cold chicken, baked ham, roast beef and duck.

CHAPTER THIRTEEN

The first line of Ruby Quarry rail track was to be laid today. It would cut across the moorland where Tommy had discovered the red shards of slate three years earlier.

There was to be a ceremony. A dignitary from the proposed Western Snowdonia Railway had already arrived, eager to talk of the design of his company's railway.

The other guests were milling around a table, which held several bottles of champagne and a light repast, prepared by the cooks in Plas Mawr.

Lord Harvey accompanied by Lady Isabelle and the four London businessmen who had invested in Ruby, were standing together, the conversation light-hearted and optimistic.

Oakley, the manager of the Garddryn, was a sceptic regarding Ruby; he had heard too many conversations between Tommy and Madoc the solicitor, and too many letters had passed his desk for him to have much faith in the outcome of the quarry, but he wasn't fool enough to express his opinion.

Madoc was standing on the fringes of the gathering with a banker from Bangor.

There was a sprinkling of worthies from the county, delighted to be transported to such a wild and remote spot and in such splendid carriages provided by the owners of the new quarry.

A hundred and fifty Irish labourers had been digging at

Ruby for a more than a year and to date there had not been a lot to show for their effort.

The task of keeping the investors, especially Lord Harvey, interested in the project and prepared to plough ahead with the improvements had fallen to Tommy. Tommy's enthusiasm albeit false had convinced Lord Harvey to increase his investment and now there were several mortgages held on Hollybeck House and the repayments were financially crippling.

It surprised Tommy that the money was holding out for so long. Lady Isabelle was no doubt forced to cut her cloth and tighten her belt but her attempts would be for nought when the truth regarding Ruby became known.

Today was the first time Tommy had seen Lady Isabelle in a while. He suspected that she was still seeing the man that she had abandoned him for. Her betrayal still had the power to anger him even though he had reinstated his affair with Sadie, the maid at Penrhyn.

Crossing to the group of investors, his shoes whispering in the dry spiky grass, Tommy came alongside Lady Isabelle and stood close enough for his trouser leg to brush against the full skirt of her yellow and black dress.

Courteous, he smiled. 'How very lovely you look, Lady Isabelle.'

Surprised, he hadn't spoken a civil word to her in months, she returned his smile. 'I thank you, kind sir.' Still finding him maddeningly attractive, she hoped that this softening on his part meant that the hostilities between them were at an end.

The champagne, the air, and the prospect of vast profits made Lord Harvey expansive. Jovial, he grasped Tommy's hand and shook it vigorously. 'What a glorious day. The weather is perfect, brilliant sunshine, not a cloud in the sky. It's ideal for laying that first important track. Ruby will be fully operational in no time. Very soon now the slate will be hauled to the dock in enormous quantities.'

Still pumping Tommy's hand, he went on, 'I don't know how to thank you for putting this great investment my way.'

Still grinning, he punched Tommy lightly on the shoulder. 'Bet you wish you'd kept all this to yourself instead of sharing it with the likes of me and my wife?'

'Not at all, Lord Harvey, I'm pleased that everything is going so exceptionally well.'

Tommy managed to free his hand. Sardonic, he said 'You never know, I might want to buy back in at a later date.'

It was the last thing that Lord Harvey wanted to happen. He had no intention of sharing the profits with another investor, not even Tommy Standish. Proving that he understood nothing of the master of the Garddryn, Lord Harvey's attempts to dissuade him were amateurish.

'I would have thought that the Garddryn would be more than enough for any one man.' He smiled ingratiatingly. 'Plus you own the lease on this land and by the amount you're charging us for the business of quarrying here, you can't really be too disappointed.'

Tommy saw through Lord Harvey's inexpert attempt to retain the largest share. The blatant avarice amused him.

His eyes shone with laughter but his tone was appeasing, as he said 'Not in the least, Lord Harvey. Everything is going splendidly and according to plan. Better than I ever expected.' Dropping his voice he was conspiratorial. 'It's so rewarding when everything begins to work out as you expected, isn't it?'

Relieved, Lord Harvey rushed his words. 'Yes, yes. I must say I can't wait to get Ruby fully operational and producing. We investors have sunk a lot of money into it.'

His liverish eyes roamed the middle distance. 'We have probably gone a bit far in putting in expensive equipment at this stage. But we have been led by you. And we agree that it would be costly to lay off men whilst new innovations are installed.'

Gesturing to the site of the new railway track, he said

'Laying the lines would be doubly difficult if we had horse drawn wagons using a separate line. Already we have fifty men preparing the land for the rail. It's costing but it'll be worth it.'

It amazed Tommy that anyone could have as little business acumen as Lord Harvey and it was incredible that he'd teamed up with four like-minded men. Accepting his word as master of the Garddryn without seeking outside professional help was sheer lunacy.

Mid-afternoon, the guests were gathered together for the journey to Plas Mawr where they were to dine. Tommy shared a carriage with Madoc. Heading for the mansion, they discussed the incredible business of Ruby Quarry.

Edward was home from his school in Cheltenham for the Christmas holidays. On the first opportunity, unbeknownst to his father, the boy headed for Corn Cottage.

Standing at the table in the kitchen, beside a blazing fire, Emily was stirring a fruit cake mixture. The table was littered with ingredients, greased tins and dough rising in a large crock. She had been baking for several hours and the debris of her labour had accumulated.

A timorous knock sounded on the front door. As she didn't expect a caller and had no wish to be caught out in such a mess, she frowned. Muttering something about carol singers and parents taking more responsibility with their offspring, she put aside the sticky spoon. Wiping her hands down her apron, she went to open the door.

Edward was on the doorstep, his slight frame wrapped in a warm tweed coat and trousers, with a red muffler around his collar to keep out the bitter cold wind.

Emily's hand went to her mouth in surprised delight.

His small face was red, eyes bright from the arctic blast the village was experiencing.

The thought of this moment had been with him throughout the lonely school term. Delighted that it was at last upon him, he beamed. 'Nana, are you pleased to see me?'

Emily scooped him up in her arms, hugging him tight.

Edward laughed, spluttering, 'Nana, I can hardly breathe!'

Drawing him into the warm room, she began to undo his coat.

'I can do this now, Nana.' Fumbling with the buttons, getting his muffler caught in his collar, Edward pulled off the coat and slung it onto his grandpa's fireside chair.

Emily bustled about the kitchen. Throwing extra wood on the already blazing fire she put the kettle to it. Only minutes before she had taken a fruit pie from the bread oven and although it had hardly cooled she took a knife and cut into it, releasing the sweet aroma of blackberries. The berries she had picked and preserved from last autumn's harvest.

Gesturing to Joe's chair, a plate in her hand, she said, 'You just sit down there, eat this, and tell your poor old Nana all your news.'

Shuffling his bottom on the shiny wooden seat, his short legs dangling towards the slate floor, he took the offered plate and spoon. 'Coor, Nana! There isn't much to tell. I went to school and now I've come home again.'

Emily laughed. 'You get more like your grandfather every day, young man. He's also lacking in the information department when it suits him. Come on tell me, what is the school like? Who do you meet there? Are the teachers nice?'

'Nana, that's boring. I'd rather you told me about the pigs. Did they have many babies? What happened to the cat next door? Did he get better after falling in the hole? I want to know everything.'

Whilst Edward sat and ate his pie, Emily brought him up to date with the welfare of the animals in the vicinity. Stretching the news to cover the time it took Edward to scoop the last blackberry onto his spoon.

Putting the plate with the other debris on the table, the visit was too important to ruin it with washing up. Emily helped him on with his coat and muffler. Taking a shawl off the door peg, she threw the ancient green woolly over her shoulders.

Braving the bitter weather they went out to see the seven young pigs. Walking alongside his grandmother, trotting to keep up, Edward chattered about the foal at Plas Mawr and the kittens born last summer in the tack room.

Reaching the pigpen, Edward climbed onto the gate, his arms thrown over the top bar. Inquisitive, the young pigs trotted towards him. Grinning at their antics, Edward threw the apple cores that Emily had brought. Squealing the young animals attacked the unexpected bounty. Delighted with the small porkers, Edward laughed gleefully.

Joe was coming to the garden gate as Edward's laughter rang out and quickening his pace he hurried towards the pen.

Emily and Edward turned as Joe approached. Leaping off the gate, Edward ran into Joe's arms.

Stooping, his arms wrapped around the small body, Joe held him close.

Releasing the boy, holding him at arms length, Joe said 'It lovely to see you, Edward, but will you get into trouble coming here?'

Edward's china-blue eyes were serious. 'There will not be any trouble Grandpa, honest. Papa is away in London.' A grin lit his small face. 'And I gave Josie a sixpence to keep the latch off the scullery window. So it'll be easy to sneak back in.'

Joe laughed. 'And who is the co-conspirator, Josie?

Edward looked serious. 'She's not a spirit, she's a scullery maid.'

Joe tried not to laugh again. 'Well, that's all right then. It seems you have organised yourself very well, you and this maid.'

Edward beamed with delight.

Emily handed the last of the apple cores to Edward and

pleased to show his grandfather the pigs' antics, he threw the cores as far as he could into the pen. Laughing as the little porkers made a dash for them.

Joe looked up at the sky. It would soon be dark. Reluctant to see Edward leave, he placed his arm around the child's shoulder.

'How about me and Nana walk you back to Plas Mawr?'

Edward climbed slowly off the gate. 'I suppose I should go but I don't really want to. I would love to stay here with you and Nana.'

Sad, Joe ruffled the boy's hair. 'That sound's lovely but what about poor little Josie, won't she be wanting her tea? Can't expect a girl to keep watch at a window and go without her tea.'

Edward sighed. 'You're right, Grandpa. I was being unkind.'

Jumping down, he took Emily's hand, held his other up to Joe. 'Come on, Grandpa. We had better let Josie have her tea,' he said, sounding resigned.

As they approached the gates of Plas Mawr dusk fell suddenly. The grey mist on the horizon glowed smoky ruby, casting tawny shades on the bare tree and fields. A moment later the day was gone, the sky and sea merging to dull, bleak grey.

Emily remembered the last time she had walked down the avenue towards the mansion. She had been alone and nervous but determined to pay her respects to Edward's mother. For many weeks after that visit she struggled to come to terms with the reality that her son was ashamed to acknowledge her. It had been hard to bear, but as Joe had said at the time 'all things pass.' Now if images of that day came to haunt her she thought of Frank; there wasn't a young man in the world that loved his mother like Frank did. She squeezed Edward's hand. Now she had this little boy to love.

Edward was determined to get into the house through the scullery window. Emily said she thought he should try a door but Edward would not be turned from his plan.

Walking stealthily around to the back of the house, Emily nervously checking behind them every few seconds, they came to the window. It was unlatched. Joe lifted Edward in.

Looking out as his grandparents, Edward's beam was as bright as a harvest moon. He whispered, 'This means that I will be able to escape at anytime and come to see you.'

Emily and Joe grinned back.

Joe gestured to the latch. 'Don't forget to lock it.'

'I won't, Grandpa. Goodnight. See you soon.'

They were treated to another broad smile before the boy dropped the latch and was lost to the gloom of the unlit scullery.

Walking back along the avenue, the bitter wind crept beneath their clothes. Joe put his arm around Emily's shoulder.

Smiling, she looked up into his face. 'The little perisher was determined to go through that window.'

Joe laughed. 'Of course he was. He'd given Josie sixpence so that he could get in through the scullery window. He wasn't going to waste sixpence, was he?'

Emily chortled. 'The little beggar.'

For several days after the visit, Joe and Emily wondered if they would see Edward again before he returned to his school at the end of the Christmas holiday. Sure that they would, Joe tried to reassure Emily. It saddened him to see her look out at the slightest sound.

Finishing work at noon on Christmas Eve, Joe forwent the usual ale at the Half-Way and strode towards home, a small bundle hidden in his coat.

Emily was standing on a chair stringing paper lanterns across the ceiling as Joe came down the path. The door opened wide and smoke came down the chimney into the room. Closing the door quickly keeping out the freezing air, Joe wiped his feet thoroughly on the doormat.

The determined wiping of feet of her men folk was in Emily's eyes a bad sign, generally heralding either a confession or a desperate request. Glancing down from the chair, she waited for either to show itself.

'I would have done that if you'd waited, Emily.'

Emily stepped down. 'I wanted it all done just in case Edward comes.' She looked towards the scullery door. 'I've got some holly and ivy and a bit of mistletoe, so you can help me put that around.'

Something moved beneath Joe's coat and they both looked at his midriff, Joe guiltily.

Emily frowned. 'Joe. I hope you haven't brought some poor creature to kill for the table, because if you have you can let the little beast go, now.'

'Course I haven't!' Undoing a couple of buttons, putting his hand into the coat he withdrew a small bundle of black fur. The puppy whimpered. 'I know what you're going to say Emily, that it costs to feed a dog, but I got this for young Edward. It's Ed's Christmas box.'

Emily's eyes didn't leave the creature. 'How on earth can he get it into Plas Mawr? You know our Tommy hates dogs.'

Holding the little animal up, Joe looked into the puppy's black eyes. 'He's not going to have to get it into Plas Mawr. Although he belongs to Edward, the dog will live here. Edward can come to see his puppy whenever he likes.'

Tears filmed Emily's eyes. 'Joe, you are a wonder, trust you to come up with an idea like that. Edward will bust a gut to come and see his puppy.'

Taking the puppy from Joe, she kissed the top of its silky head. 'Little doggy, I reckon we should find you a bowl and put something nice into it. You never know, Edward could come along at any minute and he wouldn't like to find you hungry, would he little one?' she said, carrying the pup to the scullery.

Joe marvelled at the ability of women to fall in love spontaneously. He had to admit he had been a bit worried, wondering if Emily would take to the idea of a dog in the house.

Emily came back carrying the pup and a dish; putting both down at the fireside she watched the dog eat hungrily. 'What'll we call him?'

Joe's eyes were on the short, wagging tail. 'I thought Saint Nicholas, it being Christmas.'

'It's a bit long. I can't see you standing at the door shouting Saint Nicholas, Saint Nicholas.'

'No, you're probably right; how about Nick?'

Emily glanced at the pup. 'Nick, it suits him.'

The puppy was sleeping on the hearth rug when a light knock sounded on the door.

Joe leapt up, flinging aside his newspaper.

Emily was at the table making bread sauce for the goose they would share tomorrow with Amos the book peddler and Tudor, Joe's closest friend. Fergus Holmes was coming for afternoon tea and bringing his four motherless children.

Her heart in her mouth, Emily watched Joe open the door. When she saw who stood there, she let out a loud cry, 'Edward!'

The child, his cheeks red with cold, came in clutching a bag. 'A very merry Christmas,' he said beaming.

Coming to the table, he delved proudly into his bag. Pulling out an elaborate silver and red package, he handed the box of sweetmeats to Emily.

'This Nana is for you. I bought them in a very posh shop in Cheltenham town.' His eyebrows rose. 'I bought them with my pocket money, honest.'

Emily bent to kiss his cheek. 'Thank you, Edward. It is very kind and thoughtful of you.'

Beaming again, he pulled another package from the bag and handed it to his grandfather. 'Although this didn't come from a very posh shop, I still bought it myself.'

Joe smiled. 'Thank you, Edward.' He bent to kiss the boy.

There was still another trophy at the bottom of the bag. As an exceptionally fine bottle of port was revealed, Joe noticed that there was no mention of its origins.

Untying the ribbon from around the box, Emily stripped the covering from the sweetmeats. Hearing the paper crinkle, the sleeping puppy stirred.

Seeing the small animal, Edward squealed with delight. Reaching down he hauled the tiny pup from the rug. The boy's nose touched the puppy's and pleased at the attention the puppy licked Edward's face.

'Where did he come from? Isn't he beautiful? Is it a boy?' Edward laughed as the puppy's tongue found his nose.

Joe didn't think that he had been as happy as he was at this moment for a very long time; content yes, but not brimming with gleeful happiness.

Smiling broadly, he said 'He's all yours. But it's perhaps better that he lives here and we look after him for you.'

'Mine, he's mine.' Edward's happiness boiled over. 'Has he got a name? Is he really mine?'

Beaming, Joe said 'We thought a good name would be Nicholas, because it's Christmas. He could be called Nick. But if you want a different name ...'

'Nick's perfect, Grandpa.'

Edward nuzzled the pup's nose. 'He's the very best present I ever, ever, had.'

It was mid-afternoon when Joe walked back to the gates of Plas Mawr with Edward. The puppy wrapped in Emily's shawl against the biting cold.

Joe asked Edward what arrangement had been made for the holiday tomorrow and he had been amused by the boy's reply. For days afterwards, Joe chortled recalling Edward's words.

'Papa will be at home,' he had said seriously. 'He has invited Mr Madoc and his wife to stay. Mr and Mrs Arnold are also coming. They are bringing Mrs Arnold's two nieces.

They are twins but much too old to play with. Papa says that they are twenty-four and unmarried. Mrs Arnold is trotting out her fillies. I heard Papa tell Mr Madoc this.'

With a look of bewilderment, Edward glanced up to Joe. 'What do you think *trotting out fillies* is Grandpa? I would hate not to know how to play the game if we are to play it after dinner.'

Joe was as reluctant to part with the boy, as the boy was to part with the pup. After several false starts, Edward ran to the house. Joe watched his fast progress from the avenue.

Joe and Emily, the pup sleeping between them, were talking in the dark. The puppy had whimpered incessantly on being left in the kitchen. Joe with a long drawn out sigh had brought it to bed, where it had fallen asleep immediately. They were left wide awake, chatting in the darkness, giggling at the *trotting out of fillies*.

Edward's happiness was complete, when on Christmas morning his father took him to the stable to give gifts to the stablemen. Edward, too small to see over the stalls had no idea that his Christmas surprise was hidden there.

Tommy, a rare smile on his lips, opened the half-door of the stall.

Edward started in surprise seeing a pony with a red and green ribbon tied through its golden mane.

'She's all yours, Edward,' his father said, still smiling. 'You must choose her name and take good care of her.'

Eyes shining, Edward promised to do so. 'Can I take her out?'

Tommy sniffed, 'I see no reason why not. You've been riding long enough now. One of the men will saddle her up.'

Bursting with happiness, Edward ran back to the house to change into riding clothes.

Minutes later a stable hand brought the pony to the front door.

Flushed from hurrying, Edward ran down the front steps. The brown cape he'd thrown over his coat flying behind him.

Although he was a little nervous on his new mount, Edward thought it important to introduce Holly, the pony instantly had a name, to Nick the puppy. His happiness complete, he rode slowly to Corn Cottage.

CHAPTER FOURTEEN

Tommy was in the library going over the recent report submitted by the geologist, Mr Thomas Parker. The report didn't hold any new information. It didn't differ from the initial inspection of the land almost four years previously. Ruby Quarry was viable, the area rich in slate.

Sipping coffee at his desk, Tommy reread the report reaffirming Parker's opinion. In one way it was good news; he held the lease on the land. But Lord Harvey only had to hang on for another few weeks and the huge investment, dangerous re-mortgages and added borrowing would be vindicated and Lord Harvey would become a rich man again. Lady Isabelle, damn her, would reap the benefits. Where was the retribution in that? He slapped the report down on the desktop and rested his hand upon it.

Hearing a vehicle coming towards the house he came from around his desk to look out of the window. Rivulets of rain were running down the pane. The light was quickly failing, granite clouds racing across the darkening sky. Beyond the drenched lawn the black branches of the trees were swaying in the gusting, bitter wind.

He watched an ancient black carriage draw up at the main entrance. He sighed, hating the inconvenience uninvited guests put on his personal plans and the household in general.

Two liveried footmen trotted down the front steps, shoulders hunched and necks buried in their coat collars against the slanting rain. The butler followed, opening a black umbrella as he hurried to open the carriage door.

The coachman, submerged in a cumbersome brown cape, climbed down from the box rheumatically. With his head bent to the wind, he held the bridles of the snorting, steaming horses.

Alighting clumsily, Lord Harvey glanced around before turning to assist Lady Isabelle down.

Even from the distance of the library window it was evident to Tommy that Isabelle was disgruntled and Lord Harvey appeared in no better mood.

'Now what brings that pair here?' he said aloud.

Hearing footsteps approaching the library door, he turned from the window. Shouting 'enter' the moment someone knocked.

The footman, his uniform and hair wet through, gave a perfunctory bow. 'Lord Harvey and Lady Isabelle request a most urgent meeting with you, sir,' he said nervously, expecting a severe reprimand for bringing the guests baggage into the house without his master's consent.

Although intrigued by the reason for the unexpected arrival, Tommy decided to keep the pair kicking their heels in the guest room for fifteen minutes. Then a sudden sickening thought came to him, perhaps they had discovered the contents of the report on Ruby Quarry and they knew that immense wealth was within their grasp. God in heaven, he hoped that they hadn't thought fit to come to celebrate their incredible good fortune. That would be hard to stomach.

Anxious to discover the truth, he waved the footman away impatiently. 'Yes, yes show them in. And bring tea and whisky.'

With the help of a servant, Lord Harvey divested himself of his outdoor coat in the hall. His black frock coat and grey trousers were creased from travel and his grey waistcoat rode up over his paunch. Hurrying to be away from London in the early hours, he had gone without his morning shave and he looked unkempt, locks of grey unwashed hair hanging lankly on his coat collar.

The footman coming from the library advanced on the guests. 'Mr Standish will see you at once.'

Tommy was standing beside the marble chimneypiece, a fire blazing brightly in the grate. Behind him, on the top of the bureau, an oil lamp with a white globe burned evenly and another glowed on the desktop.

The footman preceding Lord Harvey into the library gave a small bow and began to announce the guests.

Ignoring the servant, Lord Harvey crossed the room quickly. Grasping Tommy's hand, he shook it vigorously. 'It's good to see you. I hope we haven't put you out by turning up like this?'

There was a false joviality in the greeting and Tommy's misgivings began to subside.

The servant withdrew, silently closing the door.

Lady Isabelle was wearing the latest fashion, a princess-line dress. The dark red and black material drew the colour from her face and to counteract this Lady Isabelle had applied heavier rouge and brighter lip paint, which accentuated the thinness and slight puckering of her mouth.

Tommy noted that she was looking her age and the flirtatious glint had gone from her once lovely eyes.

'I had no idea that you and Lady Isabelle were in the area,' Tommy said enquiringly.

Lord Harvey looked embarrassed. 'We were not, Tommy. We have come especially to seek your advice. I'm afraid that we are in serious trouble.' He gave a long sigh. 'The bank has foreclosed on the mortgage and they wish for immediate possession of Hollybeck House.'

Although jubilant that his plans to ruin Lady Isabelle had at last come to fruition, Tommy managed to sound mournful at the news. 'Surely things can't be that bad?'

Lady Isabelle gave a harsh laugh. Glancing spitefully in Lord Harvey's direction, she rasped, 'There's another problem which my husband hasn't yet mentioned.' Her top lip curled contemptuously. 'Are you going to explain dearest, or shall I?'

Lord Harvey drooped. 'You might as well as do it, Isabelle. You've had plenty of practice reminding me of my folly during the last few days.'

Her scornful eyes didn't leave Lord Harvey's face, as she said 'My darling husband, not satisfied with mortgaging our home on one occasion, chose to do it several times using various banks. He now faces a long gaol term for fraud if he is caught.'

Wet tears were on her lashes. She turned to Tommy. 'We are on the run and that is why we have come to you.'

Lord Harvey looking like a whipped dog, tried to clutch her arm. Tearfully he said, 'Forgive me, my dear. I never thought it would come to this.'

Brushing off his outstretched hand, she sneered. 'You don't *think*, Harvey.'

Lord Harvey's red-rimmed eyes filmed with tears. Turning to Tommy, he pleaded, 'Please advise me. What are we to do? We ran in your direction as we have nowhere else to go.'

Afraid that he might be saddled with the pair indefinitely, Tommy said hastily, 'Well, you must emigrate.'

'With what? We have no money.' Lord Harvey held up his hands as though demonstrating his lack of funds.

The man's ineptness is astounding, Tommy thought, his temper beginning to simmer.

'Oh come, there must be something you can sell,' he said, finding it difficult to hide his true feeling.

He turned towards Isabelle, expecting her to make a helpful suggestion to save their skin. She remained silent, a look of raw anxiety on her face. Her small hand covering the pearls at her neck.

The pearls had belonged to Louise Bellamy. He had given them to Isabelle during an afternoon of passion, threading them through her secret womanly hair. He remembered just how hungry she had been to possess the gems.

Thoroughly enjoying her misery, he gestured to the necklace. 'Lady Isabelle's jewels could be sold.'

She flashed wet, vicious eyes. 'Oh, how could you, Tommy?'

Tommy crossed to her.

Lifting her arm he clasped the gold bangle set with six rubies she was wearing. He gave a derisory laugh. 'With such wonderful trophies, you're not likely to starve are you, Lord Harvey?'

Reticent, Lord Harvey came alongside his wife and knelt beside the chair. 'I'm so sorry, my darling, but Tommy is right. The gems will have to be sold to allow us to make a new start.'

'Oh, you are so hateful!' she sobbed.

He touched her arm tentatively. 'My love, you must see that it is the only way,' he said, trying to mollify her.

Isabelle pulled the bangle off viciously. Flinging it towards him, she shrieked 'Have it! Have it!'

Her trembling fingers went to the diamond studded clasp on the necklace and she unfastened it roughly. 'Have this too,' she said, shoving it into his hand.

The last of her strength evaporated. Holding her head in her hands, she cried plaintively 'I really can't bear the thought of being poor.'

Hiding his smirk, Tommy spoke sympathetically. 'But you won't be poor. With the proceeds from your jewels you and Lord Harvey can buy a small house, maybe somewhere in Ireland. You will be in a position to live quietly but comfortably.'

Lady Isabelle's painted lip curled. 'Oh how hateful! I suppose you want me to dig potatoes?' Sarcastically, she said 'Oh I forgot, the God-forsaken country is going through some sort of famine. Isn't it? So there's every chance that I'll starve.'

346

Tommy brushed her words aside. 'Don't be foolish. Everything will work out. You'll see.'

She waved her arm to encompass the luxurious room. 'It's all right for you, Tommy. You have all this. You are rich,' she wailed.

Lord Harvey tried to take her hand. 'Ireland is probably a very good idea. We can slip over there unnoticed.' Desperation came to his voice, 'But my darling, we must have money for a new start.'

She glared spitefully. 'Oh I suppose you want the entire contents of my jewel case too?'

Sighing, grasping the side of the chair, Lord Harvey struggled up clumsily.

Turning to Tommy, he spoke quietly, 'I would be most grateful if you could sell the jewellery for us. If it's discovered that I sold off assets, it'll go badly for me if I'm brought before the court charged with fraud.'

Tommy placed his hand on Lord Harvey's coat sleeve. 'I will buy the jewellery. I can sell it later. If we settle on a price, the money will be yours tomorrow.'

Lord Harvey sighed. 'Bless you for that. I'll accept a fair price. We only need a small home and furniture to fill it. Our needs from now on will be simple.'

He gave a wan smile. 'In many ways it will be good to settle quietly, just the two of us. I've never been truly happy entertaining and being entertained, and the theatre holds little interest for me.' Looking sad but optimistic, he went on 'Yes, all in all, this move might be a good thing. A quiet life does have a certain appeal.'

Behind him, Lady Isabelle wailed.

Tommy hid his smile.

Turning to Lord Harvey, he said quietly, 'I will have your bags taken upstairs. Lady Isabelle might like to look out her jewel box.'

Tommy was interrupted by the arrival of the butler and a footman carrying trays of tea and whisky.

Lady Isabelle turned her face to the fire.

After taking light refreshment, Tommy called for the best carriage to be brought to the front door.

On hearing the vehicle's approach, he swallowed the whisky in his glass, quickly. Patting Lord Harvey's arm reassuringly, he said 'Don't wait up for me. I could be several hours. But be assured I will not return until I have arranged a comfortable passage to Dublin for you both.'

Lord Harvey sniffed back tears. His voice breaking, he said 'I will never be able to thank you enough for all that you are doing for us, Tommy. You're a good and faithful friend.'

Tommy didn't answer, but he shook his lordship's hand warmly.

Wrapped in her misery, Lady Isabelle kept her eyes to the fire.

In the grand hall, the first footman held out Tommy's coat for him. Slipping into it, Tommy fastened the buttons before donning his black hat. A smile rarely seen by a servant flitted across his face as he took the silver-topped ebony cane from the footman. Pulling on dove-grey leather gloves, he strode to the door, held open by the second footman.

Outdoors was dark, rain lashing from a sloe-black starless sky. An easterly wind shivering the wet coats of the two ebony horses.

Euphoric with the success of his plan, Tommy trotted down the steps to the waiting carriage, hardly aware of the pitiless night.

The driver, muffled in a great coat, the collar pulled up to his hat, gave a sidelong glance to the master. Looking back to the horses' heads, his mouth moved in a silent curse. 'Who in their right mind would want to be out on such a night?' he muttered into his grey woollen muffler.

Stepping jauntily into the carriage, Tommy settled on the leather seat.

The door was closed by the footman. The servant stood,

shoulders hunched, waiting for the carriage to move, the slanting rain plastering his hair to his head.

Leaning forward, Tommy glanced in the direction of the library windows, glowing with lamp light. Smirking, he thought of the scene in the room, Isabelle furious, and Lord Harvey pacifying.

'They have only themselves to blame,' he said aloud, pulling a cigar from the inside breast pocket of his coat.

The wheels of the carriage moved, splattering water from the rain oozing from the thin layer of gravel on the driveway.

The whip cracked above the heads of the two horses and they picked up their hooves, trotting down the long avenue.

On hearing the approaching vehicle the gateman rushed from the lodge. Whilst still fastening his cape, he flung the gates wide. The glistening wet carriage passed beneath the ornate arch and turned onto the roadway.

Inside the carriage was chill. Crossing his legs at the knees, Tommy pulled his coat close. In a congratulatory mood, he smoked the Havana cigar, his eyes fixed on the rivulets of rain running down the window.

A wheel hit a rut in the road and he uncrossed his legs to keep his balance. Reaching over to the opposite seat he took hold of a folded blanket and shook it out. Covering his legs he tucked it carefully around his coat. A draught whistling beneath the door was catching his shins.

Finishing the cigar he let down the window-sash and threw the butt out into the night. Rain splashed in and he closed the window quickly, blocking out the beat of the horses hooves and the rattle of the carriage wheels.

For months he had planned this day, not just the downfall of Isabelle but the reclamation of his creation, Ruby Quarry. With Lord Harvey out of the picture and the other shareholders in arrears, he was within his rights as landowner to take back Ruby. The quarry would be solely his again before the end of the week.

He gave a self-satisfied sigh.

Coming to the outskirts of Caernarvon the coachman slowed the carriage. Although it was a miserable night there were several vehicles travelling towards the dock.

Passing between the castle and the quay wall, Tommy saw several ships moored there. Some were being loaded and would probably sail on the tide. Others were in darkness, the rigging creaking in wind funnelling down the wide river.

The driver pulled up outside the Black Boy Inn.

Tommy alighted. 'I don't know how long I will be,' he said looking up at the coachman. 'Take the horses to the stable on Castle Street and dry them off. I will come to you there, when I have finished my business.'

The driver touched the brim of his dripping hat.

As the carriage moved away, Tommy glanced down the narrow street. Three rough looking men were standing under the arch in the castle wall. Giving them the benefit of the doubt, they might not be ruffians but men sheltering from the rain, he entered the smoky inn.

The crowded room fell silent as he strode in. Ignoring the sullen and interested faces, Tommy ordered a glass of whisky from the innkeeper standing behind the counter top.

Throwing money onto the counter, he tossed his head in the direction of a corner table. 'Pour another, for Mr O'Leary.'

Shaun O'Leary, leader of the Irish tinkers, now working at Ruby Quarry, rose slowly from a wooden chair beside the fireplace, his large frame dwarfing the other men sitting there.

Moving towards the bar, he came alongside Tommy. 'What brings you out on such a foul night as this?' He smiled, lighting his pale blue eyes. 'Not just to buy me a drink, I'll wager.'

Tommy downed half of the whisky in his glass. 'No. But I'm glad to stand you a drink, O'Leary.' Dropping his voice, he leaned towards the larger man. 'I'm looking for a boat making passage to Dublin, tomorrow if possible.'

Watching O'Leary's face, Tommy took a swig from his glass before placing it back on the counter top. 'The fewer questions asked, the better. The travellers, a man and a woman, will pay the captain well.'

He smiled crookedly. 'Of course, there's something in it for you, as negotiator.'

Shaun O'Leary tipped his glass to his mouth and swallowed the contents. 'Consider it done, Mr Standish. Give me half-an-hour.' Turning, the Irishman walked to the door and without a backward glance walked out into the pelting rain.

Knowing that all eyes were on him, Tommy turned his back on the inquisitive customers and ordered another whisky from the silent innkeeper.

Before half-an-hour passed, Shaun O'Leary came back into the barroom and crossed to Tommy.

Catching sight of him in the tail of his eye, Tommy rapped the counter with his glass, calling to the inn keeper, 'A whisky for Mr O'Leary.'

Coming alongside, his shoulder almost touching Tommy's, O'Leary said 'It's arranged for tomorrow night. The passengers need to be at the quay wall at eight o'clock. The *Serenity,* it's a fishing smack, will take them out on the tide. She's not the most comfortable of boats but then *beggars can't be choosers.*'

Tommy hid his smirk. 'They'll be there in good time. They will pay on boarding.'

Tommy delved into his coat pocket and bringing out a small purse he handed it to O'Leary.

Satisfied, Tommy left Shaun O'Leary drinking at the bar.

Outdoors he pulled his coat collar up against the sloughing rain and stepped from under the eaves of the inn. Walking quickly, he came to the stables on Castle Street, to reclaim his carriage.

The Plas Mawr coachman was standing near a brazier under the shelter of an overhanging roof. Seeing his master approach, he hurried to get the vehicle ready.

When the horses were back in the traces, the carriage was drawn out of the yard and onto the roadway.

Inside the chilly carriage compartment, Tommy covered his legs with the blanket. Lighting a celebratory cigar, he went over the events, not only of the day but the last few months. Vengeance was sweet. Now with the arrangements in place, Lady Isabelle had a dull life ahead of her, with plenty of time to regret thrusting the master of the Garddryn Quarry aside for a new lover. She was now without an elite social circle, jewels, friends and Hollybeck House. Isabelle was rather like a broken and ageing doll, cast aside by those that had once enjoyed her perfection. Tommy sighed with satisfaction.

Ruby was almost his again. Tomorrow he would call in the lease. The investors were in arrears, so their partnership with him was finished. In three months time, Ruby, under his sole ownership, would be hauling out more slate than the great Penrhyn Quarry. His fortune would be made.

He drew fragrant smoke into his mouth, exhaling it into the damp chilly air. Turning the cigar in his hand, he looked at the gleaming red tip.

If only it were as easy to solve the problem of his father, he thought pensively, his good mood evaporating. Joe Standish was a thorn in his side. The old man had the beginnings of a union. If he were to go unchallenged, he might succeed. With a strong union behind him, Joe Standish could write the rules of the Garddryn Quarry. He would have power, a say. It did not bear thinking about.

CHAPTER FIFTEEN

Tommy woke on the tail of a dream and for a moment the mist of sleep tangled with reality and imagination. He believed the visit from the police had not really occurred; it was all a nightmare. The case was not going to be reopened on Henrietta's sudden death, and Millie's murder was long forgotten, impossible to prove.

The blessed relief made him sigh out loud. The sticky sweat on his clammy flesh cooling as the terror subsided. His head ached. Last night he'd drunk far more whisky than was good for him. Rising up, he rested on one elbow, looking to the Mona marble chimneypiece. A few embers glowed in the grate.

As he swung his legs off the bed, the floor came up to meet him sickeningly, and he sat holding his head in his hands. The dream fled on the searing pain. The visit from the police had actually happened. He groaned as fear crept into his belly again. He took a moment to recall all that had occurred yesterday, to get his thoughts in order before yanking the bell cord to summon his valet.

Bathed and dressed he made his way down to the breakfast room.

Lord Harvey was sitting at the table, a plate of kidneys, lamb chops, ham and eggs in front of him. He looked well rested, less dishevelled than the previous day.

Wiping his mouth on the white napkin, he said jovially 'Tommy, good morning. It's a better day today than yesterday.' Half-turning he glanced out of the long window. 'The sun's even trying to break through.'

Tommy wondered what it cost the man not to ask immediately if the trip to Caernarvon had been successful. Feeling wretched, he was in half a mind to let the buffoon go on making pleasantries throughout breakfast and not mention what he must be burning to hear.

Feigning nonchalance, Tommy also looked to the window. 'Not too bad, is it? At least it's drier.'

A footman drew a chair away from the table for him. Without acknowledging the man, Tommy sat down and waited silently for the white linen napkin to be placed over his lap. Glancing at Lord Harvey's breakfast, he wondered if his stomach had recovered enough to digest similar.

The footman poured coffee into a blue and white porcelain cup. Lifting it to his lips Tommy drank most of it.

At the sideboard the second footman dished chops, ham and eggs onto a plate. Bringing it to Tommy he placed it before him, and gave a small neat bow.

'Is her Ladyship coming down to breakfast?' Tommy asked Lord Harvey.

His mouth full of toast and egg, his lordship shook his head. Swallowing he said, 'Isabelle likes time to herself in the morning. You know what these ladies are like. They take an age to dress their hair and attend to nature's little imperfections before they dare show their faces.'

Tommy cut into a slice of ham. It was rare to hear Lord Harvey acknowledge that his wife had imperfections; normally he defended her robustly. Tommy wondered if his lordship was at last getting the upper hand in his marriage.

'Oh, by the way,' he said as though it was just a passing thought, 'I managed to get a passage organised. Tonight, suit you?'

Lord Harvey's cutlery clattered to his plate. 'Tommy, you are a wonder. Who else could have done things so efficiently? I will never forget this. You are a good friend.'

Smiling broadly, he picked up the knife and fork and cut into a kidney vigorously. Chomping, he said 'Isabelle will be so pleased.'

The hell she will, Tommy thought, hiding his smile.

The door opened and Miles appeared; walking briskly across to the table, he bent at Tommy's side. 'The gentleman, that called yesterday evening, is here again, sir,' he said confidentially.

Tommy's stomach contracted. He wondered if he could bear the shame of being carted off ignobly whilst Lord Harvey and more importantly Lady Isabelle were in the house.

Purposely lowering his voice to hide any tremor that might surface, he said 'Show him into the library.'

'Yes, sir,' Miles said, backing from the table.

Placing the cutlery onto his plate, Tommy took a sip of coffee. 'Please forgive me for leaving you at the table, but there is something important that I must attend to.'

'Think nothing of it, my boy. I will finish this toast and then go up to see my wife.'

Unable to bear the smug satisfied look on the older man's face, Tommy introduced a little poison, saying quietly 'A policeman called yesterday evening and he has obviously thought fit to return. I suggest that you and Lady Isabelle lie low until I get rid of him.'

Lord Harvey's face fell. 'Police! So they have traced us here?'

Tommy gave the impression of being in control. Throwing his napkin onto the tablecloth, he said 'I will deal with them.' Rising, he touched the cuff of Lord Harvey's coat. 'Try not to worry.'

Lord Harvey looked up beseechingly. 'Do your very best, Tommy.'

Cameron Chamberlain, the newly installed Captain of the County Police, turned from looking out of the window as Tommy entered the library.

Cameron Chamberlain did not possess the loud forceful voice that Tommy expected. He was quite surprised by the soft tone and conspiratorial quality of the man's speech. Chamberlain was of medium height, his build slim. Clean shaven, his brown hair brushed straight back from his brow, exposed strong features. But there was a deceitful look in his brown eyes examining the room, taking in every detail of the costly furniture and decoration.

Walking around his desk, Tommy sat in the chair, the leather creaking with the shifting of his weight.

Gesturing to the smaller chair opposite, he said 'Please take a seat. Mr' he waited for the man to introduce himself.

'Thank you, Mr Standish.' His eyes on Tommy's face, he lowered himself into the chair. 'Let me begin by introducing myself, my name is Cameron Chamberlain. I have recently arrived to take charge of the County Police.'

Nausea rose in Tommy's throat. His hands turned clammy. It was an effort to keep them still.

Cameron Chamberlain gave a small cough. 'I say that I have recently arrived, but not so recently that I missed the near riot yesterday evening at Bethesda. Hearing that the quarrymen of Penrhyn and your own workers were gathering together, determined to get a union sanctioned, I sent as many men as I could spare to quell any disturbance. Needless to say ...'

Tommy's gut began to relax. What was the man talking about? Quarrymen! Riot! This was nothing whatsoever to do with Henrietta's death. The relief he felt was so strong it was hard not to smile. He tried hard to concentrate on what the man was saying.

'Several heads were broken. Quarriers' heads, I might add.' He gave a wan smile. 'My own men were saved from injury.'

Tommy could not resist a barb. 'The quarrymen were not armed then?'

'Not as far as I know,' Chamberlain said frowning.

'That was lucky for your men.' Tommy smiled.

'Quite so,' Chamberlain harrumphed. 'I have the ringleaders' names. So I can bring them to justice.'

Tommy leaned forward in his seat. 'Ringleaders?' His interest was real.

'Yes, quite a few were followed to their homes by my men. Of course they were out of uniform. I thought that you as master of the Garddryn would be interested to know which men are heavily involved with forming this Society of Quarrymen. We don't have long to punish them, according to those in the know; the men will have their society sooner rather than later.' He harrumphed again. 'It seems your father was one of the men that was followed to his home.' He looked intently into Tommy's eyes. 'If you have any influence with Joe Standish, I suggest you tell him to stay clear of these gatherings and meetings.'

Rudely, Tommy burst out laughing. 'Influence with that old bugger? He's not the sort of man to be influenced by anyone, least of all me. The bugger is a law unto himself and always will be.'

Tommy looked carefully at Cameron Chamberlain. He was pretty sure he had the measure of the man. He had not come all the way from Caernarvon to discuss Joe Standish. The man had other, bigger fish to fry.

'So you have the names of the ringleaders?'

'I do.'

'That could be a useful list.' Tommy eyes narrowed.

'Imprisoning those who are heavily involved would slow progress in forming the union. It will not hold it off forever, but it'd give the quarry masters a bit of breathing space. They might even have time to employ foreign labour. The Irish for instance.'

Tommy cut to the chase. 'Is perusing the list likely to be expensive?'

'Depends on what you consider expensive. I'd say a hundred pounds would be a fair price.'

Tommy inched forward in his seat. 'It seems fair to me. Why don't you call back tomorrow? I will have the money here.'

Cameron Chamberlain made to stand.

'When you called yesterday,' Tommy said softly, 'you enquired about my wife.'

Chamberlain resumed his seat. 'We met on what must have been the last day of her life. She was travelling on the same train as myself. She had been to Denbigh to visit a relative. A most charming woman. She talked of her young son with such affection. A very strikingly beautiful woman. She must be a great loss to you.'

Tommy had never thought of Henrietta as being beautiful but hearing it from a stranger made him conjure up her face, and yes, he supposed that she probably had been beautiful.

Dismissing Henrietta from his thoughts, he rose. 'I will expect you tomorrow, Mr Chamberlain. Shall we say about five o'clock? It's a good time to sit over a drink and get to know each other.' Tommy smiled.

Yanking the bell cord, he called a footman to show out the visitor.

Alone again, Tommy went back to his desk. Sitting, stretching out his legs, he was thoughtful. Cameron Chamberlain could be bought. The man may be a useful asset in the future. For the time being it was valuable to know the names of the quarry troublemakers. Well worth the outlay of a hundred pounds.

His face darkened as he considered the nightmarish twelve hours he had just endured. How long would it be before something happened like it again? Henrietta, George and Millie Barker were dark shadows that would walk beside him until the end of his days.

The quarrymen that gathered at Corn Cottage to discuss the debacle at Bethesda left during the early afternoon.

With the closing of the front door, Emily donned her abandoned apron, hidden beneath the cushion on the fireside chair, and began to put the ingredients for supper onto the table.

Joe took his muffler and coat from the back of the door. Wrapping the green scarf around his neck, he tucked the fringed ends into the lapels of his jacket.

'I thought I'd just stretch me legs,' he said watching Emily pour white flour into a large basin.

'Don't be too long, our Joe. I'm making a meat and potato pie.' She smiled up at him, the tiny crows' feet at her eyes crinkling. 'It's your favourite.'

'So is rabbit pie, lobscouse and beef suet pudding.'

'Get away with you, Joe Standish. You're always telling me that meat and 'tato is the true favourite.'

Slipping on his coat, he kissed her brow lightly. 'Happen you're right. I won't be late. Is our Frank in for supper?'

'Aye, he said he would be.'

'That's good,' he said, opening the door. A small cloud of smoke blew down the chimney as he closed the door behind him.

Emily looked to the fireplace. 'Wind must be in the east,' she muttered, putting a lump of lard with the flour.

With his head bent, watching the toecaps of his black boots, Joe trudged towards the outskirts of the village. Passing the chapel he turned right, making for the hillside cemetery.

The grass was soggy, drenched from last night's downpour. Thank God it had not rained like that all day, he thought. The outcome of the gathering of the quarrymen had been bad enough, without the bleak mountainside being the target for a deluge.

Twenty men had been injured in one way or another; most were knocked about the head by stick wielding policemen.

'Barbarians!' he rasped.

Slightly out of breath, he stopped and looked out over the mountains to the plateau of Carneddau and the peaks of Carnedd Dafydd and Llywelyn, the outlines stark and clear in the wet air. Turning his head, he gazed at the grey sea, imagining the land of Ireland beyond the horizon.

Climbing again he came to the stone wall surrounding the small cemetery. Opening the plain wicket gate, he went amongst the gravestones.

Ahead was a large tree, the branches spread to where his darling Chloe rested in perpetual childhood.

Stooping he read the inscription for the thousandth time. Chloe Standish 1843-1846. Tears rose to his eyes. The pain had never eased nor ceased. She was still his darling girl, with the violet pansy eyes and baby lips.

Kneeling, he told her of yesterday, painting a picture with words of the mountainside, grey with the coats of men. The air thundering with their words, hopes and dreams. They would have a union, a society for quarrymen, and it would not be that long in coming. Then men would be free of the shackles of unscrupulous masters.

'We have almost won, my little one, almost won. It's a great achievement, something for all men to be proud.'

Tears filmed his eyes. 'I would have conquered the world for you, lass,' he sighed. 'Conquered the world.'